Hkae

SARASOTA DREAMS

THREE MENNONITE COUPLES
FIND LOVE IN FLORIDA

DEBBY MAYNE

BARBOUR
PUBLISHING

Print ISBN 978-1-62836-167-4

eBook Editions:
Adobe Digital Edition (.epub) 978-1-62836-984-7
Kindle and MobiPocket Edition (.prc) 978-1-62836-985-4

Published by Barbour Publishing, Inc., P.O. Box 719, Uhrichsville, Ohio 44683, www.barbourbooks.com

Our mission is to publish and distribute inspirational products offering exceptional value and biblical encouragement to the masses.

Member of the
Evangelical Christian
Publishers Association

Printed in the United States of America.

Dear Readers,

Welcome to Pinecraft, a delightful Mennonite and Amish community in Sarasota, Florida. I've been there several times, and during each visit I learn something new. I'm thankful to the many people I met who were willing to answer questions for my books. One such person, Lee Miller, always took my calls and shared his vast knowledge to help with keeping these stories grounded in reality.

Although I'm not Mennonite, I discovered that the people I wrote about share the same human conditions we all do. They experience joy, sadness, confusion, and all the other emotions that have us turning to God and trusting in His greater understanding. Some of the folks in Pinecraft choose to continue living the simple life, while others have embraced some modern conveniences. The population of this community increases significantly during the colder months as winter visitors come down to bask in the Florida sunshine.

If you ever take a trip to Florida, please plan to visit Sarasota and have a hearty lunch at Yoders Restaurant. They have some of the best pies you'll ever taste. After lunch, stroll around Pinecraft, where you'll find produce stands, candy stores, gift shops, and some very friendly people who love the Lord.

Blessings to you and your family,
Debby Mayne
www.debbymayne.com

SHADES OF THE PAST

Dedication

This book is dedicated to my daughters, Lauren and Alison,
and my granddaughter, Emma.

Thanks to Lee Miller and Pastor Rocky Miller for answering dozens of questions about the Mennonite community in Sarasota.

I appreciate Tara Randel's willingness to read the first few chapters and the suggestions she made to help bring this story to life.

Chapter 1

Mary Penner lowered herself to the hot, moist sand, gathered the front of her skirt, and twisted it around her shins as she pulled her knees to her chest. She carefully tucked the folds of her skirt around her to cover herself. It was only May, yet the intensity of heat from the sun reflecting off the beach in Sarasota, Florida, sent droplets of perspiration trickling down her back. But she didn't mind. Being here in a stable home, living among the Conservative Mennonite folks, and knowing her grandparents would always be there for her gave her a sense of peace—even if they wished she'd never been born.

Mary still had confusing and sometimes even bitter moments when she couldn't put her past completely behind her. Today was especially difficult because it was the ninth anniversary of her mother's death.

The gentle whisper of waves as they lapped the sand blended with the sound of seabirds on their never-ending search for food. Children scampered around blankets, sand buckets in hand. Teenagers and young adults lay sprawled on beach towels, catching the last of the day's rays, their bronze bodies showing very little modesty. Years ago she would have been among them, but now. . .well, it embarrassed her.

Mary extended her arm and studied her shadow before she pointed her index finger and drew a figure eight in the slightly moist sand. That was how her life seemed sometimes—a double circle that started out as though going someplace, yet it managed to meet back up at the beginning. Just like her thoughts.

"Mary?"

She snapped her head around at the sound of the familiar voice. "Oh hi, Abe."

He drew closer and squatted. "Nice day."

"Yeah." Mary sniffled and turned slightly away from Abe Glick. His presence had always created the strangest sensation—sort of a dread mixed with exhilaration in her chest. The stirrings of emotion confused her as always. "What are you doing here?"

Abe chuckled. "I was about to ask you the same thing." He gestured to the sand beside her. "Mind if I join you?"

She cast a quick glance in his direction, then looked back toward the water, hoping he wouldn't notice her heat-tinged cheeks. "That's fine."

He slowly sat down and stretched his long, navy-blue twill-clad legs toward the water. "It's a mite hot today."

"I don't mind."

A Frisbee zoomed a few feet past them, followed by a half-dressed teenage boy. "Sorry," he said. His gaze lingered long enough to satisfy his curiosity, then he took off after the Frisbee.

Abe nodded toward the kid, a half smile on his face, before turning to face Mary. "So what are you thinking about?" Abe asked.

Mary shrugged. "Work. Family." She paused to take a deep breath before adding, "Just everyday stuff."

"I don't think so." Abe tilted his head back and let out a deep chuckle. "Based on the look on your face, I think it's much more than that."

Mary darted a quick look in his direction, then turned back toward the water. "Is it any of your business?"

He lifted his hands. "Sorry if I offended you, but I did it innocently, I promise."

His apology deflated her short burst. "That's okay. I'm sort of touchy today anyway."

"So do you wanna talk about it?"

Mary snorted and shook her head. "You are something else, Abe. Do you ever give up?"

"Giving up isn't in the Glick vocabulary."

"Okay, so what if I tell you I was thinking about the past?" Mary leveled him with an I-dare-you-to-ask-more-questions look. "Does that make you happy?"

He looked right back at her with as much of a dare as she had. "Ever miss your old life?"

"Never." She paused as she considered his question. "I love being with Grandma and Grandpa. They're good to me."

"Indeed they are." Abe's sidelong glance at her heightened her pulse rate. "There was never any question about that." He turned completely toward her and stared until she met his gaze. "Or was there?"

He asked too many questions, and she was growing more irritated by the second. "No, of course not!"

"You don't have to be so defensive, Mary. I'm not the enemy."

A soft grunt escaped her throat. "Never said you were, Abe. What's this all about anyway?"

"Just curious, I s'pose."

"Curious? How about nosy?" Mary shifted a few inches away from him. "Why did you follow me all the way here?"

"Who says I followed you?" He lifted an eyebrow and gave her a teasing grin.

Mary mimicked his expression, then turned back to face the water. "Did you have some business on the beach?"

"Ya, I came to see you."

"See? That's what I'm talking about."

Abe laughed. "You're too easy to rile, Mary Penner."

"Is that what you're trying to do? Rile me?"

His teasing had always annoyed her.

He lifted a shoulder then let it drop. "Maybe."

"Stop trying to make me mad, Abe Glick," she tossed right back. "Sometimes it seems like that's all you live for."

"Oh there's much more to life than making you mad, Mary. I like making you laugh and getting you to think. And sometimes it's fun to scare you. Remember that snake?"

"How could I forget that snake? That *fake* snake. You got me in so much trouble, you're lucky I'm talking to you now."

"I don't believe in luck." He gave her a teasing grin. "Sounds like you're holding a grudge."

"Maybe I am."

Abe touched Mary's arm. "That was eight years ago, so if you aren't over it by now, I would suggest you start working on not holding grudges. God doesn't want us to be angry."

"That was seven years ago," she corrected, "and I'm not angry."

Abe snorted and turned to face the water. "Sure is pretty, isn't it? I can't imagine living in a place where I couldn't get to the beach once in a while."

"No one ever asked you to."

"You're still a mite touchy, Mary. I suppose I should leave you to your thoughts."

"Excellent idea."

"If you ever wanna talk about anything, I'm a good listener." He touched her arm. "I promise not to judge your past."

Mary swallowed hard and nodded. "I'll remember that."

Abe stood and brushed most of the sand off his backside. A small amount of the wet sand still clung to his trousers. "I best be getting back to the farm before the sun goes down."

She lifted a hand for a brief wave, then waited until he was out of sight before getting up. Her midshin-length skirt held more sand than Abe's trousers, but it never bothered her until Grandma fussed at her for tracking it into their tiny rented home in the Pinecraft community. She shoved her feet into the tan clogs she'd worn to work. The sand was still gritty on her feet, and it irritated her until she left the beach, took them off, and carefully brushed the tops and bottoms of her feet. She clapped her shoes together and put them back on. Other people darted past her, some of them openly staring and others trying hard not to. She'd gotten used to being noticed for wearing plain clothes, but when she'd first arrived in Sarasota, she felt awkward. Some of the Mennonites set themselves apart from the Amish by wearing brighter colors. Grandma still clung to her Amish roots, but Mary didn't mind. Her brown skirt and off-white blouse helped keep her from being noticed, which was just fine with her. Her *kapp* covered about half her head and tended to fall to one side in spite of the pins she used to secure it.

As Mary walked to the bus stop, she thought about Abe's offer of lending an ear. She'd been in Sarasota for a little more than nine years, and to this day, no one had discussed her past—at least not with her. Abe had come close a few times, but he never pressed for information, and she never offered it. They'd never actually talked much beyond the teasing and gentle jousting that he always started.

She'd always thought her teenage crush on Abe would fade, but sitting next to him on the beach proved that wasn't the case. If things had been simpler, Mary might have given in to her feelings. The anniversary of her mother's violent death continued to remind her she'd never be like other Mennonites, who'd all led godly lives since birth.

When Mary first arrived in Sarasota, she remembered the fear of facing Grandma and Grandpa after hearing all the stories from Mama about how they'd shunned her when she got pregnant out of wedlock. Her story shifted slightly with each telling, but the pain in Mama's voice was evident every time; that part never changed. Even if Mama embellished her story, Mary couldn't doubt there was a foundation of truth to what she said had happened.

As difficult as Mama had made their lives, Mary still missed her. Mama was loving and kind to Mary. She said she'd do anything to make things better, but she'd gotten herself into so much trouble, she didn't know how to dig her way out. Mary had to guess what Mama was talking about, but it wasn't too difficult to put the pieces together. The love was there, but without guidance or a parenting role model, Mama made some terrible mistakes—including one that had cost her life. Mary leaned against a light pole and squeezed her eyes shut as the memory of that awful night pounded through her head.

The wind shifted slightly, bringing her back to the moment. Mary blinked as the bus pulled to the curb, the fumes surrounding her and making her cough.

"Hey, lady, are you getting on or not?" The bus driver leaned toward her as he waited with his hand on the door crank.

"Oh. . .sure." Mary gathered her skirt up and climbed onto the bus. She found a seat near the front and plopped down then stared out the window. Mary was on her way to Grandma and Grandpa's house, just like nine years ago, only now she knew her place. Her memories had always transported her somewhere she didn't want to go, and sometimes she couldn't keep the demons away. If Mama had told her more about her father, she might have had someone else to turn to. The times Mary had asked about him brought such sadness to Mama, she eventually gave up and created an image in her own mind of who he might be. When she was little, she pictured a prince riding in on a stallion, but as she got older, his image darkened, and he became a brooding man similar to those in Mama's life.

Mary had been puzzled the first time she met the people Mama said had shunned her. They'd both embraced her and told her she was one of them now—and she had nothing to worry about as long as she followed God's Word and His calling to be a good Mennonite girl. There were a few people who weren't as open, but Grandpa reminded her that no one was perfect. Occasionally Grandma would mutter something about having another chance at raising a daughter—only this time they wouldn't make the same mistakes.

Abe arrived at the old family farm in time to send his hired workers home and finish putting away some of the tools for the day. His grandfather had resisted the transition from farming celery to dairy farming and growing citrus, but after Grandpop passed away, Abe had managed to make the changes when he returned from college, where he got his business degree. Dad was pleased with Abe's work, and he retired from farming after Mom died. He had moved into the Pinecraft community in town so he could live among other Conservative Mennonites.

A grin played on Abe's lips as he reflected on the last time he'd visited Dad in town. He'd been on the shuffleboard court and didn't seem to want to be interrupted. If Abe didn't know better, he'd think Dad preferred his new life over what he'd done the first almost fifty years of his life. Although Dad had once loved farming, the combination of all the heavy lifting and the hot Florida sun had taken its toll on him. Abe still did some of the farmwork, but he'd managed to put what he'd learned about business management into practice and hired some workers to do most of the manual labor. Abe's job was to manage the farm and find ways for it to sustain itself and the people who depended on it. After a shaky year, the farm was in good enough financial shape to pay everyone, including Dad, a nice wage after expenses.

Once the last of the equipment was put away in the new barn Abe had built, he brushed off his trousers and headed into the old house that he now lived in alone. The echo of the screen door slamming reminded him of how lonely it had gotten since Dad moved out. Both of his brothers had their own places—Jake on a neighboring farm and Luke in a swanky neighborhood in Sarasota. Jake was more like Abe; he had no desire to go crazy during *rumspringa*, the one-year running-around period some of the Mennonite families carried over from their Amish ancestors. However, once Luke got a taste of worldliness, he didn't want to go back. While some families would have shunned their children, Dad never did that to Luke. Dad didn't like Luke's choices, and he'd taken every opportunity to let him know it, but he still embraced his wayward son. Abe reflected on Dad's decision and determined he would have done the same thing.

Mary's grandparents, according to the bits and pieces he'd heard, had made the traditional choice when their only daughter, Elizabeth, had gotten pregnant during her rumspringa. They'd shunned her. Although he'd just been born when it happened, he'd heard about it from the Conservative Mennonite children when Mary showed up at school. Parents used her and others who experienced something similar to remind their children how worldly allure wasn't all it was cracked up to be.

Abe had heard about the Penners' shame and how they mourned the loss of their daughter for years. In fact, until Mary came to live with them, they seemed like very bitter people. The only contact he'd had with them when he was a child had been when he went into their restaurant with his folks. He'd never seen a smile touch their lips before Mary arrived.

The very thought of Mary made him warm inside. The first time he'd seen her when she arrived at their tiny school had sent his heart racing. He laughed to himself as he remembered how difficult it had been for her to adjust to the Mennonite ways. She grumbled about everything—from the head covering she couldn't seem to keep straight to the skirt that constantly got twisted between her legs. She questioned authority and balked at some of the conservative teachings in the early years. The few times she spoke, she went for shock value and blurted things the other Mennonite kids had never heard about before. But he suspected there was more truth than fiction in her words. Dad had told him he heard that a drug dealer killed her mother when he suspected she was about to turn him in.

It didn't take Mary long to clam up and withdraw. Most of the other girls ignored her, and the boys were a little afraid to go near her. Abe wasn't scared of much, including Mary, so he teased her every chance he got. Her reactions were more exciting than any of the other girls' would have been, and he found her scrappiness intriguing. As a teenager, he didn't know any other way of showing how much he liked her.

Abe shuddered at the thought of what Mary must have seen as a child. When he was at college and learned about the evils of the world, he'd developed a keen sense of the difference between right and wrong. Mary needed a friend, and he resolved to be just that. He'd thought about Mary during college, and when he met other girls, he couldn't help but compare them to her.

He'd been stopping by Penner's Restaurant when he came to town, and each time he saw Mary, he did whatever he could to get her attention. The chemistry between them was powerful—stronger than all the common sense in Sarasota. He couldn't put together an intelligent sentence the first time she asked for his order. When she laughed at his feeble attempt, he relished the sound of her laughter. He'd had to go home and practice talking to her before going back the next day. This had gone on for more than a week before he was able to formulate a plan.

Abe had wanted to see Mary when he first came back from college, but there was so much work on the farm, he had wanted to square that away first. He'd been back from college about eight months when he first walked back into Penner's Restaurant and spotted Mary. He was struck hard by how much she'd matured.

If things worked out, maybe he and Mary could be more than friends. He'd always thought her differences made her special.

❧

"Mary? Is that you?" Grandma's voice echoed through the tiny, sparsely furnished house. She appeared by the main room, her scowl dredging up a sense of shame in Mary. "Where did you go? Your grandpa said you left the restaurant early."

"The beach." Mary was on her way to the bedroom when Grandma stepped in front of her, arms folded, her heavy eyebrows arched. "Oh no, you don't. I'll not have you tracking sand in this house after all the time I spent cleaning up today. Back outside." She jabbed a finger toward the door to drive her point harder.

Mary did as she was told. During the time she'd been with Grandma and Grandpa, she'd learned the ropes, but today her thoughts had shoved common sense to the back of her mind. She'd managed to shake off most of the sand, but Grandma took the broom to her skirt and loosened the grains that had gotten stuck in the seams and folds.

"Now go on inside and wash up and help me get dinner on the table. Your grandpa will be back soon, and I don't want to make him wait."

As soon as she stepped back inside, a sweet aroma wafted from Grandma's kitchen. She turned to her grandmother. "Peanut butter pie?"

"Ya. That's for dessert, and only if you do as you're told."

Mary sighed. She was twenty-three, yet she was still treated as a child. She'd offered to move out, but Grandma and Grandpa told her no, not under any circumstances. They said she needed them to look after her until she found a suitable husband to take care of her. Where they expected her to find someone who'd want to marry her was beyond Mary. Besides, after what she'd seen, she knew the only decent man under God's sun was Grandpa.

Grandma's expression remained stoic as she handed Mary a short stack of stoneware plates to set on the table. The two of them worked in silence, giving Mary's mind another chance to wander. Even after all these years, Mary remembered how her mother hated a quiet room so much she'd turn on a television just to drown out the silence. The quiet didn't bother Mary all that much, but she did rather enjoy hearing something besides the clatter of dishes, forks, and spoons. But her grandparents went along with the traditional Mennonite ways of not listening to music or watching TV. The only concessions they made were some of the conveniences that came with the house they rented.

By the time Grandpa walked in the back door, everything was ready. He sat down and without a word reached for her and Grandma's hands. As he said the blessing for their food, Mary thought about his humble words. "Lord, thank You for giving us this home, this food, and one another. I pray that You continue to keep us on our narrow path until we reach the gates of Your righteousness. Bless our souls, and thank You for this day. Amen."

Normally Mary would have been starving and eager to dig into Grandma's specialty meat loaf. The salt air from the beach should have given her enough of an appetite to eat, but she wasn't hungry. She'd been busy at the restaurant, and as had happened many times, she'd forgotten to eat lunch.

"Well, are you going to answer your grandpa or not?"

Mary blinked and looked back and forth between her grandparents. "I'm sorry, Grandpa, but I missed what you said."

A tiny flicker of a smile tweaked his lips. "Abe was looking for you after you left the restaurant. Did he find you?"

"Yes." Mary looked down at her plate and swallowed hard before looking back at Grandpa. "He found me at the beach."

Grandpa pushed his chair back and tilted his head as he quietly regarded Mary for a few seconds. "Ya, I told him he might find you there."

"You never told me you were with Abe," Grandma said. "I've taught you that withholding information is the same as lying."

Mary wanted to explain that she'd gone to the beach alone and left alone, but she knew it wouldn't matter. "I'm sorry, Grandma."

"Sarah," Grandpa said softly. His forehead crinkled as he shook his head at Grandma then turned back to Mary. "How long were you and Abe at the beach?"

"I was there about an hour. Abe came after I got there, and he left long before I did."

"She wasn't with Abe, Sarah. She wasn't lying. He went looking for her, and it sounds to me like she didn't give him the time of day."

Grandma shook her head and stood, grabbing her plate and Grandpa's to carry to the sink. "You'll never find a husband if you keep treating all the nice men like that."

Mary was confused. First Grandma seemed upset about her being with Abe, and now she wanted her to be nice to him. Her stomach churned, and the peanut butter pie Grandma had made didn't sound so good. Mama's angry words played in the back of her mind as she thought about how nothing she did around here seemed to be good enough. Sometimes Grandma seemed halfway happy, but Mary still hadn't figured out what it took to get a lasting smile from her. When she smiled, it was unexpected, and it flickered but quickly vanished. Mary knew Grandma loved her, but she was obviously afraid to show it.

"May I be excused?" Mary asked.

Grandma had her back to her, but she slowly turned. "I made this pie 'specially for you, Mary. Don't tell me you don't want it."

"She'll have some," Grandpa said as he stood up and walked around the table. "Just give her a few minutes for her food to settle. Why don't the two of you ladies take a break? I'll clean up the kitchen."

"I'll not have you cl—" Grandma began.

Grandpa shushed her by placing his hands on her shoulders and turning her toward the door. "I said I'll clean up. Why don't you two take a stroll around the block, and by the time you get back, I should be all done."

The last thing Mary wanted to do was be alone with Grandma, but she was too tired to argue. She looked at Grandpa, who winked and made a shooing gesture.

As soon as they got outside, Grandma started talking. "Your grandpa thinks I'm too hard on you. He's afraid you'll run off like your mother did. Is that going to happen?"

Mary allowed a few seconds to slip by before speaking. "No. I don't plan to leave."

"Neither did your mother." Grandma's voice cracked.

Mary was sick of being compared to her mother. "I'm not my mother." The instant those words left her mouth, she regretted how harsh she sounded. "I—"

"Ya. Thank the Lord."

"My mother was good to me."

"Maybe so, but look how she left you." Grandma slowed down. "Today is the anniversary of—"

"I know."

"I've been thinking about her all day. It isn't easy, you know, raising a child up in the Lord, only to have her turn on me like she did."

"She didn't mean to hurt you, Grandma."

"But she did. Very much. I may never get over it."

"Mama did what she thought she had to do." Mary cleared her throat. "I've never understood what happened, though. She tried to tell me, but some things didn't make sense."

"Do you want me to tell you?"

"Yes." Mary knew Grandma's story would likely be quite different from Mama's, but this was the first time she'd ever offered to discuss it. Grandma had obviously been doing the same thing Mary had all day—thinking about

Mama. "I'm ready to hear the truth."

Grandma stopped and squeezed her eyes shut. A tear trickled down her cheek as her lips moved in silent prayer. When she opened her eyes, Mary saw the pain etched in them.

"I'm sorry, Grandma. If it hurts too much, you don't have to talk about it."

"Neh, it's time you heard the truth." Grandma paused long enough to gather her thoughts before she began. "She wanted to go stay with some friends she met at the restaurant, in spite of my worries," Grandma began. She coughed and sniffled.

"She told me about those friends, and they didn't seem so bad."

"Those girls were horrible, and they taught her how to be disrespectful to her faith."

"I'm sorry, Grandma, I didn't mean—"

Grandma held up her hand to shush her. "Your grandpa and I have been talking about this quite a bit lately. He thinks I should tell you everything. I guess today is as good as any to do that."

"I would like to know more," Mary said softly. Mama had told her all about how Grandma had flown into a rage, telling her to leave and never show her face again.

"I'm ready to tell you our side of it." Grandma hung her head as she reached for Mary's hand. Mary's shock sent a lump to her throat. "I love you, sweet girl. Just like I loved your mother. She hurt us more than you'll ever know—unless you have a daughter of your own who storms out and never returns."

Mary swallowed hard. "But I thought—"

"Be quiet and let me tell you."

Mary forced herself to nod. She knew Mama had been hurt, and her perception had been tainted by her childish anger. After all, Mama was only sixteen when she left home. But Mary also knew Grandma's memories were slanted from her perspective—just like Mama's were. "Okay, please tell me."

Grandma pulled a tissue from her pocket and dabbed at her eyes before she opened up. "These girls were here on vacation—down from Cincinnati. Elizabeth met them when they came into the restaurant looking for something to do. Her plain clothes and different ways fascinated them, so they invited her along everywhere they went."

Mary smiled. She understood how those girls must have felt because when she first arrived in Sarasota, she'd been awestruck by the plain lifestyle.

"I didn't want her to go, but your grandpa said it would be good for her. After they left, I was relieved, but only for a short while because after they went home, they sent word that they wanted her to visit them up in Cincinnati. She'd obviously told them about rumspringa, and they wanted to show her their way of life. Again, your grandpa said we should let her go.

Besides, he pointed out that she planned to leave town, and it would be nice to know she had a place to stay, so off she went. When she came back, I knew she was different. Four months later, it was obvious she'd never be the same." Grandma slowed her pace and rubbed her abdomen. "She was pregnant with you. I said some things. . ."

"I know," Mary said. "Mama told me."

"I couldn't help it. When I had my rumspringa, things were very different." Mary smiled. "What did you do during your rumspringa?"

"Helga and I went to town and bought some lipstick. Then we went to a dance party that she heard about from some boys. The second we walked into that place, we knew it wasn't good for us, so we left."

Mary couldn't picture her grandmother wearing lipstick, and showing up at a dance party? That was unfathomable. She laughed. "Were you and Helga by yourselves?"

Grandma's stern lips turned up at the corners, and she finally allowed herself a full grin. "Ya, but we didn't leave that party alone."

"Grandma!" Mary couldn't hold back her shock. "Did you meet some boys there?"

"We knew a couple of them, ya. But don't get so alarmed. One of them was your grandpa. He and Paul got there right before we arrived, and they didn't like it any more than we did. So they offered to take us home."

It must have been scandalous at the time, but everything obviously worked out fine, since Grandma and Grandpa were still married and Helga was still married to Paul. They lived in Pinecraft, just two blocks away from the Penners. Paul had a small candy store not far from the community with a corner nook featuring Helga's crafts.

"I think your grandpa should be done with the kitchen chores by now. We need to get on back."

"Grandma, before we go any farther, I want to know something."

"Just ask me, Mary. Don't drag it out."

"If you had it to do over again with Mama, would you have done anything different?"

Grandma's soft expression instantly returned to a scowl. "It never does anyone any good to have regrets. It's too late to look back and say what I should have done, so I won't even think about it like that."

Chapter 2

Abe pulled out his cell phone and punched in the number of his favorite ride into town. It was too difficult in this modern world to drive a horse and buggy. Accidents on the highway left many of the Mennonites and Amish dead or with debilitating injuries, so he relied on the services of folks who made their living transporting those who didn't drive cars.

David answered right away. "Sure thing. I can be there in fifteen minutes."

"That'll be just fine." Abe finished getting ready, then went out to wait on the front porch.

The large white van pulled into the shell-encrusted driveway exactly fifteen minutes later. "Where to, Abe?" David asked as Abe slid into the van.

"Penner's."

David chuckled as he pulled out onto the road. "That Penner's place must have some great food for you to go there every day."

"Not every day," Abe reminded him. "They're closed on Sundays."

Abe saw the look of amusement on David's face, but at least the man had the decency not to continue this train of thought. "How's the farm doing? I can't help but notice the changes. Seems like there's something different every time I come out here."

"Ya, I've made a few changes in the last year."

"Things must be going well then."

"Can't complain. We work hard, though."

"So when do you think you'll need some more workers? I have a couple friends who are out of work."

"Out of work? Why?" Abe folded his arms and stared out the window as they whizzed past alternating farms and patches of palmettos.

David shrugged. "Layoffs. The economy's been rough lately."

"So I've heard." Abe could use another worker or two, but they had to be able to jump right in without much supervision. "Any of your friends have farming experience?"

"Probably not."

"Can't use 'em then."

"How about you meet them first, before you make a decision? I can't speak for all my buddies, but I think a couple of them would be good at farming if they knew what to do. They're hard workers, too."

Abe pondered that thought for a moment before crisply nodding. "I s'pose that would only be fair. I've already asked around the Mennonite community, and no one else is beating my door down for a job."

"Thanks, Abe. I'll send my friends your way. Is it okay if they call your cell phone?"

"Of course. How else would they get hold of me?"

"True." David snickered. "I bet you're a tough man to work for."

"No. Just fair. I expect people to earn their wages, and I pay them what they're worth."

"Interesting concept," David said. "Too bad more people aren't like you."

Abe slowly shook his head. "That might not be such a good thing. God created us all different for a reason."

"Good point." David pulled into the Penner's parking lot. "Want me to pick you up here at a certain time, or should I wait to hear from you?"

"I'll call," Abe said as he got out of the van. He handed David some cash. "Thank you for the ride, David. See you later."

David waved before he took off. Abe turned around and faced the front of Penner's. For a moment, his resolution to work his way into Mary Penner's life wavered, but he recognized his fear of rejection and dismissed it. That should never keep a man from following the Lord's plan for him, and he was fairly certain of what God wanted. Otherwise, why would God plant Mary's image on his brain so indelibly?

"Abe." Joseph Penner greeted him at the door. "Good to see you again. Where would you like to sit?"

Abe nodded toward the right. "Is Mary still working in that section?"

Joseph grinned. "She's supposed to be in the kitchen this morning, but I can send her out if you want to see her."

"Neh, don't change things on account of me." Disappointment flowed from his chest to his abdomen, but he tried his best not to show it. "I'm sure we'll see each other again soon."

"Go find a seat that suits you, Abe, and I'll have someone right over to take your order. Want coffee?"

"That would be good."

Abe had only been seated a few seconds when Mary showed up. Even dressed in plain clothes, she glowed with a unique beauty—with her deep green eyes and peaches-and-cream complexion framed by strawberry blond hair that peeked out from beneath her traditional head covering. A stray wisp hung down over her forehead, but she didn't seem to notice it.

"Grandpa said you wanted to see me?" She lifted an order pad and poised her pen above it. "Do you know what you want yet?"

Abe didn't have to look at the menu; he knew it by heart. "I'll have a tall stack of pancakes, sausage links, two fried eggs sunny-side up, fried potatoes, and a side order of buttered toast."

"Pancakes and buttered toast?" she asked. "And all that fried food?"

"Ya, that's what I said."

She licked her lips and grimaced. "That's a lot of bread and grease for one person at one time."

"But that's what I want." Abe challenged her with a stare down.

She finally took a step back, nodded, and jotted his order on her pad. "Then that's what you'll get, Abe Glick, along with a big spike in your blood sugar to go with your clogged arteries."

"Are you saying you're worried about my health?" He had to force himself not to show his amusement.

"No, of course not. I was just calling it to your attention, that's all. If you want to go to an early grave, who am I to stop you?"

He blew out a breath. "Then what do you suggest I have?"

"It's not my place to suggest what you should have. If you want—"

"Tell you what, Mary. I'll change my order if you'll consider going out with me after work."

"Why?"

"Because I want to get to know you better. I like you, Mary Penner."

Her arms fell to her sides, and her pen fell and rolled across the floor. "What?"

"I would like to take you somewhere." It was hard not to laugh.

Mary narrowed her eyes in suspicion. "Where?"

Abe bent over to retrieve her pen as he tried hard to think of someplace specific, but nothing came to mind, so he relied on what he knew she enjoyed. "You like the beach, so why don't we go there?" He held out the pen.

She grabbed the pen from his hand. "I went to the beach yesterday."

"Then maybe out for ice cream?"

She remained standing there, her stare intense, the surprise still evident on her face. "What is this all about, Abe? Did Grandma or Grandpa put you up to something?"

"Are you saying you don't trust me? Or your grandparents?"

"No, of course I'm not saying that. I just want to know why you're suddenly tracking me down, following me everywhere I go."

Abe leaned back and regarded her before saying, "I don't follow you everywhere."

"Okay, so what do you call what you did yesterday when I was at the beach? And now?"

"The beach isn't everywhere."

Mary made a low growling sound. "You know what I mean."

"What is wrong with wanting to get to know you better?"

"Nothing, except you should know me well enough after all these years."

Abe tried to tamp down the hurt. "You make it sound like torture."

One corner of her mouth quirked into a grin. "Well, sometimes it seems that way."

He lifted his hands in defeat then let them fall, slapping the table. "Okay, okay, I can tell when I'm getting the brush-off. I'll leave you alone. Now if you'll please bring me my breakfast, I can be on my way sooner rather than later."

Mary turned slightly, then glanced at him over her shoulder with a coquettish look, her cheeks a little rosier than normal. "Grandpa will probably let me leave at three o'clock when the new server comes in, if you'd like to come around then. Maybe a walk on the beach would do us both some good."

Abe's reaction was priceless. His chin dropped, and his eyebrows shot up. As Mary headed back to the kitchen, she had the sensation of floating a few inches above the floor. Grandpa did a double take as she passed him, but he didn't say a word. However, she did hear a soft chuckle, letting her know he was aware that something was up.

Ever since she had spotted Abe in the corner of the classroom when she first arrived, Mary had thought he was cute. He'd obviously noticed her, too, but not in the same way. From the moment they exchanged their first words, he seemed bent on tormenting her with practical jokes and mild, good-natured taunting. He was funny, but she worked hard not to let him know she thought so. And he hadn't changed much.

Not wanting to face Abe so soon after her emotional vault, Mary talked Shelley, one of the other servers, into bringing him his food and the message that she'd see him at three o'clock sharp out in front of the restaurant.

Shelley came back, laughing. "He was definitely disappointed to see me, but he said to let you know he'll be there on the dot."

"Good," Mary replied. "I don't like it when people are late."

"That's because you're a Penner. Your grandparents insist on punctuality, which is why there are so few of us working here."

"I'm sure." Mary also knew that the small staff had something to do with her grandparents' frugality. They didn't believe in having more than what was needed, including employees. Grandpa expected everyone to work hard, but he compensated everyone well enough to keep the conscientious people.

"So are you and Abe dating?" Shelley asked.

"Ha. Not in this lifetime."

Shelley stood still and cast a questioning glance Mary's way. "You said that awfully fast." She folded her arms and narrowed her eyes as a sly grin worked its way to her lips. "That usually means something."

Mary planted a hand on her hip and scowled. "It means nothing, except if I don't agree to go out with Abe Glick, he'll keep after me until I do, so I might as well get it over with."

"Then what?" Shelley smiled.

Mary lifted her hands. "Then we go right back to how we've always been."

"Which is?"

"Do you ever stop asking questions?"

"Okay," Shelley relented, turning back to pick up the next order. "I guess it's none of my business."

"I guess you're right." Shelley started to walk away. "Wait, Shelley."

Shelley turned around, the plates balanced on her arms. "Ya?"

"I—I just wanted to tell you how much I appreciate you trying to help."

"You really need to think about opening up and letting people in a little more."

Mary forced a smile and nodded. Shelley would never understand. Whenever people looked at Mary, she was sure they saw her mother—and in this community, that wasn't a good thing. Other people had left, and she heard the talk.

The rest of the day was busy as always. Between visits from the Mennonites and Amish from the Pinecraft community and the tourists, Penner's Restaurant did quite well. Grandma's pies were especially popular. Folks from other parts of the country had heard of her peanut butter, pumpkin custard, banana cream, and key lime pies, and once they tried them, they spread the word even more.

Around two thirty, Shelley pointed to the clock. "A half hour to go. Do you need to freshen up? If you do, I'll cover for you."

"No, I'm fine." Mary thought about how disheveled she must look after serving the busy lunch crowd. "It's just Abe."

"Abe is a very nice-looking man."

"You think so?" Mary asked. "Then why don't you go for him?"

Shelley let out a low growling sound. "You're impossible, Mary. You know I already have a man."

"But you're not married or engaged."

"Not yet," Shelley conceded. "But I have a feeling it won't be long." She tilted her head and batted her eyelashes. "And now it's your turn to find love."

"I think not. There is no one around here who would even consider getting engaged to me." Shelley was one of the few people who'd given her the time of day since they first met, so she'd understand. "People can't seem to separate me from my mother."

"That's not true. I think you're the one who can't let go of what happened. A man who has a heart for God understands what a good woman you are and what an excellent wife you will make. If I'm reading him correctly, Abe wants to court you."

"Maybe you need stronger glasses, Shelley." She wiped her hands on the dishrag and tossed it onto the counter. "I think I will go check my kapp. I wouldn't want any loose hair flying around."

"Oh no, you wouldn't want that," Shelley teased. "Heaven forbid Abe would see your hair down."

"Quite frankly," Mary admitted, "I don't care one way or another, but Grandma and Grandpa do care, and I'm not about to get them mad."

A minute later, Mary stood in front of the restroom mirror, kapp in hand, studying her hair. Her mother had always said it was her best feature, but according to Conservative Mennonite custom, she wasn't allowed to show it off. Or at least not all of it.

She removed the clip, raked her fingers through her waist-length hair, then wound it back up in a bun and refastened it. She tucked in her kapp on the sides to expose a little more of her hair before pinning it back into place. Her makeup-free face was pale from being indoors all day, so she pinched her cheeks to give them a little color. Not that she cared what Abe thought. She just wanted to freshen up a bit.

Once she was satisfied with how she looked, she tried to scoot out of the restaurant but stopped when she heard her name. "Mary, it's not three o'clock yet. Where are you going?"

Mary turned around to face Grandpa, who stood there with a knowing smile. "Um. . .I don't want to be late."

"Eager to see Abe, are we?" He was obviously working hard to hold back his laughter. "Never mind. I'm sure he's just as excited to see you."

"I am not eager or excited to see Abe."

"Of course you're not." He flicked his hand toward the door. "Go on, get out of here. You and Abe have some fun, okay? Tell him I said so."

"I will, Grandpa." Mary left without arguing. Grandpa was too old to understand anything on her mind, so there was no purpose in telling him.

❧

Abe had arrived a few minutes early. In his haste to be on time, he had David pick him up at two o'clock.

"Got a date?" David said.

"In a way, I suppose it is. Why?"

"Twice to town in one day. I'm getting used to daily, but there's definitely something going on."

"Nothing going on but getting to know a smart-mouthed woman who makes me laugh."

David tilted his head back and guffawed. "That's the best kind. You'll never be bored if she can make you laugh."

"Neh, I'd never be bored with her, that's for sure."

"So, does she like you, too?"

"Ya, I can see it in her eyes, but she doesn't know it yet. She keeps trying to put me in my place, but that won't work with me."

"Looks to me like it's working." David had turned the music down on his radio, but the sound of the bass still thumped through the van. He tapped his steering wheel in time to the music as Abe thought about what David had said.

"How you figure?" Abe finally asked.

"Figure what? That whatever she's doing is working on you?"

"Ya."

"You keep coming back for more."

Abe scrunched his face. "Never thought about it that way."

"You don't have much experience with women, do you?"

"Neh, I've spent most of my life studying and learning about the farm."

David nodded. "That's what I figured. You're a smart man, Abe. If you ever want some pointers, I'll be glad to give you some."

"No offense to you, David, but I'll try to figure her out on my own. You never met anyone like Mary Penner."

"I'm sure. If she's got you all worked up, she must be quite a woman."

Abe folded his arms and tucked his hands under his arms as he snickered. "That's one way to describe her."

Mary Penner was a smart girl. After she settled down and accepted the Mennonite ways, she was one of the best students in class. In their last year of high school, he'd asked her if she was going to college. As she shook her head no and replied that her grandparents wanted her to help with their restaurant, he could see her sadness. Mary could have done whatever she wanted, but she was loyal to the people who had taken her in. Abe admired and respected her even more for that.

As David turned the corner, Abe caught sight of Mary standing outside the restaurant. His pulse pounded through his body, and a lump formed in his throat.

"Is that her?"

"Ya." He unfolded his arms and gripped the armrest.

"Don't be nervous, man. When a woman waits for a man, it means she likes him."

Abe nodded. "That is what I'm thinking. Now I need to find a way to make her see that." He cleared his throat. "Can you slow down a bit?"

David snorted. "Don't worry, you'll be just fine. Want me to pick the two of you up later?" He pulled to a stop about ten feet from the curb where Mary stood.

"Can you wait here? We want to go to the beach, and I think we might need a ride."

"Okay." David gestured toward Mary. "You better go, or you might lose her before you have her. I'll be right here."

Abe got out and strode over to Mary, who quickly glanced away. "Been waiting long?"

She turned back to face him, her face flushed and her hands in a tight clasp in front of her. "Yup. Too long. What were you and that man talking about?"

"That's David. He's one of the folks who picks up some of the farmers when we need to come to town. He wanted to know when to pick us up."

She tilted her head and smirked. "Is that all?"

"I don't know." Abe rubbed the back of his neck with one hand and extended the other hand toward the van. "Come on, Mary. David can take us to the beach."

She hesitated. "I don't know David."

"But I do. The beach is too far to walk."

"I generally ride a bus that has a route and other people."

"I've been using David as a driver for a long time, and I trust him." He gave her the best assuring look he could. "Why would we ride the bus when David's right here?" Abe glanced over his shoulder and saw the amused expression on David's face. He didn't know what to do, so he just stood there, looking back and forth between Mary and David.

"Oh all right," Mary finally said as she forged ahead toward the van. "I'll have you to protect me if anything happens."

Abe opened the door for Mary; then he climbed in after her. "Mary, this is my friend David."

"Nice to meet you, Mary." David nodded to Mary and grinned at Abe. "Buckle up, and we'll be on our way."

They were at the beach ten minutes later. Abe helped Mary out of the van and handed David some money.

"What time do you want me to pick you up? The wife has plans for us tonight, so I'll need to be home by seven."

"We won't be that late. I'll call you."

"My evening will just be getting started." David gestured toward Mary. "See you two soon."

Abe and Mary stood on the sidewalk and watched David drive off before Abe turned toward her. "David is a good man."

"Yes, he seems to be." Mary shielded her eyes from the western sun. "There sure are a lot of people out today."

"That's because it's nice out." Abe wasn't sure what to do next, so he reached for her hand and placed it in the crook of his arm. "Let's enjoy ourselves this afternoon, okay?" For a moment, he thought she might remove her hand, but when she didn't right away, he relaxed a little.

They took a few steps on the sidewalk, then stopped to remove their shoes. It was easier for Mary because all she wore was a pair of clogs. Abe had to remove his shoes and socks, then turned to Mary in time to see the grin form on her lips.

"So what is this all about?" she asked once they resumed walking on the sidewalk beside the road. "Why have you been so adamant about hanging around me lately?"

"I—" Abe was interrupted by the honking of a horn.

"Hey, Abe! What are you doing with her? Taking a walk on the wild side?"

"Who was that?" Mary asked.

Abe narrowed his eyes and gritted his teeth. "That's Jeremiah Yoder."

"Oh yeah, I remember him. I heard he left the church."

"He did," Abe replied. "He never came back after his rumspringa."

"That happens to a lot of people, doesn't it?"

"Ya. I s'pose once some folks get a taste of the wild life, some of them have trouble finding pleasure in plain, simple living." He shrugged. "But I think most have the sense to come back." As soon as those words left his mouth, he regretted it. Abe never wanted Mary to think he was judging her for something she had no control over.

"Yeah, it must be hard." Her voice was laced with pain and defensiveness.

Abe stopped and turned Mary around to face him. "I am so sorry, Mary. I never should have said that."

"No big deal. Don't worry about it."

Chapter 3

Mary tried her best to hide the lump in her throat. What Abe just described was exactly what had happened to her mother.

He continued shaking his head. "I would never want to say mean things to you, even when you aren't nice to me. I understand—"

She reached up and gently touched his lips. "Don't."

Before she had a chance to retract her hand, he reached for her wrist and held her fingers to his lips. Her heart hammered as he kissed her fingertips, one by one, until her knees almost buckled beneath her.

Abe's expression was tender as he looked down at her. Mary's dry mouth prevented her from speaking at first. She yanked her hand back and covered it with her other hand.

"I'm sorry, Mary." He grimaced then shook his head. "No, I'm not. I take that back. I'm not sorry in the least."

Mary managed to find her voice. "So what was that all about, Abe? Were you trying to distract me? Or are you in cahoots with Jeremiah and his buddies?"

"No. Never. I have nothing to do with Jeremiah."

"I don't think that's so good either." Mary shoved her fist on her hip and leaned away from Abe.

"What? Did I say something wrong?"

"So you believe in shunning people who leave the church?"

"Don't be so touchy, Mary." Abe widened his eyes as he took a step closer to her. Before she had a chance to react, he reached out and closed his fingers around her wrist again. "I never said that I believe in shunning. What I do believe in is doing what is right and standing up for someone I care about. I can't let someone say such things about you, Mary." He bent his elbow toward her and placed her hand back in the crook of his arm where it had been. "Come on. We're supposed to be walking on the beach, and that's what I intend to do."

Mary's confusion deepened. She wanted to appreciate Abe's chivalry, but she still didn't know why he'd bother with her when there were plenty of other Mennonite girls who would love to be with him.

"What's on your mind?" he asked as they stepped off the sidewalk onto the warm sand.

"What makes you think anything is on my mind?"

Abe rubbed her knuckles with his other hand. "That's my girl. I like when you answer my questions with a question of your own."

She paused at his comment, *That's my girl.* "But why?"

He beamed down at her. "You make me think. I like to be with people who make me think."

"Sometimes thinking is overrated." She stumbled over some uneven sand, and he quickly reached around to steady her. "I can be so clumsy."

"It may be overrated to you, but it keeps our minds sharp. And you are not clumsy—just a little unsteady, having trouble navigating the sand today."

Yeah, she was unsteady, but it had nothing to do with the sand. It was all about the butterflies flapping around in her abdomen every time Abe touched her or looked at her with those light brown eyes with golden flecks that sparkled in the late-afternoon sun.

They walked about a quarter mile before Abe tugged on Mary. "Let's take a break. I want to slow down and enjoy our time together." He tucked his fingers beneath her chin and tilted her face up.

Her stomach lurched, and she stepped back. Another tender moment would send her senses to a place she wasn't ready to go. She had to change the mood—quickly. "There's something else I don't understand, Abe. You went away to college and got your degree in business. What do you plan to do with your education?"

He shrugged. "I s'pose I'm doing it."

"Working on the farm? You didn't have to go to college to do that. You could go into business if you wanted to."

"What business?"

"Banking?" She couldn't think of anything else.

"Neh, not banking. I like farming. Besides, who says I'm not in business? I run one of the biggest and most productive dairy farms on the west coast of Florida. I've managed to convert the last of the celery crops to citrus, and we expect to have our best yield next season."

Mary was impressed, but her insides still swirled from Abe's nearness, making it difficult to hold an intelligent conversation. She extended her foot and glided it across the sand, smoothing out a section.

"Do you want to walk some more or sit down for a while?" he asked.

"Um. . .I didn't bring anything to sit on."

Abe laughed. "That didn't stop you before. You sat right down on the sand."

Yeah, but she didn't have anything to risk. . .like her heart. "This is a nicer skirt than the one I wore yesterday."

"Ya, I s'pose you should think about your skirt." Abe held her gaze as a suppressed grin twitched the corners of his lips.

She swatted at him. "Let's walk."

"Ouch." He feigned being injured. "Apparently you didn't know we Mennonites are opposed to violence."

"If that hurt, you're a bigger sissy than I ever thought, Abe."

He pulled his straw hat down a little in the front. "No one ever calls Abe Glick a sissy."

Mary tossed him a playful glance then took off running. "Sissy, sissy, sissy! Abe Glick is a sissy!"

"Oh, you." He ran after her and quickly caught her in his arms.

As he pulled her close, she knew running had been a big mistake. Abe had never been one to back away from a challenge, and he'd never let her get away. It took him about two seconds to catch her in his strong arms, but his grip was very gentle. He was stubborn but not mean. His Mennonite heritage ran deep with Abe—all the way to his core.

When Abe turned her around, everything outside their bubble of closeness was blurry. She wanted him to kiss her, but she wasn't ready to put herself in such a vulnerable position. A memory of her mother being fondled by one of the many faceless men in her life flashed through her mind. Panic overrode her desire, so she yanked away and nearly threw herself onto the sand as she popped out of his grip.

"What happened, Mary?" The look of concern on Abe's face tweaked her heart. "Did I hurt you?"

"No," she said quickly. "Yes, but not like you think."

"Why do you talk in circles? Either I hurt you, or I didn't. I asked a direct question, and I expect a direct answer."

"Too bad." Mary tucked the loose strands of hair back beneath her kapp. "I don't have any answers to give."

"Why do you continue to shut people out, Mary?"

"I'm not the one shutting people out. In case you haven't figured it out, other people have already made up their minds about me, and there's nothing I can do to change them."

"Maybe you're imagining some of it."

"I don't think so." She folded her arms.

He glanced at her arms then looked her in the eye. "Perhaps people are afraid to get close to you because you are so standoffish. Perhaps your shame made you that way?"

"What? I am not standoffish." She unfolded her arms and lifted her hands. "I'm as open as the next person."

He gave her a lopsided grin. "Oh you are, are you?"

"Never mind. You'd have to be me to understand." She took a step back.

His once-rigid shoulders sagged. "You confuse me."

Not as much as she confused herself. All she knew was how the flood of emotion when she was around Abe rendered her incapable of logical thinking.

She opened her mouth to respond, but she had no idea what to tell him, so she shook her head and lifted her hands before letting them fall back to her sides, slapping her skirt.

They studied each other for a moment before Mary looked down at the sand. Abe took a few steps toward the water, his hands in his pockets, his hat tipped low in front. She had a brief flashback to what Jeremiah had hollered as he drove past them honking. Did Abe really like her, or did he have an ulterior motive in wanting to be with her?

She remembered Mama saying once that everyone wanted something. Was Abe looking to take a "walk on the wild side," as Jeremiah had so crudely put it? Or did Abe feel sorry for her? These were questions she had to ask herself, and she'd never be satisfied until she knew the answers.

"Abe?" She squared her shoulders and tried to put on a brave front.

He spun around and took a couple of steps toward her. "Ya?"

Mary licked her parched lips. As he looked into her eyes, her bravery faded. She offered a closed-mouth grin. "Never mind."

Abe awkwardly offered his arm, but she pretended not to notice. He quickly retracted. "Ready to head back now?"

"Yeah." Mary turned to face the water before adding, "You should call David now."

"That's exactly what I'm about to do."

Mary heard Abe let David know they were ready for him to come pick them up. After he flipped his cell phone shut, she remained standing with her back to him.

"If I knew what I did wrong, I could apologize."

"You did nothing wrong. Where is David picking us up?"

"Where he dropped us off," Abe replied. "He said he'll be there in fifteen minutes."

"Then we best get going."

Since they hadn't gone far, they were able to saunter back. Quite a few people—most of them tourists—stared at them. Mary thought she was used to it, but now it bothered her. She didn't like feeling like a sideshow. She wanted to be accepted for who she was deep down—not for something she was trying to be. The problem was that she wasn't sure who she was.

David was waiting for them when they arrived. "Glad you finished up early. The wife called and said to come home as early as possible."

"It's always a good idea to make the wife happy," Abe said as he helped Mary into the van.

David chuckled. "That's a wise comment coming from a single man."

This discussion made Mary very uncomfortable. After buckling her seat belt, she shifted and faced the window. Abe left the seat next to her empty, and he took the one by the opposite window. She didn't want to admit it, even to herself, but she enjoyed having him close. His quiet strength gave her a sense that nothing bad could happen.

Instead of chatting, David turned up the music a little louder. The oldies song on the radio brought her back to a time she constantly tried to forget. Good thing they didn't have far to go.

The van slowed down a few feet from the walkway to the restaurant. "Nice meeting you, Mary."

She smiled and nodded. "Thank you."

"Could you wait here a minute while I walk Mary inside?" Abe asked.

David glanced at his watch then nodded. "Take your time. I don't think a few minutes will make that much difference since you called so early."

Mary got out and turned to face Abe. "You don't have to walk me inside. I know the way."

"But I want—"

"No, I'm perfectly capable of taking care of myself." She realized her tone was harsher than she intended, but she didn't feel like apologizing. Seemed lately she spent a lot of time explaining herself, and she was getting tired of it.

"Yes, I'm sure you can, Mary, and you may have your way this time." He tilted her head up to face him. "But remember that I don't give up easily."

Mary turned her back and walked toward the restaurant, knowing Abe watched her. As soon as she was inside, she heard the van door slam. Grandpa stood there waiting, but he didn't say a word. All he did was nod as she breezed past to get her things.

She started to go out the back door to her three-wheeler, but then she decided to go ahead and get the discussion over with. She put her tote on the counter and plodded toward the front of the restaurant.

"We had a very nice time at the beach, Grandpa," she said.

"Good." He grinned and widened his stance. "So will you be going out with Abe again soon?"

"I doubt it."

A frown replaced his smile. "Did he say anything inappropriate?"

"No, Grandpa. We're just both very busy people with not enough time."

"Don't say that, Granddaughter. You have to make time for what is important in life. What are you, twenty-two?"

"Twenty-three," she corrected.

"Old enough to fall in love, get married, and have children of your own."

"I'm not ready for anything that serious, Grandpa. I'm comfortable living with you and Grandma, and working here makes me very happy. I get to serve people who appreciate it."

"Ya. And you are very good at it. But this isn't what your life should be about. The Lord blesses two people who fall in love, and that's what I want for you."

Who said anything about love? "Thank you, Grandpa. Maybe someday."

"Ya, someday." He nodded. "Maybe soon."

"I'm going home to help Grandma with supper. See you at the house in a little while."

"Ya. Eleanor can close the restaurant. Tell your grandmother I'm bringing home some pie for dessert so she won't make more."

Mary left out the back door, grabbing her tote off the counter on her way out. She tossed it into the basket and hopped on her three-wheeler.

❧

David didn't say much as they rode to the Glick farm. He apparently sensed that Abe needed some quiet time. However, right before they turned onto the long shell road leading to the house, he spoke up.

"So how was your walk on the beach with Mary?"

"It was good."

They hit a bump as they turned, so David slowed down. "Don't wanna talk about it, huh?"

"There's nothing much to say."

"Is this a relationship that may lead to something bigger?"

"Bigger? Are you asking if there's romance?"

With one of his customary chuckles, David nodded. "Yeah, I guess that's what I'm asking."

Abe inhaled deeply then slowly exhaled. "That's what I would like, but I'm not so sure about Mary. She seems to still be hurting from her past."

"I take it you know something about her past that would bother her."

"Ya, but mostly what I've heard from other people, and that was a long time ago. She can't seem to let go of her past, and she thinks other people are holding it against her. I have to tread very lightly on that subject when I'm with her."

"How long have you known this girl?"

"Nine years. I met her when she arrived to live with her grandparents. She wasn't Mennonite before coming here. Her first day of school, she walked in looking so lost and scared." Abe's heart twisted at the memory. "She wore plain clothes, but everyone could tell she was uncomfortable in them, especially her kapp. She kept fidgeting with it."

"I can understand someone having a tough time getting used to the customs," David said. "No offense meant, though. All I'm saying is change is tough for most people."

"No offense taken. Ya, I'm used to this, but I can see how someone who was never around the plain and simple way of life might be uncomfortable. But that's not what bothered me."

"Obviously, something did bother you." David pulled to a stop in front of Abe's house. "Wanna talk about it? I have a little time."

"I thought you were in a hurry."

"I can spare a few minutes."

Abe pondered discussing something so personal with someone outside the faith and decided it had some advantages in this case. "Ya. I would like to talk."

David turned off the ignition and turned around to face Abe. "So tell me what's on your mind."

"Most of the other girls didn't understand all she'd been through. All they knew was what they'd heard, and they didn't give her much of a chance. There was one girl, though, who tried to help her. That's Shelley, who works for her grandfather at the restaurant."

"Did the other girls make fun of her or say mean things?"

"Neh." Abe shook his head and leaned against the door. "It might have been easier if they had. They didn't say much of anything to her. I imagine Mary felt like an outcast."

"How about you? Did you talk to her?"

"Ya. Mary and I became friends."

"Friends, huh?" David nodded. "That's how my wife and I started out, until I got the nerve to tell her how I really felt. I was so in love with that girl, I never knew which way was up."

"I know what you mean," Abe said. "I've felt that way around Mary since before I went off to college. I thought I would forget about her, but when I came back and saw her working for her grandfather, it felt like my world got brighter." He cast his gaze downward. "I just don't know what to do next."

"Sounds like the real thing to me, Abe. So what's stopping you from just coming right out and telling her what you told me?"

"It isn't that easy. She's very touchy about getting close. I think she still has problems trusting people."

"That's understandable, after the reception you said she got when she came here."

"I think it's even deeper than that. Something happened in her past that she has never told me about."

"Do you know this for a fact?"

"Neh, but I sense it. I can imagine how she feels about people ignoring her, but she shuts me out when anything comes up about what happened before she came to Sarasota."

"Why do you care so much?" David asked. "It's not like there aren't more than enough Mennonite girls to go around."

Abe's lips twitched into a smile. He'd heard this before from his father, who kept after him to find a wife when he first returned from college. "I don't want just any girl. She has to be special."

David nodded his understanding. "I getcha, and I agree. You deserve someone special."

"I don't know about deserve. I'm happy with whatever the Lord provides, but I can't help but think He brought Mary into my life for a reason."

David's forehead crinkled, and he grew silent for a few seconds before he asked, "Any way you can find out what's bugging her?"

Abe thought for a moment, then shook his head. "I don't know." He opened the door and got out. "Thank you for listening. Have fun with your wife tonight."

David lifted his hand in a wave. "I intend to. Take care, Abe."

After Abe went inside, he fixed himself a grilled cheese and ham sandwich to keep his stomach from rumbling later. If David had more time, Abe would have ordered something from Penner's, where the food was filling and delicious.

If he hadn't set his mind and heart on winning Mary over, he could be married by now, and dinner would be a feast, no matter what she prepared. Like David had said, there were plenty of unmarried girls who would be happy to find a husband with land and a good future.

⌒

"Mary Penner, you haven't said more than five words since you got home." Grandma stood at Mary's bedroom door glaring at her. "You can at least tell me what you and Abe talked about."

"We didn't say much, Grandma. We mostly just walked on the beach and looked at the water."

"Did he tell you why he asked you out on a date?"

Mary stiffened. "It wasn't a date."

"In my book, when a man asks a woman to go somewhere with him, it's a date. What do you call it then?"

"Just a walk on the beach."

Grandma placed her hands on her wide hips, closed her eyes, and slowly turned her head from side to side before looking directly at Mary. "Walking on the beach with a man is the same as going out to eat with a man. Either one is a date. What's wrong with you, Granddaughter?"

The same sensation she'd always felt when her mother used to shame her into conceding flooded Mary. "Nothing is wrong with me, Grandma. I don't know what all this fuss is about me going to the beach with Abe."

Grandma lifted a finger and shook it. "I tell you what's wrong, Mary. You're a woman now. A twenty-three-year-old woman who should start con- sidering her future. Abe obviously cares enough about you to go out of his way to be with you."

Mary pursed her lips. Nothing she could say would make a difference in what her grandparents thought.

"Mark my words, Granddaughter, Abe is not going to wait around for you forever. I just happen to know several young women who think he would make a good husband."

Mary gasped. "I'm not even thinking about getting married."

"Maybe it's time you started thinking about it. I don't want you to become a lonely old woman with no one to love you. Your grandpa and I are all you have. If we could have had more children, you would have aunts, uncles, and cousins. As it is, after we're gone there will be no one left but you."

"Yes, Grandma, I realize that. But you and Grandpa are very healthy, and I expect the two of you to be around for a very long time."

"Only the Lord knows, Mary. Just remember that."

Yes, and only the Lord knew what Mary should do. Now if He'd only find a way to let her know how to handle Grandma and Grandpa's nudges toward what she wasn't sure of. She'd seen plenty of successful relationships since being in Sarasota, but images of the past her mother had tried unsuccessfully to shelter her from continued to haunt her.

"I made some beef stew, and it will be ready when your grandpa comes home from the restaurant."

"I'll help you get it on the table," Mary said. "Just let me know when."

After Grandma left, Mary bowed her head and prayed. *Lord, I am so confused. I like Abe very much, and he makes me feel things no one else does. But does that mean I should do something different from what I'm doing? I want to do Your will, but I don't know what that is.* She opened her eyes then slammed them shut again. *I don't want Abe to feel sorry for me or pity my past. I do care for him, but not enough to complicate his life or mine. I would be such a burden to him, and I would never feel worthy of his name.*

Mary repositioned the kapp on her head and carefully pinned it to prevent more hair from escaping. It was almost summer, when the Florida humidity created stray frizz that would form a halo around her face. After she pulled herself together, she went to the kitchen to help Grandma get dinner on the table. Grandpa walked in with a big smile on his face.

"After you left, I heard from some people who saw you and Abe this afternoon." He turned to Grandma. "I suspect we might be planning a wedding soon."

"According to our granddaughter, that isn't likely."

Grandpa cut his glance back and forth between Mary and Grandma and finally settled on Mary. "Then you best not be cavorting with Abe anymore, or you risk ruining your reputation."

Grandma spun around and faced Mary. "Cavorting? What did you and Abe do?"

Chapter 4

Mary was temporarily tongue-tied. Grandpa plopped down in his chair and picked up his fork. "It isn't a good idea to show affection for someone in such a public place, Mary."

"Grandpa, I didn't do anything wrong. Abe and I walked on the beach. H–he took my hand and—"

"You don't need to make excuses," Grandma said. "If you did something wrong, the Lord knows about it. If not, then you have nothing to worry about or explain."

With her emotional stirrings already creating confusion, Mary couldn't argue. She tightened her lips and nodded.

Grandpa motioned for them to join him at the table. "I believe she knows what the Lord wants, Sarah. We need to trust our Mary. She's a good girl."

Although Mary was happy Grandpa defended her, he was the one who'd started this to begin with. Mama's words kept ringing in her ears. *Men can't be trusted. They only come around when they want something.*

"Mary?" Grandpa tilted his head forward and lifted his eyebrows. "The blessing."

Grandpa took her hand, gave Mary's fingers an extra gentle squeeze, and winked at her. She forced a smile and lowered her head. As he said the blessing, she tried to push Abe's image from her mind—but it was impossible.

As soon as they filled their plates, Grandpa started talking about how busy they'd been with the summer crowd lately. "It's starting early this year. I'd planned to add more to my food orders in another month, but it looks like I need to do it this week."

"I can stay later in the afternoons," Grandma offered.

"That would be good." Grandpa turned to face Mary. "Anyone you knew in school who might need a job?"

Mary slowly shook her head as she wondered why he'd even bother to ask. Both Grandma and Grandpa knew that very few of the people she knew in school would give her more than a few passing words.

"Ya, I didn't think so." Grandpa took a bite of his yeast roll and chewed as he thought about it. "Perhaps we can ask some people at church tomorrow. Eleanor is working out very well, but it's difficult for her to manage the kitchen while she's on the floor taking orders."

"Good idea," Grandma said. "This is potluck Sunday, so we'll be there longer."

Mary always felt out of place at the church potluck, and she dreaded the second Sunday of every month. After the service everyone gathered outside, unless it was too hot or rainy. Then they'd meet in the fellowship hall instead. No one was outright mean to Mary. In fact, some of the older members were very polite, but the people her age had maintained their old habit of ignoring her.

Abe had been to a couple of the dinners since he'd been back from college. She wondered if he'd be there tomorrow. A sliver of hope was dashed by dread at the thought of Grandma's eagle eyes watching her talk to Abe, waiting to pounce if she stepped the slightest bit out of line.

After dinner Mary told her grandparents that she could clean up the kitchen alone. "It's your turn to go for a walk with Grandma," she said to Grandpa.

He laughed and rubbed his belly. "Ya, that's probably a good idea after such a hearty meal."

As soon as they left the house, Mary scurried around the kitchen, washing dishes and cleaning all the counters and the table. She wanted to be done with all the work when they got back.

⸻

Abe got up early and made sure all the cows were fed before going back inside to get ready for church. One of his workers had set up a table at the farmer's market in town yesterday, and he'd left the money by the back door. Abe was pleased by the fact that everything had sold. This looked like it would be a busy tourist season, which he thanked the Lord for after hearing about the past two seasons being so lean.

He intended to go to the potluck after church with the hope of talking to Mary. So far his plan to pique her interest seemed to be working. Perhaps over a slice of one of her grandmother's delicious pies, they could find some common ground and maybe he'd get a step or two closer to breaking down her wall.

Mary Penner was quite a challenge, which would have had his mother asking if that was her appeal. Abe remembered his mother's spunk. She never backed down from anyone, and she always had a quick quip. Dad had married the same type of woman Abe knew he wanted.

With a chuckle and a lighter step, Abe dressed in his Sunday finest trousers, a white shirt, and a vest he'd pulled out from the back of the closet. The one he wore last week had become frayed from age.

He stepped out on the front porch in time to see the cloud of dust billowing as his ride turned onto his property. David was right on time. As soon as the car stopped, Abe ambled over and got into the passenger seat. He snapped the seat belt in place.

"I appreciate you picking me up again, David. I know it's a lot to ask a man to work on Sunday."

"My pleasure. I'm starting to feel like we're old friends."

Abe adjusted his shirt and vest as David pulled onto the asphalt beyond the long driveway. His mother had made him this shirt years ago, but he hadn't worn it much because she wanted him to save it for something special.

David glanced at him then turned back to face the road. "You look nice, Abe. New duds?"

"Same kind of thing I always wear." Abe kept his focus straight ahead.

"Right." David snickered. "Will she be there?"

"If you're talking about Mary, yes, I imagine she will be. I don't think she or her grandparents ever miss church."

"My wife always goes to church, and sometimes I go with her to make her happy."

Abe turned to face David. "That seems strange to me. Why wouldn't you want to go all the time?"

David shrugged. "It's just not my thing."

"What if the Lord were to think the same of you?"

As they came to a stop sign, David nodded. "Good point. I never really thought about it like that."

"If you only do what is. . .your *thing*, then some of the important things might not get done." Abe paused, and when David didn't say anything, he continued. "God created us and gave us these lives, so why wouldn't we show our appreciation and worship Him as He instructed us to?"

David grinned. "Have you been talking to my wife? You sound just like her."

"Your wife is obviously a wise woman. Maybe you should listen to her more."

"I think I just might do that. In fact, I'm going to go straight home after I drop you off and tell her I'm going to church with her. She might fall over dead from shock."

"Or jump up and down with joy," Abe countered.

"That would be good. Thanks, buddy. I think you're good for me."

"The Lord puts people into our lives for a reason. You and I are good for each other."

"Yeah, we are." David stopped the van in front of the church, where several families had already gathered. "What time do you want me to pick you up?"

"Mind if I call? I plan to stay for the potluck afterward, and that can go on for a while."

"That's fine. I'll make sure I turn my cell phone on after I get out of church so I don't miss your call. I'll be taking a few people home right after church, but I should be available."

Abe got out, closed the door, and waved to David before turning and walking toward the church. Ruthie, one of the girls from school who was still single, shyly lifted her hand in a greeting as he approached the front door.

"Hi, Ruthie. Nice day, eh?"

"Ya, it's a very nice day." Her sister standing behind her nudged her, causing her to lose her balance.

Abe reached out and gave her a steadying hand. "Whoa there, Ruthie."

Ruthie looked flustered as she glanced back at her sister, who stood there grinning. "Thank you, Abe. I—"

"Hi there, Abe!" a deep voice from behind bellowed.

Abe turned around to see Joseph Penner, followed by his wife, Sarah, and Mary trailing behind. He was sure Mary saw him, but she didn't look him in the eye.

"Excuse me, Ruthie, but I want to talk to someone."

"Ya, it was good seeing you, Abe."

As he walked away from Ruthie, he overheard her sister asking why she didn't say more. Ruthie was a nice girl, but she didn't have the ability to send his senses soaring the way Mary did.

Joseph stopped in front of Abe, and Sarah glanced over her shoulder, where Mary stood fidgeting with the folds of her skirt. Abe wanted to step past Mary's grandparents and talk to her, but he wasn't about to be rude.

"So how's the farm coming along?" Joseph asked.

"Bumper crop. Cows are all producing. Couldn't be better." Abe's gaze locked with Mary's, and he saw a tiny twitch of amusement. His mouth suddenly went dry.

"That's good. The Glick farm has always been a good producer."

"Let me know what you need for the restaurant, and I'll make sure you have it."

"Thank you. You're a fine man, Abe."

Abe flashed a polite smile at Joseph before leaning around to look at Mary. "Will you be staying for the potluck, Mary?"

"Yes," she replied. "What else do you think I'd be doing?"

"Mary!" Sarah glared at her granddaughter before shaking her head as she looked at Abe. "I apologize for my granddaughter."

"Oh that's quite all right. I understand."

Mary narrowed her eyes as her lips puckered. It took every ounce of self-restraint for Abe not to laugh.

"We best be getting inside," Joseph said. "You and Mary can talk later."

Throughout the service, Abe cast occasional glances Mary's way. Once or twice he thought he might have caught her looking back at him, but she'd become a master of avoidance. He understood, based on her past and all, but he wished he could break through her shell enough for her to trust him. That was his first goal, and he knew it wouldn't be easy.

After the sermon, some children went up front and sang a cappella. The sweetness of their voices moved Abe. When he glanced at Mary, his heart melted at the sight of tears glistening in her eyes, obviously the result of her emotions tugging at her as his did him.

⋙

Mary's heart ached at the memory of her own childhood and how much she missed out on. Instead of being here with other children, singing, she'd been darting about, running away from men with her mother. Sunday mornings had been the only time they'd spent together, but never in church. A few times Mama had tried to explain who God was, but her attempts were awkward. Until Mary came here to live with Grandma and Grandpa, all she'd thought about God was that He was cruel, and His only intent was to punish anyone who strayed from the very narrow path He'd laid before them.

Abe's lingering gaze did little to quell her sadness. He'd been just like those children, singing his heart out for the Lord while the adults listened with rapt attention. All this did was serve as another reminder of why she and Abe weren't meant to be together. No matter what Grandma and Grandpa said, Mary still didn't quite fit in. But she wasn't cut out for her former life either.

Mary still felt like an island—so alone and without anyone who could see how much she hurt inside. And she didn't dare let anyone know, in case her mother had been right. When she was younger, she thought that if anyone had any idea of all she'd seen, she'd be cast out of the community and never allowed back in. Now that she was older and realized she wasn't being shunned, all she felt was shame.

Grandma and Grandpa loved her. They knew her mother had done some bad things, and they even knew what some of those things were. But if they had any idea how much unmentionable decadence Mary had been exposed to, even they would have reason to pause before letting her into their home. She'd covered for her mother by lying to bosses and other men. They'd run away in the middle of the night a couple of times, and once when a man came looking for her mother asking for money he said she'd stolen, Mary had told him a string of lies to make him go away. Mary shuddered. She'd been an accessory to many evils that she never wanted anyone to know about. But the Lord knew, so she'd never be able to completely escape her shame.

Grandpa tried to show a soft side with her, but Grandma's sternness was real and there all the time. Mama had loved Mary, but she obviously didn't have the judgment or discernment she needed to take care of a child. As much as Mary loved Mama, she wished she'd started out with the safety and shelter she now knew.

Abe caught her attention and smiled. She tried to smile back, but her chin quivered, and she had to look away.

Mary was relieved when the children finished the last of their songs. Music stirred her spirit to the point of dredging up even more of her past than she wanted to remember. After the singing was over and the pastor ended the service, everyone filed outside where the men had set up the tables and Grandma and a few of the other women had begun arranging the food. Mary tried to stay invisible as she helped.

Before she even heard his voice, Mary felt Abe's presence behind her. "That was a very touching service," he said softly. She turned to face him, and he lowered his head so only she could hear him. "I saw that you felt it, too. How sweet the sound of young, innocent voices."

Mary managed a small smile, and she nodded. "Yes, they were very sweet."

"I vaguely remember standing there singing for the congregation when I was a boy. If I knew then what I know now. . ." Abe chuckled. "Famous last words of many a man."

"Abe!"

They turned to see Grandpa heading toward them. "Don't look now, but I think we're about to have a chaperone."

"Mary, your grandmother needs you over by the dessert table." He looked at Abe. "You don't mind, do you?"

"For the sake of my sweet tooth, by all means, please see what your grandmother needs." Abe gestured toward the food. "I don't think anyone will leave hungry."

"I'll go see what she wants," Mary said as she took off toward the cluster of women arranging pies, cakes, and cookies. Deep down she was glad to have something else to do. All that talk about the innocence of children conjured up memories that had kept her up many nights.

Mary passed one table laden with various versions of potato salad, coleslaw, and an assortment of other cold vegetable dishes. The table on the other side hosted platters of roast beef, ham, and chicken. Abe was right. No one would go hungry today.

She'd barely arrived by her grandmother's side when the older woman shoved a platter of cookies toward her. "Take this to that extra table we're setting up." Grandma pointed to a bare table about twenty feet away. "We got more desserts than we expected."

Mary busied herself with mindless tasks, helping get everything organized. As people filled their plates with what had been laid out earlier, quite a few more dishes seemed to appear by the minute.

After the women were finished, the pastor asked everyone to gather so he could bless the meal. Everyone held hands. One of the children who'd sung earlier stood on one side of Mary, and Grandma's friend Helga was on the other. After the blessing, the little girl let go and scampered off, but Helga squeezed Mary's hand and pulled her in for a hug.

"You are a good girl, Mary."

"Thank you." Mary leaned away, but Helga still didn't let go.

"You do realize your grandparents love you very much, don't you?"

"Yes, of course."

"Your grandmother still struggles with Elizabeth's departure. Please understand how difficult that was for her."

Mary nodded as she wondered what Grandma had told Helga. She didn't know what to say, so she remained quiet.

"Sometimes I think Sarah is a little bit too stern with you, but I think she's afraid to loosen up for fear of something bad happening."

"I understand," Mary said softly.

"Do you really?" Helga released her grip and placed one hand on Mary's shoulder. "I know it can't be easy when you feel like someone is always angry. My mother was like that, after my sister left and never came back."

"I–I'm sorry. I didn't know about that."

Helga dropped her hand from Mary's shoulder and tilted her head. "Some people don't understand how blessed they are, and they go looking for happiness outside what brings true joy."

"Yes, I know."

"You'll be just fine, sweetheart. Now what's this I hear about Abe courting you?"

"Oh, we're just friends."

Helga leaned back and laughed. "Sure you are. Mary, you need to open your eyes and see how that man looks at you. He's smitten, even if you're not."

Once again Helga had rendered Mary speechless. She smiled and shrugged.

"Looks like the rest of the men are all in line now, so let's join the others, shall we?" Helga didn't wait for an answer before taking Mary by the hand and leading her over to the crowd around the tables.

After Mary filled her plate, she glanced around until she spotted Abe sitting at a table with some of the children. There was an empty place next to him. She wondered if he might be saving it for her. She was about to walk toward him when Ruthie plopped her plate on the table, and she sat down next to Abe. A stabbing sensation shot through Mary's chest, and she forced herself to turn away.

"Over here, Mary," Helga said, her hand lifted in the air. "We saved you a spot."

Thankful for a place to go, Mary darted over to where Helga, Helga's husband, Paul, her grandparents, and a few other people their age sat. As she passed some of the people she knew from school, some of them looked away as though pretending they didn't see her. Before sitting down, she looked around for Shelley.

"Who are you looking for?" Helga asked.

"Shelley. Do you know if she's here?"

"Her brother is sick, so she left right after church to help his wife," Grandma replied without looking up.

Mary suspected the reason Shelley was so kind to her was that her older brother had left the church before Mary met her, so she knew some things were out of Mary's control. Shelley still didn't understand all Mary had experienced.

"These rolls are excellent, Sarah," one of the other ladies at the table said to Grandma. "What's your secret?"

"Butter," Grandma replied. "Lots of it."

"Butter makes everything better."

"Looks like the tourists are coming early."

"Ya," Paul said. "And they like their ice cream."

Everyone smiled and nodded. "Your ice cream is the best there is."

"So I've been told." A few people laughed.

"You better make some pies and freeze them, Sarah. With all these tourists coming to Sarasota, they'll be wanting dessert every day."

"I might have to teach my granddaughter how to make pies instead of having her wait on tables, taking orders."

Mary nodded. "I'll do whatever you need."

Helga nudged her. "I don't know if it's such a good idea to stick Mary back in the kitchen. She's still a young girl. She needs to be around people."

Grandma snorted. "She's around people in church. I don't think she needs to be around all the customers."

Mary squirmed. She hated people talking about her. Helga reached for her hand and offered a conspiratorial smile before turning to face the others. "I hope this weather stays nice for a while."

That was all it took for the conversation to turn to weather. "It's gonna be a hot summer," one of the men said.

Helga leaned toward her and whispered, "Abe keeps looking over here. I bet he wishes you were there instead of Ruthie."

"I'm sure he's just fine sitting next to her." Mary used every ounce of self-restraint to keep from glancing in Abe's direction.

❧

Abe strained to see around some people who stood between him and Mary.

"I haven't been to your family farm since you added the barn," Ruthie said. "I hear it's huge."

"Ya." Abe stuffed another bite of roll into his mouth, chewed it, and glanced over toward Mary. "It's big, but I have a lot of cows. I need a big barn."

"A dairy farm is a good business, according to my father. He says a man who has land and animals will never have to depend on anyone else to survive."

"I s'pose your father is right."

Ruthie put down her fork, placed her hands in her lap, leaned back, and sighed. "It's such a beautiful day. Perfect for a long walk, don't you think, Abe?"

"Ya, it is indeed a very nice day." He knew what Ruthie was hinting at, but he didn't want to go for a walk with her. He wanted to be with Mary, who wouldn't even turn around and look at him.

"Would you. . .um. . ." Ruthie swallowed and fidgeted.

Abe took advantage of her nervousness and stood. "Thank you for your company, Ruthie, but I have to talk to some people. See you around, okay?" He smiled as warmly as he could.

She looked dejected, but she quickly recovered. "Ya. See you around. Will you be in church next week?"

"You know I'm always in church on Sunday."

"Ya, that is true."

"Bye, Ruthie." Abe felt terrible. He hated hurting people's feelings, but he couldn't justify sitting there letting Ruthie think something might happen between them when he really wanted to be with Mary instead.

He suspected Ruthie was watching him as he made his way over to where Mary sat with her grandparents and all their friends. One by one, they looked up at him as he arrived.

"Hi, Abe. Did you enjoy the potluck?" Helga asked as she leaned back to give him a clear view of Mary.

When his gaze met Helga's, he saw the depth of her understanding. A smile crept across her face, and her eyes twinkled as she grinned. He couldn't help but smile back.

"Yes, it was delicious." He turned to Mary. "Would you like to take a walk with me, Mary?"

"Um. . ." She looked at her grandpa, who gave a crisp nod. "That sounds good." Then she paused for a moment. "But I have to help the women clean up."

"Here," Helga said, handing her some plates. "Take these to the sink in the church kitchen and consider your part of the cleanup done."

"I'll help," Abe offered.

Before anyone said a word, he walked around the table and gathered some plates. Several of the men got up and started helping out as well. This started a snowball effect as everyone pitched in. In less than fifteen minutes, most of the yard had been cleared away.

"C'mon, Mary, let's go." Abe placed his hand on her shoulder and led her away from the crowd.

Chapter 5

The streets were beginning to fill with cars, with license plates from a variety of northern states and Canada. The first of the summer tourists had made their mark on the town. Occasionally one of the members of the local Mennonite or Amish community passed them on a three-wheeler. Mary didn't have much experience in Mennonite communities outside the one in Sarasota, but she'd heard about the horse and buggies in Ohio and Pennsylvania, where many of her grandparents' friends were from. Some of them came from communities where they rarely had contact with Yankees. Here in Sarasota, that was impossible.

Once they were a block away, Abe looked down at Mary and grinned. The softness in his gaze turned her insides to mush.

"What's wrong, Mary?" He slowed down his pace a bit.

"Nothing's wrong. It's just that. . ." How could she explain that whenever he gave her that look, she felt the world was spinning, but she enjoyed the ride? How could she tell him how much she loved being with him, but she didn't know what to think or how to act? Abe got her senses all out of sync. And then there was the issue of not knowing what he wanted. And all men wanted something, didn't they?

"You can talk to me, Mary. I want to get to know you better."

"We've known each other nine—"

"I know." Abe snorted. "You keep reminding me. We've known each other a long time, but how well do we really *know* each other?"

"Well, I know you have a big farm." Mary held up one finger then lifted another. "And you like to eat at my grandparents' restaurant." She raised a third finger. "You love bread and lots of grease."

"Not that kind of stuff, Mary. I'm talking about knowing someone deep down." He made a fist and touched his chest. "Things that really matter."

"I don't know. There are some things we probably shouldn't know about each other."

"Like what?" he asked.

"Why would I tell you anything?"

"Because I care?" Abe stopped, gripped her shoulder, and turned her around to face him. "Because I've liked you since I first met you."

"So you've said." She couldn't help her eyes widening as he continued to watch her, almost as though waiting for something. "But why?"

"I wish I knew. It's strange. When you walked into the classroom years ago, I saw something in your eyes that grabbed my heart."

Mary had to stifle a gasp. "I don't understand what you're saying, Abe."

"Okay, let me spell it out for you. I like you a lot, Mary Penner, and I want to spend time with you and see if you're the woman God wants for me." He held her gaze, making her insides flutter again. "I think you and I are meant to be together."

"I don't think you know what you're saying."

"Oh, but I do. Do you not like me?"

"I like you just fine, Abe."

"Then what's the problem? I like you, you like me. We can share our thoughts and feelings, and maybe. . ."

"What if you find out some stuff about me that makes you not like me anymore?" she asked.

"Or what if you find out something you don't like about me?" He tilted his head and snickered. "That could happen, you know." He took her hand and led her to a more secluded spot, away from the street.

Her heart thudded. "I'm sure it could."

"Mary Penner, I have a question for you."

She tensed. Questions generally led her someplace she didn't want to go. "What is it?"

"Do you mind if I kiss you?"

Mary slowly turned her face up toward his again. As he lowered his lips to hers, an odd sensation ripped at her stomach. She pulled away. "No, don't."

A wisp of hair escaped her kapp and fell across her forehead, then covered one of her eyes. Abe lifted it and gently tucked it behind her ear.

"You're beautiful, Mary."

No one had ever told her she was beautiful. She was momentarily paralyzed and speechless. Abe continued staring down at her face, his gaze traveling from her eyes to her mouth then back to her eyes.

A shiver washed over her as her mother's words popped into her mind. *Never believe a man who flatters you, Mary. It just means he wants something.* She shuddered.

Abe tilted his head. "Are you cold?"

She shook her head. "No, but I need to get back."

"What just happened, Mary?"

"Nothing." How could she explain the turmoil inside her—the sensation of wanting to be with Abe but not trusting his intentions? As much as she wanted him to kiss her and hold her close, her mother's voice continued to play in her head.

He stood staring at the ground for a few seconds before he offered a hand. "C'mon, I'll walk you home."

"I think I'd rather walk home by myself."

"But—" Abe stopped himself then frowned. "Okay, but I don't understand. You are a very confusing woman."

"I'm sorry." She turned away from him and started half-walking, half-running toward her grandparents' house with a heavy heart.

"I don't give up easily," he called out. "You'll see me again soon, Mary Penner."

She broke into a full run until she was nearly a block away. Then she stopped, sucked in a breath, and looked around at the tiny houses that surrounded her. Pinecraft was home now, but she felt isolated, even in familiar territory. Memories of her childhood continued to flood her mind. The first thing she remembered was when she was very small—maybe three or four years old. Her mother had just handed her over to a woman who took in children while their parents worked the night shift.

"I'll be back in the morning," Mama had said in her usual weary tone. Mary watched her mother walk away, shoulders sagging as the weight of her life dragged her down. Even now, nearly twenty years later, she remembered feeling an overwhelming sadness and despondency.

As Mary slowly trudged home to her grandparents' house, more images and scenes popped into her head. Through the years, Mama had a variety of jobs, but she'd discovered the highest-paying ones were in bars, which had turned out to be a disaster for both of them.

When Mary turned twelve, Mama announced that she trusted Mary to stay home alone. "Just stay inside and don't answer the door. You'll be asleep while I'm gone, so everything should be okay."

But everything wasn't okay. Mary always had a tough time falling asleep in the tiny one-bedroom apartment they'd managed to keep for almost a year. They'd been booted out of all their other homes because her mother couldn't afford the rent when it came due.

Vivid scenes of men coming and going made Mary sick to her stomach. She suspected she missed quite a bit while she was in school, and she was thankful for it. As it was, she saw more than a child should see in a lifetime. But the one scene that she'd dreaded remembering came crashing through her mind, and she couldn't stop it. It was the night when her life completely changed.

Mama had left for work a little after nine and told her to go on to bed—said that she'd be back when Mary got up. As always, Mary lay in bed with the covers pulled to her chin, shivering from fear of darkness, waiting for sleep to come. . .to overtake her and pull her from the conscious nightmare she'd suffered ever since Mama had taken that job at the bar down the street. Mary didn't know what Mama did, and she didn't want to know.

She'd started to feel the wooziness that preceded drifting off to sleep when she heard the loud banging on the door. At first she didn't want to answer it, but a low voice from the hallway let out the code word she and Mama had established. So she wrapped the blanket around her shoulders and made her way to the door. She left the chain latched as she opened the door a few inches. The man handed her an envelope through the tiny opening, then took off running.

After he was out of sight, she closed the door and fastened the dead bolt then turned on the light in the living room. The outside of the envelope had the words *In case of emergency, deliver to my daughter, Mary* scrawled across the front. Mary ripped it open and pulled out the pink-lined paper. The note was in her mother's handwriting. With shaky fingers, she read that she was to call Big Jim at the phone number beneath his name.

The details of that night remained a blur. All she remembered was calling Big Jim and learning her mother had been killed. It had something to do with a drug bust and her mama being an informant. She didn't believe him, so she dropped the phone and ran to the bar to find her mother. Instead she found Big Jim in his office that reeked of cigar smoke and stale beer. Big Jim gave Mary some money, bought her a bus ticket, and told her he'd sent word to Elizabeth's parents letting them know their fourteen-year-old granddaughter was on her way. He added that he'd tried to warn her mother that she was in dangerous territory by agreeing to help the police, but she thought the money the police promised her would help make a better life for her and Mary.

"Go home and get your things. I'll pick you up and take you to the bus station," Big Jim said before pausing and turning. "Oh, I almost forgot. I have something your mother wanted me to give you." Big Jim's son, Jimbo, sat on the floor in the corner of his dad's small office, glaring at Mary with beady eyes and a scowl. She shivered at the memory.

Big Jim had handed her a small box and instructed her not to open it until she was safely with her grandparents. He even made her promise. As she nodded her promise, she couldn't help but notice the smirk that had formed on Jimbo's face. She shuddered at some of the memories she had of that horrible boy.

To this day, she still hadn't opened the box. She'd lived this long not knowing what it was. Why would she want to do anything that would bring back such horrible memories? But they were still in her head. And that tiny box lay on the floor in the corner of her closet, serving as a reminder that she had a past no one in Pinecraft would ever understand.

⁓

Frustrated and perplexed, Abe stood on the street, waiting for his ride. David had sounded surprised to hear from him so soon.

"I just dropped off the last family, so your timing was good."

Abe opened his mouth to say something but quickly closed it. Then he sighed.

"I don't have to ask what happened," David said as soon as Abe got into the car. "It's written all over your face." He shook his head. "Women."

"Something happened to her," Abe said. "She seemed fine to a point, but when I asked her. . ." He looked down at his hands steepled in his lap. "I asked her if I could kiss her, and she just. . .well, she acted frightened."

"That's where you went wrong, buddy. If you wanna kiss a girl, you don't ask, you just do it. That way she can't turn you down."

"Mary is different."

"Maybe so, but it looks to me like she wouldn't mind if you kissed her, as long as it happens by surprise."

Abe stared at David. "What makes you say that?"

David cast a quick smile in Abe's direction. "I've seen how she looks at you. She likes you, Abe. In fact, she likes you very much."

If Abe could be sure David was right, he'd be willing to take his advice. But David obviously didn't know how bad Mary's past experiences might have been, and he certainly didn't want to be the one to tell him.

"Give it a shot, Abe. You like her, she likes you. What have you got to lose? She's Mennonite. She won't slap you, right?"

David had a point. "Ya, I don't think she'll slap me."

"Now that we've got that settled, my wife wanted to know if you planned to have some of your delicious vegetables at the produce market on Saturday."

"Ya, I always do. I'm not sure yet who will be working it."

"If you're in the same place, I'll just tell her to go there. She said your citrus was better than anyone else's." David turned at the farm entrance. "I'd like my wife to meet you one of these days."

"Why?"

David grinned. "She's fascinated by the things I tell her about you."

"I don't know what would be so fascinating about me. My life is very plain and simple."

"Plain, maybe," David agreed before lifting an eyebrow. "But not simple." He came to a stop and repeated, "Definitely not simple. You seem to have pretty much the same issues people who aren't Mennonite have, only you have a different way of dealing with them."

Abe opened the car door but paused before getting out. "Matters of the heart are never simple, are they?"

"You got that right." David waved as Abe got out of the car.

∽

"I'm not hungry, Grandma," Mary said. "I think I'll pass on supper tonight."

Grandma gave her a sideways glance. "I don't want you tossing and turning all night because your stomach starts rumbling."

Mary patted her stomach. "I don't think that'll happen. I ate enough at the church to last the rest of the day."

Instead of responding, Grandma turned back to preparing the food. Mary left the kitchen and went outside. As she stood in the front yard, she glanced around at the children playing in the yard a few houses down. Occasionally she thought about having her own family, and there were even times she longed for a husband and children. The women in the neighborhood seemed content in their marriages.

Mama's words about men always wanting something rang through her mind constantly, but sometimes Mary wondered how true they were. It was obvious that Mama's experiences had been different from these women's. However, Mary also remembered what Mama had told her about being shunned by her own community, and there was never any doubt her mother had told her the truth—at least from her perspective. They hadn't exactly been warm and welcoming to Mary in the beginning. A few people, like Shelley. . . and Abe. . .treated her well, but many of the others acted as though she had some disease they might catch if they so much as had a conversation with her. No one had been openly mean, but even now people seemed afraid to hold a conversation with her. She thought about what Abe had said—that her shame made her standoffish, which in turn kept people away.

She stood in the front yard and watched a couple of neighborhood children playing ball. The older boy was kind and considerate of the younger one's lack of coordination. Seeing these boys playing made her think about all she'd missed as a child. She wondered if she'd ever be a mother, and if so, how she'd handle questions about her past.

Mary watched the boys until their mother called them inside. Then she headed back into her grandparents' house. Grandma and Grandpa were in the kitchen reading their Bibles. The aroma of Grandma's homemade vegetable soup still hung in the air.

"Join us, Mary," Grandpa said, patting her place at the table. "We were just reading from the book of Luke."

"Luke 21:34," Grandma added. "You may read next if you like."

Mary nodded as she pulled her Bible from the small shelf Grandpa had built next to the table. She flipped through the pages and began to read.

"Be careful or your hearts will be weighed down with carousing, drunkenness and the anxieties of life. . ."

As the words flowed from Mary's lips, she could feel the intensity of how relevant they were to her life. She'd seen the results of what happened when people got caught up in sins of the flesh. What a bitter existence. The life she had now was one of simplicity and very little focus on worrying about things. At times like this, the peace that washed through her soul reminded her of how blessed she was.

She finished the verse and glanced up in time to see Grandma wipe a tear from her cheek. Grandpa's foot lightly touched Mary's beneath the table. As their gazes met, she saw how concerned he was for Grandma.

Mary started to get up, but Grandpa motioned for her to sit back down. "Your grandmother and I have been talking. . . ." He glanced over at his wife, who nodded for him to continue. "What happened to us the day you arrived was both tragic and joyful. We lost one daughter—for the second time—and gained a granddaughter we always longed to see. But the most tragic thing that happened was losing our daughter the first time—back when she found something she preferred over what we offered her."

"I–I'm sorry," Mary said.

"You shouldn't be sorry," Grandpa said with a forced smile beneath glistening, moist eyes. "You are the joy that came out of the sadness. We love you very much, and we want you to be as content as we are. The Lord has blessed us greatly."

Mary turned to Grandma for a check on her reaction, and she was surprised to see her also smiling. "Ya, we love you very much, Mary. I know I don't always show how much—"

"She knows you love her, Sarah." Grandpa looked at Mary with his head tilted toward her. "We're concerned about you, though. There is no joy in your life. All you do is go to the restaurant and then come home. We were hoping you and Abe. . .well, that maybe you two would hit it off."

"Abe is a fine man," Grandma added. "He will take care of you, and you will always know you're safe."

Mary looked down at her hands clasped tightly in her lap. She wasn't sure if she'd ever feel safe—no matter where she was or who she was with. Even here with Grandma and Grandpa, in her mind the safest place on earth, there were times she wasn't sure she was wanted.

Grandpa shifted in his seat, capturing Mary's attention. "I know you have some painful memories, Granddaughter, and there's nothing we can do about that except pray. But it's time you learned to trust other people."

Mary nodded. "I trust both of you."

"Ya," he said, "but you need to trust that the Lord has put Abe into your life for a reason." He paused before adding, "And you need to trust Abe with your heart."

Mary knew Grandpa meant well, but it was easier for him to say than for her to take his advice. "I'd like to," she whispered.

"Let's pray about this," Grandpa said as he pulled one of her hands from the other. He reached for Grandma's hand, and they all bowed their heads.

After the prayer, Grandpa released her hand. Mary kept her eyes squeezed shut and silently added her own thoughts and feelings. *Lord, I want to be the woman You want me to be. Please show me the way, and I'll try. . .no, I'll make it my plan to do Your will.*

When she opened her eyes, both of her grandparents had gotten up.

Grandpa had left the room, but Grandma was over by the sink with her back turned toward Mary.

"I'm washing the pot I left to soak after supper," Grandma said.

"Need help?"

"No, I'm almost done." Grandma dumped the water from the pot and dried it with the dish towel before putting it back in the cupboard. "I heard you talking to that little boy. Maybe someday you'll have children of your own."

"Maybe."

Grandma sighed. "I would have had a houseful if I could. Your mama was such a cheerful little girl, I thought a dozen more just like her would be perfect." She sniffled and wiped her cheek with her sleeve. "The Lord obviously didn't feel I should have more children. When we lost Elizabeth, your grandpa and I felt like our breath had been taken away. Worldly living does that to so many people. I didn't want her to go up to Cincinnati to stay with those girls. I was afraid she'd never come back. When she did, I was so happy, I sang all the time. Then. . ." She hung her head. "As each day passed, the light in your mama's eyes faded a little bit more. I knew something was wrong, but until I realized what she'd done and that she was pregnant, I couldn't figure it out."

Mary wanted to hear more about the specifics of what happened on the day Mama left from Grandma's perspective, but she didn't want to push for answers. She didn't want to create tension.

"Mama missed you and Grandpa," Mary said, her voice catching on emotion.

"Did she tell you that?" The expectant look on Grandma's face tempted Mary to lie, but she couldn't.

She shook her head. "No, she never actually came right out and said that, but I could tell. She was lonely." And she cried when she didn't think Mary could hear her.

"So was I. Some days, every time I heard a sound outside, I ran to the door, hoping it was my Elizabeth."

Mary wanted to ask more questions—like what would have happened if she and her mother had shown up. But it seemed that questions caused Grandma to clam up. She was much more open when she spoke of her own volition.

Grandma folded the towel and hung it from the drawer handle, then turned and looked Mary squarely in the eye. "I used to worry that when you turned sixteen, you would do what your Mama did."

Mary slowly shook her head. "No, I would never have done that. It wasn't a good life."

They held gazes for almost a minute before Grandma closed the gap between them and wrapped her arms around Mary. At first Mary was so stunned she froze. Then she slowly relaxed, melting into Grandma's embrace and allowing the older woman's warmth to provide the comfort she needed. They held on to each other until Grandma finally let go and gently held Mary at arm's length.

"You are a delightful young woman, with a lot to offer the right man."

Mary gulped. "I want to do what God calls me to do." She dropped her gaze to the floor.

"Yes, I know that now." Grandma lifted Mary's chin and looked her in the eye. "Do you ever think what it would be like to find a husband and have your own home?"

Chapter 6

Mary lay in bed staring at the ceiling with the light from outside casting a faint glow through the thin curtains. Usually before she fell asleep, she reflected on the day and how far she'd come from her past. Tonight was different. She'd had some sort of emotional connection to Grandma that she never thought possible. Grandma's question about whether or not she wanted a husband and home of her own played through her mind, and Abe's image instantly appeared.

She squeezed her eyes shut and asked the Lord to give her the wisdom she needed. Abe had already made his intentions clear, and Grandma seemed to think she should try to have a normal Mennonite life.

Mary wanted a normal life, but it never seemed possible for her to have one. Her rough early years haunted her everywhere she went. When she'd first moved to Sarasota, she doubted everyone's motives for talking to her, including Grandma and Grandpa's. It hadn't taken long to learn to trust Grandpa. Even though Mama had said men always wanted something, Mary sensed a strong relationship between Mama and Grandpa that her mother missed, or at least hadn't told her about. Mama had complained about Grandpa being cold, but Mary didn't see that in him. Grandma was a different story. According to Mama, Grandma was a vindictive old woman who didn't understand what it was like to be young. At first, after coming to live with her grandparents, Mary agreed with Mama, but through the years, she occasionally saw a softening that escaped Grandma's stern facade for a few minutes or seconds. Until recently.

Now everything was different. After Grandma's talk with her during their walk, her demeanor had gradually softened even more. Mary's thoughts swirled around all the conversations she'd had with Abe and how her grandparents were encouraging her to be with him. As her swirling thoughts gradually slowed, Mary finally relaxed and allowed sleep to wash over her.

She awakened the next morning with the determination to explore her relationship with Abe. Her feelings couldn't be denied, and she needed to put a stop to the negative thoughts that crept into her head. Mama's words had been spoken during the worst of all times. Mary was now much older than Mama had been when she'd left the safety and security of her family's home. Their lives were totally different.

Grandma stood at the stove stirring something in a small pot. Without turning around, she asked, "Want some oatmeal before you go in to work this morning, or would you rather eat there?"

Mary pulled a bowl from the cupboard and set it down next to the stove. "I'll eat before I go in." She leaned against the counter. "I've been thinking about our conversation last night."

Grandma sighed. "Sometimes you think too much. If you keep doing that, you'll talk yourself out of happiness."

Mary laughed. "Not this time. I've decided to get to know Abe better and see how things go with him."

"You've known that boy for nine years, child. How much longer do you need to know him?"

Abe's words from when she'd cast out the same argument flittered through her head. "I want to know more about him as a man. If I went on the way he acted when we were kids, I'd run fast in the other direction."

Grandma cast a dubious look at Mary, then went back to stirring. "He couldn't have been that bad."

"He wasn't, but at the time I didn't like it. His teasing irritated me."

"Hand me your bowl." Grandma took the bowl from Mary's hands and scooped some oatmeal into it. "So what do you plan to do to get to know Abe better?"

"I'll start by accepting when he asks me to do things."

"I thought you already did that."

"I did, but I didn't make it easy for him. I've been very defensive around Abe. That will change now."

"Good. Now eat your oatmeal and get out of here so you can help with the breakfast crowd. I'll be in after I get the kitchen cleaned up."

Mary gulped down her oatmeal then rinsed her bowl. She got her tote from her room, went outside, and put the bag in the basket of her three-wheeler.

She'd always enjoyed the ride to work in semidarkness, when Sarasota still seemed like a sleepy little town. In just a couple of hours, they'd have bumper-to-bumper traffic and the sounds that went with it.

From the moment she walked into the restaurant, Mary was busy waiting on tables, busing tables, and helping out in the kitchen. Her focus was on giving her customers—mostly tourists—what they needed.

"Mary."

The soft male voice behind Mary stopped her. She slowly pivoted until she was looking into Abe Glick's warm brown eyes. Her lips twitched as she smiled at him.

His eyebrows shot up as surprise registered on his face. "You must be having a good morning."

"Yes." Mary nodded as she held his gaze. "A very good morning."

Abe nodded toward a booth in the back. "Mind if I seat myself over there?"

"That would be just fine. I'll bring you a menu. Want coffee?"

"Don't worry about the menu. I know what I want. Just bring coffee, and I'll give you my order."

"Okay, I'll have it to you in two shakes of a horse's tail."

Abe leaned away and grinned. "You certainly are in a good mood this morning. I don't know if I've ever seen you like this before."

Suddenly it struck Mary. Maybe Abe wouldn't like her if he didn't feel like he had to cheer her up. "Is that a bad thing?"

"Neh. I like it."

"Well, good. Go have a seat, and I'll be right there."

Mary didn't waste any time getting Abe his coffee. She laid the napkin-wrapped fork, knife, and spoon on the table in front of him before lifting her order pad.

"So how would you like your sugar and grease this morning, Mr. Glick?"

The corners of his eyes crinkled as he chuckled. "What would you think if I told you I'll eat whatever you think I should have?"

"Doesn't matter what I think. The question is, will you really eat it?"

Abe leaned back and studied her. "I think so. Just make sure there's an egg or two on my plate, and I'll eat pretty much anything."

She jotted that down and gave him a clipped nod. "Coming right up. Mystery breakfast with an egg or two."

⁓

Abe had entered Penner's with the intention of observing Mary then going home for the rest of the day. However, the way she was acting led him to believe things had changed. He thought she might be open to doing something with him later.

He sipped his coffee and watched Mary wait on other customers while the folks in the kitchen prepared his breakfast. He didn't have to wait long before she brought him a plate laden with fresh fruit, one of her grandmother's famous bran muffins, and two poached eggs.

"No gruel?" he asked playfully.

"Nope. It's all good for you, and it tastes good, too." She took a step back and smiled over her shoulder. "Anything else I can do for you, Abe?"

"Ya."

Mary stopped and turned completely toward him. "Okay, now what?"

"You can go with me to have some ice cream later. I know you have to work, but maybe after lunch?"

"Um. . ." She placed her index finger on her chin as a smile spread across her lips. "Sounds very good. I'd love to go have ice cream with you."

He tried not to show the shock over her lack of resistance. "I have to go home to do a few things on the farm, but I will be back. What time can you go?"

Mary glanced around at the crowd. "We're busy today, but I think things will slow down around three. I'll check with Grandpa before you finish your breakfast and make sure it's okay with him, but I think he'll be fine with that."

Abe picked up a muffin and held it up to her. "Sounds good."

He watched Mary scurry around the restaurant as he ate his breakfast. It wasn't as filling as what he was used to, but he thought it was sweet that Mary was conscious of his diet. Most people couldn't eat as much grease and sugar without increasing the size of their girth, but Abe was so busy on the farm, he worked it off. He'd be hungry again in a couple of hours, but he'd ask David to stop somewhere so he could grab a slice of ham and biscuit on the way back to the farm.

Before he was finished, he called David and asked if he could pick him up in ten minutes. David said that would be fine since he had some other people to pick up and drop off not far from the Glick farm.

After Abe paid, Joseph Penner approached him and put his hand on Abe's shoulder. "I'm happy to hear that you'll be back to see Mary later. I told her she could leave at two thirty if that's better."

"Neh, three o'clock is fine. I have to do some things on the farm, and that gives me just enough time to get back to town."

"I'll tell Mary," Mr. Penner said.

Abe saw David pull into the restaurant parking lot. "I gotta go. My ride is here. I look forward to seeing Mary this afternoon."

A couple of people were in the back of the van, but they were engrossed in conversation. Abe hopped into the front passenger seat.

As soon as Abe clicked his seat belt, the questions started. "Well? What did she say?"

"I'm coming back this afternoon and taking her out for ice cream."

"Good job, man. It won't be long before you're announcing your engagement."

"That would be good, but one thing I know about Mary is that she can't be rushed. I have to let her get used to the fact that she and I are meant to be together."

David snickered. "You're pretty sure about that, aren't you?"

"Never been more sure of anything in my life." Abe paused and faced David. "How about when you met your wife? Weren't you sure?"

"I knew I loved her, but the thought of it being a forever kind of relationship sort of scared me."

"What's to be scared of?" Abe asked. "Marriage is a sacred commitment between a man and woman."

David cleared his throat. "I think that's what scared me the most—that sacred commitment thing."

Abe shook his head. "Commitment is a good thing. It keeps us focused on the Lord's will."

"I wish I could be more like you, Abe. Your life is so simple and easy to figure out. I bet you don't have any debt, do you?"

"Nch, I only buy what I can afford. Why? Are you in debt?"

"Oh yeah. To the max."

"But why?"

David shrugged. "I dunno. It just sort of started with us wanting a car we couldn't afford, then it progressed to other things."

"You can do something about that if you want to."

"We're working on it. It took some doing, but I finally got my wife on board with the concept of following the biblical financial plan they offer at our church." He turned onto the shell road and pulled to a stop in front of Abe's house. "After she dragged me to church, I found the one thing that interested me was the financial program they offered."

Abe got out, reached deep into his pocket, and handed David a few extra dollars. "Add this to your fund, David. Get out of debt as soon as you possibly can, and you'll be much happier."

"You don't have to do that," David said as he looked at the wad of bills in his hand.

"I know I don't, but I want to."

"You're a good man, Abe—a very good man who will make some woman a wonderful husband. I hope things work out between you and Mary."

"I have to trust in the Lord's will. If Mary and I are meant to be together, it will happen. See you this afternoon around two thirty?"

David nodded. "I'll be here."

Abe closed the door, turned, and walked toward the house. He heard David's van heading back toward the highway.

As Abe walked up the path to his front door, one of his workers ran up to him with a question. The rest of the morning and early afternoon seemed to fly by, which suited Abe just fine. It kept his mind off Mary.

David arrived at two thirty, only this time he was in his car. "Where's the van?" Abe asked as he buckled his seat belt.

"The wife has been after me to hire someone to help me branch out and increase business, so I finally did. He has the van." David looked over his shoulder as he backed up to turn the car around. "I've found that my wife is generally right, but when you meet her, don't go telling her I said that."

Abe laughed. "It might be a good idea for you to tell her that."

"What? And let her think she can win all the arguments? Where's the fun in that?"

"I don't know about you, but I don't like to argue. I find it very upsetting. When I get married and my wife tells me something that helps, I will tell her."

"I'm sure you will." David focused his attention on the road until he was about a mile from Penner's. "Wanna call me when it's time to pick you up?"

"Neh, I'll be ready around four thirty."

"See you then," David said as he pulled to a stop in front of the restaurant. "If anything changes, you know how to get ahold of me."

Abe waved to David then turned around and found himself about three feet from Mary, who had an amused look on her face. "Good to see you again, Abe. Now let's go get some ice cream." Without another word, she reached for his arm and tucked her hand in the crook of his elbow.

❦

It took all of Mary's self-restraint not to laugh at Abe's reaction. His eyes widened, and his chin dropped. "So how's the farm? Anything new?" she asked.

"Ya. Just this morning one of my workers told me about a new bull that's for sale. I told him to look him over and buy him if he thinks it's a good deal."

"A new bull, huh? How about that?"

"We just cleared the land for some more grapefruit trees, too."

Mary smiled. Abe's dedication to his farm was admirable.

The blaring sound of a honking horn snagged their attention. Mary scrunched her eyebrows. "Is that Jeremiah again?"

"Afraid so." Abe shook his head. "Ever since he left the church, he's been sort of wild."

"Sort of?" Mary snorted. "He came into the restaurant with some of his friends earlier. Grandpa had to ask them to quiet down or leave."

"He used to be such a good guy, but I do remember him talking about outsiders and how much fun they seemed to be having."

Jeremiah pulled to a stop beside them. "Hey, Abe. Wanna go for a ride in my new wheels?"

"Neh." Abe glanced down at Mary. "I'm on a date."

Mary started to grin, but Jeremiah's hoot cracked her joy. "Can't say I blame you. She's hot."

"Don't talk about her like that, Jeremiah." Mary saw Abe's jaw tighten. "She's a nice girl who deserves respect."

"Did you ever ask her about what she did before she joined the plain clothes brigade?" He cackled. "I bet she saw some action that would make you a very happy man."

Abe started to advance toward Jeremiah, but Mary held him back and walked up to Jeremiah alone. "You're a terrible man, Jeremiah. Just because you turned your back on God doesn't give you the right to try to pull someone as nice as Abe away."

"Wait, Mary, I can handle this," Abe said as he gently took her hand then stepped between her and the car. "Jeremiah, you better move along. You know I can't fight you, but I can contact the authorities."

Mary held her breath as she watched Jeremiah's expression go from jeering to acceptance. Finally he nodded. "I'll talk to you about it later, Abe. I don't want you missing out on a golden opportunity, now that you've got yourself a live one." He sped away, hooting and hollering and saying disrespectful things.

"I'm so sorry, Mary. You should never have to hear such words."

She flicked her hand. "It's nothing I haven't heard before."

"In your past?" he asked softly.

"Well, yeah, then, but I still hear things that you wouldn't believe. People come into the restaurant and say all kinds of things."

"Surely not from Pinecraft people."

She shook her head. "No, not from any of the Mennonites or Amish. Mostly just rude outsiders."

"That's terrible. Maybe you should put a sign on the door telling people to leave those things outside." He offered a teasing grin. "Think that'll work?"

She tilted her head back and laughed. "About as well as telling Jeremiah to behave. You know he'll do that again."

"Of course he will. And I'll just have to be ready for him next time."

"What can you do about it?"

Abe shrugged. "I'll search through scripture and come up with some verses to put him in his place in a God-pleasing way."

Mary thought for a few seconds, then nodded and laughed. "If nothing else, he'll stop just to shut you up."

A woman on a three-wheeler bumped up on the lower part of the curb in front of them. Her skirt barely covered her knees, and the ties on her kapp lifted with the breeze. The basket in front of the handlebars was laden with bags from various stores and behind her rolled a wagon filled with jars. The final bump sent a couple of the jars flying off the wagon and crashing onto the sidewalk.

She got off her three-wheeler, extracted a bag from the side of the wagon, and picked up some of the broken pieces. Mary and Abe ran up to her and helped.

"Hello, Abe. Thank you." The woman nodded and darted her gaze toward Mary. Her eyebrows lifted, but she didn't address Mary. "Nice afternoon for a walk." She tucked the bag filled with broken glass into the side of the wagon and hopped back up on her three-wheeler.

"Yes, Mrs. Troyer, it's a very nice afternoon." Abe wanted the woman to acknowledge Mary, but he wasn't sure what he could do to make that happen.

"Looks like you have quite a load there, Mrs. Troyer," Abe said. "Would you like me to take the wagon somewhere for you?"

Mrs. Troyer looked flustered but finally relented and nodded to Abe. "That would be nice. . . ." She tentatively glanced at Mary. "That is, if you don't mind. I'm having a very difficult time."

"No problem at all," he said. "Mary, you don't mind, do you?"

"Of course not."

Abe untied the wagon from the back of the three-wheeler. "We'll follow you." As they fell in behind the woman, with Abe pulling the wagon behind him, he winked at Mary. "As soon as we deliver the load, we'll go get our ice cream."

Mary's opinion of Abe soared even higher. The man was kind to everyone, smart, educated, handsome, and tenacious. To top it off, each time she was with him, the fluttery feelings in her tummy increased.

They arrived at the woman's house, where she hopped off her three-wheeler and pointed to a patch by the door. "Just leave the wagon there. What do I owe you?"

Abe's forehead wrinkled. "Nothing. It was our pleasure."

She grinned. "You are a very sweet man. Thank you." Then she glanced at Mary. "I hope you realize what a fortunate young woman you are to be with a man like Abe."

"I'm the fortunate one for Mary to be with me," Abe said. "If you don't need us anymore, we'll be on our way."

Mary and Abe walked in silence until they came to the end of the block when Mary turned to him. "You didn't have to say anything."

"I know I didn't, but I felt it was the right thing to do."

"I'm used to it, though. In fact, I've come to expect people to think the worst of me."

"That's not right, Mary. Maybe she doesn't think badly of you. Some people simply don't say much."

"Or they want to shun me for what my mother did."

"Mrs. Troyer wasn't shunning you, if that's what you're implying. She is just one of those quiet, shy women. I saw her look at you, and there didn't seem to be any animosity in her eyes."

"So what are you saying, Abe?"

He squeezed his eyes shut for a few seconds as though he might be sending up a brief prayer. Then he looked directly at her. "Perhaps you're the one holding on to the grudge. It's not like your mother was the first to leave the church."

Mary shook her head. "I don't feel like people respect me around here, no matter what I do."

"I think you're a wonderful woman, and I'm sure others do, too." Abe stopped in the middle of the sidewalk and turned her around to face him. "You should never be treated with anything but the utmost respect."

"Thank you." Mary gulped as she looked up into Abe's eyes, which flickered from the reflection of the afternoon sun. He lowered his head toward her and looked like he was about to kiss her, making her heart hammer so hard she feared Abe would hear it.

But he didn't kiss her. Instead, he took her hand and turned her back around. "I'm hungry for some ice cream. Let's go."

At the moment, Mary didn't care if she never saw ice cream again. She'd much rather have a kiss. Disappointment rolled through her.

When they arrived at the tiny ice-cream shop, Abe asked her what she wanted. "I'll just have whatever you're having." She folded her arms and tried to hide her feelings.

He squinted as though confused by her answer, then turned to the woman behind the counter. "We'll have two double vanilla cones please." After she scooped the ice cream and Abe paid, he handed Mary one cone and licked the other. "Mmm. This is good."

Mary turned her cone around and studied it before tasting it. A tiny drop of ice cream splashed onto her hand, and she licked it off. "Yeah, it is good. Perfect, in fact."

"What just happened back there, Mary?" he asked as they ambled down the street. "You suddenly acted strange."

She paused mid-lick. "Strange? How so?"

"After that conversation when we left Mrs. Troyer, you gave me an odd look. Did I do something wrong?"

"No, Abe," Mary said slowly, wondering if she should leave it at that or explain. "It's just that. . .well. . ."

"You can talk to me about anything, Mary. I want you to trust me."

"Oh I do trust you, Abe." She swallowed deeply and looked down at the sidewalk before meeting his gaze. "Much more than I do most people. It's hard for me, you know."

"Yes," he said as he reached out and brushed a lock of hair that had escaped her kapp with his free hand. "I do know."

A pinching sensation in her chest and the urge to let Abe know how she felt about him battled with the warning bells going off in her head. Telling him her feelings would leave her vulnerable and exposed. Did she dare do that? She wanted to very badly, but in spite of Abe admitting he was romantically interested in her, the fear of being hurt was still lodged in her heart.

"Mary?" he asked, bending over and tilting her face up to meet his gaze once again. "Talk to me, okay?"

She pulled her lips between her teeth and nodded. Her heart felt as though it would jump out of her mouth if she didn't say something. If ever there was a time to release that fear, this was it. Finally, she sucked in a deep breath, squared her shoulders, looked Abe in the eye, and blurted, "Kiss me, Abe."

Chapter 7

Abe blinked, and the ice-cream cone toppled from his hand and fell to the ground. Did Mary just tell him to kiss her? Neh, couldn't have. Not Mary with the standoffish sarcasm and strong-arm defense.

She held her ice-cream cone up with one hand, jammed her other fist on her hips, and leaned forward, lips puckered, eyes narrowed. He had to bite the insides of his cheeks to keep from laughing.

When he didn't do anything, she folded her arms and pouted. "Oh, so you don't wanna kiss me now, huh?"

"Oh I didn't say that. You just caught me by surprise."

"Okay, so do you want to kiss me or not?"

Abe pondered the thought, then slowly nodded. "Yes, I'd love to kiss you, Mary, but not here."

"What's wrong with here?"

"This isn't exactly the best place for us to have our first kiss."

Mary lifted her free hand in surrender. "So you get to pick where we kiss?"

Abe gave himself some time to gather his thoughts before speaking. "Mary, when I kiss you, I want you to understand it's because I have feelings for you. It's not something I take lightly."

"Who said anything about taking it lightly?" She frowned as she took a lick of her ice cream. She shook her head. "Don't tell me you agree with that mean Jeremiah."

"No, this has nothing to do with Jeremiah. What it has everything to do with is letting you know that a kiss means. . .well, it means. . ." He glanced down then back up at her, slowly shaking his head.

Mary lifted an eyebrow in amusement and tapped her foot. "Go on, Abe. I want to know what it means."

"Let's just say it's very special to me. A kiss is not like a handshake or even a hug. It means we're more than just friends."

"I'm okay with that." She held his gaze as though challenging him. "I thought that's what you wanted."

That was exactly what he wanted, but the timing was off. Kissing on command seemed forced and cold. But he didn't want to risk hurting or embarrassing Mary—not after her attempt to be more open and trust him.

"Let's take a little walk, okay?" He extended his elbow, hoping for the best, and to his delight, she took it.

"Sorry about your ice-cream cone," Mary said.

Abe laughed. "I should have held on to it better."

"Want a lick?" she asked, offering her ice-cream cone.

Abe laughed. "No thanks. I'm not about to take your ice cream."

"That's okay, I don't mind. I sort of lost my appetite."

"You don't have to finish it."

They walked in silence for another block then turned up a side street behind some of the small shops at the edge of Pinecraft. Abe pointed to a lonely tree holding court over a tiny patch of grass in the center of a circle of palmettos. "Let's get some shade."

Mary pivoted and headed straight for the tree without a single word. Abe was right behind her. They passed a trash receptacle, and she tossed her dripping ice-cream cone. "I can't eat any more."

Abe leaned against the tree and extended his arms. "Come here, Mary," he said softly.

She took a step toward him then stopped. "Oh, so now you want to kiss me?"

He closed his eyes, retracted his outstretched arms, and silently chuckled. When he opened his eyes again, she was so close, all he had to do was open his arms and she was in them. "May I kiss you now, Mary Penner?"

She turned her face up to his with her lips puckered and her eyes closed. This time he leaned down and touched her lips with his for a couple of seconds. When he pulled away, she slowly opened her eyes and smiled up at him.

"So that's what a kiss feels like," she said, her voice barely above a whisper. A quick flash of her mother being kissed and groped darted through her mind. A few times men had attempted to touch her, but her quick reflexes and whatever lies she could make up saved her. Mary shuddered as she forced herself to stay in the moment. Abe was nothing like those men, and she knew this was different.

Abe couldn't help but laugh. "Disappointed?"

"Nope. I liked it. Let's do it again." She puckered her lips and closed her eyes.

He dropped a brief kiss on her lips then the tip of her nose. "I think I better get you back before this gets out of control."

"Well," she began slowly as she looked at him coyly. "I have plenty of self-control. It's you I'm worried about."

He chuckled. "I'll be fine."

"Good. Now that we've got that settled, when are we going out again?"

"Now look at you. When I first wanted to get to know you better, you acted like I was the enemy, and now you want to rush things. Why don't we take things nice and slow?"

She shrugged. "What's the point? You like me, and I'm pretty sure I like you."

"You don't mince words, do you, Mary?"

"Why would I do that?"

Her abrupt turnaround both delighted and startled Abe. Something had happened since the last time he'd seen her. "You're acting different now."

"Maybe I am different."

Abe shook his head. "People don't change that quickly. What's going on, Mary?"

"Don't be so skeptical. Nothing's going on, except I've had time to think about us."

"Oh yeah?" He glanced down at her as they walked side by side on the narrow sidewalk. "What were your thoughts?"

"To start with, I know that you're a very nice man, and you seem honest."

"Ya, I like to be nice to people, and honesty comes natural. But plenty of people are nice and honest."

"Oh but not like you, Abe."

He knew some people were puzzled by Mary, and even after all this time, some of them may still have held her past against her. But he hadn't seen anyone being intentionally mean except Jeremiah—even Mrs. Troyer, whose mind seemed to be elsewhere.

"Has anyone said or done anything to hurt you?" he asked. "Besides Jeremiah, that is."

"Not really. I've gotten used to being ignored. But you've never ignored me. You've always acted like I was any other Mennonite girl."

"Trust me," he said with a chuckle. "You're not like any other Mennonite girl."

She gave him a look of pretend hurt then grinned. "I'll take that as a compliment."

"Good. You should." They continued another half block toward her grandparents' house. "It's still not enough to explain why you're suddenly demanding kisses. Why did you ask me for a kiss today?"

Mary contorted her mouth and pondered the thought. Finally she shrugged. "Why not?"

"There you go again, answering my question with a question."

She shrugged. "I wanted a kiss, so I asked for it."

He studied her. "Okay."

"Besides, I like the way I feel when I'm with you."

Now they were getting somewhere. "How do you feel when you're with me?"

"I...well..." She pursed her lips and sighed. "I think I've already told you too much. Since you want to take things more slowly, I think I'll keep some things to myself."

Abe grinned. "You are such a mystery, Mary Penner."

"Is that a problem?"

"Neh, I think I like it."

"Good. Then my hunch worked out." They'd gotten to the block where her grandparents lived, so she stopped and turned to face him. "Thank you for the ice cream and kiss."

He tilted his head toward her. "And thank you for spending some time with me. . .and the kiss. I'll see you soon."

⌐∾

Mary was pretty sure Abe couldn't see her hands shaking. It had been difficult to hide her nerves, but it was better he didn't know how he affected her. Ever since their lips touched, she felt as though the earth had tilted just enough to throw her off balance.

"Mary, is that you?" Grandma called from the kitchen. Before Mary had a chance to answer, she added, "Come on back and tell me about your ice cream date with Abe."

"I'll be right there, Grandma. I have to put my stuff away first."

As Mary deposited her tote on her bed, she took several deep breaths to get a grip on her nerves and gather some thoughts on what to say about her time with Abe. Maybe Grandma wouldn't ask too many questions.

That hope was quickly shattered when Mary joined her grandmother in the kitchen. "How was your date with Abe?" Before Mary had a chance to say a word, Grandma added, "You're back awful early. Did something happen?"

Mary reached for the flour canister and moved it to a different spot on the counter so she could help with dinner. "No, nothing happened."

"I thought you'd be home before dinner, but not this early." Grandma pointed to the other canister. "Hand me the sugar, please."

"We got ice cream and went for a walk. That doesn't take very long."

Grandma paused and looked directly at Mary. "You and I need to have a talk. There are obviously some things you don't understand about courting."

Mary's cheeks flamed. "I think I know enough."

"Dating someone you're thinking about spending the rest of your life with involves more than getting ice cream and going for a walk."

"Who said anything about spending the rest of my life with him?"

Grandma shook her head. "Are you saying you're not interested in marrying Abe?"

Mary let out a nervous laugh. "That's not what I'm saying. Things like that take time. Besides, I'm not sure I ever want to get married."

Grandma placed one fist on her hip and shook her other finger at Mary. "Don't ever say that again. If the Lord puts the right man in front of you, who are you to say you don't want to get married?"

Mary knew better than to argue with Grandma about the Lord's will. It would be a losing battle since Grandma knew the Bible front to back. Mary had studied tenaciously since she'd been in Sarasota, but she knew she didn't know scripture like Grandma did.

"I'm not saying you should marry Abe, but don't rule it out. It's not like every Mennonite boy in Sarasota is beating our door down for you." Grandma turned back to the cobbler she'd been working on, leaving Mary to ponder her words.

They sifted, stirred, and rolled dough in silence as Mary's mind wandered from the kiss and Abe's intentions to her motives. Grandma was right. The only man who'd shown any romantic interest in Mary was Abe. If she had her choice, would he be the one she'd pick? Without having the experience, how would she know?

"Mary?" Grandma's voice was soft and tender. "I didn't mean to say you should marry Abe because you can't do better. It's just that your grandpa and I are concerned about you, and Abe is such a nice boy. He's a hard worker, and he has land that would be ideal for a large family."

Grandma and Grandpa had always wanted a dozen children, but Mary knew that for some reason they hadn't been able to have more than one child. Mary couldn't imagine having a houseful of kids underfoot. All the babies and toddlers she'd seen required so much selfless work. And her mother's voice rang through her head. *If I didn't have you to worry about, my life would be so different.*

"I'm not so sure that's what I want," Mary said. "A big family is a lot of work."

"Anything worth having is a lot of work," Grandma replied. "Including Abe."

Mary wanted to end the conversation, so she racked her brain for a new topic. She was about to mention the seasonal crowd at the restaurant when she heard the front door. "Grandpa's home. Eleanor was off today, so he must have left Shelley in charge of closing."

"Hello, ladies," Grandpa bellowed as he entered the kitchen. "Beautiful, sunshiny day."

"Ya." Grandma paused with her hands hovering slightly above the finished cobbler. "Mary got home early from her date with Abe."

Grandpa looked at Mary and winked. "I'm sure she has her reasons."

"Said it didn't take long to eat ice cream."

Mary wished they didn't talk about her as though she weren't there. She wanted to run from the kitchen, but that would make the situation more uncomfortable when she came back.

"She's right," Grandpa said, surprising Mary. "Besides, I think it's a good idea for them to take it easy. We don't want Abe getting the wrong idea, thinking Mary is too eager to find a husband."

"I'm not even looking for a husband," Mary blurted.

Grandma made a clucking sound with her tongue, and Grandpa chuckled. "Good girl. It's harder to find one when you're looking," he said.

"She's not getting younger, Joseph."

He nodded. "I think she knows that. How much longer before supper's ready? I'm starving."

"Not much longer," Mary replied. "The ham and sweet potatoes are ready. As soon as the rolls are done, we can eat."

"In that case, I'll go do some weeding. Let me know when it's time to sit down at the table."

Silence fell between Mary and Grandma after Grandpa left the kitchen. Mary sometimes wondered why Grandpa came home acting as though he might starve to death after working in a restaurant all day. Even though he was surrounded by food, Mary or Shelley sometimes had to remind him to eat lunch. He worked as hard as his employees did, so Mary was more than happy to do what she could to help out at home.

After the rolls came out of the oven, Grandma pointed to the door. "Go let your grandfather know it's time to wash up for supper. Then you can help me put everything on the table."

Mary's skirt swished as she turned around and headed for the back door. She shielded her eyes as she stepped outside on the western side of the house.

Grandpa glanced up. "Supper ready?"

"Yes," she said. "It'll be on the table in a few minutes."

Grandpa nodded. "I'll be there in a moment."

Mary went back inside to help Grandma finish the meal preparation. She sliced the maple-citrus-glazed ham and set it on the table then slid the hot, buttery rolls into the napkin-lined basket. Grandpa liked buttermilk with dinner, so she poured him a glass and set it at the head of the table. Grandma placed a pot holder on the table before putting the dish of sweet potatoes on top of it. The aromas blended and would have had Mary's taste buds on high alert if her stomach wasn't so off-kilter after the afternoon with Abe and the conversation between her grandparents.

"Get the lemonade," Grandma ordered. "I'll get the glasses."

By the time the women had everything laid out, Grandpa appeared. "Have a seat, ladies."

They sat and bowed their heads for the blessing. Mary held her breath as he thanked the Lord for the beautiful day and the food they were blessed with, hoping he wouldn't mention Abe. When he finished with "Amen," she let the air out of her lungs. She opened her eyes to see him staring at her. He winked, and she managed a slight grin in return.

❧

Abe stared at the sandwich on the table. He was getting sick of eating the same old thing every night for supper, but he felt guilty for his dissatisfaction because he never had to go hungry. Although he knew how to prepare a meal, it seemed pointless to go to so much trouble for only one person.

After he and his brothers grew up, his mother mentioned the same thing about cooking for two. "But if I don't prepare a meal for your father, he might wither up and die, then I'd have only myself to cook for."

Abe felt an emptiness in his heart as he longed for the days when his whole family was in the house, eating a lavish dinner prepared by his mother's loving hands. He took a bite of his sandwich and slowly chewed before swallowing and repeating until it was gone.

He carried his plate to the sink, washed it, dried it, and put it away. Next time he went into town, he needed to get something from Penner's to go.

It was still daylight out as he stepped onto the front porch and deeply inhaled the fresh air. The workers had gone home for the day, so here he was, in the middle of his family farm, alone and confused—not only by the way Mary Penner was acting but by how he felt about her. As much as he liked her, he should have been happy to kiss her, but when she ordered him to do it, he was startled.

Then when they finally did kiss, it was even better than he'd expected. He still wondered why Mary had changed toward him so abruptly.

The sound of an automobile turning onto the shell driveway caught his attention, and he turned in the direction of the main road. A bright orange car came barreling toward him. The only person he knew with a car that color was Jeremiah Yoder. Tension rose from his core and extended throughout his entire body. Why would Jeremiah be coming all the way out here?

Abe stepped down off the porch and into the yard. He placed his hands on his hips and glared as the automobile drew closer. He could see Jeremiah's face had a look of determination.

The orange car came to a skidding halt about twenty feet from where Abe stood, and Jeremiah got out. "Hey, Abe. Got a few minutes to chat with an old friend?"

"What are you doing here, Jeremiah?" Abe had to hold back the anger that brewed in his chest.

Jeremiah lifted his hands in surrender. "Hey, man, I just wanted to make amends. I feel bad about what I said in town earlier."

"You do?" This didn't sound like the Jeremiah of late. Abe couldn't help but be suspicious.

"Yep. I was being a class-A jerk, and I'm sorry."

Abe's faith ran deep, and he knew that when a man was sincerely sorry for what he did wrong, he needed to be forgiven. But it wasn't always easy.

"Want some coffee?" Abe asked.

"Nah, I can't drink coffee late in the day or I'll be up all night."

Abe smiled. "Based on what I've heard, being up all night is normal for you these days."

"Yeah, afraid so. But I'm getting older, ya know?"

"I do know. So you've apologized, and you're forgiven." Abe took a step back, hoping Jeremiah would get back into his bright orange car and leave.

"I'd still like to talk"—Jeremiah glanced around—"unless there's something else going on, and you can't."

"Nothing else is going on."

Jeremiah continued standing in the same spot, kicking at the sandy soil beneath his feet, looking uncomfortable while Abe watched and waited. Something was up, and Abe couldn't tell if it was good, bad, or neutral.

"What do you want, Jeremiah?"

Jeremiah shrugged and shook his head but didn't say anything. Instead, he looked everywhere but at Abe. Finally Abe decided someone needed to speak up, so he gestured toward the house. "Do you wanna come inside?"

With a nod, Jeremiah took a step toward the house. Abe led the way in silence, wondering all the way what was so important for Jeremiah to have to talk now.

"Have a seat at the kitchen table," Abe said. "I would offer you something besides coffee, but since I live here alone, I don't generally keep much extra food lying around."

"I didn't come here to eat." Jeremiah pulled out a chair and glanced around before sitting. "This place hasn't changed a bit since we were kids, except for a few missing decorations."

"There's no reason for it to change. I put the decorations away, but I still have them."

"True, there isn't a reason for change." Jeremiah let out a nervous laugh. "But some people like change just for the sake of something different."

"Not me."

"I realize that, and it's the reason I wanted to talk to you."

Abe sat down and leaned back in his chair, arms folded, eyes narrowed. Since he had no idea what Jeremiah wanted to talk about, he didn't know of any questions to ask.

"This isn't easy for me, Abe, so bear with me."

"I'm listening."

"You know I left the church when I realized how much fun I could have." He cleared his throat. "Or how much fun I thought I could have."

"What do you mean by that?"

Jeremiah rolled his eyes upward and looked around the room before settling his attention back on Abe. "It's really strange how enticing the world can be, but when you get smack-dab in the middle of it, there's something not right. It doesn't feel as good as it looks."

"What happened, Jeremiah?"

"Nothing really happened. It's just that I was seeing this girl. Amy. She's very cute and funny and a little bit wild. I knew that, and I was okay with it at first. But the more I got to know her, the more I realized how lost she was. Amy lives for the moment and had the philosophy that if it feels good, it's okay."

Abe never expected to have this kind of conversation with Jeremiah. He could see the man was troubled, so he nodded his understanding and encouragement to continue.

"Amy's a sweet girl but very misguided. She's been around the block a few times, ya know?"

Abe tilted his head. "Around the block?"

Jeremiah chuckled. "She's been with other men. At first I tried to be cool with it, but as we got deeper into our relationship, I realized how much it bothered me."

"Ya, that would bother most men, I think."

"Not all men, but in spite of the fact that I left the church, my Mennonite roots run deep. I couldn't deal with Amy's wild ways anymore, so I broke it off with her."

"I'm sure that's a very good idea."

Jeremiah tilted his head and gave Abe an odd look. "Don't you worry about that with Mary?"

"Why should I worry about Mary?"

"Well. . ." Jeremiah lifted his hands and let them fall on the table. "You know where she came from, and chances are—"

Abe shot up from his chair. "Don't you ever say another word about Mary's past. She's a good Mennonite girl."

"Okay, okay, I'm just thinking there might be some things you don't know about her. Remember when we first met her? There was some talk about her mother and where she came from and all."

"What happened to Mary was out of her control. She was fourteen when she came here, and since I've known her, she hasn't done anything wrong." Abe's jaw tensed, and he sat back down to try to regain control of his emotions. "Mary is a very sweet woman who is committed to the Lord."

Jeremiah closed his eyes and pursed his lips. He was obviously a very frustrated man.

"I'm still not sure why you came here, Jeremiah," Abe said. "Did you want advice about Amy or to deliver some lies about Mary?"

"Neither."

"Then why are you here?" Abe asked.

Jeremiah sucked in a breath, blew it out, then leveled Abe with a look of determination. "Do you think there's any chance I can come back to the church?"

Chapter 8

The next day Mary's nerves were on edge. Each time she heard the bell on the restaurant door, she jumped.

"Expecting someone?" Shelley asked.

"Abe."

Shelley smiled. "I thought so."

"Something must have come up, or he would have been here by now."

"Lunch isn't over yet. Maybe he had some things to do on the farm."

"I'm sure." Another customer walked in and sat down in Mary's section. "At least we're busy today. All these customers are keeping my mind off him."

Shelley laughed. "Who are you trying to fool, Mary? A bomb could explode in the room, and you'd still be thinking about Abe."

Without a response, Mary turned toward her customers. Shelley was right. Nothing would get her mind off Abe—not after that kiss that still had her lips tingling.

After the lunch crowd dwindled, Grandpa approached Mary and handed her the phone. "It's for you," he said.

She answered it with a tentative, "Hello?"

"Is this the Mary Penner who lived in Cincinnati?" The man's voice was barely audible, but it had a familiar tone to it.

Mary's legs nearly gave out, so she lowered herself into the nearest chair. "Who is this?"

The man let out a sinister laugh. "You're good at hiding. It took some work to find you."

"Tell me who you are, or I'm hanging up," Mary demanded.

She heard him laughing as the call disconnected. Whoever that was didn't sound nice at all.

Shelley approached before she had a chance to stand back up. "You okay, Mary?"

Mary blinked and nodded. "That was the strangest phone call. Some man asked me if I was the Mary Penner who lived in Cincinnati, but he didn't tell me who he was or why he wanted to know."

"That truly is strange. Let me know if you need something. I need to check on my customers."

"Thanks." Mary stood and crossed the restaurant to hand the phone back to Grandpa, who was busy filling some late lunch orders. She was glad he didn't have time to talk to her, or he would have asked questions about the call.

At about three thirty, Grandpa walked up and put his arm around her. "Why don't you run on home and tend to the garden so I don't have to?"

Grandpa loved his garden, so she suspected he was trying to help get her mind off Abe. She started to say she could stay a little longer, but instead she offered a brief nod. She untied her apron and hung it on the rack.

She was almost to the door when she heard Grandpa call out to her. "Don't rush things, Granddaughter. The Lord knows what's on your heart, and He'll make everything all right."

Mary forced a smile. "Yes, I know that."

"Oh, here, take this to your grandmother," he said as he pulled the last of the cake from the shelf. "I told her you'd bring home whatever dessert was left."

She took the cake, covered it, and went out the back door. After carefully positioning the cake in the basket of her three-wheeler, she hopped on and pedaled home.

Grandma wasn't in the kitchen, so Mary set the cake on the counter and opened the oven door. It was hot, but nothing was in there. *Strange.*

"Grandma, are you home?" she called out. No answer. "Grandma?" She spun around and looked on the message board by the door. Nothing there.

Mary's heart raced. Something wasn't right. She couldn't ever remember a time when Grandma left without telling someone or at least leaving a note. Her head swirled with all kinds of thoughts of what could have happened— particularly after the odd phone call that afternoon. Mary didn't have a cell phone to call Grandpa, so she started to head back to the restaurant. She'd barely mounted her three-wheeler when she spotted the van Abe often rode in when he came to town as it pulled up in front of the house.

Both Abe and Grandma got out. "Where are you off to, Mary?" Grandma asked while Abe went around to the other side of the van and pulled out a big brown box.

"I was—" Mary stopped when the van door slammed. Her jaw dropped, but she quickly recovered and pursed her lips.

Abe carried the box to the curb and set it down before placing his hands on his hips and looking at Grandma. "Where do you want this?"

"By the back door, if you don't mind."

Abe lifted the box and brought it around back while Grandma followed. Mary was right behind them with her three-wheeler.

"Come on inside," Grandma said. "Mary, you can set the table."

Mary glanced back and forth between Grandma and Abe after she placed the dishes on the table. "You weren't here, and I was. . ." Her voice trailed off when she saw the look of amusement on Abe's face. "What's so funny?"

"Nothing," Abe said. "I just think it's sweet that you were worried about your grandmother."

Grandma flicked her hand. "Oh, she wasn't worried about me."

"I was," Mary admitted as relief washed over her. "Did you know you left the oven on?"

"Uh-oh." Grandma made a face. "That's not good."

"I'm afraid it was my fault," Abe said in her defense. "I stopped by and talked her into going with me."

"Where did you go?" Mary asked.

Her grandmother's gaze darted from Abe to Mary. "Abe came by after I got home from the restaurant. We started talking, and next thing I knew, he was taking me out to his farm to show me what he's done."

"Ya," Abe said. "She hadn't been out there since my mother passed away. I wanted her to see how well the citrus was growing."

"Maybe you can go see the farm sometime, Mary. Abe is doing quite well." She bent over the box, opened it, and extracted some of the fruit. "This is from the last of the season's citrus," she explained before turning back to Abe. "I think we can put it to good use around here. Thank you, Abe."

He grinned. "My pleasure, Mrs. Penner."

"You'll be staying for supper, won't you?" Grandma said.

Mary quickly cut her gaze over to Abe, who'd given her a questioning look. He opened his mouth then narrowed his eyes before nodding. "Yes, that would be very nice. I don't normally have a very good supper, so this will be a treat."

"Mary, set an extra place for Abe."

Without a word, Mary did as she was told. Her spirits had been lifted, but she didn't want anyone to notice—particularly not Grandma, who would most likely have something to say about it later.

"Is there anything I can do to help you?" Abe asked.

Grandma shook her head, but Mary pointed toward the back door. "Grandpa asked me to tend his garden, so you can help me out."

"Mary!" Grandma gave her a scolding look. "Abe is a guest!"

"That's all right, Mrs. Penner. I don't mind as long as Mary's with me."

Mary avoided looking directly at Grandma for fear of a reprimanding glare. Instead, she marched straight out to the backyard before turning to face Abe.

"I wondered where you were today when I didn't see you at the restaurant."

Abe grinned. "Do you always worry about people when you don't see them?"

"Who said I was worried? All I said was—"

Abe quickly narrowed the distance between them. He took hold of her gloved hand and held it between both of his, creating a flutter inside her. Mary glanced over toward the window and was relieved not to see Grandma watching. But she pulled her hand back anyway; she didn't want to press her good fortune.

When she glanced back at Abe, she knew he'd seen her look. "I—"

"She knows," Abe said softly. "I told her I wanted to see more of you."

Mary's jaw fell slack again. "And what did she say?"

"I have her blessing. Your grandpa's, too."

"When did you talk to him?" She averted her gaze and bent over to pull a weed from the edge of the garden.

"This morning before you got to the restaurant. I wanted to make sure they understood my intentions before we got too carried away."

Mary shot straight up and planted her weed-filled fist on her hip, then looked directly at Abe. "You didn't tell them I asked for a kiss, did you?"

Abe laughed. "That's the Mary I remember. No, I didn't mention the kiss, but I did say you were spirited and full of surprises."

"Surprises? Me? How about you? So tell me what's going on."

"I want to court you, Mary. I thought I told you I wanted us to get to know each other better."

"You did, but you didn't say anything about courting."

"You're a smart woman. If you thought about it more, you would have figured it out." He lightly touched her cheek then pulled back. "I want to be with you every chance I can."

That was exactly what she wanted, too. But deep down, her mother's words still haunted her, dredging up just enough fear to concern her.

"What if we find out we can't stand each other?" she challenged.

"I doubt that will happen."

"It might. What then?"

He shrugged. "If that's the case, I s'pose we'll know that we're not meant to be together."

That was exactly what Mary was afraid of. But the more she thought about it, she was afraid they *were* meant to be together. And then what? Mary had no idea what to do in a real relationship with a man, and even though she wanted to have a relationship, she feared she wasn't capable of fully trusting him—or any man—with her heart.

She moved faster through the garden, frantically yanking out the spindly, green intruders, tossing them into the bin her grandpa had set by the garden.

"Whoa, there," Abe said. "You're gonna hurt yourself if you keep up this pace. Let me give you a hand." He narrowed his eyes and studied her face. "Is something else going on?"

Mary hesitated but decided to let Abe know about the call. She explained what had happened, and he listened. After she finished, he shook his head.

"That is very strange. I wonder why the man wouldn't tell you his name. Are you frightened?"

"At first I was," she said as she resumed her weeding, going more slowly now that she'd let some of the worry be known. "But I prayed about it, and now I know I'll be fine."

As Abe joined her in weeding, Mary forced herself to calm down. She wanted to believe her fears were uncalled for, but at the moment, they were stronger than her desires.

"God will protect you, but that doesn't mean you have to let down your guard," Abe said. "Please be careful and let people know where you are at all times."

Mary chuckled. "Grandma and Grandpa pretty much know my whereabouts every minute of the day."

"Next time you decide to walk on the beach, you might want to have someone go with you." He grinned. "I'll be glad to volunteer."

"I'm sure." She smiled back at Abe.

"Mary."

She glanced up toward the sound of her grandfather's voice. "I got a late start, but Abe's helping me, so I'm almost done."

"You don't have to do any more, Mary. I didn't intend for you to put our guest to work."

Abe straightened. "She didn't put me to work, Mr. Penner. I insisted."

"That's fine, but come on inside. You're our guest, and I want you to feel welcome. Sarah told me you gave us some fruit. We should be weeding your garden, not the other way around."

Abe grinned. "I don't expect anything in return."

Grandpa gave a clipped nod. "I understand, but both of you, come on into the house and wash up for supper."

Mary tossed the last of the weeds into the bin then removed her work gloves. She dropped them on the table on the back porch. Abe was right behind her.

After they washed up for supper, Mary helped Grandma finish getting the food on the table. They all sat down and joined hands.

Grandpa said the blessing. He gave Mary's hand a squeeze before letting go. "This looks delicious, Sarah."

Grandma made a clucking sound with her tongue. "I know what you like to eat."

Conversation was all about the food, which suited Mary just fine. She didn't feel like answering personal questions—particularly with Abe sitting right across from her. And she was glad he didn't bring up the phone call.

"This is good, Mrs. Penner," Abe said. "I haven't had a meal like this in. . . well, since my mother died."

Grandpa held his fork midair as he gave Abe a comical look. "Not even at the restaurant? We like to think the food there is as good as home cooking."

Abe chuckled. "Well, other than the restaurant. I should have clarified."

"That's okay, Abe," Grandpa said as he belted out a laugh. "I was just teasing. My Sarah is the best cook in Sarasota, and no restaurant food can even come close."

"Mary is a good cook, too," Grandma added. "I've been teaching her."

"Maybe I'll have the pleasure of eating something she cooks sometime," Abe said as he stabbed another bite with his fork. He cast a quick glance in Mary's direction, and she saw the humor in his eyes.

Grandma lifted her eyebrows and exchanged a glance with Grandpa, and neither of them said a word. The idea of cooking for Abe was pleasant, but an awkward silence hung in the air.

After Abe got home, he pondered the conversation while they were weeding and how different she was during supper. He sensed that Mary was worried about the call, but he couldn't imagine anything happening to her in Pinecraft.

Mary didn't say much during the meal, particularly after his comment about her cooking something for him. Her sensitivities were different from most people's. Abe suspected it had everything to do with her past. Until he could get her to open up more and talk about it, he'd never know what happened to make her so skittish. Her scars ran deep, and he knew that until she faced her past, it would forever darken her world. He decided to back off and stop trying so hard to court Mary. If it turned out to be the Lord's will, she would come around naturally, but at the moment Abe didn't see that happening.

The day had been long and tiring, so Abe didn't have any trouble sleeping. He awoke the next morning to the sound of someone banging on his front door. He opened it and found himself looking at a middle-aged man he'd never seen before.

"I'm Jonathan Polk," the man said. "David said you were looking for workers, and I need a job."

"Can you give me a few minutes?" Abe asked.

"Sure. If you don't mind, I'll wander around and take a look-see at your land."

Abe went to his room and dressed then to the kitchen to make some coffee. When he went back outside with two mugs of coffee, Jonathan was standing by the split-rail fence, looking out over the property.

"Nice place you have here," Jonathan said as he took the mug.

"Ya. I like it."

"How long have you been farming in Florida?"

"All my life." Abe sipped his coffee. "I'm the third generation. My father moved here with his parents and started a celery farm. Have you ever worked on a farm?"

Jonathan slowly shook his head. "No, but I've worked with my hands plenty, I'm handy with machines, and I learn quickly."

"I can't pay a big salary."

"That's fine," Jonathan said. "I'll just be happy to have regular work."

Abe nodded his understanding. At least the man was looking for work—not handouts.

"If I hire you, I'll need you to learn all aspects of farming. We work hard, and we don't specialize in any one thing around here."

Jonathan turned away from Abe and looked out over the farm again before speaking. "There's something refreshing about working hard outdoors. Even though the only outside work I've ever done has been yard work at home, I think it would be good for me." He paused before adding, "And for you. I'm honest, reliable, and loyal. I'm pretty good at fixing things."

Abe needed someone soon, and he hadn't been able to find any Mennonite workers. Jonathan sounded like a man of integrity, plus he'd been referred by David, who knew what Abe needed.

"Can you start tomorrow?" Abe asked.

Abe could tell it took a few seconds before the question registered with Jonathan. Suddenly he grinned. "You mean it? I'm hired?"

"Ya. Come back tomorrow, and I'll start teaching you all about dairy farming."

They walked toward Jonathan's car, where he handed Abe his mug. "What time do you want me here in the morning?"

"Six thirty." Abe thought for a few seconds before correcting himself. "Make that six. I'll need to show you a few things to get you started."

Jonathan nodded. "I'll be here earlier than that if you need me."

"No need to be earlier. Six is just fine."

Abe stood with both mugs in his hands as he watched Jonathan pull away from the house. After the car disappeared from sight, he headed inside to wash the mugs and get ready to go to town. David was supposed to pick him up at nine, and he'd overslept. He'd spent a good hour chatting with Jonathan, touring the farm, and discussing cows and citrus, and it was already a quarter to eight.

∾

Mary had just served a large party of ten when she spotted Abe walking through the restaurant door. Grandpa pointed toward her and said something to him.

Her heart fluttered as Abe got closer, but she forced herself to glance away. She took her time making her way to him. He'd turned down the menu enough times she knew he didn't need one.

"What would you like this morning, Abe?" She had to take a deep breath to steady her nerves and keep her hand from shaking as she held the pen above the order pad.

"What do you think would be good for me?" he asked with a teasing tone.

"It's up to you. Would you like a boiled egg, oatmeal, and some fruit, or do you prefer ham, eggs, and fried potatoes?" She scrunched her nose as she finished the question.

Abe leaned back, folded his arms, and smiled as their gazes met. "I'll take the healthy breakfast. . .that is, if it makes you happy."

She tried to keep her emotional balance as she jotted that down on the pad and stepped away. "Good choice," she said as she left and walked toward the kitchen.

"You look good when your eyes twinkle," Shelley said.

"I have no idea what you're talking about." Mary refused to look directly at Shelley, who was obviously having some fun.

"Don't tell me you don't know how much you light up whenever Abe's around."

"He's just another customer." Mary couldn't prevent the grin that tweaked her lips.

Grandpa chose that moment to round the corner and walk toward them. "I'm glad Abe is here. I was beginning to wonder when he'd come back after he said he wanted to court you."

Mary kept her focus on her task. "He's just hungry."

She heard Shelley snicker as she brushed past to get the next order up.

Abe's food was ready a couple of minutes later. Shelley had returned to the kitchen, and she gestured toward Mary's kapp. "You might want to straighten up a bit before you go back out there."

"I'm fine," Mary said, determined not to do anything different just because Abe was there. If he wanted to get to know her better, he might as well get used to the fact that her kapp was often at an angle. Even after all this practice, she still struggled with getting it just right on her head.

She pulled the plates from the counter and carried them to Abe. "Here's your fruit," she said as she placed the bowl filled with strawberries, blueberries, and cantaloupe in front of him. "Be careful with the oatmeal." She put that down beside the fruit bowl. "It's very hot. I'll have your boiled eggs right out."

"No hurry," he said. "Are you able to take a break and join me?"

Mary quickly shook her head and spun around to get the rest of his meal when a little boy running past tripped her. Embarrassment flooded her when suddenly she felt herself being scooped up by a firm, strong arm.

"Whoa there, Mary." Abe caught her and set her back on her feet. "You okay?"

She took the opportunity to straighten her kapp and run her hands down the sides of her full skirt. "I'm just fine. Thank you for catching me. . .again."

"Children need to be taught manners before they're allowed out," Abe said. "When I have my own, that's one of the first things I'll teach them."

"I–I'm sure you will." Mary allowed a brief sidelong glance in Abe's direction before she scurried toward the kitchen again.

"If Abe hadn't been there, you might have been hurt." Shelley handed Mary a glass of water. "You've been working so hard, Mary. Why don't you sit down for a little while? I can handle the crowd."

"I can't do that to you, Shelley. I'm fine."

Grandpa handed Abe's boiled eggs to Mary. "Take these over to Abe and have a seat at his table." He leveled her with a firm gaze. "I'll bring you something to eat."

"I—"

He tilted his head forward and gave her an even sterner look she couldn't argue with. She carried Abe's eggs to him. "Is the offer still open to join you?"

Abe gestured to the seat across from him. "Ya. I'd be honored for you to sit down with me."

Mary had only been seated about a minute before Grandpa came over with a cup of coffee and a bowl of fruit for her. "Would you like some oatmeal?"

She nodded. "Yes, please."

"I'll have Shelley bring you some. Why don't you relax for a while and enjoy Abe's company? I'm sure Abe wouldn't mind, right?"

"I would love that, but I can't stay long. I have a new worker coming out to the farm tomorrow, and I have to get everything ready for him."

Grandpa seemed pleased. "It's nice to hear that you're doing well enough to hire more people. Isn't that right, Mary?"

"Yes." She fidgeted with the napkin in front of her.

"Shelley will be right over with your oatmeal." Grandpa turned and headed back to the kitchen to turn in her order.

"You seem rather glum today, Mary." Abe cracked his egg and began to peel it.

Mary didn't know what to say. Her crazy, mixed-up feelings for Abe were enough to send her to the funny farm, as Mama used to tell her. "I'm not glum."

"Good. I was worried I might have said or done something to upset you."

"No, you've been very kind, Abe."

He put down the peeled egg, placed his forearms on the table, and leaned toward her. "Then what is going on? Just when I thought we were getting along—as friends, of course—you started acting strange."

Chapter 9

Abe watched Mary as she fidgeted with the napkin. All sorts of thoughts flowed through his mind.

"Do you want me to leave you alone?" he asked. "You're confusing me, Mary. I tried very hard to show you how much I care, and I think you know I'm willing to be your friend even if you don't want more."

Mary's gaze locked with his. She slowly shook her head. "No, Abe, that's not what I want. I guess I'm just skittish because I never understood why you would want to court me in the first place. Surely you could do much better than me."

"I don't know about that." He sighed. Mary's tight grip on her past still frustrated him. "There isn't any reason, besides the fact that I like you, Mary—very much."

"But why?" She tilted her head and gave him a look that broke his heart.

"Why wouldn't I? You seem faithful to the Lord and to the people you love. I always see you in church, praying and helping others. The look on your face when you worship is pure. You never fail to do whatever your grandparents need you to do. You're sweet beneath that shell you use to hide your heart."

Her eyes fluttered closed, then they instantly widened, sending a bolt of shock through him. There was something else between him and Mary—something he couldn't explain because even he didn't understand it.

"Why do you pay so much attention to me in order to know all this?" she asked. "What have I done to deserve your attention?"

Abe lifted his hands in surrender. "I have no idea. Maybe it's just a feeling I have."

"There are some things. . ." She met his gaze as he lifted one eyebrow. "Some things you don't know about my past."

When she stopped talking, he urged her to continue. "I'm willing to listen if you want to tell me, but I doubt there's anything that will make me change my mind."

"I saw some very bad things before I came here, Abe." She lowered her head as if in shame. "Bad things I can't talk about to anyone. I suspect no one in this community has ever experienced what I did at a very young age."

Abe reached across the table and placed his hand over hers. "That was something you couldn't help, Mary. And I believe others here might have had some bad experiences they don't talk about, too. I want you to trust me."

"I'm not completely blameless, either. I lied my way through life many times."

"You were a child, Mary. You did what you thought you had to do. No one is holding that against you."

"Maybe you're right."

"Even if you don't want more than friendship, I still want you to trust me."

Mary licked her lips and looked him in the eye. "I want to trust you, too."

Abe took a deep breath, glanced around the room, then turned back to Mary and exhaled. "The Lord brought you here nine years ago, and I felt something then, but I was too young to know what to do. After all that time, I aimed to find out if I was in His plan to be a part of your life, now that we're adults. I've never been interested in any woman besides you, Mary. I wanted to get to know all about you and what makes you the person you are."

A tiny smile tweaked the corners of her lips. She put down the napkin she'd shredded.

"I'm very happy to be with you, but I don't understand so many things about myself, I can't imagine you ever figuring them out."

"Oh, but I'm willing to try." Abe didn't add the fact that her challenging ways intrigued him even more. He didn't want to say anything that might be misconstrued. "As a friend, of course." Abe still wanted more, but he knew it was out of his hands.

Shelley arrived and placed a bowl of oatmeal in front of Mary. "Topped with brown sugar and apples, just the way you like it."

"Thank you, Shelley."

After Shelley left, Abe leaned forward and inhaled the aroma wafting from Mary's bowl. "That smells delicious."

"It is." Mary lifted her spoon and swirled the fruit into the cereal. "Mama used to eat her oatmeal this way." She closed her eyes to say a quiet blessing.

Abe studied her face until she opened her eyes. "You don't talk much about your mother, Mary. I'd like to know more about her."

She frowned. "Like what? If all the rumors about her are true?"

"No, I'm sure most of the rumors are just that. Rumors. But I would like to know what the two of you did together and where you lived."

Mary shrugged. "Mama and I mostly just found ways to survive. After she left here at sixteen, she didn't know what to do. At least that's what she told me later. It wasn't easy, being a teenage mother with no one to help her."

"I'm sure."

They sat in silence as Mary lifted a spoon half filled with oatmeal to her mouth. Abe didn't want to push, but she'd told him just enough to create more questions in his mind.

"What?" she asked after her next bite. "Why are you looking at me like that?"

This obviously wasn't a good time to ask questions. "I'm sorry if I upset you. It's just difficult for me to know what to say to you sometimes."

"Maybe it's best not to say anything." She put her spoon into the bowl and stood up. "I better be getting back to work now. I've taken enough time off already."

Abe stood until she left, then he sank back down into his seat. Just when he thought he'd made a step forward, he said or did something that made him slide back. If he didn't feel called by God to continue, he would consider backing down. But every time he thought he might be better off with someone else, something happened to pull him back in Mary's direction. The memory of Mary demanding a kiss brought a smile to his face and joy to his heart.

<hr/>

Mary managed to finish her shift without crying, but it hadn't been easy. After Abe brought up her mother, that familiar lump formed in her throat, and she wanted to run out of the restaurant and hide.

As sweet as Abe had been to her, Mary couldn't push her mother's words from her mind. If she hadn't seen her grandmother's anger firsthand, she might have thought her mother's words were childish rebellion. But after Mary moved in with Grandma and Grandpa, she'd overheard some conversations between them that made her think she wasn't wanted. Their talks late at night when they thought she wasn't listening used to worry her, but she eventually became numb to comments about how unexpected her arrival had been and how difficult it was to raise a child at their age. Mary felt secure as long as she stayed on their good side, and now she wondered if Grandma and Grandpa had taken her in to try to redo the mistakes they'd made in the past.

Mama's stories continued to haunt her. She sensed that the only man her mother ever trusted was Grandpa, and even that trust had been shaken when he hadn't protected her from everyone's wrath.

Instead of going home after work, Mary took the bus back to the beach. She decided she'd walk along the water rather than sit this time.

The beach was even more crowded with tourists. "Hey, Mommy," she heard a little girl say. "Why is that lady dressed like that?" Her mother's reply was in a hushed tone, and Mary couldn't make out what the woman said.

Most of the locals were used to seeing Mennonites around town, but many of the tourists weren't accustomed to their presence. She wanted to be invisible, but with her kapp and long, full skirt, that was impossible. What if she secretly changed into Yankee clothes once in a while, just to hide from the world? The irony of shedding clothes in order to hide gave her a chuckle.

Half expecting to hear Abe's voice behind her caused her to glance over her shoulder every once in a while. But she didn't. All she heard were the sounds of water washing up on the beach, birds calling out to each other, and the high-pitched sounds of kids playing.

The sun was hotter than last time, so she didn't stay on the beach long. After a brief walk, she went back to the bus stop and waited. The flurry of emotions continued swirling around her, escalating her confusion. She no longer fit into the outside world, but she'd never felt like she fully belonged in the Mennonite community. She felt like a misfit, no matter where she was.

She boarded the bus after it stopped. No one else was on it, so she took a seat toward the front. Mary felt very alone.

A few stops later, Mary got off the bus a block from the restaurant. In order not to be seen, she darted between buildings and went straight around back to get her three-wheeler. She was about to take off when the sound of someone sniffling caught her attention.

Mary glanced over her shoulder and saw Shelley by the garbage cans behind the restaurant, dabbing her eyes, her body racked with sobs. She hopped off the three-wheeler and ran over to her friend and coworker.

"What happened, Shelley? Was a customer mean to you?"

Shelley stiffened as Mary gripped her arm. She looked up to Mary with red-rimmed eyes and shook her head. "Peter told me he's marrying Clara."

"But I thought—" Mary stopped herself before blurting that she thought Peter was about to propose to Shelley. "Clara who?"

Shelley sniffled again and blew her nose. She cleared her throat. "Clara from Pennsylvania."

"Do we know her?" Mary asked.

Shelley shook her head. "I saw her talking to Peter once, but I just thought they were acquaintances."

"How can he do that, after courting you for so long?"

"He said he and I were just very good friends all along and that I should be happy for him. I feel so stupid now."

"Join the club," Mary said. "I feel that way most of the time."

"I thought I did everything right. Whenever he wanted to do something, I was always right there, willing to do it with him. When he needed help with the food drive, I jumped in and volunteered. At the potlucks, he always wanted to sit with me, so I saved him a place. Wanna know what he asked me to do?"

Mary shook her head. "No telling."

"He wants me to be in charge of the food for his wedding."

"Peter isn't as smart as I thought he was."

"No, Mary, I think I'm the one who isn't very smart. Now that I think back, I can't remember a time when Peter ever said anything about getting married."

"Didn't he tell you he loved you?"

Shelley shook her head. "Never. Not even once. All he said was that we were about as close as two people could get without being husband and wife. I read into it too much."

"Everyone thought you two would get married."

"I know. He said something else I didn't expect. He told me he always felt sorry for me because of William."

Mary gasped. "William is so sweet and such a blessing."

"Yes, I know. I thought Peter understood that, too. But he's just like the rest of the people we knew in school, even though he's a couple years older."

Mary dropped her arms by her sides. This just validated her mother's words about men even more. Even from her vantage point, Peter had appeared smitten with Shelley. When they were at church, he never let Shelley out of his sight. He even came to the restaurant asking where his girl was.

"This is terrible, Shelley, but you're a strong woman. You can stand up to him and show you're not the least bit fazed by his silliness and. . ." She wanted to say *stupidity*, but she held back. She'd already said enough.

Shelley let out a tiny half giggle/half sob. "Mary, you are such a good friend. I'm glad you came back when you did." She blew her nose then stuffed the tissue back into her pocket. "By the way, where did you go? Your grandfather said you left, but when I came out here, I saw your wheels."

"Sometimes when I need to think I catch the bus and go to the beach." Mary tugged Shelley away from the spot where she'd been standing. "Why don't you come to my grandparents' house with me? I'm sure Grandma wouldn't mind you staying for supper."

"No, I have to cook for William. Our parents are up in Ohio visiting family." Shelley took hold of Mary's hand. "Thank you for caring. I don't know what I would have done if you hadn't come along when you did."

"You would have done the same thing for me," Mary said. "In fact, you have. Sometimes when I feel lost or all alone, you say something or give me a look that lets me know I'm not."

Shelley squeezed Mary's hand then let go. "I need to get on home now. William is probably worried about me."

"Tell William I said hi." Mary hopped back up on the seat of her three-wheeler. "Speaking of worry, I need to get home and help Grandma with her chores. I don't want her to worry about me."

On the way home, Mary thought about the similarities between her life and Shelley's. Although Shelley had never left the community, her older brother had fallen away from the church and her younger brother had Down syndrome, which made some of the other kids in school very uncomfortable. At first Mary wondered why Shelley was such a loner, but after she went home with Shelley a few times, she learned.

Sometimes life just didn't seem fair. Mary had done nothing to cause other people to pretend she didn't exist, yet some still did.

Mary's mother had shared her faith with Mary, but she always mentioned the inconsistencies she'd noticed from some of the people who attended church. Not all of them, but some had twisted the Gospel to fit their agenda.

Shelley somehow maintained her sweetness, and her zest for everything she did gave her the ability to overlook other people's pitying glances. She was the only person who'd actually gone out of her way to be nice to Mary. Perhaps she understood how Mary felt on some level.

What Peter had done was incomprehensible. As Mary reflected on how much time Shelley had put into that relationship, she had no doubt Peter had strung Shelley along, knowing what she expected. Mary knew she wasn't supposed to be angry. The Lord would want her to turn her anger over to Him and simply pray His will be done. It wasn't easy, but as soon as she pulled into her grandparents' yard, that was exactly what she did. Mary had just closed her eyes and begun to speak to the Lord, asking for help in knowing how to comfort Shelley, when she heard Grandma.

"Mary, is that you? Come inside right now. I need you to give me a hand in here."

"I'll be right there," Mary called back. She closed her eyes again, finished her prayer, and said "Amen" aloud before hopping off her three-wheeler and going inside to see what Grandma wanted.

"Grace Hoffstetter is sick, and her husband, Bernard, needs some supper. I fixed them a little something, but I can't leave the house. I want you to take this over to them." She pointed to a casserole cooling on the counter. "You can stop by the restaurant and see if there's any pie left from today that you can take with you. Tell your grandfather I said it was okay."

Mary nodded. Grandpa wouldn't have minded if she'd taken pie, even if Grandma hadn't said anything, but she didn't need to mention that. "Is it just for Mr. Hoffstetter?" Mary asked.

"As far as I know. I don't think Grace can eat yet." A pinched look came over Grandma's face. "Josephine still hasn't returned."

Mary had overheard Grandma telling Grandpa about Josephine Hoffstetter leaving the church. No doubt it brought back haunting memories of their own earlier lives.

As Mary and Grandma got a basket loaded with some bread and other items to take with the casserole, Mary tried to make conversation. "What's wrong with Mrs. Hoffstetter?"

"Don't know exactly."

"Is it serious?"

"Don't think so."

Grandma's clipped words let Mary know she wasn't in the mood to talk. They finished packing the food in silence.

"Don't stop anywhere except the restaurant," Grandma said. "I want this food to still be warm when you get to the Hoffstetters'."

Mary bit her bottom lip. Grandma still treated her like she didn't have the sense to know what she needed to do.

After everything was all packed up, Grandma touched Mary's arm, stopping her. "Your grandfather and I have been talking. We think it's time for you to get a cell phone so you can let us know where you are."

"I can just tell you where I'm going," Mary said. "I don't need a cell phone."

"We'd like for you to have one, even if it's on one of those prepaid plans. You make plenty of money in tips, and you don't have anything else to spend your money on."

"I'll think about it," Mary said. "Let me get this to the Hoffstetters now so I can be back in time to help out with our supper."

Grandma nodded. "You are right, Mary. We don't need to worry about you." Her expression softened. "I will give you credit for being a good girl. . . at least so far."

Stunned, Mary lifted her eyebrows. "I try to be."

"Now go on, get outta here. I'm sure Bernard is half-starving by now." Grandma shooed her out the door.

After carefully placing the casserole and other items in the basket, Mary got on her three-wheeler and pedaled toward the restaurant to pick up some dessert for the Hoffstetters. She'd turned the last corner near the restaurant when she caught a glimpse of Abe bent over a car, talking to someone through the side window. He obviously didn't see her, so she scooted around back.

She found a safe spot for her three-wheeler, secured it, and walked into the restaurant, where Grandpa was finishing the late afternoon cleanup. "Grandma told me to pick up some dessert for the Hoffstetters. Got anything good?"

"Ya." He pointed toward the pie case. "Take your pick. Give them enough for tomorrow, too."

Mary found a couple of to-go containers and carefully placed some chocolate cream pie in one and some coconut cake in the other. As she left, she lifted her hand in a wave. "See you in a little while."

"Does your grandmother want me to bring something home?" he asked.

"She didn't say, but I'm sure that would be good."

He nodded. "Okay, I'll bring some cornbread and the rest of the chocolate pie—that is, if you left any."

"Oh there's plenty left," Mary said. She shoved the door open with her backside and slipped out.

She couldn't help but look for Abe when she got outside, but she didn't see him. That was just as well. She needed to get this food to the Hoffstetters and then head straight home to help Grandma.

It was a gorgeous day, with a blue sky and a few fluffy clouds that had drifted in from the Gulf of Mexico. A couple of seagulls called out as they flew over. The palm trees lining both sides of the road completed the postcard-perfect setting. The gentle breeze lifted the hair that had fallen beneath her kapp and fluttered the leaves of the trees.

Mary sighed. She was blessed to be here in Sarasota, even though memories continued to haunt her. Grandma's occasional softening gave her hope, but it rarely lasted long. She knew it was time to let go of her past and allow herself to appreciate God's blessings and forgive anyone who chose to treat her poorly, but it was harder than simply making the decision to do it.

After Mary made sure both of the Hoffstetters were fed and comfortable and the dishes were washed, she left their house. She'd turned the corner past the restaurant when she spotted Abe getting out of the car she'd seen him standing beside earlier. She was about to call out to him when the driver's side door opened and out stepped Jeremiah. It wasn't the same car she'd seen Jeremiah in earlier.

Alarm bells rang in Mary's head. What was Abe doing with Jeremiah?

Chapter 10

Mary's heart lurched as she saw Abe and Jeremiah talking and laughing together as though they were good friends. Jeremiah stepped beside Abe on the sidewalk, and they went off in the other direction.

She stopped pedaling and tried to process what she'd just seen. All this time Abe had seemed appalled by Jeremiah's behavior and the things he'd said. Now, however, he looked perfectly fine with the man who'd fallen away from the church and said those horrible words about her.

Mary's mother's words drifted back into her mind. During the past several days, Mary had convinced herself that Abe was different and that he was the one man besides Grandpa who could be trusted. Now she doubted herself and her ability to discern anything about anyone.

She began pedaling as fast as she could, dodging people on the sidewalk as she headed home. By the time she arrived, she was hot and sweaty, and her face flamed.

Grandpa had obviously just arrived home. He stood not far from the kitchen door, smiling, but she didn't bother saying a word as she brushed past him.

"Mary!" Grandma's voice echoed through the tiny house. "Come here right now. Don't you just tear through the house like a spoiled child. What happened?"

Mary could hear Grandma getting closer. She was tempted to close her bedroom door, but that would only make the problem worse.

Grandma stopped in the bedroom doorway and glared at her. "What's got you in such a dither?"

Mary slowly shook her head. "Nothing that matters."

"If it doesn't matter, then I need you to come help me in the kitchen. I've been waiting for you. I expected you home a while ago. You were supposed to drop off the food and come right back."

"Mr. Hoffstetter said his wife might eat a little if I took it to her, so I did. Then she asked me to make some lemonade with some lemons Abe dropped off earlier, and—"

"Stop." Grandma held up her hand. "I get the picture. You helped the Hoffstetters, which was the right thing to do. Now let's get moving so we can get supper done with before it gets dark." She issued a stern look before going back to the kitchen.

Mary sucked in a deep breath and slowly blew it out. She hoped she could get through the evening without losing her composure. Until seeing Abe, she hadn't realized just how much she'd begun to think something might work out between them. He'd made it clear he wanted to advance their relationship, and it was starting to sound mighty good. But now that he was buddying up with Jeremiah, there was no way she could trust him.

The tiny houses rented by the Mennonite and Amish families in Pinecraft were wired for electricity, so most of them, even those from the Old Order, used it sparingly. But Grandma and Grandpa preferred not to any more than necessary, which was why they tried to eat dinner before it got dark. They occasionally used candles, but with the large picture window across the back of the wall in the kitchen, it generally wasn't necessary.

Mary went into the bathroom and splashed water on her face, hoping to cool off. By the time she joined Grandma in the kitchen, she was able to think more rationally. Grandpa was out in the backyard, surveying his tiny garden.

"Crumble up that sleeve of crackers, Mary, and sprinkle them over the casserole. We can stick it back in the oven for a few minutes and have a nice crust." Grandma stirred something on the stove then turned down the burner. "Oh, by the way, we're having company for supper, so you'll need to set an extra place."

"Company?" Mary asked. "Who?"

Grandma's lips twitched into a smile. "Abe."

Mary's arm stilled, and her ears rang. "Abe is coming over for supper?"

"Ya. Your grandfather saw him after closing the restaurant, and he invited him to come eat with us. I thought you'd like that."

What could Mary say? She forced herself to continue preparing the cracker-crumb topping for the casserole.

"We have a special key lime pie for dessert. I thought that would be nice to serve company," Grandma said.

"Yes, it's very nice."

"Mary, turn around and look at me."

Slowly, Mary did as she was told. She tried hard to wipe any expression from her face, but she didn't think she succeeded.

"What are you so unhappy about?"

"Nothing. It's just that I enjoy spending time with you and Grandpa—just the three of us."

Grandma scowled. "Stop being selfish. Abe goes home to an empty house every night. He appreciates having a good meal with a family. Maybe someday soon he'll have a wife and then a family of his own." The harshness on Grandma's face softened.

"Maybe." Mary couldn't tell Grandma about the shock and the emptiness in her heart after seeing Abe with Jeremiah. She wouldn't understand.

Not much surprised Abe, but when Jeremiah had come to his house and asked what he could do to get back into the church, he was taken aback—particularly after the comments Jeremiah had shouted from his car. When Abe cornered him about that, Jeremiah seemed sincerely sorry for acting out in such a childish way.

"I guess I've formed some bad habits that I'll have to break," Jeremiah had explained.

"Ya, I guess you have."

Jeremiah had talked for more than an hour about his life outside the church. He said it was fun at first. Someone gave him a job, and shortly after that he'd learned to drive. When he had enough money saved, he bought his automobile. With the freedom of his own wheels came some things he said he was ashamed of.

"I don't think I need to go into the details," he admitted, "but I can tell you it's not anything that made me a better man."

Abe asked why he wanted to come back to the church if being on the outside was so much fun. The look of anguish on Jeremiah's face touched Abe.

"It's really not as much fun as I originally thought. There's a lot of trouble and insecurity in this world."

"Ya. There is that, but you won't be able to completely get away from it. Even if you come back to the church, you might still see it."

Jeremiah folded his hands on the table. "The difference is with the church, you know there's hope."

"Have you prayed about this?" Abe asked.

"I tried. But it felt awkward."

Abe led Jeremiah in prayer then told him it was time to go see someone from church who could counsel him. But first he had some work to do on the farm. Jeremiah offered to help. After they finished, they went back into town to see one of the church elders.

The initial meeting with Franz Bartel, the church elder, had gone much better than Abe had expected. In fact, Franz said the folks at the church had been praying for Jeremiah.

"But I hope you understand that we must be very cautious about proceeding," Franz had explained. "We don't want our members to think we have a revolving door that you can come and go through on a whim."

"Yes," Jeremiah said as he hung his head. "I understand."

"Are you willing to answer questions?" Franz asked. "Some of them may be quite personal, but we want you to repent of all the sins you've committed during this. . .extended rumspringa."

Jeremiah nodded, but the pain on his face was evident. Abe didn't feel sorry for him, though, because he'd made the choice while others remained faithful to God.

After they left the Bartels' house, Abe asked Jeremiah if he'd like to have some coffee at Penner's Restaurant. "They shouldn't be crowded since it's still about an hour before people arrive for dinner."

"Sounds good," Jeremiah said. "I can take you back home afterward."

As soon as they walked into the restaurant, Joseph Penner greeted Abe but gave Jeremiah a curious look. When Jeremiah got up to use the men's room, Joseph made a beeline for Abe's table and asked what was going on. Abe explained Jeremiah's desire to return to the church.

"Praise the Lord," Joseph said, "but be very careful. The serpent knows the Gospel as well as you and I do, and he's not afraid to use it to his advantage."

"Ya, that I do know," Abe agreed. "Mr. Bartel already explained that it will take some time for people to accept him back."

"Would you like to join my family for supper tonight?"

Abe wanted to jump at the offer, but he still needed a ride home, and he wasn't sure David was available. Before he replied, Jeremiah came back to the table.

"Hello, Mr. Penner. Good to see you again."

"Ya, son, it's been a very long time." Joseph placed a hand on Jeremiah's shoulder. "I'm happy to see you, too."

Abe cleared his throat. "I have a special favor, Jeremiah. Would you mind picking me up at the Penners' after supper?"

"Or you may join us for supper, if you like," Joseph added. "Sarah and Mary always make plenty of food."

Jeremiah grinned. "I think it would be best if I didn't surprise Mary just yet, so I'll take a pass on supper. But I'll be glad to pick you up afterward, Abe. What time?"

Abe glanced at Joseph, who shrugged, then he turned back to Jeremiah. "Mind if I call you?"

"Sure, that's fine."

Joseph left the table. Shelley stopped by to refill their coffee. At first she didn't look Jeremiah in the eye, but then Abe mentioned that Jeremiah was trying to come back to the church.

"That's nice," she said.

To Abe's surprise, Jeremiah spoke up. "I heard about what happened with Peter. He made a very big mistake."

Shelley gasped. "I. . .uh. . ."

"I'm sorry," Jeremiah said. "I guess I shouldn't have been so direct. It's just that I always thought you were very sweet." He paused before adding, "And I. . .when we were younger, I wanted to be your boyfriend."

After Shelley recovered from shock, with cheeks still tinged pink, she smiled at Jeremiah. "Thank you." She held up the pot of coffee. "I'll check on you in a little while, in case you want more coffee."

Abe's heart went out to Shelley. Even he was surprised at Jeremiah's audacity to be so outspoken about his childhood feelings. "I think we've had enough coffee."

After she left, Abe snickered. "Did you mean what you just told Shelley?"

"Absolutely. In fact, one of the reasons I went so wild was from jealousy of Peter. I never could understand what she liked about him."

"You can't blame someone else for your indiscretions, Jeremiah."

"Yes, I'm aware of that. What I did was my own fault."

After they finished their coffee, Abe paid Joseph on their way out. Abe and Jeremiah went out to the parking lot. "Mind if I make a couple of stops?" Jeremiah asked. "They're on the way to the Penners'."

"That's fine."

After pulling through the teller window at the bank and dropping off some mail at the post office, Jeremiah turned to Abe. "Why don't you bring some of this fruit to the Penners? I can't eat it all."

"Are you sure you don't mind? I gave it to you."

"Take it. It's the least I can do for someone who's going to all this trouble to help me win favor with the people I never should have left."

"Ya, that would be good then. Mrs. Penner can certainly use some of it in her cooking."

"Now I have a favor to ask of you," Jeremiah said. "Would you mind talking to Mary for me? I want to apologize, but I doubt she'll even give me the time of day."

"You're right," Abe said. "And I can't say I blame her. Good thing I'm not a fighting man, or you would have had your face rearranged."

Jeremiah let out an embarrassed chuckle. "I knew that, which was one of the reasons I was so brave."

"Not so brave," Abe corrected.

"You got that right. More like stupid."

Jeremiah drove toward the Penners' house, but Abe asked him to stop a half block away. "I don't want to alarm Mary before I have a chance to talk to her."

"Good idea." Jeremiah pulled up to the curb. "There's a bag in the backseat. We can transfer some of the fruit to that for me, and you can take the box with the rest of it to the Penners."

After Jeremiah pulled away from the curb, Abe stood with his hands on his hips for a moment as he considered how he'd bring up the subject of Jeremiah. It wouldn't be easy after some of the comments Jeremiah had shouted from his car.

Finally, Abe lifted the box and went to the Penners' front door. Before he had a chance to knock, Joseph came around from the back of the house and called out his name.

"Abe, I'm glad you could make it. Sarah was happy when I told her you were joining us."

"Good. I don't want to go where I'm not wanted."

Joseph opened the door and walked inside. Abe followed.

Mary appeared, but she wouldn't even glance at Abe. He watched as she scurried around the kitchen, working around her grandmother, filling serving bowls and setting them on the table.

Joseph came up beside him. "Let's go outside for a moment, Abe."

Abe followed the older man out the back door and into the yard. "Nice garden."

"Ya, but that's not what I wanted to talk to you about. It's Mary. I don't have any idea what's gotten into her. She's acting very strange."

"I think there are quite a few things about Mary that we may never understand."

"I know." Joseph kicked his toe on the ground. "It's difficult watching her deal with her problems. I wish I could fix everything for her."

"That most likely wouldn't be good. Mary needs to learn how to fix her own problems."

Joseph pursed his lips and nodded. "I'm sure you're right. Just don't let her mood tonight bother you."

"Trust me," Abe said. "I've seen her in much worse moods than this."

"Why do you bother with her, Abe?" Joseph narrowed his eyes and gave Abe a piercing stare. "There are plenty of young women who would be happy to be courted by you."

Abe chuckled. "I'm not so sure about that, but even if that's the case, I've always had a soft spot for Mary."

Joseph folded his arms, never averting his gaze. "But why? Is it just a physical attraction, or do you really care about her?" Before Abe had a chance to answer, Joseph continued. "Mary is very special, but she's been through more in her short lifetime than many other girls in our community. I don't want her to get hurt. Can you be there for her, even when she doesn't want you there?"

"That's a lot of questions," Abe said.

"Then just answer the first one. Why do you have a soft spot for Mary?"

"I sure wish I could tell you. I've often wondered that myself. Sometimes I lie awake at night thinking about all the things she says and does, and I try to come up with reasons to move on and look for someone else. But when I wake up the next morning, I'm that much more determined to do whatever it takes to make Mary trust me."

"She trusts you as much as she has ever trusted anyone. And I think she might even love you, Abe." Joseph relaxed his position slightly.

"Love me? I doubt that."

Joseph chuckled. "She just has a difficult way of showing it. Her grandmother and I suspect she saw some very bad things—worse than we can ever imagine—that still haunt her."

"I'm sure you're right. Mary is a hurting woman, but behind that wall of steel is a sweet woman who loves the Lord." Abe grinned. "Every now and then I catch a glimpse of it, like when she's serving a family in the restaurant or when she speaks of you and Mrs. Penner."

"That's nice to hear," Joseph said as he gestured toward the house. "Let's get back inside before the ladies think we've abandoned them."

"Abe, you sit over there," Mary said as she pointed to her regular chair. "Grandma and I thought it might be better since you have such long legs."

He was surprised she spoke to him after the cold shoulder he'd gotten earlier. "I'll sit wherever you want me to."

"Let's say the blessing now," Joseph said.

They all joined hands and bowed their heads and listened while Joseph thanked the Lord for the blessing of such a beautiful day, having Abe for dinner, and for the food they were about to eat. It was simple but heartfelt.

"So, Abe, how many hired workers do you have on the farm now?" Joseph asked as they passed the food around the table. "I hear you just hired someone new."

Abe explained how David had come to him about his friends needing jobs. "I brought one man on recently—Jonathan—and he seems to be working out just fine. He's worked with his hands before he got his office job, so I just had to teach him some of the basics of farming."

"Think he might stay?"

"I'm not sure. Farming is one of those things you either love or really dislike. After he gets comfortable with what I taught him, I'll have a better idea."

Joseph shook his head. "Too bad so many of our Mennonite boys aren't more interested in farming."

Abe was about to put a forkful of food into his mouth, but he stopped. Was this a good time to risk mentioning Jeremiah? Silence fell over the table. A few seconds later, Abe decided he might as well mention it now. He had nothing to hide, and Mary would find out eventually. "Jeremiah wants to come work for me."

Mary scowled at Abe. "How can you suddenly become such good friends with such a vile man?"

Her grandfather reached for her hand, but she pulled away. When Joseph turned to Abe, the look of helplessness on the older man's face was evident.

Abe looked directly at Mary. "I hesitated at first, but we've chatted a few times. He wants to come back to the church. I took him over to Franz Bartel's to discuss having him come back to the church today, and Franz thought that was a good idea."

Mary played with the food on her plate, pushing her vegetables around but not eating them. When she looked up at Abe, he saw a flicker of angst. "That man can't be trusted. Aren't you concerned he might do something to sabotage you?" she asked.

Abe shook his head. "Not really, although the thought that he might be using me crossed my mind."

"There is that," Sarah said. "Plus the fact that he has a history of bad behavior might make you think twice."

Joseph looked at his wife. "But Sarah, through the Lord, Jeremiah can be made a new man. Don't forget about the prodigal son."

"I do think the Lord's timing is an indication of what I'm supposed to do," Abe said. "The farm has expanded, and I need more people. Jeremiah's timing was perfect. I prayed about it when Jeremiah first came to me, and everything seems to be falling into place."

Mary put her fork down and placed both hands in her lap. Her eyes appeared glazed as she stared down at the wall. Her shield had returned. Abe wished he'd waited to discuss this with her first before having a conversation about it with her family, but once again the Lord's timing had kicked in, and he followed what he felt led to do.

"Blessings," Joseph said. "I'll pray that Jeremiah is able to help you with your farm and that he follows the examples the Lord has set before him."

"Thank you," Abe said. He glanced over at Mary, whose body appeared rigid as she moved her gaze to something on the table. When he looked up, he saw that her grandparents had noticed it, too.

Sarah's chair screeched across the floor as she stood. "Anyone ready for dessert?"

Abe rarely skipped the opportunity for something sweet, but at the moment it didn't appeal to him. He stood up and carried his plate to the sink. "No, thank you, Mrs. Penner. I appreciate the delicious meal, but I need to be heading back home. I have an early morning tomorrow."

"I understand," Sarah said softly.

"Excuse me while I go call for"—Abe looked at Mary then at Joseph, who offered a slight smile—"my ride." He went outside and punched in Jeremiah's phone number. "Can you pick me up in a few minutes?" he asked.

"I'll be there in about ten minutes," Jeremiah said.

Abe went back inside and thanked Sarah again for the food. Mary was nowhere in sight, but Joseph offered to walk outside and wait with him.

Once they were on the front lawn, Joseph spoke up. "We need to pray for Mary and her forgiving spirit. This is obviously very difficult for her, but she needs to realize that most people aren't judging her about her past."

"Yes, I know," Abe agreed. "I'll do my best to help her, but I have to admit it will be much easier if she would open up and talk to me about how she feels and what she's thinking. She started to, but something is holding her back."

Joseph shook his head. "I wouldn't count on her ever opening up completely. Mary is a very private young woman."

Jeremiah pulled up at that moment. He waved to Joseph, who waved back. Once Abe was in the car and buckled up, Jeremiah took off toward the farm.

"How'd it go?"

Abe wasn't sure what to tell Jeremiah, but he wasn't going to lie. "I talked about hiring you for the farm."

Jeremiah snorted. "Oh, I bet that went over like a lead balloon." He cleared his throat. "Sorry."

~

No matter how hard Mary tried, she couldn't let go of the pain from her past. She sat on the edge of her bed, staring at the box she'd pulled out of the closet and placed on her bed. Until now she'd avoided it, but all the emotional stirrings had lately brought it to mind. A knock on the door interrupted her thoughts.

"Mary," Grandma said. "Mind if I come in?"

"I don't mind." Mary shifted to face the door as it opened. "Did you need me for something?"

Grandma's stern face softened as she saw the box on the bed. "No, Mary, but I think you need me." She sat down next to Mary and took her hand. They sat in silence for several minutes.

"Grandma, if it weren't for Mama getting pregnant with me, do you think she'd still be here?"

Her grandmother's chin quivered before she lifted her head and looked directly at Mary. "We cannot do that, Mary. Going back and trying to figure out what might have been will only weaken and eventually destroy our faith."

"But if Mama hadn't gotten pregnant, you wouldn't have told her to leave."

A flash of confusion flickered through Grandma's eyes. "Is that what you think? That I told your mama to leave?"

Mary hung her head and slowly nodded. "Isn't that what happened?"

"No, not at all." Grandma's eyes glistened with tears, but she reached out and gently stroked the side of Mary's face with the back of her hand. "When she admitted what she'd done, we were very upset. I said some things that upset her. . .things I shouldn't have said, but I never told her she had to leave. In fact, I told her she couldn't leave. She had to stay home."

"But—"

Grandma lifted a finger to shush Mary. "We told her that as long as she lived in our home, she was to follow our rules. She told us our rules were archaic, and she stormed out." Grandma allowed a tear to escape. "That was the last time we saw her."

Grandma's version of what happened was quite different from Mama's, but Mary knew how time altered things. Even some of her own memories had blurred.

"Mary?"

Mary glanced up. "I don't know what to do now. . .or what to think."

"Why don't you go ahead and open the box? There might be something in there that can help you through this time." Grandma brushed a tear from her cheek. "And if there's not, I'll be here for you, no matter what."

"It just doesn't seem right," Mary said softly. "Mama isn't here anymore, so what's the point?"

"She obviously wanted you to have whatever it is. If it were me. . ." Grandma's voice trailed off as she turned back to look at the box. "But it's not me."

Mary took a chance and studied her grandmother's face. The pain she saw was as intense as the ache in her own heart. For the first time, she considered what the impact of her mother's actions had on Grandma. She had to fight the tears to keep them from falling, but a couple still escaped. Now she realized that the box she'd kept in her closet meant as much to her grandmother as it did her.

"Mary, you're a grown woman now. It is time to deal with your past."

Grandma was right. Mary nodded. "Yes, you're right." She paused.

"Would you like me to open it?" Grandma asked.

Mary stood, swallowed hard, and shook her head. "No, I think I can do it now."

"Do you want me to leave?" Grandma's quavering voice shook Mary even more.

"Please stay." Mary lifted the box and turned around to face Grandma, whose gaze locked with hers. "Let's open it together."

The box was sealed tightly with packing tape. Mary picked at one end of the tape while her grandmother snagged the other. They pulled at the same time, releasing the flaps that had been shut for many years.

Grandma stilled Mary's hand. "Let's pray about this before we look."

Mary nodded and squeezed her eyes shut. As Grandma prayed for the emotional strength and understanding of the meaning behind whatever Elizabeth had placed in this box, tears managed to stream their way down Mary's cheeks. When they both said "Amen," Mary opened her eyes and saw that Grandma's eyes were misty.

"Ready?" Grandma asked.

Mary opened one flap, and Grandma lifted the other. Grandma gasped as the plain white kapp came into full view.

"It's Elizabeth's kapp—the last one she wore before she. . .before she left." She pointed to some initials on the back. "Your mother always liked to monogram her kapps, and this time she used green thread because she ran out of brown."

Mary leaned over the box to see if there was anything else inside. There was—a sealed envelope with her name on it. She pulled it out, turned it over, and cleared her throat.

"Go on, Mary," Grandma urged as she hugged the kapp to her chest. "Open it."

Mary fumbled with the envelope flap until she finally ripped it open. She pulled out a brief letter addressed to her.

"Read it to yourself first," Grandma said. "Then if you don't mind my reading it, I will."

"I'd like to read it aloud the first time if you don't mind."

Grandma glanced down, sniffled, then looked back at Mary, nodding. "If that's what you want to do."

"It is." Mary lifted the letter and studied it for a few seconds before she began.

> My dearest Mary,
>
> I want you to know how much I love you. Your life hasn't been easy, and it's my fault. I am terribly sorry for all I've put you through, but I never knew what to do.
>
> When I was sixteen, I was very foolish, and I left the church for a life that seemed very exciting. And it was for a while. But then you came along, and I didn't know the first thing about how to raise a child. All I knew was that I longed for my old, simple life, but instead of going back and begging for forgiveness, I let my pride take control, and I tried to follow the ways of the world.
>
> I've kept my kapp as a symbol of who I used to be and what I still wish I could be. However, the mistakes I've made have snowballed out of control. If you are reading this, I'm probably not in this world any longer. However, I want you to know that I've never stopped praying, so perhaps the Lord will have mercy on me and allow me into His kingdom.
>
> All the things I told you about Grandma and Grandpa are true, but they're the truth from a rebellious teenager's rationalization. Now that I'm an adult with my own daughter, those truths are somewhat blurry. I wish I had been a better mother and found a way to bring you back to where I came from—back to a safer place where you'd be protected and surrounded by love. But I was scared. I never want you to have the fears I faced all my adult life, so please study your Bible and listen to your grandparents, whom I am sure will welcome you with the love of Jesus and love you as much as I do.
>
> Trust me, dearest Mary, when I say I wanted to take you home, but the shame I felt kept me away. Tell your grandparents how much I cared about them and appreciated all the love they gave me. Your grandfather

tried numerous times to contact me in the early days after I left, but I was too stubborn to accept his calls. Even my Yankee friends begged me to return home, so I pushed them out of my life as well. When you were much younger, asking questions about family, my words were only half truths. I left out the part about God's grace and mercy as it came through my parents—your grandparents. Until I had you, I never understood my own mother, but after I was faced with so much responsibility, I realized what she did was out of love.

Please keep this kapp as a symbol of who I wish I was and know that I loved you with all my heart. Pray every day and never turn your back on your Creator.

Love,
Mama

A flood of unfamiliar emotions washed over Mary as she looked up into Grandma's stunned eyes. They remained transfixed until Grandma's shoulders began to shake as tears rolled down her cheeks.

Chapter 11

Jeremiah pulled the car up to the front of Abe's house. "I hope I don't blow things for you with Mary."

Abe opened the car door but remained sitting. "Mary is a very complex woman. Until recently I thought we might be making progress in our relationship, but there's something about her I can't figure out."

"You might never figure it out."

"Maybe you're right, brother."

"Women."

"Ya." A flurry of emotions swarmed through Abe. "I care about her too much to forget about her, but I've reconsidered trying to make her my wife."

"Wife? Dude. That's serious."

"You're right. It's very serious. But when the Lord calls me to do something, I know I'm supposed to submit to His ways. I have to admit, lately I haven't been sure what He wants me to do."

"I'm probably not the one to tell you this, Abe, but you might be over-thinking your relationship and trying too hard with Mary. Even if she is the one for you, try just letting things happen."

Abe swung his legs out, then stood. "Thanks for the ride, Jeremiah. I'll see you soon."

"Hey man, I appreciate all this time you're spending with me, but don't risk your relationship with Mary just for me."

Abe bent over to look at Jeremiah. "If doing the Lord's calling and helping you get back into the church hurts my relationship with Mary, it's clear the relationship isn't right for me." He started to turn and walk inside, but he stopped. "Oh, and Jeremiah, you need to apologize to Mary soon."

"I will." Jeremiah smiled and lifted his hand in a wave. "See ya, Abe."

After Jeremiah pulled away from the house, Abe went inside and looked around at the sparse furnishings. His mother's feminine touch had long since been replaced by utilitarian design. Everything in the house had a purpose. It was all easy to maintain.

But it seemed so empty—like Abe's heart.

He rinsed his coffee mug from earlier before walking back to his bedroom, where he got ready for bed. The sheets were slightly cooler than the air that had already started getting muggy from the humid Florida heat. He pulled the blanket off and slid beneath the top sheet. As his eyes closed for his evening prayer, images of Mary flitted through his mind.

He thought about how the softness of her face weakened his knees when they were together, but the abrupt changes frightened him. He thought about Jeremiah's words. Had he been trying too hard? Had he assumed the Lord's intentions for him and Mary, just because he'd always had those feelings for her? Feelings like that were temporary while the Lord's plan was eternal.

As Abe prayed for guidance, he tried to push everything else from his mind. His upbringing had taught him to rely on the Lord and not his own desires. Now he needed to follow the path God set before him.

It had been a long day full of emotional highs and lows, creating an exhaustion that was stronger than any physical tiredness Abe had ever experienced. As sleep came, he kept his thoughts on the Lord.

Mary awoke the next morning feeling like a weight had been lifted off her. Her mother's kapp lay on her otherwise bare dresser. She got out of bed, walked over to the dresser, and stared down at the pristine white kapp that would forever remain a symbol of her mother's desire to return to her faith.

After Mama's death, Mary realized that all this time she had blamed herself and Grandma for everything. If it weren't for her, Mama would still be alive and living in the faith she'd grown up with. Now, after hearing Grandma's side of the story, she wasn't sure about anything. It was so easy to blame Grandma for Mama having to struggle so hard, but Mary remembered the stubborn streak that had been the main source of conflict between her and her mother. Mary suspected Grandma's words held a stronger ring of truth than Mama's version.

After dressing, Mary went into the kitchen, where Grandma stood in front of the stove frying bacon. "I thought you might be hungry," she said. "You didn't eat much of your supper last night."

Mary still wasn't all that hungry, but she didn't tell Grandma. Instead she poured herself a cup of coffee and asked what she could do to help.

"Nothing. I told your grandpa you might be a little late this morning."

"Why would I be late?"

Grandma shook her head. "I wasn't sure how you'd feel after last night."

The soft side of her grandmother was disconcerting to Mary. She'd grown used to her sternness, but she'd seen Grandma smile more, show sorrow through tears, and express her feelings, all in the last few days. Maybe those sides of Grandma were there before, but Mary chose not to notice. That revelation hit Mary hard.

"Grandma," Mary began, "you and Grandpa have been very good to me. I want you to know how much I appreciate everything."

"We love you, Mary." Grandma didn't look up from the pan as she dabbed at her cheek with her sleeve. "After your mama left, we felt as though the sun would never shine on our house again. People from the church talked to us and assured us that the Lord was watching over your mother, but we doubted that."

"I think the Lord understands. What you went through must have been terrible."

"It was."

"Mama was good to me," Mary said, hoping to comfort Grandma—at least a little. "She didn't always know what to do, but she let me know she loved me."

Grandma swiped at her cheek with her sleeve. "This will be the first time I ever said this aloud, but during that time, we let our grief swallow up our faith."

"I understand, and I'm sure the Lord does, too."

"Ya, He is much wiser than any of us will ever be. For that I am grateful. And I'm thankful He brought you home to us. Your mama might have conceived you in sin, but you've turned out to be a precious child of the Lord."

When Grandma handed Mary a plate filled with bacon and eggs, Mary looked at it. "I'll eat as much as I can, but this is a lot of food."

"Don't go to work hungry."

Grandma sat down with her mug of coffee. "I know this is difficult for you, but it's time we talked about something."

Mary put down her fork. "About Mama?"

"Neh, this is about Jeremiah. He has asked Abe to pray with him. Abe told us that Jeremiah said some things to you that were upsetting."

Mary tried to hide her feelings, but she knew Grandma could see right through her steely expression. "Do you believe Jeremiah?"

"It's not up to me to believe him, but I do know that God is forgiving. If Jeremiah is sincerely repentant, the Lord will welcome him back into His fold." Grandma reached for Mary's hand that had stilled on the table. "Just like He would have welcomed back your mama."

Grandma's point hit hard. "It's not easy," Mary said.

"I know. It's never easy for us, but we have to hold on to our faith and trust Him. As long as we're right with the Lord, His plan, which is greater than anything we might want, will prevail."

After breakfast, Mary washed her plate and left for the restaurant. Grandma had some shopping to do, and she said she wouldn't be able to get there until right before the lunch rush.

Shelley was gathering an armload of plates when Mary arrived. "Oh good. You're just in time to give me a hand with these." She nodded toward a couple of plates on the counter. "If you don't mind."

"Of course." Mary pulled a clean apron from a hanger, slipped it on, and tied it before lifting the plates. "I'm right behind you."

Once Shelley's customers were served, Grandpa asked Mary to help finish up with the biscuits before taking over her station in the dining room. She was used to the chaos, and today she was happy she didn't have time to think. That would come later.

Mary had just finished rolling and cutting the last pan of biscuits when Grandpa came back to the kitchen. "There's a strange man out there asking about you."

"A strange man? What did he ask?"

Grandpa lifted his hands. "He wanted to know if I knew Mary Penner. I told him you were my granddaughter."

"Did you ask his name?"

"Ya. He gave me this." Grandpa pulled a slip of paper from his pocket. "Jimbo." He tilted his head in confusion. "Do you know anyone by that name?"

Mary's heart thudded. The only Jimbo she knew was Jim Jr., son of Big Jim, the man who owned the bar where Mama had worked. She had only a few vague memories of Jimbo, who was about four or five years older than her.

The first time she saw him was when Mama had just gotten the job working for his dad. He had a foul mouth, and he told her his dad was the most important person in town—that she needed to be nice to him or her mother wouldn't have a job. Another time he'd pressed her against a wall and touched her in places that made her cringe. She managed to get away, but he told her if she ever mentioned it, he'd make sure her mother was fired. Mary managed to avoid him after that, except the few times he'd been in the bar when Mary went with her mother to pick up her paycheck. And that night when his dad, Big Jim, had given her the bus ticket to Sarasota.

"Mary?" Grandpa asked softly as he placed his hand on her arm. "Do you want to go see what he wants?"

"No," she said. She had to grab hold of the counter for balance as her awful memories threw off her equilibrium.

"Who is he?"

Mary pulled her lips between her teeth as she tried to find a way to let Grandpa know without going into too much detail. Finally she blurted, "He's the son of Mama's old boss."

Grandpa's forehead crinkled. "Then why don't you want to see him? Did he do something to hurt you?"

Shame prevented her from telling everything. "He's just not a very nice man."

"That was a long time ago, Mary. Maybe he's changed."

She doubted it, but she'd seen much stranger things. Her thoughts flew back to her mother's kapp on her dresser. "Maybe."

Grandpa frowned and shook his head. "If he's dangerous, I don't want you talking to him yet."

Shelley charged through the doorway. "It's a zoo out there. Looks like tourist season has hit hard this year." She clipped her order to the board. "Are you almost finished with the biscuits, Mary?"

"I'll be out there in a minute," Mary said. After Shelley went back out to take more orders, Mary turned to face Grandpa. "Where is he sitting?"

"Over in the front corner by the window." He paused then strode toward the door. "I'll have Shelley wait on him. You take the other side."

"Thank you."

After Grandpa left the kitchen, Mary bowed her head. *Lord, give me the wisdom and strength to handle whatever is about to happen.* She opened her eyes then shut them again. *I pray that nothing happens.*

Mary sucked in a deep breath, squared her shoulders, and marched out into the dining room. She tried hard not to look at the man she wanted to forget.

The crowded restaurant was a blessing for Mary. All the tables between her and Jimbo were filled, and a couple of tall customers blocked her view from most angles. But still, his presence loomed and brought a sense of foreboding.

Mary scurried around the dining room, trying to focus on her customers, but the one time she allowed a glimpse in Jimbo's direction, she caught him staring at her. Her mouth went dry. He hadn't changed much—just a few extra pounds, a few lines on his face, and some stubble on his chin. He had the same sinister look in his eyes that had always given her a creepy feeling.

Grandpa caught up with Mary in the kitchen. "I see him watching you."

Mary shuddered. "I can only imagine what he wants."

"I'll go talk to him and tell him you're too busy."

"I doubt that will matter to Jimbo." Mary snorted. "Mama used to say he would grow up to be a thug, and it looks like she was right."

"You can't judge a man by the way he looks, Granddaughter."

Shelley brushed past Mary. "Some guy out there is determined to talk to you, Mary. Every time I pass him, he asks how much longer." She hesitated a few seconds then added, "Some of the other customers are starting to get annoyed."

Mary pressed her finger to her temple. Jimbo was disrupting business for her grandfather and making Shelley's job more difficult. "I'll talk to him then."

"I'll be right behind you," Grandpa said.

She started to tell him no, she'd deal with it on her own, but a flashback of last night's conversation with Grandma stopped her. "Let's go then."

Mary charged right up to Jimbo's table and stood in front of him, arms folded and feet shoulder-width apart. "What do you want with me, Jimbo?"

He glanced up at her and started cackling. "You are one ridiculous-looking chick, Mary."

"What do you want?" she repeated.

Jimbo's gaze darted behind her, where she suspected her grandfather stood, then he looked back at her. "I don't need an audience."

"Too bad. You came here and said you wanted to talk to me. Now talk."

"Not with the old man staring at me." Jimbo leaned back in his chair and extended his legs across the space between his table and the next one. "I'll just wait right here until we can have a private conversation."

Grandpa stepped up. "Whatever you have to say to my granddaughter, you can say in front of me."

"No offense, Gramps, but this is a private conversation."

Mary turned toward Grandpa and saw his face redden and his fists clench at his sides. He was obviously infuriated, but his Mennonite faith wouldn't allow him to act on it—at least not with his fists.

"Grandpa," she whispered as she took hold of one of his fists and tugged at him. "Let's leave him alone now. He's obviously just trying to upset us."

"I cannot allow anyone to talk to my granddaughter like this."

"It's just words," Mary said. "C'mon."

Jimbo snorted. "Look at the baby run away with her cowardly grandfather. No wonder your mother couldn't stand it here. What kind of people are you, anyway?"

Anger boiled inside Mary, but her Mennonite teachings popped into her mind. *Lord, please forgive me for these feelings, but I'm only human.* She felt her grandfather resist, so she pulled even harder. "He's just trying to make you do something you'll regret," Mary whispered.

Grandpa's jaw remained tight as he nodded. "You're right."

"I'm not sure how we're going to get him to leave," Mary said on their way back to the kitchen. "Looks like he's determined to make our lives miserable."

They'd barely reached the kitchen door when Grandpa softly said, "I'm calling the police. I can't allow him to threaten you."

"He didn't exactly threaten me," she reminded him. "He just said he wanted to talk to me privately."

"I'm still calling the police." Grandpa pulled his cell phone from his pocket and stepped toward the back door.

Mary glanced across the dining room and spotted Abe and Jeremiah sitting in her station. She felt as though her world was imploding. She wasn't ready for these two very different pieces of her life to meet.

Shelley gently touched Mary's arm. "Is there anything I can do?"

"I don't know," Mary admitted. "I never expected to see anyone from. . ." Her chin quivered, and she sniffled and glanced down.

"You don't have to say anything," Shelley said. "I just want you to know I'm praying for you."

"Thank you," Mary said. She forced a shaky smile. "Isn't it amazing how we seem to be taking turns needing the other one to hold us up?"

Shelley nodded. "That does seem to be the case. I'm glad we have each other."

Mary noticed Shelley's eyes refocusing on something behind her, so she glanced over her shoulder and saw Grandpa approaching. "Did you call the police?"

"Ya." Grandpa looked frustrated. "They said unless there was a blatant threat, they can't really do much. They'll let the patrol officers know, and they'll come out when they get a chance." He cleared his throat. "Something about this not being a high priority."

With as much confidence as she could muster, Mary lifted her head. "I'm sure we'll be just fine. I'm not going to let some mean man from my past make me afraid."

"Would you like to go on home?" Grandpa asked from behind her.

"No, we're too busy. I'll work until the crowd settles."

"Let me know if I need to do anything, okay? I'll keep a close eye on you." Grandpa paused before he gestured toward the dining room. "Oh, one more thing you need to know. Abe's here with Jeremiah."

"Yes, I know," Mary said.

"You okay with that?"

She smiled to ease the angst she saw on Grandpa's face. "Yes, I am just fine."

"You're a strong woman, Mary," Shelley said.

An expression of pride replaced the one of worry on Grandpa. "That's because she's my granddaughter."

Mary and Shelley both laughed. "I don't know about my personal strength, but I'm fortified with friends and knowing the Lord is with me, no matter what."

"Ya." Grandpa patted her and Shelley on the shoulders. "Now I gotta go see how we're doing on the breads."

Mary stared at the door to the dining room then took a deep breath. "Time to go face the lions."

"You go see what Abe and Jeremiah want. I'll try to deal with that strange man," Shelley said.

After Shelley disappeared into the dining room, Mary went toward Abe and Jeremiah's table. She lifted her order pad and pencil. "Have you decided what you want?"

Abe glared at Jeremiah, who cleared his throat. "Um. . .Mary, I want to. . ." He tossed a helpless look in Abe's direction, but Abe looked away. Mary couldn't help but notice Jeremiah's discomfort.

"You want to what?" she asked.

"Look, Mary, I'm really sorry about those things I said to you that weren't respectful. I was just being. . .well, I was being a jerk."

Mary blinked then turned toward Abe, who nodded. "He means it," Abe said softly.

From the first time they'd met, Jeremiah had never been nice to her. When he'd shouted those comments from the car, Mary was shocked at how crude he could be.

"Please, Mary. I want us to be friends," Jeremiah continued. "I don't think I'll ever be able to make it all up to you, but I'd at least like a fresh start."

The swirl of thoughts in Mary's head nearly made her dizzy. Too much was happening too fast.

Abe glanced up, and his eyes widened. He pointed to something behind Mary. She spun around and found herself face-to-face with Jimbo. Her mouth instantly went dry.

"I told the old man I wanted to talk to you, and I'm not taking no for an answer," Jimbo said as he placed his face inches from hers. "You have something of mine that I want."

Fear welled inside Mary's chest. "You don't know what you're talking about, Jimbo. I don't have anything of yours."

His eyes narrowed, and a smirk covered his lips. "I was there. I saw my dad give you that box."

The box. Mary's mind went back to that day when Big Jim had broken the news and given her the bus ticket and box. Jimbo had been with him.

"What's in that box is not yours," Mary said.

"Oh, but I believe it is. My father gave you something that's rightfully mine. He's gone now, and now I've come to claim it."

Mary was more surprised than frightened. "That box—"

Jimbo didn't give her a chance to finish her statement before grabbing her by the arm so tight she let out a yelp. "You're giving me whatever was in that box my father gave you, and I'm not leaving until I have it."

Before Mary had a chance to react, both Abe and Jeremiah stood. One of the chairs crashed to the floor, sending a startling collective gasp over the guests in the restaurant.

Next thing she knew, Abe was on one side of Jimbo, and Jeremiah was on the other. Abe's large frame towered over Jimbo, and with stocky Jeremiah on the other side, he looked terrified. They each took one of his arms and lifted him off the floor. Mary stood with her mouth gaping open as they walked Jimbo to the door, where they nearly slammed into a pair of uniformed police officers.

Chapter 12

W e got a call to stop by here," one of the officers said. "We were a few streets over. Do you need some assistance?"

Jeremiah looked at Abe and nodded. "Yes, sir, this man threatened one of the women who works here," Abe said.

The officers exchanged a glance before one of them spoke up. "We understood this wasn't a physical threat."

"There wasn't a physical threat when Mr. Penner called, but that has changed. This man grabbed Miss Penner right before you arrived."

The officers both nodded then stepped forward to take over with Jimbo. Abe's muscles were still tight, but he let go. Jimbo kicked one of the officers and tried to flee, but Abe was quick. He caught Jimbo and returned him to the police officers within seconds.

"Sir, you just made one big mistake."

Joseph had made his way over to them by now. "I didn't think we'd see you any time soon," he said to the officers. "Thanks for coming when you did."

One of the officers grinned. "You've been good to us, and we were in the neighborhood."

The men followed the officers outside where they handcuffed Jimbo, read him his rights, and put him in the back of the police cruiser. Joseph, Jeremiah, and Abe each told the officers what had happened. After the officers left, Abe patted Jeremiah on the back. "Thanks for helping out."

"Yes, I want to thank you, too." Mary's soft voice came from behind. Abe and Jeremiah turned to face her, and she looked directly at Jeremiah. "I want you to know that I accept your apology, and I want to apologize to you, too."

Jeremiah smiled and kicked at the ground with his toe. "Thank you, Mary, but you didn't do anything wrong. I'm the one who should do all the apologizing. If I hadn't acted so selfish, we could have been friends." He extracted his hand from his pocket and extended it.

She smiled, took his hand, then turned and met Abe's gaze as Jeremiah let go and stepped back. "Abe, I'm sorry I was so abrupt with you last night," Mary said. "I've been. . .well, out of sorts lately. Can we be friends, too?"

Abe hesitated but eventually nodded. "Ya. I think that's a very good idea, Mary. We can be friends." He felt as though a piece of his heart had been chipped away. He still wanted much more than friendship with Mary, but he'd settle for what she was willing to offer.

"Well, I better get back inside and tend to my customers," Mary said.

Joseph wedged himself between Abe and Jeremiah and put his arms around them. "You fellas want something to eat? My treat."

"Thanks, Mr. Penner. We need to get back to the farm. Jeremiah is starting today."

⌒

Mary had been back in the restaurant for nearly an hour when someone from the police department called Grandpa. After he got off the phone, he motioned for Mary to join him in the small office beside the kitchen.

"They have a statement. Apparently Jimbo was very talkative, and they have some information they said you might want to hear."

"Any idea what it is?"

He shook his head. "Neh, but I don't think we'll need to worry about him coming around here anytime soon. He's in jail now, and if he even steps foot on the restaurant property when he gets out, he's going back to jail."

"I wonder why he wanted that box from my mother."

Grandpa cupped her chin. "I'm sure he must have thought it was something it wasn't. I can't imagine a Yankee man wanting a Mennonite woman's kapp. The officer who called asked if we wanted to go to the police station or if it would be better for someone to come here."

"I hope you said they should come here."

"Ya. It's much easier since they have the cars." He pulled her into a hug. "I want to be there with you when they tell you whatever that evil man said."

Her throat swelled with love for Grandpa. "Thank you."

The crowd had died down, so when the police officer arrived to see Mary, they were able to sit at an isolated booth in the corner where no one else could hear. Shelley said she'd seat people as far away as possible for as long as she could. Grandpa brought some mugs and a pot of coffee to the table, and the three of them sat down—the officer, Grandpa, and Mary.

"I'm not sure how much of this is true or how much he made up, but we backed some of it up by calling the police station in Ohio," the officer began. "James McCollum Jr. gave us a statement that we thought would interest you."

"James McCollum Jr.?" Grandpa said.

Mary nodded. "Jimbo."

"Oh." Grandpa turned back to the officer. "Please continue."

"Apparently his father, James McCollum Sr., and your mother were in a relationship. He'd agreed to be involved in a drug sting, and apparently your mother got caught in the crossfire when it fell apart." He paused for a moment when she gasped. "You okay?"

Mary stared at the officer who told her a completely different story from what she'd always believed. She had no idea her mother was in a personal relationship with Big Jim, and she'd thought her mother had been killed because she was an informant. "Please continue."

"James Jr. said he was in the office when his father presented you with the bus ticket and a box. After you left, he asked his father what was in the box, and he was told it was something of great value, but he never said what it was, except it was rightfully his." The officer shifted in his seat. "You wouldn't by any chance still have that box, would you?"

Grandpa's head whipped around to face Mary. "You don't have to—"

She covered his hand with hers. "No, that's okay." Then she looked at the officer. "Yes, I do have the box, and Big Jim was right. It is the most valuable possession I own."

The officer looked extremely uncomfortable as he fidgeted with a sugar packet. Finally he looked at her. "I've been asked to take a look at it if you do so I can let them know what was in it. They think it might be a clue in a case against a drug ring."

Mary grinned. "I doubt that, but I'll be glad to show you what was in it."

Grandpa stood. "Why don't the two of you go on to the house now while we're slow here?"

The officer and Mary left the restaurant and rode in silence. As they pulled up in front of the house, Mary looked around at the place she now called home. It was hard to imagine what her life would have been like if things had been different.

Grandma greeted them at the door, her eyebrows knit in concern. "Come on in. Would you like something to eat, Officer?"

"No, thank you, ma'am. I just want to take a look at the box and let them know what I see."

Mary led the way, with the officer and Grandma bringing up the rear. She knew her grandmother was there to protect her from whatever she might have to deal with.

When they got to her room, Mary pointed to the dresser. "There's the box." She moved her finger to the right, where the kapp lay on top of the note. "And that's what was in it."

He crossed the room and lifted the box. After he turned it upside down and thoroughly inspected it, he focused his attention on the kapp and note. "Mind if I read this?" he asked.

Mary's breath caught in her throat. As difficult as it was, she nodded. "That's fine." She had to turn away to keep from breaking down.

The room grew quiet as the officer read the letter. When he finished, he returned the paper to her dresser and gently placed the kapp back on top of it. "Ms. Penner," he said softly. "I am so sorry about all this. I'll let them know it was only a couple of personal items and nothing of interest that would affect the drug ring case."

Mary had to fight the tears as she nodded her thanks. Grandma put her arm around Mary and pulled her close.

The ride back to the restaurant was as silent as the ride to the house. But when they pulled up at the curb, the officer turned to Mary and handed her a card. "Take care of yourself, Ms. Penner. If anyone ever tries to bother you again, call me."

"I will," she said as she opened her door. "Thank you for being so understanding."

Mary walked back into the restaurant and into Grandpa's arms. "Do you feel like working, Granddaughter? If you need—"

"I need to work. This is where I belong."

He let go and gestured toward the kitchen. "Then go get your apron on and get to work."

Mary did as he said. It was already early afternoon, so most of the lunch crowd had left. A few people lingered, and occasionally a group would enter for a late lunch or dessert. Mary was glad for the distraction of work.

She'd finally finished serving the last person on her shift, hung up her apron, and started talking to Shelley when she heard loud voices in the dining room. "I wonder what that's all about?" Shelley asked.

Mary rolled her eyes. "No telling, but after today I think I can handle anything."

Grandpa rushed into the kitchen. "There's been an accident on the Glick farm!"

Her ears rang. With all the turmoil of the day, she'd managed to push Abe to the back of her mind.

Grandpa motioned wildly. "I tried to call Abe's cell phone, and he didn't answer. We need to go see about him."

Mary nodded as her heart raced. "I'm coming with you."

One of Grandpa's regular Yankee customers, Phillip, offered to drive them to the farm. On the way, Grandpa kept asking, "Can't you go faster?"

Mary was glad Phillip remained steady. "No, sir. I'm going the speed limit."

When they pulled onto the road leading to Abe's house, they saw the ambulance. Mary's heart raced even faster. Grandpa took her hand and bowed his head. *Lord, I pray for Your mercy on Abe.*

Phillip pulled the car to a stop beside the ambulance. Mary hopped out and ran to see if Abe was in it.

"Mary," she heard from behind. When she turned around and saw Abe standing there, her knees started to give way. Abe reached out to steady her. "Are you okay?"

She gulped and nodded. "What happened? I thought you were hurt."

"Neh, it was Jonathan Polk's son. He came to help out for a few days, and I hadn't given him the safety talk yet. He went to the old barn and tried to move something. One of the rafters fell down on him, but it looks like he'll be fine. They're taking him to the hospital for x-rays, but they don't think anything is broken."

Abe started to let go of Mary, but she pulled him closer. "Please don't let go. I was so worried something terrible had happened to you, and it scared me, so when Grandpa said he was coming out to check on you, I wanted to come with him, and now I'm—"

"Whoa, Mary, slow down." Abe held her at arm's length and looked in her eyes. "So you were worried about me, huh?"

She nodded and opened her mouth, but nothing would come out.

Abe broke into a grin. "This might sound strange, but I'm glad to know you were worried about me."

Mary pulled back and scowled. "What? You like to worry me?"

"Now that's my Mary. Feisty and direct."

"Why would you want to worry me?"

He caught her off balance as he pulled her back to his chest. "I don't want to worry you, but I'm happy you care enough to check on me."

Mary finally sighed as she thought about how her mother's pride created regrets that could never be overcome. She couldn't make the same mistakes. "Abe?" She looked up into his eyes.

As their gazes locked, her knees went all wobbly again. He steadied her.

"Now I'm worried about you," he whispered. "Would you like to come inside and get something to drink? I'm thinking the heat might be getting to you."

"No, Abe, it's not the heat," she whispered. "It's you."

A grin continued to play at the corners of Abe's lips, but his eyes showed concern. "Are you sure, Mary? I don't want you to get sick."

She closed her eyes and prayed that she wouldn't regret what she was about to say. Then she sucked in a breath and blurted, "Abe Glick, I love you. I've shut you out for so long, I don't know why you even bothered with me."

"You have been a bother," Abe teased. His expression quickly became serious. "But I see something in you, Mary—something that let me know that beneath your shield is a loving, spirited woman."

"So what now?" she asked.

Abe glanced around then took her by the hand. "There are too many people here. Let's go find a private spot so I can show you what now."

Mary's heart raced as she followed Abe to the back of his house. As soon as they were out of sight, he spun her around to face him.

"I've loved you for as long as I can remember—even when we were kids," he said. "I wanted to protect you from everything that might ever hurt you. When I went away to college, thoughts of you helped me through the most difficult times, so the first thing I wanted to do when I returned and saw you again was to make you love me, too."

"Why did you wait a whole year?"

"I didn't want to be in too big of a hurry, and I wanted to make sure everything was just right for us."

"Why did the Lord let me continue being so stubborn?"

"I don't know," Abe replied.

"So what now?"

He let go of her and shoved his hands in his pockets. "The very thing that attracted me to you also scared me. It still scares me. Sometimes you're not easy to approach."

Mary laughed. "So I've heard."

"I wanted everything to be perfect—" Abe glanced around then settled his gaze on her. "But nothing we do can ever be perfect, so. . ."

The look in Abe's eyes melted Mary's heart. When he gently took her hand and tenderly kissed the back of it, her knees turned to jelly. She grabbed hold of Abe's shoulders to keep from falling.

Concern again flickered across his face. "Let's go inside."

"No," she said as she steadied herself. "I like how this is going. I wanna stay and see what happens next."

Abe's laughter was delightful—a sound she knew she'd never get tired of hearing. "Mary Penner, you are so full of surprises."

She jammed the fist of her free hand on her hip and widened her eyes. "So are you, Abe Glick." Then she gestured for him to continue. "Okay, keep going."

He again kissed the back of her hand, never taking his gaze off hers. "Mary, how would you like to live on a farm?"

Mary contorted her mouth and narrowed her eyes. "All depends on what farm we're talking about."

"This farm. With me."

"Hmm." She tapped her chin with her index finger.

Abe placed his hands on her shoulders, his face inches from hers. "Mary Penner, will you make me the happiest man in Florida and be my wife?"

She offered him a teasing look. "Just Florida?"

He grinned as he lifted his arms and gestured wide. "If you say yes, I'll be the happiest man in the world!"

She forced herself not to smile or jump up and down with joy. Instead, she leveled him with as stern a look as she could manage. "What took you so long to ask? Of course I'll be your wife."

"Abe? Mary?"

They glanced up toward the voice. "Grandpa!" Mary gave Abe a quick wink then ran over to her grandfather. "You'll never guess what just happened!"

Grandpa smiled. "Oh, I think I can."

Abe joined them. "I'm sorry, Mr. Penner, I should have spoken to you about this first. With your permission, I would like to marry your granddaughter."

"I'm speaking for Sarah and myself," Grandpa said as he hugged Abe. "You have our full blessing." He turned around to face Mary. "But now we need to get back to town. We have work to do."

Abe waited until Grandpa turned his back before he leaned over for a kiss. "I love you, Mary. You've just made me a very happy man."

"I love you, too, Abe." Mary couldn't believe how easily those words rolled off her tongue.

As the car rolled away from the farm, Mary looked around and thought about how this would soon be her home. Grandpa winked at her and squeezed her hand. The joy between them was so powerful, neither of them had to say a word.

Note to the Readers:

Shades of the Past is set in the Pinecraft community of Sarasota, Florida, a beach town south of Tampa Bay. Most of the Pinecraft homes are rented by Mennonite and Amish families who have decided to settle in Florida to enjoy the mild winters and white sandy beaches. The houses are small, but they are wired for electricity, which many of the inhabitants enjoy, even if they come from a sect that doesn't typically use electricity.

With Sarasota being a busy beach town, it's difficult to care for large animals, so instead of the traditional horse-and-buggy transportation, most of the Mennonite and Amish residents get around on adult-sized tricycles called bikes or three-wheelers—some motorized and some pedal powered. They attach baskets and boxes to haul larger loads for errands and short trips around the neighborhood, and they use city buses and independent drivers for longer distances.

Some visitors may have a difficult time telling the difference between Amish and the most conservative Mennonites. Most of the Amish women wear kapps with strings, while Mennonite women have a wider variety of head coverings, including crocheted pieces. Mennonite men may have mustaches, while Amish men are likely to only have beards.

Sarasota hosts a variety of Mennonite and Amish orders from other areas, creating a blend of old and new traditions that have evolved during the years. The language tends to be more contemporary than that of some Conservative Mennonite groups.

A few Mennonite and Amish farms still thrive on the outskirts of Sarasota. On most Saturdays, Pinecraft hosts a farmer's market, and roadside stands dot the area on weekdays, with local citrus being the most common produce available.

TRUSTING HER HEART

Dedication

In loving memory of my mother-in-law, Bobbie Mayne,
who exemplified Christian love every day of her life.

This book is dedicated to Mary Crawford, a kind, generous,
and sweet-spirited friend of the Mayne family.

Chapter 1

Mary Penner Glick's gaze darted to something behind Shelley, and a grin twitched the corners of her lips. "Guess who's walking in the door now."

Shelley Burkholder spun around as Jeremiah Yoder scanned the near-empty restaurant. The breakfast crowd at the small diner had dwindled, and the lunch crowd hadn't arrived yet. Her pulse quickened at the sight of Jeremiah, but she froze in place.

"Want me to seat him and take his order?" Mary offered.

"No, that's not necessary. You need to run along. I'm sure Abe doesn't want to be kept waiting."

The sound of Mary's laughter rang as she firmly placed her hand on Shelley's shoulder. "I miss working here, so it's my pleasure. Take a minute to gather your thoughts, and I'll make sure everyone is taken care of."

Ever since Peter had surprised Shelley with an announcement that he was engaged to someone else, she knew better than to let any man have even a sliver of her heart. Besides the hurt, the emotional investment took more time and energy than she had, so she saw this as a sign from God that she had no business falling in love anyway.

"Shelley, would you mind getting another pot of coffee brewing?" Joseph Penner called out, interrupting her thoughts.

"Sure, Mr. Penner." She scurried toward the beverage station.

Mary joined her as she poured the water into the coffeemaker well. "I just put Jeremiah's order in. Want me to stick around and deliver it when it's done, or can you handle him?" She reached up and adjusted her kapp, making Shelley smile. Mary had always had a difficult time keeping her kapp on her head.

"No, no, run along. You've already done more than you should around here."

"If you're sure. . ." Mary took a step toward the door. "I'll check on you later to see how things go with Jeremiah."

Shelley forced a smile. "Stop worrying about me. I'll be fine. Jeremiah is the least of my concerns."

With a teasing glance, Mary chuckled. "Okay, if you say so."

Shelley waited until Mary left the restaurant before sighing. If Jeremiah hadn't been such a rebel, she might be flattered by his advances, which had started right after Mary and her husband, Abe, got married. But Jeremiah had left the Conservative Mennonite church once, and she wasn't sure he wouldn't do it again. Her childhood crush on Jeremiah Yoder was part of her past and needed to stay that way—out of her present and future—if she wanted a peaceful life. Between her mother's recent mood dips and trying to help out with her younger brother, William, who had Down syndrome and a penchant for running away when he was upset, Shelley had little time for matters of the heart. Perhaps the Lord wanted her to stay single. It certainly seemed that way.

"Shelley, your order is up." Mr. Penner smiled. "Want me to bring it over to him?"

She inhaled deeply, squared her shoulders, and forced a smile. "I'll do it."

As she took the plate from the pass-through counter, Shelley said a silent prayer for the strength to face Jeremiah. If she hadn't been so attracted to him, waiting on him wouldn't be so difficult. And if he hadn't stayed away from the church for so long, none of this would matter. When he'd made it clear that he was interested in her, fear of losing her heart to the wrong man had forced her to erect a shield of protection.

Shelley carried the plate filled with eggs, ham, and biscuits over to the table where Jeremiah sat alone. "Here you go. Anything else I can get for you?"

He took a sip of his orange juice, set it on the table, and smiled at her, his light-brown eyes sparkling as they crinkled at the corners. "Some coffee would be good. Can you join me?"

"Neh." She hadn't meant the word to come out so quickly and with such sharpness. "I mean, I can't sit down while I'm working."

"Don't you get a break?"

"Ya, but I already took it."

His lips formed a straight line as he nodded. "I understand. Maybe some other time."

"Maybe." She took a step back before adding, "I'll get your coffee. Want cream with that?"

"Yes, please." The gleam in his eye made her tummy flutter.

She went to the beverage station and poured some coffee into a carafe, but the cream pitcher was empty. Shelley scurried toward the kitchen to get some cream, happy for a chance to gather her thoughts. Jeremiah's politeness would be stifling if she didn't know him well. He'd always been such a tease for as long as she'd known him, from back before they'd even started school. They both grew up in the Pinecraft community of Sarasota, a neighborhood of small houses rented by Conservative Mennonite and Amish families. Jeremiah had left the church right after high school and decided not to come back after getting a taste of the outside world. From what she'd seen and heard, he'd completely turned his back on his faith during that time. And now he wanted to come back. Shelley wished she could be so sure of his intentions, but it happened too fast. . .and at a bad time for Shelley. She didn't think she could face more heartbreak so soon after Peter announced he was marrying someone else.

On her way to Jeremiah's table she grabbed a cup from the beverage station, and then she filled it with coffee at Jeremiah's table and set the carafe down next to it. "Let me know if you need anything else, okay?"

He nodded but didn't say another word.

<del></del>

Jeremiah watched Shelley as she directed customers to tables after they walked into the family-owned restaurant lined with booths on each side and rows of laminate-topped tables in the middle of the floor. There was very little decor in the dining area to pull his attention away from Shelley. She appeared self-conscious when he talked to her, but her grace and assuredness returned the instant she turned her back on him. No matter what he said or did to show how much he cared for her, she appeared to keep an emotional distance.

As she glided around with ease in her midcalf-length full skirt, he couldn't help but notice her graceful, fluid movement. The crocheted kapp perched atop her braided chestnut-brown bun showed off her long, elegant neckline, which was devoid of any jewelry. Yes, he was physically attracted to her, but Jeremiah knew her heart was right with God. That alone compelled him to be near her, particularly at this time of his life as he prayed for forgiveness and mercy.

One of the many people who hadn't accepted Jeremiah when he first came back was Shelley, but she was the one he really wanted to be happy. When Jeremiah first went to Abe to ask for help in coming back to the church, he'd been surprised at the quick acceptance from Abe and a few of the other church members. Shelley seemed pleased at how he'd helped Abe protect Mary from a man who'd tried to harm her, but now she acted like he'd somehow hurt her.

Abe told him it would take some time to win her over, but to Jeremiah it seemed as though that may never happen. He'd been working with some of the other hands tearing down Abe's old barn to prevent another accident when Abe approached him and said to go pick up some things in town, since Jeremiah still had transportation. He'd traded in the shiny sports car he'd used to impress girls for a barely functional automobile that wouldn't impress anyone. And he'd donated his stylish clothes to a charity thrift store and embraced the plain wardrobe filled with neutral-tone trousers and shirts.

As Jeremiah was about to get into his car, Abe advised him to stop off at Penner's Restaurant for breakfast before returning, since they'd be working until sundown. What he suspected Abe wanted was for him to have some face time with Shelley. Now he wondered at the wisdom. Perhaps he needed to make himself scarce for a while, so she wouldn't get annoyed with him.

He stared down at his nearly empty plate. Ever since he'd started working on Abe's farm, his appetite had practically doubled.

"Can I get you something else?"

The sound of Shelley's sweet voice caught his attention. He slowly looked up and met her blue-eyed gaze to see her studying him with concern. He shook his head. "This is already more food than I'm used to."

Shelley nodded as she glanced at his plate. "Ya, I can imagine. How are you able to be away from the farm so long?"

Jeremiah had to stifle a smile. This was the most she'd chatted with him since Abe and Mary's wedding. "Abe told me to have a big breakfast while I'm in town picking up supplies."

"You still drive your car?"

"Yes."

The look of disapproval on her face told him more than words possibly could.

"So if you ever need a lift somewhere, just call me."

She shook her head. "I rarely have a need to ride in a car."

He held up both hands. "I'm just offering rides when you need them."

Shelley's long, dark eyelashes fluttered for a moment as she closed her eyes and then opened them, meeting his gaze. She smiled. "Thank you, Jeremiah. Let me know when you're ready for your bill. I have to go see about my other"—she glanced over her shoulder before turning back—"my other customer."

⤐

The other customer happened to be one of Shelley's regulars—Blake, a truck driver who stopped off at Penner's whenever he was in town. The first time she and Mary had seen Blake, they were frightened by the man's oversized arms and the multiple tattoos he didn't bother hiding. But he was polite and expressed his appreciation for what he called "good home-cooked food like Mama used to make, rest her soul." And he'd left a tip bigger than his bill.

"Hi there, Shelley. What's the lunch special today?"

"Meatloaf, but it's not ready yet. It should be done in just a few minutes."

"Okay, then I'll wait." He closed the menu, folded his arms, and leaned back in his booth. "Who's that guy staring at you?"

"Oh, that's just Jeremiah. He's an old classmate." Shelley tried to act nonchalant, but she didn't think she did a good job of pulling it off.

"Old classmate, huh?" Blake's laughter was deep and resonant. "Looks to me like he carries a torch for you." He wiggled his eyebrows. "Want me to make him jealous?"

Shelley hopped back from the table. "Neh, that wouldn't be good."

"Don't worry, honey, I'm not gonna hurt you. I might look tough, but that's just a front. In the line of work I do, I gotta have an image."

"I know that," Shelley said with a forced smile. "Would you like something to drink while you wait for lunch?"

"Yeah, I'll have some sweet tea."

As Shelley turned toward the beverage station, she caught Jeremiah glaring at her. Blake was right. He was clearly jealous! The look on his face was one she'd never seen on him before, but she recognized it from studying other people.

Jeremiah quickly shoved his plate away, took another swig of coffee, stood, and reached into his back pocket for his wallet. As soon as she delivered Blake's tea, she brought Jeremiah his bill. Shelley wasn't short at five-foot-seven, but Jeremiah's broad six-foot frame made her feel small. He handed her a ten-dollar bill and said, "Keep the change."

"Thank you."

He started toward the door but stopped and spun back around to face her. "When do you generally take a break?"

"It varies. Most of the time right after the breakfast crowd dwindles, but I still don't like to take too long."

"I'll remember that." With a nod, he left.

As soon as the lunch special was ready, Shelley served Blake and waited on customers as they trickled into the restaurant. Shortly after eleven they were fully staffed, so Shelley didn't have to cover the whole dining room by herself. By noon the place was packed and stayed that way for a solid hour and a half. After Mary had gotten married and moved out to the Glick farm with Abe, Mr. Penner had hired another waitress, Jocelyn. Shelley liked the girl, but she was a bit silly—even for an outsider. Mr. Penner told Jocelyn she wasn't allowed to dress in clothes that showed too much skin, so she wore short skirts over pants and tank tops over T-shirts. It took more convincing to get her to tone down her makeup, but after Mrs. Penner talked to her, Jocelyn instantly gave up her thick eyeliner and bloodred lipstick. Shelley didn't know what Mrs. Penner had said to Jocelyn, but it obviously worked.

"So what's kickin'?" Jocelyn asked once business slowed down.

"I beg your pardon?"

"Anything new happenin' in your life?"

Shelley slowly shook her head. "No, not much that I can think of. Everything pretty much stays the same for me." Even if something were happening, Shelley couldn't imagine sharing it with someone like Jocelyn.

"I've got some great news I'm bustin' to tell someone." She grinned. "My sister is pregnant with twins."

"You have a sister?"

"Well, half sister. My mom had her after she left me and Dad."

"Oh, um. . ." Shelley wasn't sure what to say or how to react.

Jocelyn smiled. "She contacted me a few years ago, and we've started getting close."

"That's very good news," Shelley agreed. "Children are such a blessing in a marriage."

"Oh, my sister isn't married. She's not sure she's ready to settle down."

Shelley let out a gasp. "But why—" She stopped herself from asking what she considered the obvious.

"Oh, I know how you people feel about that, but I thought you'd at least be happy I'm gonna be an aunt."

"I'm sure you'll enjoy them very much." Shelley scurried toward the door to seat some late-arriving customers.

Things had changed around Pinecraft, and Shelley found it quite unsettling. In the past, Mr. Penner would never have hired anyone who wasn't Mennonite or Amish. But as people moved away or left the church, he'd been forced to bring in outsiders to help out. Even so, not many people were lined up for jobs, so he had to accept anyone who had the slightest bit of experience. His wife said they'd be better off shorthanded, but as good as Shelley was, she couldn't handle the restaurant alone during the busiest of times. At least Mrs. Penner came around to check on things more frequently now. Mr. Penner had a soft spot in his heart for the downtrodden, regardless of their faith or lack of it. Jocelyn had been unemployed for a long time, and when she'd told him she was a week away from living on the street because her dad wasn't able to support her anymore, he gave her the job.

❧

It was late spring, and the temperatures were rising but hadn't reached the nineties yet. The winter visitors, also called snowbirds, had gone home, so the highways and businesses weren't nearly as crowded as they were as little as a month ago. The Pinecraft community in Sarasota played host to Amish and Mennonite visitors who preferred the mild winters in Florida over wherever they came from. Many of them stayed with relatives who lived in the tiny rental houses, while others had short-term leases of their own for the season.

As Jeremiah drove down the long, narrow, shell-covered driveway toward the Glick farm, he spotted Abe standing outside the old barn with a couple of the other workers. Jonathan Polk and his adult son, Charles, were part of the crew Abe had put together from a group of farmhands to take down the barn.

Abe lifted a hand in greeting, but he continued talking. One of the things Jeremiah appreciated about his friend and boss was his no-nonsense approach to everything he did. There was never any guessing or wondering where he stood. If Abe said something, that was exactly what he meant.

Jeremiah opened the trunk of his old black car and pulled out some of the supplies for the farm. By the time he'd set everything down, Abe had sent the other men off to do their chores, and he'd joined Jeremiah.

"Did you stop by Penner's?" he asked.

"Yes, but Shelley still seems distant."

Abe shook his head. "Give her some time. After your behavior in the past, I can understand her reluctance."

"Don't forget, Abe, I helped you with that bad dude, Jimbo, when he came after Mary. Shelley was there, so she knows I helped."

Abe tilted his head forward and gave Jeremiah a stern glare. "I'm sure Shelley is well aware of your good deeds, but you need to remember to exercise some humility. Don't boast about what you do because you want people to notice. The Lord sees everything, and He's the only one whose judgment matters."

Jeremiah lowered his head. "Yeah, you're right. I'm still struggling with some things."

"Don't put too much pressure on yourself or rush your relationship with Shelley. Let the Lord do His work in His own time."

"Thanks, Abe." Jeremiah turned toward the pile of supplies. "I'll go get the wheelbarrow, so I can bring this stuff in one load."

Abe placed a hand on Jeremiah's shoulder. "Trust that Shelley will eventually come around and see what a good man you are and that you've left those unruly years behind." He paused before adding, "That is, if it's the Lord's will."

Jeremiah nodded.

For the next couple of hours as Jeremiah worked with his hands, he allowed himself to reflect on his past. Abe was right. The acts he'd committed during the years that he had spent away from the church needed quite a bit of forgiving. He'd fallen into the trap of chasing the wrong kind of women, pursuing more material objects than he'd ever need in a lifetime, and being the kind of man who'd frighten someone like Shelley. In his own mind at the time, he'd managed to place some of the blame for his indiscretions on Shelley. He'd had a crush on her since they were teenagers, but she never had time for him. She was always running home saying she needed to help her mother and younger brother. At the time, he saw it as a personal rejection, but now he knew she was being an obedient daughter.

~

Shelley preferred walking over riding the three-wheeler around the community as so many of the other neighbors did. Her adult-sized tricycle stayed tethered to the pole in the carport unless she needed it to haul groceries or other items from the store. Since she worked the early-morning shift, she generally went home after the last of the lunch customers left.

As she rounded the last corner toward the house her family rented, she slowed down and said a prayer that she'd find her mother in a better mood than when she'd left. Ever since her younger brother, William, was born with Down syndrome, her mother suffered from depression, and her father retreated further into silence when he wasn't working. When William got upset, he liked to be alone, so sometimes he took off without telling anyone where he was going, which upset their mother even more. Her older brother, Paul, left the church as soon as he was old enough to find a job to support himself. At first their parents were so disappointed they didn't want him coming around, in case Shelley might get ideas to do the same. After he and his wife had their first child, the allure of grandparenting had been so strong that they'd accepted him and his family with the hope that Paul would return to the church and bring his family with him. Paul's wife, Tammy, had a sweet disposition, and Shelley adored her niece, Lucy, and nephew, Grady. Shelley wondered if she'd ever have children of her own someday, but as time passed, she wondered if most men wouldn't want to take a wife who'd ultimately wind up with the responsibility of a mentally challenged brother who would need care for the rest of his life. If Paul had stayed with the church, he would have taken William in, but Shelley was the only option. Until Peter let her down, Shelley had thought there might've been hope, but now she'd settled back to her old way of thinking.

The side door by the carport was unlocked. As she entered the house, the eerie silence disturbed her. William went to school and then an afternoon group work session during the week, and he wouldn't be home until the van dropped him off right before dinner. A single dinner plate and a glass were in the sink, letting Shelley know her mother had eaten alone. Her father had tried to talk her mother into getting a part-time job, just to get her out of the house and more socially active, but she'd insisted she needed to be home in case William needed her. She set the takeout box filled with cake on the counter before leaving the kitchen.

"Mother," Shelley called out. "Are you home?"

She was met by silence, so she made her way through the tiny three-bedroom house, glancing in each room, praying her mother would be awake. When she got to the nearly dark master bedroom, she saw movement in the bed. Recently, her mother had started napping and waking up after Shelley got home from work.

"What time is it?" her mother asked. "I didn't mean to sleep so late."

"It's a little past two."

Mother sat up in bed and patted the hair that had come loose from her bun. "Oh, good. I've only been asleep for an hour." She shoved her feet into the clogs by the bed and slowly stood. Shelley couldn't help but notice her mother grabbing onto the nightstand for support.

"If you're not feeling well, why don't you lie back down?" Shelley said. "I can finish the chores."

"There isn't much to do, since I'm the only person here all morning."

Shelley was exhausted from the busy morning at Penner's, but she thought about her father's attempts to cheer up her mother and decided she should at least try to advance his cause. "Would you like to take a walk with me now?"

"Isn't it awful hot to be walking?"

"The rain last night cooled things down a bit, so it's not too bad. We can just stroll around the block and get some fresh air."

Her mother's hesitation let her know she didn't want to do it, but she couldn't think of a good enough reason. Finally, she sighed and nodded. "Okay, but just around the block."

"I'll put a few things away while you get ready," Shelley offered. "Mr. Penner sent me home with some dessert. He said he and Mrs. Penner haven't been eating as many sweets since Mary got married and moved out."

"Just give me a few minutes, and I'll join you in the kitchen."

Shelley left her mother alone to do whatever she needed to get ready for their walk. She put her tote on the hook in her room and then went to the kitchen and put the cake in the refrigerator so the cream-cheese icing wouldn't spoil. Then she washed the dishes in the sink and wiped the crumbs off the table.

"I'm ready."

Shelley glanced up and spotted her mother at the door wearing a different skirt and some hard-soled shoes. "Don't you want to wear comfortable shoes?" Shelley asked.

"Neh, these are fine. I'm used to them."

Shelley had her doubts, but she didn't push. Her mother grabbed the key off the hook, and they took off.

"Anything interesting happen at work today?" Shelley's mother asked.

Shelley pondered mentioning Jeremiah but made a quick decision not to. "No, pretty much a normal day."

"I had a visitor this morning, shortly after William went to school."

When her mother didn't continue, Shelley slowed her pace and turned to look at her mother. "Well? Who was it?"

"Hannah."

Peter's mother. The downside to growing up in a community where everyone knew everyone else made it difficult getting over the man she once thought she'd marry. "Did she say anything I need to know about?"

Her mother shrugged. "She doesn't know if Peter is happy."

"What gives her that impression?"

"He seems restless."

Despite the fact that Shelley had thought she was madly in love with Peter before he'd informed her he was marrying someone else, she'd gotten over him. "I think Peter's always restless," Shelley said.

"Hannah seems to think Peter regrets his decision and that he's considering calling off his wedding."

If there had been any doubt about things turning out for the best in Shelley's life, it was gone. After the breakup, she'd realized that Peter always wondered what he was missing, and he was seldom satisfied with what he had.

"He might just be holding a torch for you."

"I don't think so," Shelley said.

"You wouldn't know though, would you?"

"Mother, even if Peter wants me back, I don't think we're meant for each other."

"You're not getting any younger, Shelley. I don't want you to miss out on a chance of finding a suitable husband. Peter is a good man, and if he wants to reconsider his decision, you should—"

"No, I shouldn't. I don't love Peter."

Her mother frowned. "Peter will be a good provider, and you know him very well."

"Not as well as I once thought."

"You should give him another chance."

"Considering the fact that he hasn't asked for another chance, that's a moot point," Shelley said. She noticed that they'd slowed way down. "Are you okay, Mother?"

"My feet are tired."

Shelley stopped. "Why don't you take off your shoes and walk barefoot?"

"I'll give that a try for a little while." She placed her hand on Shelley's shoulder to steady herself as she took off each shoe with the other hand. "Now what were we talking about?" Silence fell between them for a few seconds. "Oh, Peter. So would you like me to ask his mother if he might want to stop by the house soon?"

Had Mother not heard a single word she'd said? "I'm not interested in Peter anymore." Shelley turned and started walking again. Traffic had begun to pick up, so she had to wait at the corner before crossing. A black automobile slowed as it approached, and she glanced at the driver—Jeremiah.

The car stopped, and Jeremiah waved. "Hey, Shelley. Mrs. Burkholder. Want a ride somewhere?"

If Shelley had been alone, she would have turned him down, but her mother's feet were hurting. "Mother?"

Her mother audibly sighed and then nodded. "Yes, I think a ride would be very nice."

Chapter 2

Jeremiah wasn't sure what just happened, but he had to smile. One minute he was driving home from work, and the next minute he spotted Shelley and her mother walking down the street. Mrs. Burkholder had been limping. He'd stopped with the intention of offering a ride, but he wasn't sure they'd take him up on it. He was surprised when they accepted. Shelley's mother got into the front seat next to him, and Shelley slid into the backseat.

"Where to, ladies?"

"Home, please," Shelley said.

Jeremiah tried to make small talk as they drove to the Burkholder house. He could tell they were both uncomfortable, so he decided to take a low-key approach.

"Nice day for a walk," he said.

Mrs. Burkholder cleared her throat but didn't say anything. He glanced in the rearview mirror and saw a pained expression on Shelley's face. She mouthed, "I'm sorry."

Okay, so conversation would be rough. At least their house wasn't too far. As soon as he brought the car to a complete stop, Mrs. Burkholder unbuckled her seat belt, flung open the door, and jumped out. She glanced over her shoulder and scowled at Shelley before darting into the house, leaving Jeremiah and Shelley alone.

"I guess I came along at the right time, huh?" Jeremiah said.

"I guess you did. You do realize the only reason I got in your car with you was because my mother's feet hurt."

So that explained the limp. "Then I'm glad I came along when I did."

Shelley nodded. "Ya, your timing was good."

She remained in the car, so he pondered for a few seconds whether or not he should take advantage of the situation. *Might as well*, he thought. "Would you like to go out with me sometime?"

"I don't think so," she said. "You should know that by now."

"I was hoping you'd changed your mind about me."

"What makes you think I'd ever change my mind?"

"C'mon, Shelley. I was young and restless, but that's in my past. You know I see things differently now. I've turned my life back over to the Lord."

"What's to say you won't change your mind again?"

Jeremiah challenged her with a firm gaze in the mirror. "What's to say you won't do what I did?"

"Well," she began as she reached for the door handle. "I don't have the history you have. Even before you left, you were somewhat of a rebel."

"Yeah, I'll give you that."

"People don't change." She opened the door, but she didn't get out yet.

"Not unless the Lord chooses to change them," Jeremiah countered. "What can I do to prove to you that my heart is right with the Lord?"

"I'm not the one you have to prove anything to."

"I know that, but I want you to see that I've returned to my faith. And I want you to believe it as well." He glanced up and spotted her mother peeking around from behind the drapes. "Someone's watching us."

She pushed the car door all the way open and started to get out before turning back to face Jeremiah. "I'm happy you came back to the church, Jeremiah, but only for you. It has nothing to do with me."

"You're right. It's all about the Lord's direction. He's in charge of my life now, and I want to serve Him well."

Shelley finally cracked a smile. "I hope that's truly the way it is. We'll see how things go when you start to get restless again. But now I better go inside. I'm sure my mother has plenty to say about me sitting here with you."

"I'll see you soon, Shelley."

She got out and slammed the car door shut. Jeremiah sat and waited until she was safely inside her house.

$\approx$

As Shelley walked inside, she was surprised her mother wasn't standing by the door waiting for her with a long lecture, but instead she was met by silence, which brought confusion and worry. Her mother seemed more fragile recently, so she tried very hard—most of the time—not to upset her.

She sighed and went into the kitchen to start supper. As tired as she was after working such a busy shift, walking with her mother, and talking to Jeremiah, she knew that her father and William would be hungry when they got home. William liked to set the table, but her father expected to sit right down to a big meal after a long day working at the hardware store.

She'd just placed the pork chops into the oven when she saw a shadow by the door. She turned around and offered her mother a guarded smile.

"What did you and Jeremiah talk about?"

Shelley shrugged. "Not much. He just wanted to remind me that he's changed."

"Just remember, Shelley, the temptations of evil are powerful."

It took everything Shelley had not to roll her eyes. "Nothing evil happened. Jeremiah was actually very sweet to stop and pick us up."

"That's how it starts."

Shelley let out a deep sigh. Even after Jeremiah had saved her mother from having to walk back home with aching feet, she still hadn't softened. "Look, Mother, I'm not going to do anything I shouldn't do. Jeremiah says he's committed his life to the Lord, and from my perspective, it appears that he has." Even though Shelley rarely outwardly rebelled, she wasn't about to openly admit her own doubts about Jeremiah.

Silence fell between them for a moment. Shelley felt as though the conversation didn't stand a chance of having any resolution, so she thought it best to end the discussion. Her mother apparently thought otherwise.

"So you're saying that you don't have any doubts about Jeremiah's motives on coming around again?"

"No, I'm not saying that." Deep down, Shelley feared that what her mother was saying was true, and she would have been on her mother's side if she'd been talking to Jeremiah. But when he looked at her as he had a half hour ago, she wanted to believe him, even though she wouldn't let him know. "I just think we need to give him the benefit of proving himself."

"Shelley, you can be so naive."

"He helped Abe when that awful man came to hurt Mary," Shelley reminded her mother.

"Don't base your opinion of him on a few good deeds. He was away from the church for a number of years, and it'll take much more than that to show he's changed for the good."

Shelley didn't have an argument for that, so she finally backed away. "We need to finish preparing supper so Father and William have something to eat when they come home."

The cloud of their conversation hung over them as they finished cooking. By the time William walked through the door, Shelley was exhausted more from what wasn't being said than from what was.

"Can you take me to the park before supper?" William asked.

"Not now," Shelley replied. "I'm busy."

William's face scrunched into a pout. He opened his mouth to say something, but Shelley noticed their mother giving him a look that stopped him.

Shelley wished Mother would give William a little more room to explore on his own. After all, he was seventeen. But unless he was at school, work, or in the van that took him to work, Mother insisted someone from the family be with him.

~⁂~

Jeremiah appreciated the physical labor of farmwork. It enabled him to reflect on not only his conversation with Shelley two days ago but also conversations he'd had with some of the church elders over the past several months since he'd come back to his Mennonite roots. He was constantly being questioned about his motives and why he'd chosen this time to come back to the church. The reasons didn't seem clear, although he had no doubt that the Lord sometimes painfully taught him lessons that steered him back. He explained that to Abe, who seemed to understand, but his answers didn't satisfy everyone.

The people who never questioned him were Jonathan and his son, Charles, a couple of outsiders Abe hired to help out on the farm. Jeremiah enjoyed working with them.

"Watch out, Jeremiah," Jonathan said with a teasing tone. "A man who thinks too much can get hurt."

Jeremiah chuckled. "You're right. I've been thinking too much lately."

"Care to talk about it?" Jonathan raked his fingers through his half-gray, half-brown hair. "Not saying I have all the answers, but sometimes it helps to talk."

"If I had any idea what to talk about, I'd probably welcome the opportunity, but my thoughts are so jumbled they don't even make sense to me."

Jonathan nodded his understanding. "I know exactly what you're saying. This world is confusing, which is why I brought my son here to learn what's really important."

Jeremiah glanced over at Jonathan's son, Charles, who was busy hauling lumber from the old barn to the scrap pile. "Charles seems to be in his element here on the farm."

"He and I are both much happier than we've ever been. No high-powered executive job has ever left me with the sense of accomplishment that I get from working here."

"I know what you mean."

"Yes," Jonathan said with a nod. "I know you do. And one of these days, others will see that in you. Some people just need to get burned a few times before we come to our senses."

"That's a good way of putting it. I needed to get burned before I understood what I had. And now I want that back. The Lord's favor is all that matters to me right now."

"It's okay to want the girl, too," Jonathan said.

Jeremiah grinned. "Am I that obvious?"

"Yes, you definitely are. Any chance you'll be letting go of the car?"

"Abe and I have been talking about it. I already traded in my sports car for the plain one, but it's hard to give up transportation."

"I know what you mean. Charles and I have been talking about that. He seems more amenable to it than I am, but if I ever decide to embrace the lifestyle, it seems the right thing to do. My wife isn't ready yet, but she seems happier already now that we've decided to try and sell the house."

The clanging sound of the triangle signaling lunchtime got their attention. "I'm starving," Jeremiah said as he patted his belly. "Another cool thing about working here is being able to eat anything I want and not having to worry about an expanding waistline. It seemed like no matter how much time

I spent at the gym before, I always had to loosen my belt a notch or two after a big meal."

After they finished the bag lunches they'd brought from home, Abe approached Jeremiah. "Do you mind taking me to town? I have to deliver some produce to Penner's."

"I'll be glad to."

"I thought you might." Abe turned to Jonathan. "Tell your wife we enjoyed her pineapple upside-down cake. Mary would like the recipe."

"Lori will be flattered," Jonathan said. "I'll have her jot down the recipe."

Abe gave a clipped nod. "Good. Jeremiah, let me know when you're ready to go."

Jeremiah finished the last of his sandwich and rose from the picnic bench. "Time to take the boss to town."

"I'll save some of the work for you when you get back," Jonathan said as he stood. "Drive carefully."

As soon as Abe got into Jeremiah's car, he started talking. "I heard you created quite a stir in town on Monday."

Jeremiah frowned as he reflected. He didn't know what Abe was talking about. "I did?"

"Ya. Shelley's mother was very unhappy about you showing up."

"Oh, that. Well, I didn't mean to cause any trouble. It's just that I saw Shelley and her mother walking, so I thought I'd offer them a ride."

"Just remember that it takes a while to earn forgiveness from people who have been hurt. When you left, you upset some folks."

"That wasn't my intention."

"It doesn't have to be. It just happens that way sometimes."

When Jeremiah had to stop for a light, he turned to Abe. "What can I do to make things better?"

"If you're asking how you can hurry things along, I don't have any answers. But if you want to make amends with individual people, you can talk to them and explain your reasons for coming back. They need to know you have no motive other than to please the Lord and do His calling."

Jeremiah wished it were that simple, but he knew it wasn't. He'd always cared for Shelley, but she'd always seemed leery of him even when they were younger. That's why he'd been surprised when she'd gotten into his car on Monday.

"If you want to court Shelley, you need to make things right with her parents first."

"I doubt they'll bother talking to me," Jeremiah said.

"Have you tried?"

"No."

"Then do that first. You knew coming back wouldn't be easy."

"True." Jeremiah accelerated as the light turned green. "Something I've been wondering, Abe."

"What's that?"

"You didn't put me through the paces when I wanted to come back. Everyone else has one question after another, but you accepted what I said from the get-go. Why was that?"

Abe shrugged. "I s'pose I've always been a direct sort of man, and I've known you to be that way with me. There wasn't any reason for me to doubt you—particularly after you swallowed your pride when I talked to you about your crudeness with Mary."

Jeremiah cringed as he remembered his comments. "That was totally out of line. The second I hollered at you, I regretted it. I'm afraid I picked up some bad habits."

"But you apologized, and you seemed sincere. Mary and I have both forgiven you."

"Now I need to ask a lot of other people for their forgiveness."

"Ya. That's exactly what you have to do. Some people will accept your words, and others will wait and watch your actions."

"That's a lot of pressure."

"Pressure is part of life," Abe said. "After you establish yourself back in the church, there will be something else. Walking with the Lord isn't easy for anyone."

"How about you, Abe? Do you feel pressure about anything?"

"Ya, of course I do. But I don't lose sleep over it. Mary and I pray about whatever is on our minds, and we go to sleep knowing we're in the Lord's good graces. As Christians, we are His faithful servants, even when we slip up. He has never let us down."

That was exactly what Jeremiah needed to hear. He helped Abe unload the produce from the trunk, and then Joseph Penner asked them to stick around. Abe accepted, but Jeremiah asked if he could run an errand of his own. Abe smiled knowingly and nodded.

On the way to the Burkholders' house, Jeremiah prayed for the Lord's mercy and for the wisdom to say the right thing to Shelley's mother. Pride had always been a problem for Jeremiah, but he knew the Lord was working on that.

He pulled up in front of the Burkholders' house, stopped, and said a prayer for guidance. His hands were damp and a little shaky as he got out of the car and walked up to the front door. After a brief pause, he knocked.

The silence gave him the impression no one was home, so he turned to leave. The sound of the door opening behind him caught his attention. He turned around and saw Mrs. Burkholder glaring at him.

"What do you want, Jeremiah?"

"I'd like to talk to you, if you're not too busy."

The woman tightened her jaw and narrowed her eyes. "Shelley isn't here right now."

"I know. That's why I came. I'd like to talk to you alone."

She continued to scrutinize him, making him feel small and weak. Finally, she nodded. "I suppose you can come in, but not for long. I have chores to do."

Grateful for an opportunity to talk to Shelley's mother, Jeremiah followed the woman into her tidy little house, which was almost the exact same layout as the one he'd grown up in. She led him to the kitchen, which overlooked an equally well-kept backyard.

"Would you like some coffee?" she asked.

"No thank you." He gestured toward the kitchen table. "Mind if we sit?"

She looked at the table and then took a step toward the chair. "I hope you realize I'm not in favor of you seeing my daughter."

"Yes, I'm aware of that, but I'd like to find out if there's anything I can do to prove myself."

"You've already proven yourself, Jeremiah, and I don't mean that in a good way."

"I'm working hard now, Mrs. Burkholder. Abe has given me a job on his farm, and I'm back in the church now. What else can I do to show you I'm sincerely repentant of my indiscretions?"

She pursed her lips and shook her head. "I don't think there's anything you can do for my husband and me to give you our blessing to see our daughter."

That was what Jeremiah had been afraid of. He hung his head and sent up a prayer. Finally, after a few more minutes of quiet, he stood. "I better go pick Abe up from the restaurant. I told him I wouldn't be long."

"You know your way out," Mrs. Burkholder said.

He nodded and turned to leave when the sound of someone knocking at the door echoed through the house. Mrs. Burkholder jumped to her feet and ran along behind him.

When Jeremiah opened the door, he found himself face-to-face with a sheriff's deputy. "Officer," he said in greeting.

The deputy leaned around Jeremiah. "Mrs. Burkholder, we just got a call that your son, William, has wandered off from the school. A deputy has been dispatched to search the area, but I wanted to let you know."

"I'll help," Jeremiah said without a moment's hesitation. "I'll go get Abe, and we'll get right to work."

Mrs. Burkholder was right behind him. "I'm coming with you."

The officer stepped up. "Someone needs to stay here in case William comes home."

Jeremiah looked at the woman, who now looked frail. "Why don't you wait here? I have the car, so we can cover a larger area."

Her forehead crinkled in concern, and she nodded. "I don't have any way of communicating."

Jeremiah pulled the cell phone out of his pocket and handed it to her. "I'll find a phone and call you if—when—we find him."

She hesitated before nodding and accepting the phone. "If I don't hear from you soon, I'll walk over to Penner's."

"Please stay right here, ma'am," the deputy advised. "Someone needs to be home if he decides to return on his own."

Jeremiah scooted past the deputy and ran out to his car. By the time he arrived at Penner's, another deputy had stopped by and made Abe, Mr. Penner, and Shelley aware of what had happened. Shelley was beside herself.

"Any idea where he might have gone?" he asked Shelley.

"He wanders from home sometimes," Shelley replied. "But I can't imagine why he left the school. He loves his teacher. I'm worried that something terrible has happened to him. Someone needs to let my father know."

The deputy nodded. "We've sent someone to his workplace to tell him."

Jeremiah shook his head. "I have a feeling we'll find him, but we shouldn't wait too long. Why don't you come with me?"

Shelley turned to Mr. Penner, who nodded. "Okay."

"Oh, I gave your mother my cell phone, so I'll need a way to stay in touch."

Shelley reached into her apron pocket and pulled out a phone. "I have mine."

"Then let's go. We don't need to waste any time."

Jeremiah and Shelley ran out to Jeremiah's car. "Let's swing by the school and drive around the block. We can widen our search as we go."

She swallowed hard and nodded. "My little brother is so trusting. I sure hope he didn't go off with someone."

"Who would he go off with?"

Shelley shrugged. "Maybe someone offered him something he wanted."

"How old is William now?"

"Seventeen," she replied. "Almost eighteen."

"It's not like he's a little boy someone would want to abduct. He's almost as tall as me, and he looks strong, so I doubt anyone could force him to do anything."

"Ya, he's very strong."

"Then let's not worry. We'll find him."

There was no activity in the school yard. "Looks like the teachers are keeping the kids inside." Jeremiah circled the block then turned down another street to widen their search. "Any thoughts about where he might be?"

Shelley tapped her chin with her index finger. "He loves ice cream, so he might have gone to one of the ice cream shops."

"Does he know how to find them?"

"I'm not sure. One of us is usually with him."

"Let's check out Slater's Creamery. That's the closest to the school."

"Good idea," Shelley said. "He likes their vanilla bean."

Jeremiah pulled up in front and waited in the car while Shelley ran inside to ask if anyone had seen William. Hope welled inside him until she came back to the car shaking her head.

"Neh, they said they haven't seen him since we were there last week."

Jeremiah drove to a few more places Shelley suggested, but they continued turning up empty. "He can't have gone very far since he's on foot."

Shelley's chin quivered. "But what if he's not on foot? What if he got into someone's automobile?"

"He wouldn't do that, would he?" Jeremiah asked as he continued driving slowly and looking down the side streets. "I mean, you and your parents have taught him it's not safe to wander off with strangers, right?"

"Of course, but he's still so trusting. William is one of the sweetest people in the world, so if someone said the right thing, he might have gone off with them."

Jeremiah pulled over to the curb. "Before we go on, let's say a prayer."

Shelley nodded as a tear trickled down her chin. Jeremiah put the car into PARK and took hold of both of her hands. He prayed for William's safety and that he'd be found soon so everyone could stop worrying. After he said, "Amen," he opened his eyes and saw Shelley staring at him. Shortly after their gazes met, she lowered her head.

He reached out and tucked his finger beneath her chin. "Shelley, I want to be there for you—now and after we find William. Will you at least give me a chance?"

She opened her mouth but quickly closed it. A few seconds later she said, "I don't know, Jeremiah. Everything is so confusing right now. All I can think about is finding my little brother."

Yes, of course. What had Jeremiah been thinking? He wanted to kick himself in the backside for being selfish enough to turn things around to his feelings for Shelley.

"I'm sorry, Shelley. My timing was off. I just want you to know how much I care and that I have confidence we'll find William."

"What if we don't this time?" she asked, fear evident in her expression.

"We will." He took her hand and squeezed it. "We always do. We just have to trust the Lord."

Chapter 3

He'd driven a few hundred feet when Shelley's hand flew to her mouth. "I think I might know where he is. Turn here," she said, pointing to a narrow road to the right. "He has been asking me to take him to the park when he gets home from school lately, but I was always so busy."

As soon as the park came into view, Jeremiah spotted movement near the flower garden. "That looks like him over there."

"It is. Stop the car."

As soon as the car came to a stop, Shelley handed Jeremiah her cell phone, jumped out, and ran toward the boy. Jeremiah placed a call to his cell phone, which Mrs. Burkholder answered on the second ring.

"We found him," Jeremiah said. "He's at the park. Shelley is talking to him now. We'll bring him home in a few minutes."

"Praise the Lord," Mrs. Burkholder said breathlessly. "I'll let my husband know."

"I'll call the police now," Jeremiah offered. "Then I'll call Abe, and he can tell the others."

❧

"What are you doing here, William?" Shelley asked as she approached her younger brother. "Everyone is so worried about you."

William frowned before turning to pick another flower to add to the fistful he had in his left hand. "Mother is so sad. Pretty flowers will cheer her up."

"I'm sure they will, but why didn't you wait until I could bring you here?"

"I've been telling you I wanted to come here, but you never have time." William leaned toward another cluster of flowers. "Look at those purple flowers, Shelley. Aren't they pretty?"

"Yes, they're very pretty, but you need to come with me right now."

"But I want to pick more flowers to make Mother happy." His eyes brightened as he looked at something behind Shelley. "Hi, Jeremiah. Look at the pretty flowers I picked for my mother."

"Very nice," Jeremiah said. "Your mother will be very happy to see you. . . and the flowers. Are you ready to go home now?"

William plucked one more bloom then walked toward Jeremiah. "I don't want to be late for work, but I can't remember how to get back to school where they pick me up."

"I'll take you to work," Jeremiah offered.

"Oh, I don't think you need to worry about work today," Shelley said. "You'll need to stay home after scaring Mother like you did."

A look of alarm came over William. "Did something happen to Mother?"

Shelley glanced at Jeremiah, who offered her a comforting smile. "Yes, William, something terrible happened to Mother. She thought she'd lost her youngest child. You scared her and us half out of our minds by taking off like that."

"Was I bad?"

Before Shelley had a chance to respond, Jeremiah spoke up. "No, William, you weren't bad. But you should always tell someone where you're going before you leave. People worry when they don't know where you are."

William hung his head. "I'm sorry."

"Come on, William. Let's get you home to Mother. She's waiting for you."

Shelley started to buckle William into the front seat with Jeremiah. He scowled at her.

"I can buckle my own seat belt," he said. "Stop treating me like a baby."

Shelley let go of the seat belt and got in behind him. As they drove toward home, she listened to the conversation between the two men and marveled at how sensitive Jeremiah was. She'd seen brief glimpses of this with Jeremiah in the past, but just when she'd thought he had a sweet side, he'd do something to quickly erase that impression. Now she waited for it to happen again.

He pulled up in front of the house, turned off the car, and came around to help with William. Mother came running outside, and the instant William was all the way out of the car, she flung her arms around him, alternately kissing his face and fussing at him for taking off without telling anyone.

Jeremiah stood to the side, watching and waiting—for what, she wasn't sure. When they looked at each other, he tilted his head forward in acknowledgment, but he still didn't say a word. She felt a flutter of something inside, but she wasn't about to let this emotion-charged moment affect her thoughts.

"Thank you for helping, Jeremiah," she said. "Mother, if it weren't for Jeremiah, William wouldn't be standing here right now."

"Well. . ." Mother's lips formed a straight line, and she clearly didn't know what to say or do.

Jeremiah lifted a hand in a wave. "I need to get back to work. I'm glad I could help. If you need anything, let me know."

He'd gotten into his car and started it when Shelley's mother spun and ran toward him. Shelley thought perhaps she wanted to thank him, but instead she held up a cell phone. "Don't forget this."

"Do you want to use it for a while?" he asked.

Her mother shook her head. "No, I prefer not having the intrusion, but I've decided I need to get my own."

Shelley was disappointed that her mother didn't thank Jeremiah for the phone, but she knew better than to say anything. Her relationship with her mother had been somewhat strained during the past several months. She wasn't sure why, but her mother seemed to be sad all the time—until now.

"You had us worried sick," Mother said over and over. "William, don't ever run off like that again."

William innocently held up the bouquet he still gripped, several of the more fragile blooms drooping. "I wanted to pick you some pretty flowers to cheer you up," he said. "When you're sad, I feel sad."

Mother accepted the flowers and placed them on the side table without a word. When it was obvious she wasn't going to do anything with them, Shelley picked up the bouquet. "I'll put them in some water. Aren't they pretty, Mother? William picked them just for you."

Still her mother said nothing. William appeared confused as he was ushered toward his room.

Shelley busied herself with cutting the bottoms of the stems and placing them in a glass they didn't use often. Her mother didn't keep vases because she said they were unnecessary and took up valuable space. The sparsely filled shelves could use something new, but her mother didn't believe in having anything around that wasn't used often. Although the plain life made sense, there was still room for something fun and interesting.

The house was so quiet Shelley could hear the low murmur of voices coming from the bedroom area. Her father had remained at work even though he was aware of what had happened. Shelley knew he was just as worried as the rest of them, so she wondered why he hadn't come home.

She puttered around the kitchen for a little while until finally her mother joined her. "William doesn't understand why I don't want him to go to work."

Shelley turned and faced her mother. "Why can't he?"

Her mother frowned. "Don't tell me you don't understand. He had me worried sick."

"But he's fine. I'm sure he understands that he shouldn't wander off like that now."

"I thought he knew that before." Mother closed her eyes and shook her head then let out a long-suffering sigh as she looked Shelley in the eye. "We can't take any more chances with him."

"What do you plan to do? Keep him home all the time?"

"If I have to."

Shelley lifted her eyebrows. "And what will that accomplish? Do you think the Lord wants you to live in fear like that all the time?"

"It's more out of protection than fear. If I know where he is at all times, I'll never have to worry."

"Oh, I'm sure you'll find something to worry about. You always do." The instant those words left Shelley's mouth, she regretted saying them.

"And what is that supposed to mean?"

"Mother, I know you love William. I love him, too. But he can't live in a bubble all his life. School and work are important to him. He has friends."

"He can see his friends at church."

Frustration washed over Shelley as she realized her mother wasn't about to budge. "What will he do if you can't take care of him anymore?"

"That's where you come in," her mother replied. "Your father and I already thought about this before, and we decided that since Paul left, you're the logical person to care for your brother."

"Is that—" Shelley stopped herself before asking if that was why her mother was averse to her being around Jeremiah. Perhaps they thought she'd go off and leave William. She cleared her throat and started over. "You know I'll always be there for William no matter what, Lord willing."

"I certainly hope so."

"Jeremiah was very sweet for taking me to look for William. If he hadn't, I imagine it would have taken longer for us to find him."

"Just because Jeremiah happened to be here when William got lost…" Her mother's voice wandered off as she gazed out the window over the backyard.

Shelley studied her mother for a moment before speaking her mind. "Jeremiah was a big help, and I think we should be grateful that he jumped in and helped without having to be asked."

"I'd rather not discuss Jeremiah."

≈

On Saturday the farmworkers finished taking down the last of the old barn. Now that Jeremiah was used to the manual labor, he was able to work without tiring as quickly as he had when he'd first come back. Since Abe was counseling him on issues related to the church, he hung around until everyone else had gone home.

"Seen Shelley lately?" Abe asked.

"Not since we found her brother and brought him home on Wednesday. Her mother still can't stand the sight of me."

Abe chuckled. "Mrs. Burkholder is a fair woman. I'm sure she'll eventually come around."

"Back when I was a betting man, I would have bet against that."

"Good thing you're no longer a betting man."

Jeremiah nodded. "I have some things I'd like to discuss with you."

"About Shelley?"

"We can talk about Shelley, but there's something else that's bothering me."

Abe gestured toward a chair on his porch. "Have a seat, and let's talk."

Once they sat down, Jeremiah opened up. "Before I decided to come back to the church, I did some things that I'm not proud of."

"Ya, I know that."

"There are some things you don't know."

Abe turned and looked at him, waiting patiently in silence.

"I took out some big loans that will take years to pay back."

"You are a hard worker, and you live with your parents," Abe said. "You'll pay those loans back in due time."

"There's more." Jeremiah hated sharing everything, but he needed to come clean rather than have Abe find out later. "One of the men I worked with said some unsavory things about a woman I was dating, and I"—Jeremiah sucked in a deep breath—"I punched his lights out."

Abe tilted his head. "What do you mean by that?"

"I decked him." Jeremiah paused before clarifying. "I hit him with my fist."

"That is not good."

"And I spent three days in jail for unruly conduct."

Abe shook his head. "I hope the man you hit wasn't seriously injured."

"I broke his nose, which is why he pressed charges. Going to jail got me fired from my job, but I found another one."

"You need to ask the Lord for His forgiveness before you can move on."

"I've asked over and over, but I can't stop worrying about what happened."

Abe looked out over his land then turned back to Jeremiah and leaned forward with his elbows on his knees. "You need to trust that the Lord has forgiven you and move on. If He knows that you have sincere repentance for what you did, He will forgive you. From now on, you are to live as a peaceful man who will do no harm to anyone."

"That's what I intend to do," Jeremiah said. "But what if Shelley and her parents find out?"

"They will come to understand that is part of your past," Abe said, "and that you are very sorry it happened."

"If they know about my past, do you think they will they ever trust me?"

Abe shrugged. "Best leave that up to the Lord. He's the only one who can bring forgiveness."

"So let's say they can't forgive me."

Abe lifted his eyebrows and nodded. "That's a possibility."

Jeremiah knew that Abe was right, but the thought of having Shelley turn her back on him for something he couldn't change stabbed him in the heart. "I want Shelley to see that I'm the kind of man who will love her and be there for her."

"Have you shown that yet?"

"I'm working on it. Like when I helped her find William."

"Just make sure you are doing things for the right reasons and not for some reward, like earning Shelley's love. She should love you for who you are rather than what you can do for her."

Abe's wisdom belied his years. No wonder he managed to prosper during times when so many others failed.

"Thanks, man. You really know your stuff."

Abe laughed out loud—a rarity since Jeremiah had known him. "I know what the Lord calls me to do, and when I am not sure, I read scripture and pay attention to what He is telling me to do. Everything you could possibly want to know is answered in the Bible."

Jeremiah stood and stretched his legs. "I need to get back home. I promised my dad I'd help him clear a section of the yard for some tomatoes and peppers."

"You can bring home anything you need from here," Abe offered. "We have plenty to share with the workers."

Shelley's feet ached from running all over the restaurant. Jocelyn had called in and said she'd be late—and she still hadn't shown up.

"Shelley!" The sound of Mr. Penner's voice booming across the restaurant startled her. He was generally fairly calm, but something seemed to be bothering him lately.

"Yes, Mr. Penner?"

"You know I like to keep the ketchup bottles filled." He wagged his finger toward the booths along the front window. "Those over there are half-empty."

"I'll do it right now," she said.

Shelley skittered around, filling ketchup bottles, checking sugar and salt-shakers, and taking orders for the next half hour. When the door opened, she started toward the front until she realized it was Jocelyn.

"Hey there," Jocelyn said as though she didn't have a care in the world. "Been busy?"

"Ya," Shelley said, trying as hard as she could to keep the annoyance from her voice. "Are you here to work or talk?"

Jocelyn made a face. "Don't get all crazy stressed on me. Give me a chance to put on my apron."

Shelley took a deep breath and slowly let it out. *Crazy stressed* wasn't the phrase for what she was feeling. It was more like annoyance that someone wasn't doing her job and expected to be treated as though she were.

Jocelyn didn't waste any time getting ready to work. When she came around from behind the wall dividing the kitchen from the dining room, she was ready to take orders. Shelley made her way toward her and whispered an apology. "I should not have taken my frustration out on you."

"Hey, no problem. I can't say I wouldn't be taking your head off if you waltzed in two hours after your shift was supposed to start. So how's the special today?"

"It's good. Mrs. Penner made some extra coconut cream pie."

"Yum." Jocelyn gave a thumbs-up. "I'll let everyone know they need to save room for dessert."

Shelley had mixed feelings about Jocelyn. In spite of her odd hairstyle, clothes, and manner of speech, there seemed to be a sweetness hidden beneath a somewhat crusty exterior. Mr. Penner probably saw that, too, but Shelley doubted Mrs. Penner did, based on the glaring looks the older woman gave the newest employee.

After Shelley's customers had been served, she let them know she was leaving for the day and that Jocelyn would take care of them. The first few times she'd done that, she'd fully expected Jocelyn to keep her tips. But she'd been surprised each time when she came in the next day and spotted an envelope with her name on it. Inside she'd found a pile of dollar bills, some change, and a note letting her know these were the tips Jocelyn had collected from her tables. At least she was honest.

Some of the local Mennonite and Amish customers seemed disturbed by Jocelyn. Mr. Penner had pretty much shrugged off their comments until he realized he might lose a few customers. He would have eventually said something to Jocelyn, but his wife beat him to it. Shelley had to admit that Jocelyn had toned her style of dress and personality down quite a bit. She wanted to ask Jocelyn what Mrs. Penner had said, but she didn't want to be rude or nosy. One thing she did notice was that afterward Jocelyn appeared to have the utmost respect for the boss's wife.

Before Shelley left for the day, Mr. Penner handed her a package. "If you don't mind, I need to get this to my wife before I come home."

Shelley took the package and hesitated in order to give him a chance to tell her what was in it. But he didn't, so she nodded. "I'll go straight there."

With a grin, he nodded. "Good girl. Now get on out of here while you have a chance."

As Shelley reached the door, she waved to Jocelyn. "I owe you big time," Jocelyn said. "Thanks for covering my tables."

Shelley smiled but didn't say anything. On the way to the Penners', she noticed that the air hung heavy with moisture, even though it hadn't started raining yet. She glanced up at the sky toward the Gulf of Mexico. A narrow row of dark clouds rolled toward land, so she quickened her step so she wouldn't be caught in a downpour. By the time she reached the Penners' house, she'd been splattered with a few large raindrops.

Mrs. Penner yanked the door open before Shelley finished knocking. "Come inside, young lady, before you get drenched."

Shelley did as she was told. It had been a while since she'd been in the Penners' house, but nothing had changed—except the absence of Mary. "I don't want to impose," she said softly.

"That's ridiculous," Mrs. Penner said in her typical stern manner. "Come on into the kitchen. I'll fix you something to eat. We can talk while the rain blows over."

Shelley had no idea what they'd talk about, but she followed Mrs. Penner. The aroma of baked sugar, cinnamon, and yeast wafted through the tiny house. Her mouth watered.

"I just made a fresh batch of cinnamon rolls for that truck driver who stops by when he's in the area. He called Joseph and said he'd be coming over before closing." She pulled a pan out of the oven, intensifying the smells in the kitchen. "Want one?" She glanced over her shoulder at Shelley. "I have to let them cool for a few minutes before I ice them, but you can wait, can't you?"

There was no way Shelley could resist once she saw the golden-brown rolls dripping in gooey syrup and dotted with nuts. "Yes, ma'am. I can wait for one of your cinnamon rolls."

Mrs. Penner laughed. "I thought so. You look like you haven't been eating much lately. Anything you care to talk about?"

Shelley slowly shook her head. "I've just been very busy lately."

"So I've heard. You need to be careful about how you stay busy and who you are busy with. Some people can take your focus off the Lord."

There was no doubt what Mrs. Penner was talking about. Shelley instantly felt defensive, but she knew better than to argue her case. The only way Mrs. Penner ever changed her mind about someone was to see that person in action.

Mrs. Penner set the rolls on a cooling rack then poured some coffee into two mugs, which she carried to the table. "Sugar and cream?"

"Yes, please."

After they both had their coffee fixed like they wanted, Mrs. Penner joined Shelley at the table. "Jeremiah has always been somewhat spirited, as my daughter once was. You know what happened to her."

Shelley looked Mrs. Penner in the eye and saw the wisdom borne of pain. "Yes, I know."

"Well? Aren't you going to tell me Jeremiah is different?" Mrs. Penner lifted an eyebrow as she waited for Shelley's answer.

"I would like to, but I'm not sure."

Mrs. Penner offered one of her rare smiles. "Smart girl. It's always a good idea to take a wait-and-see attitude before jumping into something. He's not keeping it a secret that he wants to court you. Our Mary has tried to convince us that Jeremiah is a changed man, and she reminds us that he helped Abe escort that evil monster who tried to hurt her out of the restaurant so the police could take him away." She sipped her coffee then set down her mug before looking back up at Shelley. "But it's easy to do one act of kindness in front of an audience. We need to see if he continues or if the temptations of his old life drive him away again."

"Yes, I agree."

"He needs to be consistent. I don't want you getting hurt by someone who isn't sincere."

Shelley looked at the older woman and nodded. "Even if Jeremiah is sincere, I have to help my mother with William."

Mrs. Penner leaned forward with a hint of a smile. "How is sweet William?"

"He's fine, but he's starting to show some independence, and my mother doesn't know what to do about it."

"Yes, I can see how that would be troublesome to her." Mrs. Penner stood and walked over to the counter to ice the cinnamon rolls.

"Would you like some help?"

"Gracious no," Mrs. Penner said with a chuckle. "You'd just get in the way."

Even though Shelley understood that Mrs. Penner spoke brusquely but was a good woman deep down, she was taken aback and silenced.

"Here," Mrs. Penner said as she placed a small plate filled with a fluffy-looking roll covered in icing in front of Shelley. "Taste that, and let me know if it you like it. It's a new recipe that I'll make in the restaurant if it turns out good enough."

There was never any doubt Shelley would like it. After all, it was common knowledge around Pinecraft that Mrs. Penner's cooking had put Penner's Restaurant on the map of almost every tourist who visited Sarasota.

The first words that came to mind when Shelley tasted the roll were *totally yummo*! She giggled at how much influence Jocelyn had over some of her thoughts.

Mrs. Penner spun around and scowled. "What is so funny?"

Shelley finished chewing and nodded her satisfaction. "This is delicious."

The scowl on the older woman's face faded to a hint of a grin. "That is what I like to hear." She turned back to finish icing the rest of the rolls when someone knocked on the door. "Go see who that is, Shelley. I'm not expecting anyone."

Shelley opened the door and took a step back. "Jeremiah. . .what are you doing here?"

"Who is that, Shelley?" Mrs. Penner called from the kitchen.

"It's Jeremiah," Shelley called back before turning back around to face Jeremiah.

"I stopped by the restaurant with some produce from the farm. Mr. Penner asked me here to offer you a ride home, since it's pouring out."

"Umm. . ."Shelley glanced over her shoulder then turned back to Jeremiah. "I can wait until it stops raining."

Jeremiah glanced over Shelley's shoulder. "Hello, Mrs. Penner."

Chapter 4

J eremiah, what are you doing here?"

Mrs. Penner's tone left no doubt that she didn't want him in her house.

"I. . .uh, I came to see if Shelley needed a ride home since it's raining."

"She can wait until it stops."

Shelley cleared her throat, glanced at Mrs. Penner, then turned around to face Jeremiah. His heart lurched at the quick connection he felt with Shelley. "I really should be getting home. My mother is expecting me."

Mrs. Penner tightened her lips and folded her arms. "She'll understand since it's raining."

Shelley gave her a look of apology. "Mother is having a difficult time lately, and she needs me."

Jeremiah felt bad for Mrs. Penner, despite her opinion of him. In fact, he couldn't really blame her after his past. "I promise I'll take her straight home," he said.

The woman blinked and abruptly turned as she mumbled something very softly. He could barely hear her, but he was pretty sure she said, "Promises are only as good as the person who makes them."

After walking Shelley to the passenger side of the car with the umbrella, Jeremiah ran around to the driver's side. "This rain came out of nowhere."

Shelley's eyes were focused on her hands folded in her lap. "I'm sorry about what Mrs. Penner said, but you have to understand. After what happened with Mary's mother. . .the Penners suffered quite a bit for many years."

"Oh, I do understand." He turned the ignition and smiled at Shelley before pulling away from the curb. "She has every reason not to trust me after all the stunts I pulled."

"Oh." Shelley folded her arms and stared forward. "So what are some of these. . .stunts you pulled?"

Jeremiah smiled. "I'm afraid to tell you too many details, or you'll never speak to me again."

"Why do you think that?" Shelley asked.

Jeremiah shrugged. "You're already mad at me for leaving the church. Besides, I'm asking forgiveness while moving forward. Dwelling on the past is very unhealthy."

"And dangerous," she added. They rode in silence for a few minutes before Shelley spoke up again. "Are you planning to give up your car?"

147

Jeremiah chuckled. "Abe is trying to talk me into it, but that's the only thing I think I'll miss. It's nice to not have to rely on others for transportation. I like being able to get in my car and go wherever I want."

Shelley looked at him quizzically. "Where all do you go?"

He thought for a moment before shaking his head. "Not many places. Mostly just to the farm and around Pinecraft." He paused before giving her a brief glance. "And picking up one of my favorite people, so she doesn't have to walk home in the rain."

"I appreciate the ride, Jeremiah, but I would have been fine."

"I'm sure you would have, but it's nice to be able to offer you a ride. Did you know that I had a sports car before I decided to come back to the church?"

"Yes," Shelley said. "I remember seeing your bright-orange car."

"Abe advised me to at least swap for something less flashy before talking to the church elders." He pulled up in front of Shelley's house. "Will you be in church tomorrow?"

"Yes, of course. I never miss church."

He let out a deep sigh. "I'll be there, too. Maybe we can talk afterward."

"Maybe."

"Look, Shelley, you don't have to worry about me embarrassing you."

"It's not that I'm embarrassed. . . ."

"No, but you know what I mean. I don't want to get people thinking anything you don't want."

Shelley frowned. "I'm not sure what to say to that."

He hesitantly touched her arm. She inhaled deeply, cleared her throat, and slowly let out her breath.

"I wish I'd behaved differently in the past," he said.

"Wishing away things about the past is such a waste of time."

"Yes, I realize that. But again, you know what I'm talking about. I think things would be different between us if I had been more faithful."

"Maybe, but you don't know that for sure."

"True." He nodded toward the house. "We're being watched again."

She looked at him and smiled before getting out of the car. "Thank you for the ride, Jeremiah."

He waved and drove away. After he was out of sight of her house, he pulled over and said a prayer that Shelley would eventually care about him as much as he did her. *But I know, Lord, that it will take some time to undo the damage I've done. Guide me, and keep me on the path to do Your will.*

The next day Shelley woke up before the sun came up. Since she was the first person up, she quietly got dressed and went outside to wait until time to make the coffee.

"Get up, William," Shelley said as she stood over her brother, who refused to get out of bed. "You have to get ready for church."

He sat up and glanced around with a dazed look in his eyes. "I had a bad dream."

"Oh, sweetie, I'm sorry." Shelley sat down on the edge of his bed. "Do you want to tell me about it?"

William rubbed his eyes and shook his head. "No, it's too scary."

Seeing him like this first thing in the morning reminded Shelley of when he was a tiny boy. Her heart ached for the limitations he had in life, but he didn't seem to mind. Most of the time William was very happy, and he loved the Lord.

Shelley patted him on the arm and stood. "Get up, and get ready. I'll have breakfast waiting for you." She got to the door when she heard him softly say her name. "Yes?"

"Is Mother feeling better?"

"I think so. Let's talk about that later, maybe after church."

Gray clouds hung over the Gulf of Mexico, and the humidity was high, but it hadn't started raining yet. Shelley and William led the way to church, with their parents directly behind them. She could hear her father's voice as he spoke softly to her mother.

They arrived in time to greet some of their friends. William and her father went to one side of the church, while Shelley and her mother joined the women on the other side. Her mother's silence disturbed Shelley, but she didn't know what to say. As they sat down, she lowered her head and prayed for her mother's moods to improve.

Shelley glanced up as Jeremiah entered the church. Her breath caught in her throat, and she had to fan herself. She looked in the opposite direction, hoping her mother wouldn't notice what had gotten her in such a state.

Throughout the church service, the very fact that she was in the same room as Jeremiah hung heavy in her mind. It bothered her to feel the way she did. After all, Jeremiah obviously wasn't the ideal match for her. Everyone close to her knew that, but her heart clearly wasn't getting the message.

After church they went outside, and William didn't waste any time joining Shelley and their mother. Jeremiah stood off to the side, occasionally glancing her way but not taking a step in her direction. She knew he was keeping his distance for her sake.

In spite of the fact that Shelley, William, and their mother stood by the sidewalk waiting to walk home, their father continued chatting with some of his friends. When Mary walked out of the church, she spotted Shelley and joined them.

"It's mighty humid today," Mary said. "I thought it would be pouring by now, but the storm seems stalled over the water."

William frowned. "I don't like to walk in the rain."

Shelley forced a laugh. "He hates getting his head wet."

"It makes my hair soggy."

Mary smiled. "I know that feeling."

"Where is Abe?" Shelley's mother said. "Shouldn't he be out of the church by now?"

"He's helping Jeremiah fix one of the baseboards that came loose."

Shelley's mother looked over at her husband and shook her head but didn't say anything else. An uncomfortable silence fell among them.

Finally, Abe walked outside. Mary extended her hand toward him, and he took it as he joined the women. "It was wonderful seeing you this morning, Shelley," Mary said. "I miss talking to you every day at the restaurant."

"You have no business missing anything about your old life," Shelley's mother said. "You have a nice husband who gives you a good life."

Shelley wanted to find a rock and crawl under it, but Mary smiled at her and winked. "Maybe Abe and I can have you out to the house someday soon."

"Perhaps you can talk some sense into my daughter. She's been riding in the car with that Jeremiah boy lately. Her father and I don't like it one bit."

Mary gave Shelley's arm a squeeze. "I'll stop by the restaurant soon. We'll talk later."

After Mary left, Shelley's father joined them. "Let's go home, family. I'm starving." He gazed off into space, as he did often. Once Shelley was old enough to help out more around the house, he'd found ways to be absent—both physically and mentally.

Since her mother hadn't bothered with meals lately, the task had fallen on Shelley. She was beginning to resent the fact that too much was expected of her, yet her mother found fault with everything she did.

"I like Mary," William said. "She's nice."

"And she has a good head on her shoulders, that girl," their mother said from behind. "She knew she couldn't do any better than Abe, so she latched on to him so he could take care of her."

Shelley couldn't hold back any longer. "Mother, I don't think she married Abe just because he could take care of her. Abe and Mary fell in love."

"Maybe so. But you need to start thinking about finding a man who can take care of you, and I'm not talking about Jeremiah. He left the church once, and you never know when he'll lose interest again and take off for who knows where."

Shelley glanced over her shoulder at her father, hoping for support, but he was clearly not listening. He'd dropped back a few steps, and he appeared to be deep in thought.

Since it seemed pointless to argue with her mother, Shelley decided to keep her mouth closed. William spotted a seagull as it headed toward the beach. "Remember when we were on that picnic, and a bird just like that one tried to steal our lunch?"

"Yes," Shelley said, grateful for the diversion. "Maybe if you hadn't fed him that potato chip, he wouldn't have known we had food."

"It wasn't my fault. I was trying to keep him away from the chicken."

"A bird eating chicken." Shelley shook her head. "That's just wrong."

"I like chicken," William said. "I bet the bird does, too."

"William! Chickens are birds." The scolding tone in their mother's voice startled both William and Shelley. "They shouldn't even want to eat one of their own."

William scrunched his forehead and pondered that for half a block. Finally, he seemed to get the concept. "That's gross."

Shelley laughed. "Yes, it is definitely gross."

"Why would a bird eat another bird?"

"Maybe they're not smart enough to know it's a bird," Shelley teased. "They have bird brains."

"I'm not stupid, Shelley," William said. "I know that birds have bird brains."

Shelley tilted her head back and laughed. Before he had a chance to get his feelings hurt, she threw her arms around him and gave him a big hug. "I love you, William. You are the sweetest person I know."

He hugged her back. "Nuh-uh. You are the sweetest person I know."

"You are," Shelley countered.

"No, you are." William giggled and covered his mouth with his hand. "Mother's going to get mad if we keep this up."

Shelley turned slightly and looked at her mother before turning back. "I don't think she's even paying attention to us." Before he had a chance to look around, she nudged him and pointed. "Hey, William, look at that bird with the red wings!" She had to keep him from seeing their mother, whose cheeks were stained with fresh tears.

William went into a long, detailed discussion about the types of birds in Florida, including the fact that many of them had already left for the summer. Shelley was relieved when they arrived home.

"Wanna help me in the kitchen, William?"

He looked at their father, who seemed out of sorts. "If Father doesn't mind."

Their father shook his head before heading out the back door, while their mother retreated to her bedroom.

"Looks like it's you and me, baby brother," Shelley said as she pulled a skillet out of the cupboard.

"I am not a baby."

She grinned at him. "You'll always be my baby brother, even when you're old and gray."

William touched the top of his head. "I don't have gray hair yet. You'll get it before I do."

"Don't remind me. Would you mind handing me the butter?"

They worked together in the kitchen, with Shelley cooking while William handed her ingredients and utensils. Shelley was grateful that they got along so well. She and their older brother Paul used to have a good relationship, but when he left the church, everything had changed. Paul's wife, Tammy, was a sweet woman who would do whatever Paul wanted to do, so when he used her as an excuse for not coming back to the church, Shelley knew it was more about what Paul wanted than Tammy's lack of Mennonite upbringing. At least they went to church, although their parents didn't approve of where they attended.

After lunch was ready, Shelley sent William to let their mother know. She opened the back door, stepped out onto the patio, and called for her father. He looked up from where he'd been sitting since they'd gotten home, a sadness in his eyes like she'd never seen before.

"I'll be there in a minute."

"Shelley," William said. "Mother said she's not hungry."

She pondered what to do before turning off the stove and oven. "Let me go talk to her. Why don't you go ahead and set the table?"

Shelley tiptoed to their mother's bedroom door and knocked. There was no answer, so she slowly turned the knob and opened the door to the darkened room. She could see the silhouette of her mother sitting in a chair, back straight, head bowed.

"Mother?"

"What?" Her mother glanced up, but the room was too dark to tell if she'd been crying.

"Lunch is ready. Are you not feeling well?"

"I already told William I'm not hungry."

"You need to eat something," Shelley argued.

"Just have William bring me a plate of food when he's finished with his."

"I'd really like for the family to eat together," Shelley said. "It's Sunday, and I think it's good for all of us to be together on the Lord's day."

"We can't all be together. Paul is gone, and I'm worried you're going to run off and do something stupid."

"Mother, I'm not going to do anything stupid."

"Something is different about you lately, Shelley. I think it has something to do with Jeremiah. I keep thinking you'll decide not to come home one day, and then what?"

Shelley took a few steps closer to her mother. "Is that what's upsetting you?"

"What is happening to our family?"

"Mother, our family is fine. I'm not about to leave, and Paul lives close enough that he can be here within a few minutes if we need him."

Silence fell between them. Shelley had no idea what to say to her mother, but she didn't want to leave her alone.

"I always imagined all my children getting married some day and living nearby in Pinecraft, raising my grandchildren in the church. Now that it's not happening, I'm left to wonder what will become of the lot of us."

"When—if—I ever get married, I'll live close to you and Father. And if the Lord blesses me with children, they'll grow up in the church."

"And then there's William. Who will take care of him after your father and I are gone?"

Shelley closed the distance between herself and her mother. She reached down and took her mother's hand in hers. "You know that I will always make sure William has a home and all his needs are taken care of. The Lord doesn't want us to be anxious about the future, so please stop worrying."

"I know I'm not supposed to worry."

"We're not supposed to worry, but I think it's something we all do as humans."

"I suppose so."

Shelley took a chance and tugged at her mother, hoping she'd rise to join the rest of the family in the kitchen. She held her breath for a few seconds until her mother gave in and followed.

William had the table set, with all the food in serving bowls on the table. Their father stood at the head of the table, bent over his chair, appearing to be praying. He glanced up and looked at Shelley. "I'll say the blessing for our meal."

As he prayed, Shelley forced herself to focus on his words and not on her mother, who stood rigidly by her chair. Finally, her father sat down, waited for the rest of the family to sit, picked up a platter, put a small amount of chicken on his plate, and passed it to William.

Although Mother had been through short bouts of this bad mood throughout Shelley's life, she seemed to be getting worse. After dinner, Shelley found a way to whisper to her father and ask if they could talk. He looked at her a moment and then nodded.

"Shelley and I are going for a walk," her father said. "We'll be back shortly."

Mother gave them a quizzical look and then turned back around without saying a word. Shelley dreaded having to explain later.

Once they reached the edge of the block, Father slowed down. "What is on your mind, Shelley?"

"I'm worried about Mother. She seems to be getting worse lately."

"Ya. I agree." He shoved his hands into his pockets. "I never know what to say to her."

"I'd like to talk with the pastor about it."

"Neh. Not a good idea. Your mother would be very unhappy with that kind of attention."

"But she needs help," Shelley argued. "And we obviously can't do anything to fix whatever is wrong with her."

"We can continue to pray." He cleared his throat. "That is what I've been doing."

"So have I."

"While you're at it, pray that Paul will come back to the church. Your mother blames Tammy for his leaving, but he was always so strong-willed, I doubt Tammy has anything to do with it."

This was the most conversation Shelley could remember having with her father since becoming an adult. "Ya, I'll pray for Paul, Tammy, and the children. I would like to see Lucy and Grady more often."

"So would I." Father placed his hand on Shelley's back and gently turned her around. "We need to go back home, or your mother will worry." He smiled. "In her frame of mind, I don't want to give her anything else to worry about."

William met them at the door when they got back home. "I want dessert, and Mother says I have to wait for the rest of the family."

Father grinned. "Then let's have dessert."

"Who wants lemon cake?" Shelley asked as she made a beeline for the kitchen. "Mr. Penner sent me home with some on Friday, and I saved it for today."

"I like lemon cake," William said. "So does Mother."

"I'll have a small slice," their father said.

Shelley cut the cake into slices, including one for her mother, taking a chance that she'd have a little. She set them down in front of each family member and then carried hers to the table and sat down.

William devoured his, and her father ate his slowly. Her mother stared down at it but didn't lift her fork.

"This is very good, Mother. Mrs. Penner made several of them, and all the customers raved about it."

"I'm not hungry."

The sound of a chair crashing to the floor startled Shelley. She turned toward her father and saw that he was standing, glaring at her mother, the chair tipped over on the floor behind him. Even he looked surprised at his own outburst.

"Melba, the least you can do is take a bite. Can't you see how hard Shelley's trying to cheer you up?"

"Father—"

He held up a hand to shush her. "No, I need to say this. We love you, Melba, and it pains all of us to see you in this state. You need to feel the blessings of what you do have rather than mope around for what you think you don't have. Otherwise, you'll drive our daughter away, just like you—" He stopped himself, tightened his jaw, and glanced away, rubbing the back of his neck. "Please just stop dwelling on the negative. We have two beautiful grown children still living here."

The sound of Shelley's heart pounding equaled the impact of her father's outburst. "Mother, if you're not hungry. . ."

"I–I'll try to eat a little bit of cake," her mother whispered as she picked up her fork and stabbed at the golden yellow dessert in front of her.

Jeremiah drove Abe and Mary home. They'd invited him for Sunday lunch, which made him very happy. His parents had welcomed him back into their home, but he liked giving them some quiet time alone.

Mary made small talk from the backseat, but Jeremiah's mind was on Shelley and her family. Their sad expressions had touched his heart, and he wondered what was going on. He suspected it might have something to do with him, but he didn't want to be presumptuous and assume anything. After all, his mother had reminded him the world didn't revolve around him. The thought of that made him smile.

"You didn't hear a word I just said, did you?" Mary asked.

"Um. . ." Jeremiah glanced in his rearview mirror and caught her knowing gaze. "I'm sorry, Mary. My thoughts today are taking me somewhere else."

Mary nodded. "I thought so. Is it Shelley?"

Abe turned and looked at his wife over his shoulder. "Jeremiah might not want to share his private thoughts, Mary."

"No, that's okay. I need to be more transparent. One of the things I've learned is that I have to accept accountability to other believers." Jeremiah pondered how to form his thoughts into words before continuing. "Did you notice how sad Shelley's family seemed in church this morning?"

"Sometimes people get sad," Abe said. "I'm sure they have their reasons."

"Oh, Abe, it's not that simple," Mary said. "Yes, Jeremiah, I did notice. I think something might be wrong with Mrs. Burkholder."

"Do you think she's sick?" Jeremiah asked.

Mary shook her head, shrugged, and frowned. "I don't know. Perhaps I should talk to Shelley about it."

Abe turned around again. "That might not be such a good idea. If Shelley wants to discuss her family, she'll do it in her own time."

Jeremiah listened to his friends discuss what Mary should do. As they spoke, he became more convinced than ever that Shelley had some deep troubles that no one would ever know about unless someone who cared about her—someone she trusted—pried it out of her. And the only person he thought might be able to do that was Mary.

"No disrespect, Abe, but I think that it might help if Mary offered to pray for whatever is bothering Shelley."

Abe's expression was vague, but after a few seconds he slowly nodded. "If it is done in the correct way, it might be a good idea. Would you mind doing that, Mary?"

Again, Jeremiah looked at Mary's reflection in the mirror. She looked back at him and smiled. "I'll do what I can. Shelley has always been there for me."

Jeremiah turned onto the road leading to the Glick farm. A sense of peace washed over him as he realized how far he'd come from the life he'd transgressed to right after he got out of school. "This is a beautiful piece of property, Abe."

"I'm glad you like it. Would you ever consider having your own farm someday?"

"That would be nice, but property is very expensive these days. I'm not sure if or when I'll ever be able to afford to have my own place."

"Pray about it," Abe advised. "You might discover an opportunity that you never thought possible."

Mary let out a chuckle. "Come on, Abe, why don't you tell Jeremiah what we've been discussing?"

"Maybe later."

Jeremiah pulled to a stop in front of the old farmhouse, put the car in PARK, and turned toward Abe. "What is Mary talking about?"

Mary got out of the car and waited for the men. They started walking toward the house when she turned to face them. "You two go talk while I get lunch on the table. It'll be about half an hour."

Abe grinned at his wife then turned to face Jeremiah. "My wife is a wise woman, and she doesn't believe in waiting for things."

Jeremiah ran his fingers through his hair. "Both of you are talking in riddles. Since you've decided to let me in on this one, let's talk now. I'm with Mary on not liking to wait."

Chapter 5

They walked past the barn toward a field that had obviously not been worked in years. Jeremiah looked out over the flat terrain before turning to face Abe, who shielded his eyes. "What do you think about all that land?"

"It looks good," Jeremiah replied. "Why? Are you thinking about planting some crops on it?"

"Been thinking about it."

"Any idea what you want to plant?"

Abe shook his head, removed his hand from his face, and looked Jeremiah directly in the eye. "It's all up to you."

"Me?" Now Abe was back to talking in riddles, and Jeremiah had no idea how to figure out this one.

"Ya, I'd like to sell it to you."

Jeremiah let out a nervous laugh. "If I had two spare nickels to rub together, I'd consider trying to find a way to buy it, but I can't afford to right now—at least not until my debt is paid off."

"This land has been sitting here for years. It's a shame to let it go to waste. Mary and I have been talking about a way for you to buy it, and she actually came up with a good idea. I'll put you to work on it and let you have one of the men who helped remove the barn to work for you. Whatever crops you plant will be yours, but the land will continue to be mine. As you turn a profit, you can pay me for working it. You should do well with the hundred acres I want to sell you."

"A hundred acres?"

Abe offered a clipped nod. "Ya. That's what we have here."

"I appreciate it, Abe, but that's way too generous."

Abe shrugged. "Not really. That land is just sitting there doing nothing. If you work it, once the harvest comes in I won't have to pay your salary since you'll be making money off the crops. You will also pay the man who helps you."

"But before the crops come in, I'll have to work another job."

"Ya, you'll continue to work for me. I'm sure I'll have plenty for you to do around here, but when you're finished for the day, you'll go over and tend your own crops." He gave Jeremiah a serious look. "You will have to work very long hours, but since you've been with me, I can tell you are able to do that."

Jeremiah looked back over the land, this time from a different perspective. All that land could be his if he said yes. It sure was a nice proposition.

"When do you want an answer?"

Abe gave him a puzzled look. "Why do you ask that?"

"I should probably consider it," Jeremiah said.

"What is there to consider? You want land, and I'm offering you a good deal on a hundred fertile acres that I can't use. You will be able to repay your debt much more quickly with your own crops."

Indeed. Jeremiah had become so conditioned to look for the other person's ulterior motive, he'd been afraid to give Abe a quick decision.

He pondered the pros and cons of taking Abe up on his offer. Mary hollered that lunch was ready, and Abe let her know they'd be right there.

Abe gestured toward the house. "Let's go eat. Mary always puts a lot of work into cooking, and I don't want to act like I don't appreciate her."

"Good move." Jeremiah fell into step beside Abe, and they walked in silence for about a hundred yards. Before they reached the house, Jeremiah had made up his mind. "I'll do it. I mean, if you are serious about wanting to do this deal for the land, I'd like to take you up on it."

Abe leveled him with a serious glare. "I am always serious about any offer I make." Then he relaxed.

"Yes, I know that, and I'm serious, too. This is probably the best opportunity I'll ever have, and it's definitely something I want to do."

"Good. I'm glad you want to have your own crops. I always thought it was such a waste not to do something with that land. Some commercial developers have offered me more money than I'd ever need in my lifetime, but I thought the land could be put to much better use than what they were proposing." He shook his head. "Converting farmland so close to my home could turn out to be a disaster."

"We'll be neighbors for life," Jeremiah pointed out.

"Ya, that is true."

If Jeremiah had ever doubted his decision to come back to the church he'd so abruptly left years ago, that was erased by Abe's simple statement. "Thank you, Abe. I'll do everything I can not to let you down."

"I'm not worried about that. I have faith that you'll find the right crop to work."

Jeremiah noticed the glance between Abe and Mary and then the twinkle in her eye when she realized he'd taken them up on their offer. A broad smile covered her lips as she gestured toward the table. "Jeremiah, why don't you say the blessing today?"

After the "amen," Mary handed Jeremiah the platter of sliced ham. He piled his plate with a couple of slices, a heaping spoon of scalloped potatoes, green beans, and fresh tomatoes. Abe spoke very little, except to tell Jeremiah some of the crops he'd considered for the property.

"But it's ultimately up to you," he added. "I don't want to interfere in your business decisions."

Jeremiah blotted his mouth with the cloth napkin and placed it back on his lap. "I like the idea of lemons, tomatoes, and peppers."

"We know those will do well. After you establish your crops, you can experiment with different varieties and perhaps add new plants as you get comfortable," Abe said. He turned to Mary. "What is for dessert?"

"In honor of our celebration, I made two desserts—coconut cake and peanut butter pie from my grandmother's recipe."

"I would like some of both," Abe said. "How about you, Jeremiah?"

Still feeling as though he was floating from Abe's offer, he nodded as he patted his belly. "I might regret it later, but that sounds good. I'd hate to have to decide between those two options."

"Good!" Mary hopped up from the table to cut the pie and cake. She came back with dinner-size plates for the men, and then she went back to the counter to cut herself a small slice of pie.

"This is excellent, Mary," Jeremiah said after taking a bite of each dessert. "Your grandmother taught you well."

Mary blushed and lowered her head. Jeremiah glanced over at Abe, who smiled at his wife. The love between them was powerful and evident. Jeremiah sent up a silent prayer that he'd find a life partner who was as perfect for him as Abe and Mary were for each other. He wanted that person to be Shelley, but only if she was the one the Lord had picked out for him.

After they finished eating, Jeremiah watched Abe jump into action helping Mary. His own father had never lifted a finger around the house, but he could see the advantages of pitching in. Mary clearly appreciated Abe's help, and it gave them more opportunities to interact. Jeremiah filed that in his memory bank for future use. Then he helped as much as he knew how to.

After everything was put away, Mary said she was tired and needed to lie down for a little while. Abe asked him to join him for a walk.

Once he and Abe were far enough away from the house that Jeremiah didn't have to worry about Mary hearing them, he asked, "Is Mary okay? I don't remember her getting tired in the middle of the day before."

Abe chuckled. "Ya, she's doing just fine for a woman who is going to have a baby in about six months."

Jeremiah's eyebrows shot up. "She is? You and Mary are going to be parents soon?" His heart pounded as hard as it would have if he'd been the father. "That's great! I'm happy for you!"

"We are happy, too."

"Have you told Mary's grandparents yet?"

"Neh, so if you don't mind, I'd like for you to keep that bit of information to yourself. We've been asking them to come out to see us, but her grandfather hasn't been able to get away from the restaurant since they hired that new girl, and the late-shift manager is on vacation." Abe chuckled. "He's worried that some of the people will hurt Jocelyn's feelings about the way she looks and acts."

"Jocelyn is okay," Jeremiah said. "And I think she can handle anything people say to her."

"That is what Mary told him, but he isn't ready to leave her alone yet."

"So you and Mary will have to go to town to tell them the news," Jeremiah said.

"Ya. We are going there on Wednesday."

Jeremiah looked over toward the land that would soon be his, stretched his arms out, and sucked in a deep breath. This was turning out to be a wonderful day—full of delicious food and the best news he'd heard in ages.

Although Jeremiah could have hung around all day staring at the property, he didn't want to overstay his welcome, so he thanked Abe, asked him to let Mary know how much he appreciated all the fabulous food, and headed back to his parents' house in town. As he drove, he thought about having his own land and even building a house to live in with his future wife and children. The image brought a smile to his face like nothing else ever could have—not even his hot-orange sports car that he'd had such a hard time giving up.

<hr />

Mr. Penner had asked Shelley to stick around later on Wednesday, so he could visit with Mary and Abe when they stopped by his house. The woman who worked as the late-shift manager was visiting family in Ohio, and he didn't want to leave Jocelyn in charge yet.

"Mind if I eat first before we get slammed?" Jocelyn asked.

"Sure, that's fine. I'm not all that hungry anyway." Shelley hadn't seen Jeremiah in several days. She knew he'd gone over to the Glick farm and had lunch with Abe and Mary on Sunday, so she'd planned to chat with Mary about it. But Mary hadn't come by the restaurant lately, which Shelley thought was odd.

Jocelyn leaned over and waved her hand in front of Shelley's face. "You okay?"

Shelley startled. "Um. . .ya, I'm just fine."

"You seem out of sorts lately. Anything you wanna talk about?"

"Neh. I have a lot on my mind lately."

"I can imagine." Jocelyn started walking toward the kitchen to get her meal. She stopped and turned back to Shelley. "If you ever want to unload, I'm a good listener."

"Thanks, Jocelyn."

Shelley doubted Jocelyn would ever understand anything about her life—from being Mennonite to having a mother who was falling deeper into depression and a brother who'd never be completely independent. Sometimes her life felt weighty and more than she could bear until she prayed and allowed the Lord to remind her through scripture that there was more to life than what she had on earth.

The dining room was slow, which allowed both Jocelyn and Shelley to eat a little something before the crowd arrived. Shelley had just served the customers in the corner booth when she glanced up and saw Jeremiah walking toward her. She tried to be nonchalant when she greeted him, but the instant she opened her mouth, merely a squeak came out.

"Mind if I sit over there?" he asked, pointing to one of the empty tables in the dining room.

"That is fine," Shelley replied, her voice softer than usual. "I'll be right with you as soon as I bring these orders back to the kitchen."

As soon as she got out of Jeremiah's line of vision, Shelley stopped, took a deep breath, and tried to regain her composure. After not seeing him for a while, she'd managed to put him out of her mind—at least, she thought she had.

"Want me to take over?" Jocelyn said as she breezed by.

"Whatever for?"

Jocelyn offered an understanding grin. "Atta girl. Keep that attitude, and you'll be able to fool him into thinking you don't care. Guys like girls who play hard to get."

"I'm not—" Shelley stopped herself to keep from defending herself, which would make it seem as though she was playing a game with Jeremiah. Well she wasn't, was she? She paused for a moment to think about it. No, she definitely wasn't playing any sort of game. She pushed that thought from her mind and plowed ahead.

After she felt that she could hold a decent conversation with Jeremiah, Shelley went back out to take his order. He asked for a piece of pie and some milk.

"Is that all?" she asked.

"Yes, I had dinner. I just wanted to stop by and see you."

Shelley allowed a smile to tweak her lips. "You don't have to order dessert if you're not hungry."

"I can always make room for some of Mrs. Penner's delicious pie."

"Okay, I'll bring it right out." Shelley turned and started toward the kitchen when she heard the jingle at the door. She turned around and saw Mr. and Mrs. Penner walking in, followed by Abe and Mary—all of them wearing broader grins than she'd ever seen on any of them. She glanced over her shoulder and spotted Jeremiah with the same expression. They were all definitely on to something, and she felt left out.

As Shelley placed a slice of pie on the plate and poured Jeremiah a glass of milk, she mentally lectured herself to act normal. She squared her shoulders and headed out with Jeremiah's order in both hands.

He was still grinning as she approached his table. Mary, Abe, and the Penners stood on the other side of the restaurant chatting with one of the customers.

"Here you go, Jeremiah. Will there be anything else?"

Jeremiah shook his head and gestured toward the other side of the booth. "Join me?"

Shelley blinked. "I can't do that. I'm working."

"You don't look too busy to me."

She was about to argue with him, but Mr. Penner's voice stopped her. "Go ahead and sit down, Shelley. You've worked hard all day. You've earned it."

Not one to argue with the boss, Shelley sat down across from Jeremiah, awkwardly fidgeting with the edges of her apron. She glanced at him but quickly looked down at the table.

"I wanted to share the good news with you," Jeremiah said.

Shelley braced herself. Often other people's good news was her bad news, like when Peter had told her he was engaged to another woman, so it could have been anything, including courting someone else. The notion of that bothered her more than she wanted it to.

"Do you want to hear it or not?" he asked, his smile fading as a look of concern covered his face.

She looked up at him and nodded. "Yes, of course I'd like to hear your good news, Jeremiah. Why wouldn't I?"

"I don't know. You acted sort of strange there for a moment." He put down his fork, rubbed his hands together, cast a brief glance over toward the Penners, and then faced her again. "I am about to be a landowner."

"A landowner?"

He nodded. "Abe and I have worked out a deal for me to purchase some of the land he isn't farming. I'll continue to work for him until we get everything in place."

"That's nice. I mean, you'll be able to grow crops, right?"

"Yes, and I'll continue to work closely with Abe."

"I'm very happy for you."

Shelley started to stand, but Jeremiah placed his hand on her wrist and tilted his head toward the table. "Please stay. I'm happy, and I want to tell you all about it."

Since Mr. Penner had ordered her to sit down, she decided to remain and listen to Jeremiah's chatter about what he wanted to do with the farmland. She couldn't help but get caught up in his excitement.

"I'll start out with more citrus, and since Abe has oranges and grapefruit, I'm planting lemon and lime trees. It'll take a few years before they produce enough, so I'll add tomatoes, peppers, and whatever else I can get to grow."

"Do you know how to do all that?" Shelley asked. "After all, you haven't been working on the farm all that long."

"I know the basics, and I'm still learning. But like I said, I'll work closely with Abe. He told me about a county extension course that I can take to learn some of the science of farming."

Jeremiah had come a long way in a very short time. Shelley hoped he was as sincere as he sounded.

"And as soon as I can, I plan to start building a house on the land."

She was uncomfortable as she felt his gaze lingering on her. "A house is nice."

"I want a house big enough for a family."

Shelley's heart twitched. "Yes, of course."

"Shelley? Look at me."

She slowly widened her eyes to look directly at Jeremiah, but she didn't know what to say. He didn't speak either. Their gazes locked for several seconds before Mr. Penner joined them.

"So, Shelley," the older man said. "What do you think about Jeremiah having his own farm?"

She welcomed the diversion. "I think it's wonderful. He'll be a very good farmer—I'm sure."

Mr. Penner chuckled. "I obviously interrupted at the wrong time. I'll leave now."

Shelley jumped up from the table. "Oh no. I need to go help prepare the dining room for tomorrow."

Mr. Penner glanced over his shoulder. "Ya, that's a good idea." He leaned toward Shelley and lowered his voice. "Jocelyn is still a bit slow, but she seems to be working out just fine. Now that you've worked with her for a while, how do you like her?"

Shelley considered how friendly Jocelyn had been with her and how much the customers seemed to like her. "I like her."

"Good. She's not much past twenty, and she still has a lot to learn." Mr. Penner straightened up and tugged at his suspenders. "My decision to hire her wasn't a bad one like some people thought it might be."

As Shelley took off toward the kitchen to get a couple of rags and cleaner for the tables, she heard Mr. Penner and Jeremiah exchange a few more comments. When she heard the jingle at the front door, she thought they'd all left. However, she came back out and spotted Jeremiah still sitting at the booth.

"I thought you left," she said as she wiped his table clean.

"No, I'm sticking around to take you home after you close the restaurant."

"You don't need to do that," she argued. "I can walk home."

"I know I don't need to do that, but I want to. It's important to me."

Shelley accepted the fact that Jeremiah wouldn't take no for an answer, so she finished cleaning up as quickly as she could. Jocelyn had gotten better about knowing what to do, so Shelley didn't have to give her as much instruction.

She removed her apron, placed all the rags and towels in the laundry bin, and walked out to the dining room. Jeremiah wasn't there.

"Looks like you got ditched," Jocelyn said.

"That's fine. I like walking home. It gives me time to think."

Jocelyn leaned back, narrowed her eyes, and shook her head. "If I didn't know you, I'd think you were lying through your teeth."

"Lying through my teeth?"

"Yeah, that's like lying, only worse."

Shelley couldn't imagine a lie worse than a regular lie, and she didn't see how doing it through her teeth would change it. "I am not lying."

"I know you're not. You're the real deal." Jocelyn winked and playfully laughed. "I need to get outside since my car is in the shop. My ride will be here any minute."

"Would you like me to wait with you?" Shelley asked.

"No, you go on ahead. I'll be just fine."

The second they stepped outside, Shelley spotted Jeremiah standing over by his car talking to one of his old friends. She felt awkward and shy, and she wasn't about to go up to him while he was with that stranger.

She hesitated for a split second and then stepped down off the curb, being careful not to turn around and look at Jeremiah. She'd gone about ten feet when she heard Jeremiah call out to her. She stopped and turned around.

"Hey, Shelley, hold on a sec. Remember? I'm taking you home."

"I can walk."

"No, I'm taking you home." He said something to his friend that she couldn't hear and then jogged over to her. "That's one of the nicest guys I've ever met. In fact, he's the one who advised me to return to my roots."

"I thought you did that of your own accord."

"I did." Jeremiah waved to the man. "But Kyle was the first person I told I wasn't happy in that lifestyle."

"Did he take offense?"

"No, I don't think so. He said he thought people would accept me if they were sure I was sincere."

He opened the passenger door, and she got in. Shelley stared after Jeremiah's friend until he took off in his truck.

After Jeremiah got into the driver's seat, Shelley asked, "What was your friend Kyle doing over here in Pinecraft?"

"He was making a delivery to one of the businesses."

As they waited at a traffic light, Shelley decided to get Jeremiah talking about the farm, since that seemed to make him so happy. "When will you actually have your own land?"

"Abe is working something up, so we can eventually move the property to my name. Even before that, I'll work it like it belongs to me. Once I have it paid off from the money I get from the crops, it will be all mine." He cleared his throat. "Well, mine and my family's."

"How will you do that while still working for Abe?"

Jeremiah rubbed the back of his neck. "It'll be a lot of hard work, but like Abe said, I can do it this way, wait until I have enough money saved, or never have my own land."

"What made Abe think you'd even want to do this?"

"We used to talk about it when we were kids. Even though he's a year younger, I always looked up to him because he was the smartest and most focused kid I ever knew."

"I guess I never really paid that much attention to Abe," Shelley said. "I was too busy at home."

Jeremiah squinted as he pointed toward Shelley's house. "Isn't that your brother out on the front lawn?"

Shelley turned and looked. "Yes, it's William. What is he doing?"

"I can't tell. He has his face on his knees. Looks like he might be sick or something."

As soon as Jeremiah pulled up in front of Shelley's house and stopped the car, Shelley hopped out and ran over to her brother. Jeremiah remained in the car for a couple of minutes, but William wasn't budging. He turned off the engine, got out of the car, and walked over toward Shelley and William.

"Need any help?"

Shelley was confused. "He's sobbing, but he won't tell me what's wrong."

"Let me see what I can do." Jeremiah drew closer and squatted down beside William. "Hey, buddy, what's the matter?"

William's sobbing grew softer, but he still didn't look up. Shelley felt helpless and had no idea what she should do.

Jeremiah pointed toward the house. "Maybe you can go inside and see if something is going on in there."

"I don't want to leave William alone."

"You're not," Jeremiah reminded her. "I'm right here. I won't leave until I know everything is okay."

Shelley went through the motions of walking into the house, calling out her mother's name, and getting no answer. This had happened before, but in the past William had been either in his room or out in the backyard.

Her parents' bedroom door was closed, so she knocked. There was no answer. She slowly opened the door and saw the outline of her mother under the blanket on the bed.

"Mother, are you not feeling well?"

Her mother made a muffled sound and moved a leg. Shelley walked a little closer until she could touch her mother.

"What's going on, Mother?"

Her mother moaned and then threw the blanket away from her face. "Go away. I'm not feeling well."

"Have you spoken to William?"

"Neh. He opened the door, but I told him I needed to rest."

"Where's Father?"

"He hasn't come home from work yet." Her mother pulled the blanket back over her head. "Why don't you cook something for you and William?"

"All right." Shelley tiptoed out of the bedroom and went back out to the front yard. Her mother had seemed sad for years, but lately she'd gotten worse, and nothing Shelley did helped.

When she joined Jeremiah and William outside, they were sitting on the grass talking. Jeremiah glanced up and motioned her over. "William was just telling me that your mother is very sick. He's afraid she's going to die like your grandmother did when she wasn't able to get out of bed."

Shelley looked at Jeremiah but couldn't think of anything to say. She just stood there, silently making eye contact with him for what seemed like eternity until Jeremiah got up, brushed off the back of his trousers, and pulled William to his feet.

"Come on, buddy," Jeremiah said. "Let's go inside and help Shelley cook you some supper."

Chapter 6

Jeremiah saw that Shelley was just going through the motions of cooking, so he did everything he could think of to engage William in the process. William's sweet nature and innate desire to please others made the task not so difficult.

Once they had everything in the oven and cooking on the stovetop, Shelley went back to check on her mother. That left Jeremiah in the kitchen alone with William.

"Is Mother going to die?" William asked.

Not sure what was wrong with Mrs. Burkholder, Jeremiah hesitated before answering. He finally spoke some carefully chosen words. "Only the Lord knows the answer to that, William, but I don't think so. I just think something is making your mother very sad."

"But she can't get out of bed. When my grandmother was like that, she died."

"Do you ever feel sad?" Jeremiah asked.

William scrunched his face as he thought about it and then nodded. "Ya, sometimes."

"When you feel sad, do you ever feel like being alone?"

"One time I did." William paused before continuing. "I remember when my big brother, Paul, moved out and stopped coming to see me. That made me very sad, and I wanted to sleep all the time."

"I think that's how your mother feels right now—like sleeping all the time because she's sad."

"Oh." William folded his arms, leaned against the cabinet, and frowned. "Is she still sad about Paul?"

"I don't know, but that could be part of it. As people get older and their children grow up, things change. Some parents don't know how to react to those changes."

William puffed out his chest. "I'm growing up."

Jeremiah smiled at him. "Yes you are, and although your parents are proud of you, I'm sure they're sad they don't have a little boy anymore."

A look of understanding replaced William's worried expression. "Now I get it. Mother feels like she doesn't have a child to take care of."

Before Jeremiah could say anything, Shelley reappeared. "I think Mother is doing better. She asked me to bring something to eat when it's ready."

Jeremiah pulled her to the side as William stirred the contents of one of the pots. "Where is your father?"

"He's been working evenings lately. The store is having to stay open later, and they rotate who works the late shift every six weeks."

"I think that might be part of the problem," Jeremiah said. "Not only is her youngest child about to be an adult who still needs help, but also her evening routine has been drastically changed." He glanced up at the stove. "Look at how well your brother is doing. He's such a kind person, and he doesn't mind pitching in when he knows what is needed."

Jeremiah's thoughtfulness tugged at Shelley's heart. His past transgressions still lingered in her mind, but his current actions pushed them further back.

"I'm starving," William said. "I think supper is ready."

"Then let's eat," Jeremiah said.

Shelley cast a teasing glance his way. "I thought you already ate."

"I've worked up an appetite." He handed her a serving spoon. "For scooping the beans," he explained.

Shelley laughed, planted her hands on her hips, and gave them a playful stern expression. "Who is in charge here?"

Jeremiah lifted his hands in surrender. "You definitely are."

Once again she laughed. "Good answer."

"I would never take that away from you."

William had the plates out of the cupboard and on the table. He headed back to the drawer and pulled out some flatware while Shelley handed Jeremiah some serving bowls for the food. The scenario felt right to Shelley—almost as though God had set them up as a small family. Her gaze met Jeremiah's, and she shuddered because she thought he might be feeling it, too.

"Here is a plate for Mother," William said. "Do you think I should cut her meat for her?"

Shelley was about to say no, that she'd do it, but Jeremiah spoke up. "That would be very nice, William. Thank you." He turned to Shelley and grinned.

After the food was ready for Mother, Shelley carried it to the bedroom, where her mother sat up in bed. Shelley pulled the blinds open to let in some of the early-evening light without making it too bright in the room.

"Do you want iced tea or lemonade?" Shelley asked.

"Some buttermilk would be good."

That was odd. Her father always drank buttermilk, but her mother rarely did. "Okay, I'll go get it. Do you need anything else while I'm in the kitchen?"

To Shelley's surprise, her mother smiled back at her. "No thank you. This looks and smells very good."

After she delivered the buttermilk to her mother, she joined the men in the kitchen. "Will you please say the blessing, Jeremiah?"

Jeremiah's forehead crinkled. "I already asked William to, if you don't mind."

"Of course I don't mind." Shelley was pleased that Jeremiah had taken that step of action. Her parents had never asked William to say the family blessing, which she suspected was because he was the youngest person in the family. Jeremiah was giving William more responsibility, and she could tell that made William happy.

After the very sweet, short, but heartfelt prayer, they passed the food around the table. William took larger portions than usual, but he was obviously hungry since they were eating an hour later than normal.

"The food was delicious, Shelley."

Shelley's attention shot up to the voice behind her. When she turned around, she saw her mother standing there, half-smiling, holding an empty plate.

"Mother, are you feeling better?"

Her mother closed her eyes and nodded. "Much better, now that I know my family cares enough about me to bring me food."

Shelley was surprised that her mother spoke so freely in front of Jeremiah.

"Mrs. Burkholder, why don't you join us?" Jeremiah said.

Shelley's mother blinked as though having to refocus. Her smile faded for a few seconds, but she managed to recover. "I am not so sure that's a good idea."

"Please," William begged. "It's just not the same when you and Father aren't here."

Shelley held her breath as her mother looked first at William then at Jeremiah. When her gaze settled on Shelley, she finally nodded. "I suppose I could join you for dessert." She sat down. "There is dessert, isn't there?"

"There's always dessert," Shelley said as she stood to get the banana cream pie out of the refrigerator.

"Just a small piece for me, please," her mother said.

"I want a big piece," William added.

Jeremiah lifted a hand. "Make that a big piece for me, too, and I'll do the dishes."

"All that hard work must be giving you an appetite," Shelley said as she sliced the pie and placed the servings on the dessert dishes. "Why don't you tell Mother about your plans?"

Jeremiah lowered his head and appeared bashful, something Shelley hadn't expected. She wondered if she'd messed up by talking about something he didn't want to discuss with anyone else yet. She was about to apologize when he started talking.

"I've been working on Abe's farm for the past few months. He knows I don't have enough money to buy my own farm yet, but it's something I've decided I want to do. So he offered to sell me a piece of his land that he hasn't been farming."

"If you don't have the money, how can you buy Abe's land?" her mother asked.

"Mother. . ." Shelley said, wishing she hadn't brought it up.

"That's okay, Shelley. I don't mind telling her," Jeremiah said as he lifted his hand in acceptance. "That's an excellent question." He turned back to her mother. "Abe is allowing me to go ahead and plant some crops after I finish working for him. When the crops are ready to harvest and sell, I'll pay him back with the profits."

"That's all good, Jeremiah, but after your past decisions, I'm surprised Abe has that much confidence in you. I certainly don't."

Once again, Shelley held her breath. She dared a brief glimpse in Jeremiah's direction, but he didn't look upset. He tightened his lips but nodded. "I understand why you feel that way. I've made more than my share of mistakes, so I fully expect to be scrutinized."

"At least you know that."

"Oh, I do. And I won't let Abe down. He has been very good to me."

Shelley carried William's and Jeremiah's pie to them first and then went back to get hers and her mother's. As they ate their pie, William told their mother all about how he'd helped cook supper.

⁓

Three weeks later, Jeremiah stood in front of the land he'd plowed with the help of Jonathan Polk's son, Charles, who was right next to him. They both remained silent for several minutes.

The clearing and plowing had been much more difficult than Jeremiah had expected, but now that it was done, he felt better than he had in years. He'd accomplished something without anyone standing over him. In fact, he'd been the one giving direction to a very kind person who asked quite a few questions about the Mennonite church.

Jeremiah was pleased to have someone coming to him for answers, since he was often the one asking the questions. Charles said he liked the simple life of the Mennonite people, and he was considering adopting it. Jeremiah said that was a decision only he could make, and he needed to pray about it. Charles said he had.

The land was mostly flat with a few very small hills and some trees in a cluster near where Jeremiah thought would be a good place to build a house. He envisioned a family home with a grassy front yard and a backyard where the children would run around, chase each other, and play ball.

Charles broke the silence. "Not bad for a couple of guys and some borrowed equipment, huh?"

"We got a lot done, with the Lord's help," Jeremiah said.

"Yes we did." Charles turned to him and smiled. "And it feels mighty good."

"Thank you for helping me."

Silence fell between them once again. Jeremiah knew Charles had a huge decision ahead of him, so he gave his friend a chance to think without interruption.

"Do you think I'll be accepted since I wasn't raised in the church?"

Jeremiah nodded. "After what I did and being welcomed back, I think there's a very good chance. . .that is, if you're sincere. How do your parents feel about it?"

Charles sighed. "My dad is totally okay with it. In fact, if it weren't for my mom, I suspect he'd want to do it, too."

"Your mother doesn't approve?"

"It's not that she doesn't approve. She just isn't willing to make the change herself, so my dad can't very well do it alone."

"At least you have your family's support," Jeremiah said. "And it's something you need to pray about."

"I'd appreciate it if you'd pray for me, too," Charles said. "It's a huge decision that keeps me awake at night."

"The Lord doesn't want you to stay up all night worrying."

Charles placed his hand on Jeremiah's shoulder and bowed his head. Jeremiah had no doubt his friend was sincere.

⤳

"What's got you all tight-jawed and moody?" Jocelyn asked as they cleared away a large table together.

"All what?" Half the time Jocelyn said things that made no sense to Shelley.

One corner of Jocelyn's lip slanted upward in a half grin. "Sorry. Why are you so quiet? Did I say something that bugged you?"

Shelley shook herself. "No. I've just had a lot on my mind lately."

"Is your mom feeling any better? I overheard someone saying she's been sick."

"She seems to be doing a little better, now that my father has switched back to an earlier shift at work. She likes it when we're all home at night."

Jocelyn made a snorting sound. "I wouldn't know what that was like. My parents split before I could walk."

"That must have been awful," Shelley said.

"Not really. I didn't know any better since I don't remember a time when they were together."

Shelley wasn't sure what to say to that, so she finished wiping her side of the table without talking. Jocelyn was on the other side watching her.

"You confuse me," Jocelyn said.

"I do? What do you find confusing?"

"Everything. You never lose your temper, but I know you get upset. When I mess up, you never let me have it. When I first met you, I thought you didn't know any better, but now I know how smart and aware you are. You could level me out if you really wanted to."

Shelley shrugged. "What would be the point?"

"I don't know. But most people would tell me off or at least get mad. Do you ever get angry?"

"Of course I do," Shelley replied. "I'm human."

"Well, that's a relief."

Shelley glanced up in surprise and noticed the teasing expression on Jocelyn's face. She smiled back at her coworker. "You're funny."

Jocelyn giggled. "I'm glad you think so. Let's get this place cleaned up so you can get outta here."

Shelley appreciated Jocelyn's understanding and respect for her time. After she filled the last of the saltshakers, she hung up her apron, said good-bye to the other people in the restaurant, and took off for home.

She stepped off the curb, half expecting Jeremiah to pull up and offer her a ride, but he didn't. He hadn't done that in several weeks. The only times she'd seen him were when he came into the restaurant when he was picking up something in town to take back to the farm and after church on Sundays. But even then, he was only civil toward her and offered her a few brief comments.

"I should be glad about that," she mumbled to herself as she strode home. Jeremiah had intruded on her heart, and with all the worries at home, she didn't need something else to think about. She was better off without the feelings he evoked when he was around.

By the time Shelley arrived home, she'd talked herself into thinking she was happiest without the complications of having Jeremiah in her life and acting like he was in love with her. Love? Where had that word come from?

"Shelley, is that you?" Her mother's voice pulled her from her thoughts.

"Yes, Mother. I'll be right there. Let me put my bag and shoes away first."

Shelley went to her room, hung her tote on the peg, took off her shoes, and put on some sandals as she mentally unwound from her day. Then she joined Mother in the kitchen.

"What can I do to help you?"

She was greeted with a smile. "Nothing. Have a seat, and I'll join you. Want some tea?"

Shelley slowly nodded. "Ya, that would be very nice. Want me to fix it?"

"Neh, I have the tea in the pot, and I'm just waiting for the water to boil." She carried a couple of cups to the table and set one in front of Shelley and placed one where she normally sat.

Shelley watched her mother move around the kitchen, light on her feet, as though she didn't have a care—completely opposite from her behavior a month ago. Several things had helped, including her father's shift change, William's increased doting, and being nurtured by a small group of women from the church. They'd heard about her depression, so they'd made it their mission to check on her daily.

A few minutes later, Shelley and her mother sat adjacent to each other at the kitchen table, blowing on their tea in silence. It felt nice knowing that things were going well—at least for now.

"How was your day?" her mother finally asked.

"It was good. Normal. Nothing happened."

Her mother smiled and lifted her cup to her lips, taking a sip. "Sounds peaceful."

"How about you? Did you have a good day?"

"Ya. The women from church checked on me this morning, but they didn't stay long." Mother's smile faded, and she sighed.

Shelley touched her mother's arm. "Is something wrong?"

"I'm not sure. I'm grateful to have your father home nights, and William seems happy. Paul has been stopping by whenever he gets a chance, and he's even offering to bring the children by more often." Her mother licked her lips and slowly raised her gaze. "The only thing I have left to worry about is you, Shelley."

"Me? Why are you worried about me?"

"I'm concerned about you and Jeremiah."

Shelley leaned back and shook her head. "I haven't seen much of Jeremiah lately. He's been working very hard on the land he's getting from Abe, so he doesn't have much time for anything else."

"I've heard he's doing that so he can take a wife and have a family."

"Maybe," Shelley said slowly. "But that's not my concern."

Her mother tilted her head, raised her eyebrows, and fixed her focus on Shelley. "Are you sure it is not your concern?"

"Why would it be?"

"According to one of the women from church, Jeremiah has his sights set on making you his wife."

"Something so serious requires more than Jeremiah's sights." Shelley tried to keep a light tone to her voice, but the impact of her mother's words and concern hit her hard. "And I haven't given it a thought."

"I wondered about that. Sometimes you can be so secretive I don't know what you're thinking or even doing."

"I would never do anything wrong, Mother. I thought you knew that about me."

"You are a good girl, Shelley, but I know what it's like to be a young woman. It might have been a long time ago, but sometimes the years between then and now seem so short."

"You and Father have been together a long time," Shelley observed.

"Ya, we have." An uncommon look of contentment softened her mother's features.

Shelley had never had a discussion about her parents' relationship with her mother, but now seemed like a good time to start. "Were you always in love with Father, or did you ever doubt your feelings for him?"

"Never. . . Well, maybe when we were very young, and he teased me unmercifully—I thought he was a pest. But after we became adults, he made his intentions very obvious, and I was smitten."

That sounded similar to how Jeremiah had been with Shelley, with the exception of when Jeremiah abandoned his faith. "Father was a pest?"

Her mother laughed out loud. "That is an understatement. He found ways to annoy me when we were in our early teens." She pursed her lips and blushed.

"I'd love to hear about this."

"For starters, he hid things and then asked me if I'd seen them. Once when we had a very big homework assignment, our teacher told us to put it on our desk before we went to lunch. When we came back, mine was gone. I panicked, but one look at your father let me know he was guilty."

"I remember Jeremiah doing something like that to me," Shelley blurted before thinking. The look on her mother's face made her shrink back. "But I'm sure it was different."

"Another thing your father did was jump out from behind things and frighten me."

Shelley had never seen that playful, mischievous side of her father. All she'd ever known was the stern, serious man who came home every night for supper and ate in near silence.

"But when we became old enough to consider courting, he let me know he'd acted out because he didn't know what else to do about his feelings for me." Shelley's mother smiled shyly. "And I admitted that I was flattered. After that, we knew we would eventually get married." She paused and looked Shelley in the eye. "There was never any doubt that we both loved the Lord because neither of us ever walked away and left our faith behind."

She got up and carried the teapot to the counter by the sink, ending the conversation. Shelley brought the two teacups and offered to do the dishes.

"I'll take care of this, Shelley. You've worked so hard lately. Why don't you go to your room and rest for a few minutes?"

As Shelley left the kitchen, she thought about her discussion with her mother. This had been one of the longest they'd had in a while, and she was grateful for the time. But it obviously was done for a purpose. A warning. Mother's final comment about never leaving faith behind had been directed at Jeremiah.

She closed her bedroom door, kicked off her shoes, and lay down on the lightweight summer quilt her grandmother had made. As she stared up at the ceiling, her conversation with her mother played through her mind.

Shelley knew that her parents had married young—much younger than she was now at the age of twenty-five. Most of the Mennonite couples she knew did. Their children often waited a little longer, though, so Shelley wasn't alone. The big difference between Shelley and some of the other single people her age was that she would have the responsibility of taking care of William for the rest of his life after her parents could no longer care for him, while the others could go into a marriage alone.

Jeremiah was the only man Shelley's age who actively engaged William in conversation. William clearly liked Jeremiah, but Shelley could tell when he'd heard something negative from their parents because he would always add a disparaging comment after anything positive he'd said about Jeremiah.

After a half hour of rest, Shelley got up, repinned her hair, and adjusted her kapp. She went back to the kitchen, where her mother was still busy at the stove. Without a word, Shelley set the table for four, lingering a few extra seconds by her father's place. She was grateful to have him home for meals, regardless of the fact that he rarely said more than a couple of words after the blessing.

"How is that new girl doing at the restaurant?" her mother asked, clearly trying to make small talk without making the conversation as personal as it had been.

Shelley played along. "Jocelyn? She seems fine, but she has a lot to learn."

"I can imagine. I guess I don't have to tell you how surprised everyone was that Joseph hired someone like her."

Shelley had been surprised at the time, too, but now that she knew Jocelyn better, she saw the softer side of the girl who used makeup and multicolored spiked hair as a barrier. "She's catching on very well, and the customers seem to like her."

"I'm surprised. She rather frightens me."

"Jocelyn isn't frightening at all. She's actually rather funny." Shelley smiled at the thought of some of Jocelyn's funny phrases.

Her mother looked at her with a lifted eyebrow and froze for a few seconds. "I hope you don't go getting any ideas that it's okay to dress or act like her."

Shelley laughed. "Trust me, Mother, I have no desire to do either of those things. But beneath her exterior, she's not as different from me as I thought at first."

William arrived home from school at that moment, a grin playing on his lips, even though he looked like he was trying to hide it. Shelley smiled back at him, and he looked away then laughed.

"Okay, so what are you so happy about?" Shelley asked.

"I asked Myra to marry me, and she said yes."

Chapter 7

William's joy quickly vanished as their mother shrieked, "William! No!"

He took a step back, his face scrunching up as it always did before he cried. Shelley stood there in stunned silence as her mother told him he'd never be able to marry a girl. A huge tear trickled down his cheek, and his chin quivered.

When Mother stopped her rant, William looked her in the eye. "But I love her."

"You don't understand love," Mother replied.

He blinked and wiped a tear as it escaped. "I love you, too."

Mother looked helplessly at Shelley, silently pleading for help, but Shelley had no idea what to say. She understood her mother's concern, but she disagreed with her about William understanding love. He knew better than anyone how to love a person, but she was aware that didn't erase the complications of his proposal.

Shelley took a deep breath to steady her nerves and her voice before addressing her brother. "William, where do you know Myra?"

"She works with me at the shop."

"That settles it," their mother said. "You are not going back to that place. I told your father it wasn't a good idea for you to work."

"I want to keep working," William argued. "I like having my own money."

Shelley nodded. "I understand that, William." She glanced over at their mother. "Perhaps we can discuss this more, after Father gets home."

As Mother lifted her hand to her forehead, a sense of dread flooded Shelley. That simple gesture was generally followed by a quick drop into depression that could last for weeks. In the past, it seemed to be triggered by their father's switch to late shifts, but this was something new.

"William, you are awfully young to be thinking about getting married. How old is Myra?" Shelley asked.

He puffed up his chest and smiled. "Myra is eighteen years old." His grin widened. "And she's pretty. I like her red hair."

"I'm sure she's very pretty, but you haven't been working there very long. Getting married is very serious."

"I know that," William said. "I'm serious, too."

"Do you know anything about her family?"

"She lives in a group home."

"Does she have a family?"

He thought for a few seconds and then nodded. "I think her mother lives in Tampa. I don't know where her father lives."

Shelley and her mother exchanged a glance before Shelley turned back to William. "Maybe we can meet Myra sometime. Why don't I get someone to drive me to pick you up from work on Monday?"

"I like riding the van," he argued. "Myra rides with me, and we hold hands. We drop her off at her house first."

Shelley took a step back, placed her hands on her hips, and gave him what she hoped was an authoritative look. "Well, before you make the decision to marry Myra, we need to meet her and her family. I'm sure they feel they same way." She glanced at her mother, who stood off to the side looking aghast but remaining silent.

"Why?" he asked.

"That's just the way it's done. When you marry a girl, not only are you getting a wife, but you're also taking on her whole family."

"How about her? Does she get a whole new family, too?"

"Yes, William, it works both ways."

"That is very good. Myra says she wants a family just like mine, and now she'll have one."

Shelley hoped her talk hadn't backfired, but she couldn't worry about it. What she'd said was true, and now she needed to pray about it.

"Go wash up, William. Supper will be ready as soon as Father comes home."

As soon as he was out of the kitchen, Shelley's mother sank down in a chair. "What are we going to do?"

"We are going to pray, Mother. That's all we can do. Besides, William can't get married anyway because he's too young."

"You seem to be forgetting one very important thing, Shelley. William will never be able to get married."

Shelley wasn't so sure her mother was right, but even if she was, she was fretting over something unnecessarily. "I'll talk to William about all the things involved in getting married. Maybe he'll realize it's not as easy as he seems to think it is."

"I don't think he'll understand," Mother argued.

William understood quite a bit more than most people gave him credit for, and Shelley had been amazed at how much he comprehended. "Just let me talk to him before you worry any more. By the time I finish with him, I doubt he'll want to pursue this whole thing."

"Why?" Mother asked, her expression changing to confusion. "What do you plan to say to him?"

"I'm not sure yet. I'll need to think about it."

"Don't make him think marriage is a bad thing, just because you do."

Shelley was stunned. "I don't think marriage is bad. I think it's wonderful."

"If you think marriage is good, why aren't you trying harder to find a husband?"

Shelley's mouth went dry. Couldn't her mother see the truth—that getting married was extremely difficult for Shelley based on how much she was needed at home? She started to talk, but her voice caught in her throat. Good thing, too, because if she'd said what was on her mind, there was no telling how her mother would react.

"If your talk with William doesn't work, we have a mess on our hands. It's bad enough my oldest child married an outsider and left the church. To have my baby do that, too, and in his condition. . ." Her chin quivered just as William's had.

"Tammy is a very sweet woman," Shelley said. "They're going to church."

"But they're not going to *our* church, which was my dream. I always thought my children would grow up, get married, and attend the church you grew up in. That way we can always be together as a family, and I'd get to see my grandchildren."

"Mother, you get to see your grandchildren quite often, and it's not like they live all that far away. They always come when you need them. I pray every day that Paul comes back to our church and brings his family with him because I know it means so much to you." She took Mother's hand and held it tightly. Although Paul still walked with the Lord and attended a good church, her mother's heart was set on them being together as a family.

Her mother's eyes misted as she sighed and pulled her hand away. "Let's finish up supper so we can eat as soon as your father gets home."

As they worked in silence, Shelley allowed her thoughts to wander, and they settled on Jeremiah. Even though she'd seen some big changes in him, there was no way her mother would ever accept him. Shelley figured it was futile to even consider a relationship with him. Her mother would never forget that he'd left the church once, and she'd worry herself sick over the thought he might do it again. If he'd managed to continue walking with the Lord when he left, things might have been different, and her mother might have been more accepting.

Shelley was happy that he'd found a place with Abe though, even if she'd never be able to share it with him. She sighed and then startled as she realized the subconscious thoughts she'd been harboring. In spite of her words and attempts to keep her emotional distance from Jeremiah, she'd started to fall in love with him. That simply couldn't be. She'd hurt her family if she even suggested any such thing.

⁓

On Monday morning, Jeremiah worked hard at finishing the task Abe had assigned so he could start a little early on his own crops. Abe gave him a specific task each day now and told him that once it was done, he was free. Since he didn't need Charles today, he only had to be concerned about finishing his own work.

As he walked the rows of trees, he thought about how closed off Shelley's family had seemed at church yesterday. After the services were over, the Burkholder family left before he'd had a chance to say more than good-bye to Mr. Burkholder and William. He'd seen Shelley across the room sitting in the midst of a group of women, but she wouldn't look up at him.

"Good job, Jeremiah," Abe said from behind. "You look like a man on a mission."

"I am." Jeremiah suspected Abe only knew half the mission—the part about him having his own land. The other half was still in the works—the part with Shelley by his side as his wife. It would be a challenge, but that didn't deter Jeremiah. He'd overcome much more difficult tests, so he had no doubt he'd find a way to make Shelley realize how sincere he was.

"Do you need anything?"

"Not at the moment." At least not anything Abe could help him with.

"Good. Let me know when you're done."

After Abe took off toward another part of the property, Jeremiah let his mind wander to his personal life. During the time he'd been away from the church, he'd experienced myriad emotions, starting with a sense of freedom and ending with desperation for not being grounded anymore. How anyone could get through an entire life without their faith in God was beyond him. Not being connected with his church left him with an empty feeling. He had friends, but they could only do so much to satisfy the emptiness only the Lord could fill.

Once it became evident he needed to reconnect, he'd fought God in his mind and by acting like someone he didn't know. He cringed as he remembered some of the things he'd shouted from his car when he'd seen Abe and Mary. Fortunately, they'd forgiven him and never even brought it up again. Now it was time for him to settle down and make a life for himself that was pleasing to God. He wanted a family, but he needed a wife who was interesting, intelligent, and could challenge him when he strayed in thought and word.

Shelley was perfect for him. He found her dedication to her family very attractive. Jeremiah was aware that he'd be taking on more than a wife if Shelley agreed to marry him, but he was fine with that. He liked William, and he was pretty sure William liked and respected him.

Now all he had to do was find a way to gain her family's trust. Her father was busy with his job, and her mother's emotional health seemed precarious, so it wouldn't be an easy feat. This would take considerable thought, but that was fine. He wasn't in a hurry.

After Shelley got off work on Monday afternoon, she walked to the church school. She knew that the van often waited at the school for William to get out of class, and she hoped that would be the case today. As soon as she got close enough to see the front, she saw that the van was there. She quickened her step until she approached the driver.

"Excuse me, but do you have room for one more person today?" she asked.

He turned and gave her a confused look. "I beg your pardon?"

Shelley explained that she wanted to go to William's workplace, but she didn't drive. He'd been in the area long enough to understand her situation.

"I think that would be fine, as long as it's just this once," he said. "A couple of the people are on vacation, so we're not full this week. This is my first stop, though. I still have a couple of stops to make."

"Good. Mind if I get in now?"

He opened the door for her, and she climbed into the very back seat. A few seconds after she buckled herself in, the front door of the school opened, and the kids streamed out. Only a couple of school-aged kids went to the shop where William worked, and William was the only one from the Pinecraft community, but the van was generally full at the end of the workday when the driver took everyone home.

Shelley sat and waited for William to board the van. He didn't seem to notice her at first, but she said his name, and he turned around. At first he appeared happy to see her, and then his expression quickly changed.

"Why are you here, Shelley?" he asked. "Are you spying on me?"

"No, of course I'm not spying on you. I just want to see where you work and meet some of your friends."

"You just want to make trouble for me and Myra."

"I would never do that, but I do want to meet Myra. I'm sure she's a very nice girl."

"She's the nicest girl in the whole wide world. I love her."

"Then don't worry, William. I'm sure I'll love her, too."

They arrived at the shop a few minutes later. After the kids got out, Shelley hopped down from the van, turned around, and thanked the driver.

He waved. "I'll see you in a few hours."

"Do you have to go in with me?" William asked. "I don't want anyone to think I'm a baby."

"Why would anyone think you're a baby? You have a real job, so I'm sure they won't think that."

William looked uncomfortable before he finally said, "I want to tell Myra you're coming."

Shelley understood, so she told William to go on ahead of her. "I'll just walk around outside for a little while before I come back."

"You'll have to ask the man at the door to let you in. They are very strict about people coming into the building."

"Good," Shelley said. "I wouldn't want it any other way."

She made a lap around the building, thought about what she'd say, and then walked up to the front door. Right after she opened it, she saw a man sitting on a stool behind a desk.

"I'd like to meet my brother's supervisor," she said.

The man looked her in the eye. "Do you know his name?"

Shelley knew he was inwardly laughing at her plain clothes and kapp, but she didn't care. She was used to it. "Walter, I think. Walter. . ." She couldn't remember his last name.

"Walter O'Reilly?"

"Ya, that's his name. I'd like to see Walter O'Reilly."

The man picked up a phone and punched in a couple of numbers. After a few seconds he said something she couldn't hear, and then he placed his hand over the mouthpiece. "What did you say your name was?"

"Shelley Burkholder. I'm William Burkholder's sister."

After the man said her name, he nodded, said, "I'll tell her," and then hung up. "He'll be right out to escort you to the workroom."

"Thank you." Shelley stood staring at the bare wall, feeling as awkward as she'd ever been. She rarely left the Pinecraft community, and now she remembered why. When one of the teachers at the school had recommended this job for William, the family had discussed the pros and cons and decided it would help him feel more valued and independent. Shelley knew her mother continued to have reservations, even after she'd agreed to let William work.

A few minutes later a man with a name tag that read O'REILLY came to the door. "So you're Willie's sister, huh? He said you were coming."

"Ya, I'm William Burkholder's sister." She regretted her decision to visit her brother at work, but it was too late now. "W—would it be all right if I saw his. . .um. . .work space?"

Mr. O'Reilly laughed but not in a mean way. He gestured for her to join him. "That's perfectly fine. Right this way, ma'am." As they walked down a long corridor, he explained that the employees did mostly contracted piecemeal work for local businesses. They got a variety of jobs, including assembling simple components for factories and putting stickers on packages. "I've been doing this a very long time, and I can't think of a job I'd like more," he added with pride.

"Good," she said. "Everyone should enjoy their work."

They arrived beside a large, soft-peach painted, well-lit room filled with dozens of people similar to her brother, all working side by side, soft music playing in the background, some of the workers chattering with the person next to them. It seemed very pleasant.

"Where is William?" she asked.

"Follow me, and I'll show you."

She did as she was told and quickly found herself standing behind her brother, who still wasn't aware she was there yet. "William?"

He spun around and flashed a huge grin. He was about to say something when the girl to his right turned, looked at Shelley, and started laughing.

"What's so funny, Myra?" William asked.

"That woman. Look at that funny-looking outfit. It's so ugly."

Shelley was taken aback. Mr. O'Reilly touched her arm, but William stood from his chair, placed a hand on his hip, and shook a finger at Myra.

"That woman is my sister, and she is beautiful to me."

Myra continued laughing. "Not to me."

"How can you say that, Myra? I think she's beautiful."

"She is not beautiful. She's ugly."

Mr. O'Reilly stepped forward to intervene, but he stopped when Shelley shook her head and whispered, "I think it's best to let them work this out on their own."

William scowled. "That's mean. Take it back."

"No, I will not take it back. It's the truth."

"I don't want to marry you anymore then. I love my sister, and no one is allowed to say mean things about her to me."

Myra stopped laughing and then shrugged. "That's okay by me, William. I think you're sort of funny-looking, too."

Mr. O'Reilly looked just as surprised at Shelley felt. "In all the years I've been here, I've never seen anything like this happen. I am so sorry." He hung his head. "Myra hasn't been around many Mennonite or Amish people, I'm afraid. Her family isn't from here."

"Mr. O'Reilly, may I please be moved?" William asked. "I don't want to work next to Myra anymore."

"Yes, of course, Willie," Mr. O'Reilly said. He turned to Shelley with an apologetic look. "I'm so sorry this happened, but I really need to tend to my workers right now."

"Oh, please," Shelley said. "Go right ahead. I'll just stand here and observe if you don't mind."

Shelley stood and watched Mr. O'Reilly move her brother to the other side of the room. The two men carried his tools and equipment and placed it on an identical work space as far from Myra as they could go in the room. She wasn't sure what to think about what she'd just witnessed, but it clearly showed a side of William she'd never seen. He'd stuck up for her at the risk of his own happiness. Shelley couldn't remember ever being more proud of her brother than that very moment.

She turned back to see what Myra was doing. She half expected to see a shred of sadness, but what she saw was a silly young woman laughing with the guy on the other side of her. It didn't appear to Shelley that there was any deep love lost.

After Mr. O'Reilly finished helping William get set up in his new work space, he joined Shelley. "I feel bad that happened in front of you."

"Oh, don't feel bad. I'm flattered that my brother said what he did."

Mr. O'Reilly gave her a curious glance. "And I'm sorry about what Myra said about you. She apparently doesn't understand your style of dress. And by the way, I don't think you're ugly. You're actually rather attract—"

"That's okay," Shelley said, interrupting him before he said something to embarrass himself. "I've been laughed at before. People do that when they don't understand things, and unless they've been around plain people before, there's no way they would understand."

"You are a very wise young woman, Ms. Burkholder. May I get you something to drink?"

"No thank you. I'll just go outside and wait for my brother. The van driver said he had room to take me home."

"I have a better idea," Mr. O'Reilly said. "Come with me to the employee break room. We have magazines and comfortable seating."

"That sounds good." She followed him back out into the hallway and into another room—this one smaller and very cozy. It had thin carpet but a couple of plush couches on one side of the room, a coffee area with a refrigerator and small stove in the center, and on the other side a Ping-Pong table.

"I'll let William know you're here. He gets one very short break during his afternoon shifts."

Shelley leafed through a couple of cooking magazines. She'd never seen so many unusual foods. She closed a magazine, added it to the stack beside her, and was about to carry them back to the magazine rack and pick up a few more when William walked in.

"I'm sorry about what Myra said, Shelley."

"Don't worry about it, William. You had nothing to do with that."

He closed the distance between them and hugged her. "No one will ever be allowed to talk to my sister like that as long as I'm around."

Shelley's eyes misted. Having William protecting her warmed her heart and filled it with love.

"Want to play Ping-Pong?" he asked.

"I don't know how."

"Come on. I'll show you. But I only have a few minutes before I have to go back to work. Mr. O'Reilly let me take my break first because you are here."

Shelley tried to listen to her brother as he explained how to hit the ball and make it bounce to the other person, but her mind kept popping back to how quickly he did an about-face with Myra on her behalf. William was the most loyal person she'd ever known, and she was honored to be his sister.

～

The rest of the week went by quickly for Shelley. Her mother's eyes glistened with joy as she learned how William had stuck up for Shelley and not given it a second thought. Nothing else was mentioned about Myra, and William seemed fine with that.

As the days went by and Shelley didn't see Jeremiah, she tried to accept the idea that he might have given up. That was probably for the best, she thought, since her parents would probably never accept him.

Then on Friday, Jocelyn came up from behind her as she jotted down a big order and whispered, "Don't look now, but that cute guy who likes you just walked in."

Shelley felt her cheeks flame, but she did as Jocelyn told her and avoided looking toward the door. After she finished taking a late breakfast order, she scurried back to the kitchen without looking up.

"I'll take that," Mr. Penner said as he snatched the order slip from her hands. "Now go see what Jeremiah wants."

She opened her mouth to say Jocelyn could take his order, but Mr. Penner leveled her with a no-nonsense look. She clamped her mouth shut and nodded. She could tell Mr. Penner's attitude toward Jeremiah had changed.

As she approached Jeremiah's table, her heart hammered so hard she was certain he'd be able to hear it. She stopped beside his table, her pen poised above the order pad, and waited.

"Hello, Shelley."

He didn't say anything else, so she glanced up and met his gaze. His smile warmed her, but her mouth went dry.

"I've missed seeing you," he said. "But it takes quite a bit of time to work two farms."

"I can imagine," she said softly. "Would you like some coffee?"

He nodded. "Yes, please."

"I'll go get that for you right now while you decide what you'd like to eat."

"Sounds good."

Jocelyn met her at the beverage station. "I have to run to the courthouse to take care of a speeding ticket. Mr. Penner said I could go if I can get back in an hour, so I'd better run."

That left Shelley covering the entire dining room. "Can you be back before the lunch rush?"

"That's the plan." Jocelyn tweaked her on the arm and winked. "Better not keep the guy waiting." She laughed as she walked away.

Shelley carried a cup, a saucer, and a carafe filled with coffee over to Jeremiah. "I'll be back with the cream," she said.

By the time she put the cream in front of Jeremiah, he had closed his menu. "Can you join me?"

"No, I'm sorry. I'm the only person serving at the moment."

"Too bad. I was hoping I could tell you all about my new crops."

"Maybe another time," Shelley said. "What would you like to eat?"

Jeremiah leaned back, folded his arms, and looked directly at her. "How about some pancakes and sausage?"

Fortunately, Jeremiah had worked hard all morning, so he'd worked up an appetite to eat another breakfast. Abe had wanted to talk to him when he'd first arrived at the Glick farm, so Mary had fed him eggs, bacon, hash browns, large buttermilk biscuits, and homemade marmalade, but then he'd done a couple of hours of hard manual labor.

He watched Shelley move around in the kitchen area doing whatever she did when she wasn't waiting on tables. The restaurant wasn't crowded because it was late for breakfast and early for lunch. He thought he'd timed his visit perfectly for Shelley's break, but with Jocelyn gone, he understood why she couldn't join him.

His order only took about ten minutes. Shelley had barely placed it in front of him when Mr. Penner came out of the kitchen, his face pale and his forehead scrunched with concern.

"I just got a call. There's been an accident," he said, his voice gravelly. "Jocelyn was taken by ambulance to the hospital."

Chapter 8

C ome on, Mr. Penner," Jeremiah said as he rose from the table. "I'll take you to the hospital."

Mr. Penner glanced at Shelley. "Can you handle the dining room all by yourself?"

"Of course," she said. "Go on and see about Jocelyn."

Shelley remained standing beside the table as the two men left for the hospital. Then she bowed her head and prayed for her coworker with a bad driving record.

The restaurant wasn't so crowded that Shelley couldn't handle it alone. She even had a little bit of time between taking orders and delivering meals to straighten the beverage and prep area.

Mr. Penner and Jeremiah came back right when the lunch crowd started to roll in. "How is she?"

Mr. Penner smiled. "She has a mild concussion, so they're keeping her overnight for observation. She wants to come back to work tomorrow, but I told her absolutely not. I want her to take better care of herself." He gestured to Jeremiah. "Let's get this boy some food so he can get back to the farm."

Shelley had cancelled Jeremiah's breakfast order, and now he wanted lunch. It didn't take long for the kitchen staff to prepare the food. When she delivered it to his table, he told her more about Jocelyn's accident.

"Apparently, she ran a red light and hit a truck, according to what she remembers."

"Oh no! Was anyone else hurt?"

Jeremiah shook his head. "Fortunately, she tried to stop, so the truck driver is okay. Jocelyn really does need to slow down."

"Thank you for taking Mr. Penner to the hospital. He cares about people."

"Yes, I know," Jeremiah agreed. "Including you."

"Ya. I've been working for him since I was in high school. I feel like part of his family."

A family walked into the restaurant, so Shelley left Jeremiah's table to take care of their order. For the next several minutes she was busy, but Jeremiah waited.

When he lifted his finger to get her attention, she went to his table. "May I have my check please? I need to get back to the farm."

"Neh. Mr. Penner said you don't need to worry about paying for lunch.

He's thankful you were here to help him."

Jeremiah hesitated for a second and then nodded. "I'm happy to do it. Tell him thank you from me. I'll be back soon, and I'd like to talk with you."

Shelley opened her mouth, but she couldn't think of anything to say, so she smiled and nodded. After he left, she tried to get her mind off Jeremiah, but that was impossible. She could see that he'd truly changed since he'd come back to the church, and she liked what she saw. She'd secretly liked him when they were children, but he'd pulled so many pranks and teased her that she couldn't bring herself to let on how she felt. They'd actually started getting along as teenagers, and she'd harbored thoughts that perhaps he was the boy she'd wind up with. Then he'd turned his back on the church, leaving little hope that he'd ever come back. That was when she'd turned to Peter, who'd seemed safe.

As Shelley and Peter had seen more of each other, she'd placed all her hopes on a future with him. He'd acted as though he wanted more, but when he'd shocked her with the news he was engaged to Clara from Pennsylvania, she'd doubted she would ever find a man to spend her life with.

"Shelley," Mr. Penner said from behind her. "I just got a call from Jeremiah. He offered to take you to visit Jocelyn after work if you are able to go."

She thought about how her mother wouldn't approve, but then she really wanted to let Jocelyn know she was praying for her. "I would like that," she said softly. "But I offered to help the kids at the school get ready for the singing on Sunday."

"How long will that take you?"

"Maybe an hour?"

"I'll let him know to pick you up after you are finished at the school."

Her thoughts collided and then swirled in her head. She wanted to see Jocelyn, but her parents wouldn't approve of her riding with Jeremiah.

Mr. Penner studied her face. "Jeremiah likes you very much, Shelley. At first I worried that he would be bad for you, but he seems to be a changed man."

Shelley glanced at him and saw the twinkle in his eyes, so she quickly looked away. "I hope so."

"May I tell him you will accept the ride to the hospital?"

She nodded. "Ya, I would like to see Jocelyn, but I have to go to the church and help out with the children first."

"I will let him know you said yes. Abe told him it was okay to take the time off, so I will let you leave early, and maybe you can get a head start with the children."

"Thank you." As soon as Shelley could walk away from Mr. Penner without being rude, she did.

The combination of her growing feelings for Jeremiah and the desire to see Jocelyn had Shelley swirling in a current of emotions. She needed to settle her mind before she could hope to make sense of all the changes going on. If Jeremiah truly was a changed man, she thought about whether or not she could be with him. Her mother's lack of acceptance combined with her own fears of having something else taken away made her wary. Keeping trust in anything outside her faith, family, and work was becoming more difficult by the day.

The lunch crowd kept her busy for a couple of hours, so when Jeremiah arrived to take her to the school and hospital, she wasn't quite ready. "I thought you were picking me up at the school."

"I finished early."

"It'll be a few minutes before I'm done here."

"I'll wait," he said as he stood by the door. "Take your time, and finish your work."

She was wiping a table clean when Mrs. Penner walked in the front door. "Go on, Shelley. I'm taking over for you."

Shelley knew it had been years since Mrs. Penner had waited tables at the restaurant, so she hesitated. "I don't—"

Mrs. Penner made a shooing gesture, shushing Shelley. Jeremiah stood to the side, observing everything.

⌘

Jeremiah opened the passenger door for Shelley. As she got in and strapped her seat belt around her tiny frame, he felt more protective of her than ever. He wanted to protect her from anything bad ever happening, but she had a shield that he couldn't seem to get past. Sure, she was nice to him, and she didn't seem to mind making small talk. But he wanted so much more.

"Did you see Jocelyn yet?" Shelley asked, breaking him from his thoughts.

"Just for a few seconds. Mr. Penner went in first, and he talked to her for a while before he came and got me. When the doctor arrived, we both had to leave."

"Is she. . .does she look the same?"

"With the exception of a few bruises and a scratch over her eye, she looks exactly as she always looked." He left out how Jocelyn's tough-girl exterior had faded, and she looked vulnerable and frightened. "And I have no doubt she'll be very happy to see you." Although he didn't know Jocelyn well, he couldn't miss her when he'd gone to Penner's.

"I like Jocelyn. She works hard and says funny things."

Jeremiah thought about all the girls he'd met when he was away from the church. Many of them had taken on an image of what they wanted the world to see and kept their innermost thoughts hidden. He knew it was a protective measure, but he didn't like it. And he suspected God didn't care for it either.

"I will wait in the back of the church," Jeremiah said as he pulled up to the curb in front.

Shelley went to the classroom and asked if they could start early. The teachers were happy she was there, so they gathered the kids to herd them to the front of the church sanctuary.

The children must have sensed Shelley's anxiety, and they started acting out. One of the younger boys made faces at the girl behind him.

"Turn around, and keep your hands to yourself, Zeke," Shelley said, her voice tight and on edge.

Zeke turned around, but he still didn't pay attention to her. Instead he jumped around, flailing his arms. Then the boy next to him began to squirm, creating a snowball effect with the rest of the children. This was the first time Jeremiah had ever seen Shelley lose control. He couldn't sit back and do nothing.

"Okay, that's enough." Jeremiah's booming voice behind Shelley caught the attention of the children. "Do you want to make Miss Burkholder, your parents, and the rest of the church members happy by showing your hard work and dedication, or do you want to look like a bunch of people who didn't practice when it comes time to sing?"

Zeke burst out in laughter, but he quickly stopped when Jeremiah leveled him with a stern look. Shelley stood transfixed as Jeremiah continued to lecture for a few more minutes. Finally, he turned to Shelley and motioned for her to come forward.

"Miss Burkholder, I think they're ready to settle down and get to work now," Jeremiah said as he took a step back.

She turned and gave him a private smile and then resumed singing practice. The children were perfectly behaved, enabling them to finish very quickly.

Afterward the teachers brought them back to their classrooms, and Shelley looked up at Jeremiah. "Thank you for helping me. I normally don't have that much trouble with them."

"I know. You normally do quite well with children. Kids sense when adults have something else on their minds."

They pulled up in front of the hospital entrance. "Why don't you go on up to see her?" he said. "I'll park the car and hang out in the waiting room until you're ready to go home." He gave her directions to Jocelyn's unit and then watched her until she disappeared through the automatic double doors.

Shelley hadn't changed much since they were younger. She'd always been responsible, intelligent, and straightforward. The only difference between then and now was her guardedness, which he suspected was related to issues with her mother, Peter, and possibly her brother William.

❧

Shelley's hands shook as she followed the nurse to Jocelyn's hospital room. The sounds of medical machines whirring and buzzing made her uneasy.

She'd visited people in the hospital before, but the shock of the differences from her regular life never went away.

"Here she is," the nurse said as she opened the door. "The doctor says she's doing well, so take your time, and have a nice visit."

Shelley walked slowly into the room toward Jocelyn. With the sun shining through the window behind Jocelyn, it was difficult to see her features, so her injuries weren't evident until Shelley was right beside the bed. Even then, she didn't look as banged up as she'd expected.

"Hey there, Shelley. Who's minding the shop?"

She certainly sounded like Jocelyn—not some feeble, injured person. "Mrs. Penner came in to help out so I could come here."

Jocelyn belted out a laugh and then stopped and raised her hand to her head. "Ouch. It hurts to laugh."

"Then don't do it," Shelley said. "I don't want you to hurt."

"I couldn't help it. It's hard to imagine Mrs. Penner waiting on tables and putting up with some of the. . .well, you know how the customers can be."

Shelley nodded and grinned. "Yes, I do know, but I think Mrs. Penner can handle it. She used to work there every day when I was younger. I'm sure she'll be just fine."

"So I guess you're probably wondering what happened," Jocelyn said.

"I heard you hit a truck."

"Yeah. I was going too fast, and I couldn't slow down for the light. Ironic, huh?"

Shelley tilted her head in confusion. "Ironic?"

"That I was speeding to the courthouse to pay a speeding ticket, and that's what got me into trouble. Can you believe that I got another ticket?"

"Will you be able to drive again?" Shelley asked.

"Oh, I have to drive. It's too hard to get around without wheels." Jocelyn caught herself and chuckled softly. "But I guess you know that."

"It's not all that difficult," Shelley said. "I like walking, and when I need a ride, I take the bus or hire a driver."

Jocelyn turned away, and silence fell between them. When she faced Shelley again, her face had an odd expression that Shelley had never seen before.

"So tell me what it's like to be you," Jocelyn said.

"What do you mean?"

Jocelyn gestured toward what Shelley was wearing. "I mean to wear that getup all the time and never put on makeup. You always have that little thingy on your head, and your hair is always up in a knot. And that long skirt. Does it ever bug you?"

"Bug me?"

"Yeah. Doesn't it make you nuts to never wear shorts or let your hair down or play up your eyes with some fabulous makeup?" Jocelyn leaned forward a bit. "I mean, you have some killer peepers that would look amazing with a little mascara."

Shelley was slightly puzzled by some of the words, but she caught the gist of what Jocelyn was saying. "Neh, it doesn't bother me. This is all I know."

"Well," Jocelyn said as she leaned back and fidgeted with the sheet. "That is true. If you've never experienced anything else, you wouldn't know what you were missing." She pursed her lips before adding, "And to be truthful, I don't think you're really missing all that much."

Shelley didn't know how to respond to that. She walked over toward the window and glanced out over the parking lot.

"I want to go back to work tomorrow, but the doc says I need to wait until he clears me. He's letting me go home tomorrow though, so I can pretty much do whatever I want."

Shelley turned back around to face Jocelyn. "Don't rush things."

"You're too young to be my mom, but I appreciate the maternal advice. I haven't had that since my mom found someone else and took off, leaving me and my dad to figure out how to be a family, just the two of us."

"Is your father. . .um, does he know about your accident?"

"Yeah, he knows, but he's been pretty busy lately, so I don't expect to see him anytime soon."

Shelley made some uncomfortable small talk for a few minutes before backing toward the door. "I really need to go now. My mother likes me to help with dinner. I'm glad you're doing well enough to go home tomorrow, but I don't want you to push yourself too hard. Mrs. Penner and I can manage until you're feeling better."

Jocelyn laughed and waved. "Have fun, but don't forget about me. I need that job. It's hard finding a new one these days."

"Don't worry. We won't forget about you. I'm sure Mrs. Penner will be very happy when you return."

As Shelley walked toward the waiting room, where Jeremiah said he'd be waiting, she thought about some of the things Jocelyn had said, particularly the comment about not missing something she'd never experienced. As much as she noticed the changes in Jeremiah, she wondered if he'd miss his experiences from his more worldly life as her mother had said he might. She now realized that was the source of much of her fear of getting too close to him. What if he missed it so much he decided to leave the church again?

Jeremiah stood and smiled as she approached. "Ready to leave now?"

Shelley nodded and then averted her gaze. They walked without talking, the only sounds coming from the machines in the hospital and their shoes clopping on the floor.

"Wait here, and I'll go get the car," he said after they reached the double doors leading to the outside.

"Neh, I'll walk with you."

"I don't mind," he said.

"There's no use in standing around waiting for you when I'm perfectly capable of walking." She stepped down off the curb.

After they were buckled into Jeremiah's car, he put his key in the ignition and turned. The car made a little groan and then thudded.

Shelley looked at Jeremiah. His face was scrunched up with concern. "I was afraid this might happen."

"What's going on?" Shelley had so little experience with cars—she wasn't sure if this was serious.

"Abe told me that if I insisted on having a car, I didn't need one as fancy or with as much power as the sports car I got rid of. I chose this one just to have transportation. It's a clunker."

"Are you blaming Abe? It's not his fault."

"No, of course I'm not blaming Abe. I'm the one who knows about cars. I worked in an automotive shop before Abe hired me, so I take full responsibility."

"In that case, can't you fix it?"

Jeremiah shook his head as he raked his fingers through his closely cropped hair. "No, I don't think there's anything I can do to fix this old heap. I bought it really cheap so I could pay cash, and I didn't have that much money to work with." He leaned back and shook his head. "I have some decisions to make, and it looks like it'll have to happen sooner rather than later."

"The first decision is how we're going to get home," Shelley said. "I think the bus comes out here."

"It does," Jeremiah said. "But I don't want you having to take the bus."

"Why not?" she asked. "I don't mind."

❧

Jeremiah lifted his hand and started to pound his fist on the steering wheel, but his Mennonite sensibilities kicked in just in time. He took a couple of deep breaths to settle his nerves.

"I s'pose I could leave my car here and escort you home."

"Why?" She narrowed her eyes. "I can ride the bus alone."

"Yes, I know, but"—he opened his car door—"but I have to go home, too, and I don't live that far from you, so we might as well ride together."

"What will you do about the car?"

"I'll have to call someone to tow it to a junkyard."

After they got out of the car, Jeremiah stood looking at it for a few seconds before turning to walk away. Shelley didn't follow, so he glanced around to see what she was doing.

"What's wrong?" he asked.

She looked back and forth between Jeremiah and his car. He waited for a few seconds, hoping she'd catch up, but she didn't.

"Okay, Shelley, I can tell you're thinking about something you're not saying. What is it?"

"Since your car isn't working anymore, and you said it isn't worth fixing, why don't you try going without a car?"

"You're kidding, right?"

She tossed him a puzzled look. "Kidding?"

"Are you saying you expect me to live without my own wheels?"

"Ya. That's exactly what I'm saying."

"Abe has already challenged me to do that, but I'm not sure I'm ready just yet." Jeremiah looked around at the hospital parking lot at the sea of cars. "That is an extremely difficult step to take."

"Maybe it'll be difficult at first, but I do just fine."

"Let's check with the hospital receptionist and find out where the closest bus stop is."

After she directed them to the location where they could catch the bus, they walked outside and resumed their conversation. Shelley spoke first.

"You might discover you don't need a car," she said.

She'd obviously never understand, so Jeremiah didn't want to argue with her. "Maybe. Looks like I don't have a choice, and I'll have to make do for a while—at least until I make enough money to buy a newer automobile. In the meantime, I'll go back to walking and catching rides whenever I can." Jeremiah paused before adding, "And I guess I'd better set something up with David."

"David?"

"Yeah, the guy Abe hires to drive him places that are too far to walk. Until I get my house built on the farm, I'll need him twice a day. That can wind up costing me some money."

"Will it be more than what you pay for in gas?"

Jeremiah mentally calculated the cost of gas, maintenance, and insurance. "It might actually cost a little less if David will cut me a deal."

Shelley smiled. "That would be nice."

The bus ride to Pinecraft was uneventful. There were only a few people seated toward the front, and the bus was able to go past all stops except one where a young woman waited. As they took the last step onto the sidewalk, the bus driver wished them a good day and took off.

In spite of Shelley telling Jeremiah she could walk from the bus stop to her house, he insisted on getting off the bus with her, escorting her home, and walking the three blocks to his house. They had to dodge a couple of children playing in their yards. Memories of Jeremiah's own childhood flickered through his mind, and nostalgia nearly overwhelmed him.

"What are you thinking about?" Shelley asked as they rounded the corner to her street. "You seem mighty pensive."

He shrugged. "Just about how those kids remind me of myself when I was their age."

"I remember you back then. You were quite a character."

Jeremiah laughed. "Yeah, I was, wasn't I?"

"You used to tease me unmercifully."

"That was because I liked you," he said, a grin quirking the corners of his lips.

"If that's how you act when you like a girl, I wouldn't want to see what you do when you don't like her."

"There aren't many people I don't like," Jeremiah said.

⤙⤚

Shelley's mother stood near the door as Shelley entered the house. "Where have you been? I expected you home a long time ago."

"Jocelyn was injured in a car accident, so I went to the hospital to see her."

"You should have come home first to tell me so I wouldn't worry. It is dangerous for a young girl like you to be trotting about in an area you're not familiar with."

"I wasn't alone," Shelley said. She cringed as she added, "Jeremiah was with me."

She braced herself for an outburst of all of Jeremiah's faults. She was surprised her mother's expression softened.

"That's good. At least he knows the ways of the world, and he will protect you." She started to walk toward the kitchen, but she stopped and turned to face Shelley. "How is Jocelyn?"

Shelley told her mother about the concussion and how Jocelyn would probably be back at work soon. She was surprised not to get a lecture about the evils of living in the world.

William came home shortly afterward, and Father followed. As they sat down at the table, Shelley looked around at her family and wondered what it would be like to have her own family. Then she sighed as she considered the unlikelihood that that would happen. Even if a man was in love with her, taking on the responsibility of William might make him think twice before committing to her for life. In many ways, William was easier to contend with than someone without Down syndrome. He rarely argued, and with very few exceptions, he seemed eager to please.

When Shelley started to bring up Jocelyn's accident, her mother grimaced and gestured not to discuss it. After dinner, when William and their father had left the kitchen, Shelley turned to her mother.

"Why didn't you want me to talk about Jocelyn?" she asked.

Her mother didn't look directly at her. "We don't know much about Jocelyn, and I didn't want to upset your father."

Shelley suspected it had nothing to do with her father and everything to do with the fact that her mother didn't want to constantly be reminded about Shelley's brother Paul leaving the church. The instant she thought that, it dawned on her that this was the same issue with Jeremiah. Having him around was a reminder.

"Mother, do you ever talk with Paul about his faith?"

Her mother's expression hardened. "Paul's faith—or lack of it—has broken my heart, so I don't want you to ever bring it up again."

"I just—"

"You heard me. Paul's faith is not open for discussion."

Shelley held up her hands. "Okay, I won't talk about it anymore if it upsets you that much." She carried the last of the serving dishes to the sink. "William seems to be doing well, considering he and Myra—"

"Leave the kitchen, Shelley."

"But Mother—"

Her mother stabbed her finger in the direction of the door to the rest of the house. "I told you to leave. I cannot discuss this any longer."

Shelley did as she was told. The tension in the house was almost more than she could bear. William glanced up from couch, where he sat as her father read from the Bible. His smile quickly faded as their gazes met.

"Are you mad at someone?" he asked.

Shelley shook her head as she bit back tears. All she'd wanted to do was have a meaningful conversation with her mother, but she kept getting shut out because her mother couldn't face things she didn't like.

Father put down the Bible and looked back and forth between Shelley and William. "Why don't the two of you go out for some ice cream?"

William hopped up and clapped his hands. "Let's go, Shelley. I want some rocky road ice cream."

Chapter 9

Jeremiah still hadn't replaced his car two weeks after his old one died. He'd found a junkyard that would pay him a small amount as well as tow it from the hospital parking lot. He was surprised it hadn't cost him money. He'd gone looking at other cars, but Shelley's words continued ringing through his mind. Somehow he'd managed quite well without having his own wheels. It wasn't nearly as difficult to adjust to his old lifestyle as he'd thought.

He turned around and worked on another section of ground, getting it ready for a new variety of oranges Abe wanted to plant. He felt a trickle of sweat drip down his back. Summer had arrived early this year.

"How's the planting going?" Abe asked.

Jeremiah tossed the shovelful of dirt to the side. "I'm almost finished digging this row."

"I'm talking about on your land."

Jeremiah straightened and leaned against the shovel. "I have most of the summer crop planted already, so now it's just a matter of weeding while I wait."

"Ya, that is what we have to do."

"I've been thinking about where to put a house," Jeremiah said. "I know it needs to go over by the cluster of trees, but any advice you have would be appreciated."

Abe offered a clipped nod. "We can discuss that soon. For now, I'd like you to help me unload some of the trees I just had delivered."

Jeremiah followed Abe to the truck parked at the end of the long shell-covered road that forked in two directions—one going to the house and the other to the edge of the grove. Jeremiah couldn't help but smile as he thought about how he'd have a place of his own like this one of these days.

"It might start raining soon," Abe said. "That would be good for the newly transplanted trees."

Jeremiah glanced up at the sky. It was a deep blue with a few puffs of fluffy white clouds hanging low. He didn't see any sign of rain, but whenever Abe said rain was coming, he was generally right.

They worked hard for the rest of the afternoon, finishing a few minutes before the first clap of thunder. "I hope we get a soaker," Abe said. "That will get the trees off to a nice start." He started toward his house. "Come on inside before it starts pouring."

Jeremiah followed Abe to the house. They were dampened by the first drops of rain, but they made it to the front porch before the downpour.

Mary joined them, and they stood and watched the rain for a few minutes before she finally spoke up. "I talked to Shelley a couple of days ago. I wish someone had called me, so I could help while Jocelyn was out."

Jeremiah suspected that Mr. Penner didn't want to bother Mary, so he hadn't called to let her know. "Your grandmother filled in."

A wry smile tweaked Mary's mouth. "That must have been interesting."

"Did Shelley say anything about it?" Jeremiah asked.

"No, she wouldn't." Mary glanced over at Abe, who continued to gaze out at the rain. "I have never heard Shelley complain about anything or anyone."

"Not even me?"

"Why would she complain about you?" Mary's eyes twinkled as she laughed. "I'm the one who did all the complaining about you."

"You know I'm very sorry about that."

"Ya, I do know that, and you know all is forgiven."

Jeremiah leaned against one of the poles on the porch. "Shelley challenged me to give up my car for good."

Abe whipped around, his eyebrows lifted. "So is that why you aren't driving a car anymore—to make Shelley happy?"

With the question put that way, Jeremiah immediately knew the answer. "No. She got me thinking about it, but since I'm renewing my commitment to the Lord and coming back to the church, I figured it was time to stop dipping my toes into the water and just take the plunge."

Mary laughed again. "The way you talk reminds me of some of my old customers, Jeremiah."

Abe cast a glance at Mary. "I find it rather strange."

"Strange isn't always bad," Mary said. "I think it's fun."

Jeremiah remembered a time when Mary didn't feel that way. Abe had been good for her by accepting who she was and loving everything about her. When Jeremiah first came to Abe to discuss coming back to the church, Abe's protectiveness toward Mary had been the only obstacle Jeremiah had had to overcome. Jeremiah still felt bad about the taunting and rude comments he'd hollered from his car. Mary deserved so much better than that. Fortunately, she was as kindhearted as Abe, and she'd forgiven him.

"Jeremiah?" Mary's sweet voice startled him. "Are you feeling okay?"

He shook himself. "I'm doing just fine. Every once in a while I get lost in my thoughts."

She grinned. "Love has a way of doing that to you."

"What are you talking about, Mary?" Abe asked.

Mary turned her smiling face toward her husband. "Jeremiah knows what I'm talking about, right?"

Of course he did, but he decided to change the subject rather than field questions he didn't have answers to. "With David being available to drive me back and forth to work, I think I can do just fine without an automobile."

"Ya," Abe agreed. "That is what I've been trying to tell you."

"It took my car breaking down to get it through my thick skull, but God is in control," Jeremiah said.

"Since it's still raining, how about coming inside? Mary asked me to repair a few things in the house. Maybe you can give me a hand."

"Yes, of course," Jeremiah answered. "I'll be glad to help with anything you need."

As he walked past Mary on the porch, he tried not to look directly at her knowing, smiling face. She was extremely astute, and he suspected she was aware of everything he was thinking—particularly when he harbored thoughts of Shelley.

⌒∾

The following Sunday Shelley had a difficult time getting William out of bed. Worry gnawed at her stomach as she shook his shoulder. He mumbled something she couldn't quite understand.

"Are you sick?" she asked.

"He's not sick," her mother said from the doorway. "That awful girl Myra upset him yesterday at his company's picnic."

Shelley's heart twisted. "Don't let anyone upset you this much, William. You might have thought you were in love with Myra, but if she's mean to you, she's not worth being upset over."

William turned his head toward Shelley to face her. As he opened his eyes, she could tell he'd been crying. "Everyone was laughing at me," he said, his voice hoarse. "I don't like it when people laugh at me."

"They are stupid people," their mother said sternly.

Shelley placed her hands on William's shoulders. "People laugh at others when they don't know what else to do."

"It makes my stomach hurt when people laugh at me," William said, sniffling.

Shelley knew exactly what he was talking about. She'd experienced it when she was younger and went places where people didn't understand the plain way of life. It had taken years to eventually tune out the ignorant people who made fun of anyone unlike them.

"Stop feeling sorry for yourself, William," Mother said as she backed away from the door. "Church starts in one hour. Get up and get ready." Without another word, she walked away.

"Shelley, what can I do to make Myra stop being so mean?" William asked.

"Try to ignore her," Shelley replied, wishing she had a better answer that would soothe him and make Myra stop. But she knew there was no simple answer. "Eventually, she'll stop when she discovers her words aren't getting the reaction she wants."

William slowly sat up in bed and used the edge of the sheet to dab at his eyes. "Will Jeremiah be at church today?"

Shelley froze. She hadn't seen much of Jeremiah since the day his car wouldn't start. She understood how difficult it must have been to give up the freedom from having his own car, but she'd hoped he'd make more of an effort to stop by the restaurant. In spite of her thoughts that he might not be good for her, she'd started looking forward to seeing him. After her experience with Peter leading her on and then announcing he planned to marry Clara, she'd erected a shield around her heart. Jeremiah had managed to bring back some feelings she wasn't sure she'd ever have again.

William waved his hand in front of Shelley's face to get her attention. "Well? Will he?"

"I—I would assume so." Shelley stood and eased away from the bedside. "Now get up, and start getting ready. At least we know Myra won't be at church, so you don't need to worry about her today."

William grinned. "Good thing for that."

"Yes, it's a very good thing. I have to help Mother finish making the salad and rolls for the potluck after church."

"Are you making dessert?"

"Not this time. Last potluck we had too many desserts and not enough salads."

William grinned and rubbed his tummy. "I like dessert."

She flashed a smile as she closed William's door so he could get ready. Fortunately, William had forgotten his humiliation—at least temporarily. As she walked toward the kitchen, she said a silent prayer that God would find something else for Myra to think about so William would have some peace. It was bad enough for him to have to ward off Myra's jeers about the way Shelley dressed.

Her mother didn't waste a second. The instant Shelley arrived in the kitchen her mother started issuing orders, which was just fine. It kept Shelley from having to think about William, Jeremiah, or herself.

"Where's Father?" Shelley asked.

"He went on ahead to the church. Some of the men wanted to get the grounds ready for our potluck early." She cast a frown at Shelley. "William was supposed to go with him, but your father couldn't make him budge."

Shelley needed to change the subject quickly. "This salad looks delicious."

"Do me a favor, and put the rolls in that basket over there. I'll cover them with one of the clean dish towels in the drawer."

By the time they finished getting everything together, William had joined them in the kitchen. "I'm starving."

"I set some ham and a biscuit by the stove," their mother said. "Better hurry and eat because we need to get going."

Fifteen minutes later, the three of them were on their way to church. William carried the basket of rolls, while Shelley and Mother brought the salad and the ingredients they'd have to add at the last minute.

The second the church came into view, Shelley saw Jeremiah. He stood by the corner of the building, watching in her direction.

"That boy!" Shelley's mother shook her head. "Why isn't he working with the other men?"

"Maybe they're finished," William said. "Looky over there. Father's standing around talking to his friends."

Their mother's scowl let Shelley know that no matter what Jeremiah did, it wouldn't be good enough. Too bad Shelley's pulse had taken on a life of its own. She could feel her heart beating from the top of her head to the tips of her toes.

Before Shelley even got to the church property, Jeremiah was on his way to them. "Here," he said as he reached for the oversized bowl in her mother's hands. "Let me carry that for you."

Shelley half expected her mother to yank it away and say she didn't need his help. But she didn't. Instead, she pointed to the side of the church. "That goes in the kitchen. See to it you don't get distracted by anyone along the way."

Jeremiah cut his eyes toward Shelley and made a goofy face. She had to bite the insides of her cheeks to keep from laughing.

Mother jumped in right behind Jeremiah, preventing Shelley from directly following him, clearly a method of keeping them from being too close. Jeremiah placed the bowl where he was told. After he turned around, he leaned to make eye contact with Shelley. Her face flamed as her mother spun around and glared at her.

Mrs. Penner chose that moment to appear. "Melba! I'm so glad you remembered the salad. Looks like we have too many desserts again. Come with me, and let's see if we can figure out a way to space them better, so the children won't get too carried away with the sweets."

Shelley watched as her mother made a decision between remaining between her and Jeremiah or following Mrs. Penner. The quick look her boss's wife gave Shelley let her know she had intervened on purpose. Shelley gulped.

"Oh. . ." Mother turned a frown on Shelley but softened her facial features as she nodded to Mrs. Penner. "Okay. Shelley, make sure William is taken care of and seated before you join the women."

Shelley watched her mother and Mrs. Penner weave their way through the group toward the food that was already set up. She tingled at the awareness of Jeremiah standing so close.

"Your mother loves you," Jeremiah said, "and she's trying to protect you."

"Protect me?" Shelley blinked before looking at Jeremiah. "From what?"

"From me. She obviously still doesn't trust me, and I can't say I don't blame her. I'll probably do the same thing with my daughter. . .if the Lord chooses to bless me with one."

Shelley knew he was right, but she didn't want to continue with this conversation, which took her to an uncomfortable place in her heart. "It looks like we'll have plenty of food for the potluck."

Jeremiah tilted his head back and laughed. "Was there ever a time when we didn't? The women in this church like to make sure everyone is well fed."

"And what is wrong with that?"

"Nothing." Jeremiah grimaced. "Why do I feel like I said the wrong thing?"

Shelley sighed. "You didn't. I didn't mean to come across so harsh. It's just that. . .well, I don't know what to say right now."

"You could say that you will go to the museum with me when I have some time off from work."

Now she was totally speechless. When she tried to think of a response, nothing came to mind.

Jeremiah gave her a look of understanding. "Think about it. I'll stop by the restaurant next week, and we can talk about it then."

She nodded.

"I'd better go help the men finish setting up the tables, or they'll send out a search party for me."

Shelley watched Jeremiah walk away to join the group of men pulling tables out of the church and setting them up on the lawn. Exerting their wisdom and authority, the older men directed the younger ones. She was happy to see William pitching in and carrying chairs. He'd managed to overcome his own sadness to help others. Shelley sent up a short prayer of thanks for her younger brother.

As Shelley worked with the women, she occasionally cast a glance over toward the men. A few times she noticed Jeremiah talking to William and explaining something to him. The sight of William being treated like a man was comforting and elevated Jeremiah in her mind. She wondered if her mother noticed this.

Throughout the church service, Shelley resisted the urge to look at Jeremiah. She didn't want her mother to think he was pulling her away from her faith. When she was sure her mother wouldn't notice, she stole a glance in Jeremiah's direction and saw that he and William were leaning into each other. Father was on the other side of William, clearly oblivious to his own son's affection for Jeremiah.

Shelley thought about how she'd be with her own children. She'd certainly try to care about their feelings and innermost thoughts without trying to impose her own dreams for them.

After church was over, Mother didn't waste a single second. She took Shelley by the hand and pulled her toward the room where the food was stored. "We need to get the salads, vegetables, casseroles, and meats outside right away, or the men and children will think they can start with dessert."

Shelley seriously doubted that most of the men would do that, but she went along with her mother. Every few minutes she caught herself looking for Jeremiah. When she spotted him, a sense of satisfaction and gladness washed over her.

As soon as the food tables were full, the pastor said the blessing. There was a brief stampede toward the tables, with the younger men claiming their spots first in line, followed by the older men and children. The women hung back until the lines dwindled, and then they filled their plates. There was never any concern about not having enough food because most families brought enough to feed more than the people they came with.

Shelley had a very small appetite, so she didn't pile her plate with as much as she normally did. Before she sat, she took another look in Jeremiah's direction. William was about to sit next to him. She hoped Jeremiah didn't mind; it looked as though he was fine with William clinging to his side.

Mother, Mrs. Penner, Mary, and a couple of the other women were clustered around one end of a large table for twelve. Shelley assumed the empty chair next to Mary was for her, but she asked before sitting.

Mary pulled the chair back. "I saved the seat for you." Mary looked at Shelley's plate and grinned. "Oh good. I see that you got some of my ambrosia. Abe says it's the best he's ever tasted, so I thought it would be good for today." She leaned over and cupped her mouth as she whispered, "It's the recipe the cook at my grandparents' restaurant uses, but Abe says mine's better."

Shelley scooped up a bite of the ambrosia and tasted it. "I think it's better, too. Did you put something extra in it?"

Mary shrugged. "Just a tad more sugar, maybe, and an extra handful of coconut."

Shelley laughed. "Then this is a Mary Glick original. You have turned out to be a very good cook. I would never have thought to change a recipe."

"I can't imagine following any instructions precisely as they are written. Where's the fun in that?"

Shelley couldn't imagine not following directions for fear of a disaster. "Everything you attempt turns out better than the original."

Mary snickered and shook her head. "You only say that because I don't share the flops. And there are plenty of them."

The changes in Mary since Shelley had met her were phenomenal. When Mary first came to the school nearly ten years ago, she had a perpetual scowl on her face. Shelley suspected Mary had been shy but covered it by acting as though she didn't care about making friends. In spite of that, Shelley had forced herself upon Mary, and they gradually grew to be as close as Mary would allow. Some of the other kids had been afraid of Mary because of her shell, yet Mary thought they were shunning her. Fortunately, she now understood and had become friends with many of them.

"After you're done, try my grandmother's mixed berry cobbler. She added some vanilla, and that makes it even better than her original recipe."

"Mm." Shelley's appetite instantly spiked at the mere mention of Mrs. Penner's cobblers, which she was known for. "I can't imagine anything better than the original."

"Just wait," Mary said. "It'll knock your socks off." She winked as Shelley laughed. "I thought you'd enjoy that."

Shelley loved how Mary had embraced her life as the wife of a Mennonite farmer without losing all of herself. It must have been difficult knowing what to keep and what to let go. After all, the first fourteen years of Mary's life had been in the lowest trenches of the secular world—not knowing who her father was and with a mother who did who-knows-what to support her. Although Mary rarely mentioned anything about her life before she joined her grandparents in Pinecraft, she had shared some of the grief over her mother's death at such a difficult age.

After the older women at the table rose to bring out the desserts, Mary leaned toward Shelley. "Jeremiah can't take his eyes off you."

"How would you know?" Shelley asked.

"Because every time I look up, he's staring in this direction, and I'm certain he wouldn't be looking at an old married woman."

"I'm older than you," Shelley countered to cover her embarrassment.

"In years only. Once you get married, you get a leg up on aging." Mary let out a contented sigh. "And I wouldn't trade it for anything in the world. I sure hope you are able to experience the joy of being married to a wonderful husband."

"I thought I would with Peter," Shelley said, instantly regretting mentioning his name. "Sorry."

"Peter made a huge mistake, and I'm pretty sure he knows it now," Mary said. "Clara recently told him she wasn't sure she wanted to stay in Florida because she misses Pennsylvania. When Peter refused to follow her up north, Clara broke off the engagement."

Shelley leaned away from Mary and regarded her with interest. "How do you know all this?" Peter and Clara had started attending a different Mennonite church on the other side of Pinecraft, where Clara's parents attended when they were in town.

"Peter got a job at the lumber store, and Abe talks to him on occasion."

"Good for Peter. I knew he wanted to work there."

"So," Mary began as she folded her arms, "would you want to take Peter back if he was interested?"

"Do you know something?"

A conspiratorial smile formed on Mary's lips. "Maybe."

Shelley slowly shook her head. "After what Peter did to me, I'm not sure if I could ever trust him again."

"Why? The two of you weren't engaged, and from what he told Abe, he didn't realize you expected anything from him."

"Abe didn't tell him—"

"No," Mary said, interrupting her. "But some other people from the church did. He told Abe that he regretted many things, one of them being not noticing how you felt."

"It doesn't really matter now. A lot of time has passed."

"And you're no longer interested in Peter, are you?"

"I have no desire to resume any sort of relationship with Peter. . .well, except maybe friendship."

"Friendship doesn't preclude a more. . .romantic relationship," Mary said. "Unless, of course, you have your sights on someone else." She tilted her head toward Jeremiah. "And that someone else is heading this way."

Shelley instinctively turned in the direction of Mary's nod. She met Jeremiah's gaze as he walked toward them with determination.

Mary placed her hand on Shelley's arm. "I need to go see if Grandma needs help."

Jeremiah reached Shelley's side right when Mary left. "I hope I didn't run her off."

"No," Shelley said. "She wanted to go help her grandmother. I think I should probably do a little cleaning."

"I'll help," Jeremiah said without a moment's hesitation. "Maybe we can visit the Ringling Museum of Art afterward."

To Shelley's surprise, her mother didn't argue when Shelley asked if it was okay to go to the museum with Jeremiah. All she'd said was, "Be home before dark."

Jeremiah had obviously been there many times because he knew his way around. He pointed out some exhibits and joked around, making her laugh and forget about anything else. When he took her hand on the bus ride back to Pinecraft, Shelley could almost imagine their relationship being normal.

❧

The next morning Jeremiah hopped out of bed with more of a spring in his step than usual. Working beside Shelley yesterday had given him purpose and the feeling that there might be hope for a deeper relationship. To his surprise and delight, her mother hadn't voiced a single objection. He and Shelley had had a real date that had been over way too soon to his liking.

David, the driver he'd arranged through Abe, picked him up at the same time he did every day. "It's good to see you so chipper this early on a Monday morning," David said. "Did you have a good weekend?"

Jeremiah's grin widened. "I sure did." He told David about the potluck after church, the museum date, and how he felt that he'd made some headway with Shelley. "But I need to take this very slowly because her mom still can't stand me."

"I'm obviously speaking as a complete outsider, but it's been my observation since getting to know many people in your church that most are very forgiving if they know you're sincere."

"Yes, I'm sure that's true most of the time with Mrs. Burkholder, but I'm not so sure when it comes to her daughter. She's very protective of her family."

David told Jeremiah about the courtship with his own wife years ago. "Her dad hated my guts at first, but after we gave him a grandchild, things gradually changed. I think he appreciates me now, but it took years."

Jeremiah paid David and thanked him for the ride before setting up a time to be picked up. "There's nothing to do on my own land today, so I thought I'd swing by Shelley's house after she gets off work."

David waved before taking off. Abe joined Jeremiah on the lawn to give instructions for the day. Jeremiah was glad to have something to do to stay busy and yet have the freedom to think about what he'd say to Shelley.

At two o'clock, Abe walked up to Jeremiah. "Why don't you leave early today? Mary said she thought you might want to walk Shelley home from work."

"Thanks, Abe. I'd better call for a ride now then."

"No need. I called David about fifteen minutes ago, so he should be here any minute."

David arrived five minutes later. "Ready to go see your girl?"

"Let's hope that's how it all turns out. The more I'm with her the more I realize she's the woman I want to be with."

All the way into town, Jeremiah shared his thoughts and feelings about Shelley. "She's one of the most intelligent girls I've ever met, and she has heart. Her younger brother, William, has Down syndrome, and she's very good to him. I understand that she will be responsible for him after their parents can no longer take care of him."

"How do you feel about that?" David asked.

"I'm cool with it. William's a good kid, and he doesn't mind helping out with stuff. I think he likes me, too."

"So all you need to deal with is Shelley's parents?"

"Seems that way," Jeremiah replied as they pulled up in front of the restaurant. "Thanks for the ride." He pulled some bills out of his pocket and handed them to David.

Jeremiah straightened his shirt collar, squared his shoulders, took a deep, cleansing breath, and strode into the restaurant. He glanced around looking for Shelley and spotted her standing by the back corner booth, deep in conversation with someone. She glanced up at him but didn't acknowledge his presence, so he walked toward her. When he got close enough, the person in the booth turned around and looked at him. It was Peter, the guy Shelley had once thought she was in love with.

Chapter 10

Hi, Peter." Jeremiah lifted his chin, hoping his trepidation didn't show. "Jeremiah," Peter said as he stood. "I was just having a nice chat with Shelley, hoping she'd go out with me after work. Would you like to join me for a cup of coffee while I wait for her to finish her shift?"

Jeremiah felt as though he'd hit a wall head-on at full speed. He glanced at Shelley, who didn't look him in the eye. Her discomfort was obvious.

"Uh. . .I was. . .uh, on my way home from work, and I wanted to. . .uh. . ." What was wrong with him? He cleared his throat. "I really need to get home."

Shelley lifted her gaze and looked at him with an expression he didn't recognize. She wasn't happy about something, but he wasn't sure if he'd caused it, so far be it for him to stick around and risk being a nuisance.

"I guess I'd better go now." He lifted his hand in a half wave and let it fall back down by his side. "See ya."

"Bye, Jeremiah," Peter said as he sat back down. "It's good you're back. I'm sure you'll be much happier now that you've come to your senses."

A year ago Jeremiah would have fought for the woman he loved. He had to use every ounce of self-restraint to keep his temper under control. Jeremiah wanted to know why Peter was suddenly coming around again, but he was too stunned to see him now to ask. He needed to regroup and figure out what to do next.

Jeremiah walked outside into the bright sunshine, which reminded him the day was still in full swing. He glanced to the left and then to the right as he decided where to go. He didn't want to go home just yet. His father was still at work, and his mother had her quilting group over on Mondays.

He started walking in the opposite direction from home. It was already hot out, even though summer was still weeks away. He could go to the beach, but he didn't feel like facing the curiosity seekers, so he decided against that. For the first time since his car had stalled, he wished he'd bought a replacement.

After several blocks, he found himself at a bus stop. Maybe a ride on the bus would do him some good and at least kill some time.

The bus arrived about five minutes later. Jeremiah boarded the bus and rode for a while, hanging his head, thinking about his options. Seeing Peter with Shelley and knowing their history made his stomach ache. It simply wasn't right. Jeremiah knew for a fact that Peter was no good for Shelley, and he had no right to come back into her life as though he'd done nothing wrong. Jeremiah wasn't perfect, and his past had been checkered with things he regretted, but he'd never hurt Shelley as Peter had.

The biggest problem was how to show Shelley he was better for her than Peter. Until now, he'd felt that he was making some headway with her. The look on her face when their eyes had met flickered in his mind. She didn't seem happy—maybe she was even a touch annoyed—with him stopping by the restaurant. Perhaps he'd deluded himself into thinking she had even a sliver of interest in him.

Jeremiah glanced out the window and spotted a used-car dealership. Maybe he'd check out the lot and see if there was anything he'd feel good about driving. He let the bus driver know he wanted off at the next stop.

As soon as he reached the car lot, the salesman approached. "What can I help you with today, sir? We have some great automobiles in stock just waiting for the right person to drive one of them home."

Jeremiah scanned the rows of cars in all sizes, shapes, and colors. He pointed. "How about that gray one at the end?"

The salesman frowned as he glanced at Jeremiah's watch, the only thing he kept from his time away from the Mennonite church. "I don't know about that one. It's a little weathered and beat up—okay for a kid but not for someone who likes to ride in style. How about this fire-engine red sporty number right over here?"

Jeremiah didn't even look in the direction the salesman pointed. He knew he'd be weak if the right words were said. "No, I want to test-drive the gray car."

With a snort, the salesman backed toward the tiny sales office. "If you insist. I'll go grab the key so you can take it for a spin."

The second the salesman went into the office, Jeremiah allowed himself a brief glimpse of the sports car. His throat tightened, and his skin tingled at the thought of being behind the wheel of that gorgeous piece of machinery. Without hesitation he approached the red car and gently stroked the hood. He could imagine himself cruising the streets of Sarasota, looking all. . . He stopped, shuddered, and took a step back.

"Hey, I see you've come to your senses," the salesman shouted. "Let me go back inside and get the key so you can drive the car of your dreams. And you won't believe your luck today. We have a special—"

"No thanks," Jeremiah hollered right back. "I've changed my mind. I don't need to drive any car right now."

"Are you sure?"

Jeremiah didn't bother answering the overly exuberant man, desperate to sell him a car. Instead, he strode as quickly as he could for nearly a quarter of a mile before his resolve crumbled.

That red car sure would be fun to drive, and nothing said he had to buy it. He mentally pictured himself gripping the steering wheel, pulling out onto the highway, testing the engine by pressing his foot harder on the accelerator. After living seventeen years without a car, he'd thoroughly enjoyed the freedom with one. Letting go of his bright orange sports car had been difficult, but he'd had a mixed mission—to reunite with his church and to fulfill his longtime dream of making Shelley his wife. Now, with Peter in the picture beside Shelley, the other half of his mission seemed less attractive.

He did an about-face and walked straight back to the dealership. The little guy who was wiping the windows of a car on the edge of the lot glanced up and did a double take before grinning. "You're back. Does this mean—"

"I'd like the keys to the red sports car," Jeremiah said. "And do you have financing?"

"Yes, of course we have financing. We take care of all your car-buying needs."

Jeremiah watched the man practically skip to his office. He grinned. It didn't take much to make some people happy. He wished he could be one of them.

⌘

"I'm sorry, Peter, but I need to go straight home after work," Shelley said.

"How about tomorrow?" His voice sounded urgent. "Maybe we can take a picnic dinner to the beach and—"

"No, not tomorrow either."

"So are you saying you're not interested in me anymore?" Peter tilted his head and stared at her. She wished he wouldn't be so persistent. Although her feelings for him had faded shortly after he'd announced his engagement to Clara, she disliked being put on the spot in such an uncomfortable way, and she didn't feel that she owed him an explanation.

"Peter, I don't need to explain anything to you."

"But we had something special."

She had to take a couple of deep breaths to keep her anger in check. "So special you could get engaged to someone else, leaving me wondering what I did wrong?"

"Nothing, Shelley." He held her gaze for an uncomfortable moment. "You did nothing wrong. I want you back in my life."

She narrowed her eyes. "Where is Clara?"

His jaw tightened for a split second, and then he forced a smile. "She moved back to Pennsylvania. I—I chose not to go with her."

His confession solidified her opinion of him. "It is too late for us. I don't want to be with someone I can't trust."

"I am so sorry, Shelley. After I realized you and William were a package deal, I wasn't sure we were meant to be together." He looked down at the floor and then back up at her with sadness.

Shelley lifted her eyebrows in shock. "Are you saying you lost interest in me because of William? My little brother?"

He nodded with a look of contrition. "I know I was wrong. William is okay. It's just that—"

"You absolutely were wrong." Shelley knew for certain that there was no way she'd ever want to be with Peter now. William was a wonderful human being who would never do anything to hurt anyone. "My brother is the sweetest person I know, and he makes you look like—"

Peter's attention suddenly shifted to something behind her. She spun around and saw Jeremiah behind the wheel of a bright-red sports car as he pulled to a stop in front of the restaurant.

"I thought he decided he didn't need a car," Peter said with a smirk. "Is that what he told you?"

Shelley nodded. She'd half expected him to give in to his desire for another automobile, but she didn't think it would be one like he was now driving. It certainly hadn't taken him long to fall back to his old ways.

She turned around and looked at Peter, who continued standing in front of her smiling. "I'll give you some time to think about us, Shelley, and I'll be back later."

"No, Peter. I've done all the thinking I need to do about us."

"Think some more." With that, he didn't waste another second before striding toward the door.

Without turning around she knew that as Peter left, Jeremiah came inside. His footsteps were soft, but she saw his shadow as he approached.

Jeremiah didn't speak right away, so Shelley slowly turned to meet his silent gaze. "Hi, Jeremiah."

He smiled at her, but she couldn't hide her disappointment. His smile quickly faded. "I just wanted to find out what's going on with us."

Shelley's breath caught in her throat, so she took a step away from Jeremiah to place some distance between them. "With us?"

Jeremiah nodded. "Yes. With us." He shuffled his feet and glanced around the restaurant before settling his gaze back on her. "And between you and Peter."

"I'll answer your last question first. There is nothing going on between Peter and me."

He visibly relaxed. "That's not how it looked, but if you say nothing is going on, I believe you."

"Do you really?" she asked.

"I'm trying." He looked down at her with a closed-mouth grin.

"Now for your first question, that's not quite so simple. I'm not even sure I understand the nature of it."

"C'mon, Shelley, you know how I feel about you."

She thought she knew, but after assuming Peter's intentions, she wasn't about to make the same mistake again. "I'm not positive how you feel, Jeremiah."

"I feel. . .well, I feel like you and I get along really well, and I like being with you." He shoved his hands in his pockets and cleared his throat. "No, I take that back. I *love* being with you. When I'm with you, I feel like I can do anything."

Shelley had to try hard not to smile. She'd been hoping Jeremiah felt this way, but there was still the one issue of her parents not approving. She suspected if she could get her mother to come around, her father might follow.

"Well?" he asked. "Aren't you going to say something?"

She lifted her hands to her sides. "I'm not sure what to say, Jeremiah. But honestly, this probably isn't the best place to discuss it."

"What time are you getting off today?"

"Soon. I'm waiting for Mrs. Penner to arrive."

"I'll wait." He sank down in the chair directly behind him.

"But first," she said slowly, "where did you get that car? Is it yours?"

He looked at her and then cast his gaze downward. "No. . .well, at least not yet. I'm thinking about getting a new set of wheels, and that car just happened to be sitting in the car lot, and I—"

At least he hadn't yet bought the car. Relief flooded Shelley before she considered the fact that she didn't have the right to approve or disapprove of what automobile Jeremiah drove. Or if he even drove one at all.

"What do you think?" he asked softly.

"Does it matter what I think?"

"Yes, of course it does."

Shelley folded her arms and shook her head. "I didn't think you'd be able to resist buying a car, but I have to admit I'm disappointed in the one you chose."

"Too flashy, huh?" His expression was contrite and rather impish.

"Ya. It's very flashy. But who am I to cast judgment?"

"I value your opinion, Shelley. If you think the red car is wrong for me, I won't buy it. It's really not that important."

"Then why are you driving it?" She paused before adding, "How important is any car? I thought you were doing just fine without one."

"I guess I have been. It's just that. . ." He lifted his hands and let them slap his thighs. "I don't know. I came in here and saw you and Peter, and it was frustrating." He hung his head and looked back at her with soulful eyes. "I just reacted."

"That is a concern, Jeremiah. Reactions from bad emotions often involve bad decisions. What happens when something really awful happens? What will your reaction be then?"

Jeremiah grew pensive and rubbed his chin. "That's a good point, Shelley. I suppose I've been reacting all my life."

Shelley knew that. Jeremiah had a tremendous number of good qualities, but the one bad thing about him negated much of the positive. "You need to practice self-restraint."

"I'm working on it."

"I'm sure it takes time."

Jeremiah didn't respond to her last comment. Instead, he gestured toward the door. "Okay, so I probably won't buy the car, but would you like to go for a ride in it before I bring it back?"

She glanced outside at the shiny red car that held no appeal for her. "No, I'd better not."

⌦

Jeremiah sensed that he'd taken a step back in his quest to pursue Shelley, simply by showing up in a sports car. He wanted to kick himself a thousand times for not thinking through his decision to stop by during his test-drive. He knew he needed to do something to salvage even a shred of hope to see her again.

"I'm returning the car now, and I'll take the bus home." He took a couple of steps toward the door, stopped, and turned back to face Shelley. "I'm fine without my own wheels. It's just fun sometimes to drive a car like that." Why did he have to keep talking? That last statement eliminated anything he'd done to improve his situation. "But it means absolutely nothing to me."

Shelley grinned at him as though she understood. "I'm sure that's not the case, or you wouldn't be so excited about driving it."

He figured he'd better quit before he dug any deeper. "I'm still returning it. Can we talk soon?"

"Yes, that would be good." Shelley took a step back. "Come back tomorrow." She spun around and was barely past the kitchen door when the bell on the door jingled.

⌦

"Jeremiah, what are you still doing here?" The sound of Peter's voice grated Shelley.

"I was just leaving," Jeremiah replied.

Shelley hovered behind the kitchen door, trying to decide what to do. Mr. Penner approached and startled her.

"What is going on, Shelley?" he asked. "You look pale."

"N–nothing. I was just checking to see if Mrs. Penner was here yet."

"She should be here any minute. If you need to leave now—"

"Neh!" Shelley swallowed hard after her sudden outburst. "Sorry, but I can wait for her to arrive."

He pursed his lips and narrowed his eyes as he regarded her. "Is there something I need to know about?" He leaned past her, opened the door to the dining room a couple of inches, and peeked. "Oh, I see the problem. You don't want to leave with Peter, is that right?"

Shelley nodded. "I know I shouldn't worry you with my personal concerns, but I had no idea he was coming back."

"What happened to Clara?"

She explained what she knew. Mr. Penner made a face. "Sounds to me like he wants everything his way."

"I don't know the details about what happened between him and Clara, but I do know that I am no longer interested in him."

"Then tell him you want to go home alone. I've found that it's always best to be direct."

"I already told him that, but it doesn't seem to matter," Shelley replied.

"Would you like for me to talk to him?"

"Neh, I don't think that would be a good idea."

Mrs. Penner arrived from the back. "It doesn't look terribly busy today," she said. "Why don't you go on home now, Shelley? I can take over from here."

Shelley glanced back at Mr. Penner, who nodded. "Have one more talk with Peter, and let him know that in no uncertain terms you aren't interested in a relationship with him anymore."

Mrs. Penner planted her fists firmly on her hips and glared first at her husband then at Shelley. "What's the matter with Peter? He'd make some girl a fine husband." She frowned for a moment. "Wait a minute. I thought he was engaged to Clara."

"Why don't you run along, Shelley?" Mr. Penner said. "I'll explain everything to my wife."

Happy to be let off the hook, Shelley removed her apron, grabbed her tote, headed for the back door with only a brief hesitation, and left. She made it nearly a block before she heard Peter's voice behind her.

"Wait up, Shelley. I'll walk you home."

"That won't be necessary, Peter." She quickened her pace, but he caught up with her.

Peter laughed. "You're very independent, as always. I hope Jeremiah doesn't hold on to this silly notion that you would ever be interested in him."

"That's not your concern, Peter."

"Oh, but I think it is. I already told you I made a mistake, and I want to make it up to you. I feel terrible that I hurt you."

"People get hurt all the time. I'm over it."

"I stopped by and saw your mother this morning," Peter said.

Shelley stopped and turned to face Peter. "Why did you do that, Peter?"

"Calm down, Shelley. I care about you and your family, and I thought it would be the right thing to do."

"The right thing to do is leave me alone. You made your feelings for me and my family very clear when you became engaged to Clara. Now let things be."

Peter looked down at the sidewalk and then lifted his gaze to hers. "I can't, Shelley. I'm not getting any younger, and I need a wife."

"Oh, so that's it." She tried to hold back the sarcasm, but it erupted anyway. "You think it's time to get married, and you figured I'd be an easy catch."

"No, that's not it at all." He placed his hand on her shoulder. "You are the ideal woman for me, Shelley. You're everything I want in a wife, and I plan to marry you."

"You should have felt that way months ago. It's too late now."

"I don't think so. Your mother told me she would welcome me into the family."

Shelley felt fury well in her chest. "You told my mother you wanted to marry me?"

He tilted his head to the side. "Yes, I feel it's important to make my intentions clear from the beginning—especially after what happened before. I don't believe in hiding anything."

"You should have asked me first." She started walking again but not as quickly as before. "Now I think you should turn around and leave me alone."

"I can't do that, Shelley. I promised your mother I would join your family for dinner."

"You what?" The shrieking sound of her own voice startled her, so she steadied herself before continuing. "You have no business doing that, Peter. I do not want to marry you."

"Your mother invited me, and I don't want to disappoint her," he argued. "She seems to approve of me as a suitor."

Peter's underhandedness confirmed what she already knew from the moment he'd announced his engagement to Clara—marrying him would have been a huge mistake. They walked the rest of the way to her house in silence.

⌒

Jeremiah had just gotten off the bus after returning the car to the dealership when he spotted Shelley and Peter walking toward her house. Curious, he followed them from a distance until they reached the sidewalk in front of Shelley's house. His heart sank, and once again he had to use every bit of self-restraint not to confront them. He didn't think Shelley was trying to deceive him about not wanting to be with Peter, but maybe she wasn't ready to let him go.

Competition had always brought out the worst in Jeremiah, but he couldn't let Shelley go without at least trying to win her over. He'd have to come up with a plan before acting, though, because he knew from experience that acting on impulse would bring him the opposite result of what he wanted.

Jeremiah took a couple of steps toward home when he heard the commotion behind him. Without another thought, he spun around and spotted Shelley's mother frantically waving her arms, sobbing, and trying to talk to Shelley. Peter hung back while Shelley reached out to comfort her mother. Something bad had obviously happened.

Rather than leave, Jeremiah made the hasty decision to see if there was anything he could do to help. He took off running toward the Burkholder house.

Peter's lip curled as he spotted Jeremiah running toward him. "What are you doing here, Jeremiah?"

Jeremiah ignored Peter and focused his attention on Shelley and her mother. "What is going on?"

Shelley's arm remained around her mother's shoulder as she looked at him. "William has disappeared, and no one has any idea where he could be."

"I'll help look for him," Jeremiah said without hesitation.

"We don't need you to help," Peter said. "I think we have this covered without you."

Mrs. Burkholder's expression changed to one of confusion. "That was out of line, Peter. We need all the help we can get."

"Y–Ya, ya, of course," Peter said. "It's just that. . .I don't know if Jeremiah knows enough about William to be of much help. He might even be a hindrance. . ." The look on his face showed that he was aware he didn't have any idea what he was talking about, and he was floundering.

"Where was he last seen?" Jeremiah asked. "And do you remember what he was wearing?"

Mrs. Burkholder sniffled and wiped her nose with her hankie. "He went on break at work, and he didn't come back when the time was up. He was wearing a purple shirt that someone at work gave him. I remember because I wanted him to wear his white shirt, and we argued about it."

"Thanks. I'll start in the area around where he works," Jeremiah said. "Shelley, would you like to come with me, or do you need to stay with your mother?"

Shelley turned to her mother. "What would you like me to do?"

Again, Peter spoke up. "Don't pull this nonsense, Jeremiah. She's needed at home."

Instead of sticking around for a battle of words with Peter, Jeremiah waved. "That's fine. Instead of wasting time talking, I'm going to go look for William now. Someone needs to let all the neighbors know, so they can be on the lookout."

Mrs. Burkholder lifted her finger. "I got a new cell phone. Let me give you my number."

After Jeremiah added her new number to his phone, he sprinted to the bus stop. He rode across town and got off at the car dealership where he'd seen the red sports car. The salesman grinned at him until he realized who Jeremiah was, and then he scowled and shook his head.

"I need a car right away," Jeremiah said.

"You said you weren't in the market for a car," the salesman reminded him.

"I'm not. I just need to borrow one for a little while."

"Unless you're in the market for a car, I can't let you test-drive one. We're not in the business of loaning cars," he said, his voice harsh.

"This is an emergency," Jeremiah said. As he explained what was happening, he witnessed the man's expression softening.

"How do I know you're telling the truth?" the salesman asked.

"I have no idea, but I don't have time to argue. Will you let me use a car or not?"

The man swallowed hard and then nodded. "Tell you what. If you can give me a description, I'll take another car and search for him, too." He glanced down at his feet. "Business has been slow lately, so I don't have anything better to do."

Jeremiah nodded and described William. As soon as he had the keys to one of the cars on the lot, he took off for William's workplace.

William's supervisor gave him all the information he had and handed Jeremiah a card. "If you find him, please call my cell phone."

Chapter 11

Jeremiah drove in circles, starting with the block of William's office building. He gradually widened the circle until he spotted the entrance of a city park. On a hunch, he turned and slowly made his way through the mangroves and toward a small clearing of trees. Someone with a purple shirt sat on a picnic bench, so he turned the car toward the small parking area nearby.

As he approached the clearing, he saw William sitting there with his face in his hands. "William?"

The sound of his name caught William's attention, and he looked up. "What are you doing here, Jeremiah?"

"I came looking for you. What's going on?"

William's chin quivered, and he wiped his eyes with the back of his hand. "I had to get away."

"Did something happen?" Jeremiah joined William at the bench.

"Myra tricked me."

"Myra?" Jeremiah pulled the cell phone out of his pocket. "Give me a minute to let everyone know you're okay, and then I want to hear all about what Myra did."

Jeremiah called Mrs. Burkholder first. The instant she heard that William was safe, she broke down crying and handed the phone to Shelley.

"Is he hurt?" Shelley asked.

"Not physically. I'll take him home as soon as I can."

After he got off the phone with Shelley, he called William's supervisor. "He seems fine."

"That's a relief. We take our job here very seriously, and we don't like to lose our workers."

Next on the list of calls was the salesman from the car dealership. "I found him," Jeremiah said. "As soon as I take him home, I'll return the car."

"Why don't you keep the car for the rest of the day? You might change your mind and decide to buy it." He cleared his throat. "Even if you don't want to buy it, maybe it'll come in handy."

"Thanks," Jeremiah said. "I'll bring it back before you leave."

"I'll be here until seven or eight."

Jeremiah punched the OFF button and turned his full attention to William. "Okay, so tell me what happened with Myra."

William grasped the front of his shirt. "Myra gave this to me yesterday and said she thought I would look better in purple instead of my ugly white shirt Mother always wants me to wear." He sniffled. "She says I have funny-looking clothes, and that is why she didn't want to marry me."

Jeremiah understood what William was going through after experiencing it most of his life. "Why did that make you run. . .er, leave work?"

"When she saw me wearing this shirt, she said I was still funny-looking."

"That was a very mean thing for her to say," Jeremiah said.

"I know. I wanted to take off my shirt and throw it at her, but I didn't have anything else to wear, so I kept my shirt on and left."

"Sometimes people say mean things to me, too."

"Does that make you cry?" William asked.

Jeremiah leaned over and propped his elbows on his thighs as he pondered how to answer the question without being condescending. "It used to, but as I get older and hopefully wiser, I realize when people do that, they're crying out for help."

"What are you talking about?"

"It means that when people say mean things, they aren't talking about you. It's more how they feel about themselves. Happy people who have a good understanding of everyone's differences generally don't try to make other people feel bad."

William's forehead crinkled, and the corners of his mouth tightened. Finally, he nodded. "I believe you."

"When Myra said those mean things, did she make sure other people could hear her?"

"Ya. Everyone heard her, and that's what hurts my feelings."

"I don't think she would have said that to you if no one else were listening. I think she was just trying to show off." Jeremiah straightened up and propped his forearm on William's shoulder. "She was trying to make herself look smart by putting you down."

William turned to face Jeremiah head-on. "Myra has always been a show-off."

"I bet everyone knows that, so they don't think any less of you for what she said."

"Everyone does know," William admitted before growing silent.

"You realize you have a lot of people worried about you, don't you?"

William frowned and nodded. "Ya, but I didn't think about that when I left."

Jeremiah stood and gestured for William to follow. "Let's get you back home with your family, and I'll return this car to the dealership."

"Can I ride up front with you?" William asked.

"Yes, of course you can."

William's mood instantly changed as he expressed his excitement over riding in the car. "How fast can you go?"

Jeremiah chuckled. "The speed limit is only forty-five, so that's as fast as we're going."

By the time they arrived at the Burkholder house, William's tears had dried. His mother and sister waited anxiously in the front yard. Peter was nowhere in sight.

Shelley approached the car, flung open the passenger door, and wrapped her arms around William. "We were sick with worry. Don't ever do that to us again."

"Excuse me, Shelley, but I can't get out with you standing in my way."

Shelley laughed and scooted to the side. "Then come on. Mother wants to hug you, too."

After William walked around Shelley toward their mother, Shelley leaned over to talk to Jeremiah. "Thank you for finding my brother. How did you know where to look?"

"I didn't know for sure, but I remembered that he went to a park last time he wandered off, so when I saw the park, I took a chance he might have gone there."

Shelley smiled. "We need to have a long talk with William about not wandering off."

"Or maybe you need to have some way of him letting you know when he needs to get away by himself."

Shelley's smile faded as she shook her head. "He should never be by himself."

"Every man needs to be alone once in a while to think—particularly when he has woman trouble."

"Does this have anything to do with Myra?" Shelley asked.

"I'll let William tell you. But don't force him just yet. He and I talked, and I think he still needs to sort out a few things first."

Shelley's eyes narrowed as her voice deepened. "The only thing he needs to sort out is not scaring our mother half to death."

"Shelley. . . ," Jeremiah began, but he couldn't bring himself to tell her to back off. If something like this had happened to his own family, there was no telling what he'd do.

"Thank you for bringing him home to us. We can take it from here." Shelley held his gaze for a few seconds before joining her mother and brother.

Jeremiah sat and watched the Burkholder family huddle before he pulled away from the curb. All the way to the car dealership, he thought about how little he was trusted—even when he did everything in his power to make things right again.

Lord, I don't know how to make Shelley and her family see that I'm sincere.

I've done everything I can think of. If there is anything else I can do, please show me. . .and make it obvious because I'm blind to subtle messages.

He alternated between praying and talking to himself. Ever since he'd left the church, his life had seemed very shaky. He never doubted that coming back was the right thing to do, but having to constantly prove himself was getting tiresome.

⋐

"Someone needs to let Peter know that we've found William," Shelley's mother said after William went to his room. "Shelley, why don't you call him?"

Shelley didn't want to talk to Peter, but she did it anyway so he wouldn't continue looking. When he answered the phone, she could hear the background noise.

"Are you at Penner's?" she asked.

"Um. . .yes," Peter replied. "William isn't here."

"I know that. He's here with us."

"Oh good." She didn't hear an ounce of conviction in his voice. "I thought he'd probably find his way home."

"He didn't come back by himself."

"Hey, Shelley, I gotta run. Mrs. Penner just put my plate in front of me, and I don't want my food to get cold."

She clicked off the phone without another word as annoyance coursed through her. Peter didn't care anything about William, or he would have been out there looking for him. Her mother needed to know.

"Did you get ahold of Peter?" Mother asked.

"Yes." Shelley tried to loosen the muscle in her jaw before continuing. "He was at Penner's getting something to eat."

"Poor Peter. He must have worked up an appetite looking for our William."

That was the final straw. "No, Mother, Peter wasn't the least bit worried about William. All Peter thinks about is what Peter wants."

"Shelley! I will not have you talk about Peter like that. He's a fine young man who lost his mind temporarily but finally came to his senses about you."

"That's not true," Shelley said, working hard to keep her voice calm. "He wanted to marry Clara, but she wanted to go back to Pennsylvania, and he wasn't willing to follow her."

"That's because—"

Shelley interrupted her mother. "That's because Peter couldn't have everything he wanted, so he gave her an ultimatum—either Pennsylvania or him. And Clara had the sense to choose Pennsylvania."

"And how would you know this?"

"Peter told me. Mother, I once thought I loved Peter, but now that I look back on our relationship, I realize it was all about him. As long as I made him happy and he got his way, he came around. Clara came along and showed him a little interest, and he turned his back on me like I meant nothing to him."

Mother studied Shelley as though she understood, but that didn't last long. "Like I said, he's come to his senses, and he sees what he almost gave up."

"There's another thing I don't think you realize," Shelley continued. "Peter has never wanted to take on the responsibility for William."

"He doesn't have to."

"If he marries me, he will. I love William, and I will never turn my back on my little brother."

"I love you, too, Shelley," William said from the hallway. "I will always be your little brother." He closed the gap between them and pulled Shelley in for a hug.

As Shelley enjoyed William's embrace, she looked over his shoulder at their mother and wondered what all he'd heard. "How long have you been listening to us, William?" she said softly as she stepped back.

"The first thing I heard you say was that you love me." His grin melted her heart. "I love you, and I love Mother, and I love Father." His chest rose and fell with a deep breath before he added, "And I love Jeremiah. Did you know that he likes to go to the park to think when he has a bad day?"

"Enough of that," Mother said. "William, go back to your room and think about what you did. We will call for you when it's time for supper."

A flash of pain shot across William's face, but he did as he was told. As soon as he was out of the room, Shelley spun around and faced her mother.

"Did you even bother to hear why William took off?" Shelley asked.

"Neh." Mother folded her arms and scrunched her face. "There is no reason to bother with that. He needs to understand that he is never allowed to run off like he did today."

"Maybe if we took the time to listen to him, he wouldn't feel the need to run away like he does."

"There is never any reason for him to run away. William has as good of a life as we can possibly give him. In fact, I think perhaps we give him too much. I'm going to talk to your father about taking him out of that silly work program."

"You can't do that!" Shelley couldn't believe her mother would even suggest such a thing. "He loves working and having his own money."

"If he loves working so much, then he shouldn't have left and scared us half to death."

Shelley could see that they weren't getting anywhere, so she decided to use a different tack. She took a cleansing breath then gestured toward the kitchen. "Why don't we put our heads together and try to figure out some way to help him through this problem he's having with that girl who keeps tormenting him?"

"If it's not her, it will be someone else. Instead of wasting all our time on figuring out how to help him deal with this, we should have him come straight home after school."

Shelley knew how much William valued the small paycheck he brought home, so she decided to stop trying to convince her mother and talk to William. "I'll help you start supper, and then I think I'll go have a chat with William."

"Good idea," Mother said. "Perhaps you can talk some sense into that boy. If he keeps this up, he'll drive me to an early grave."

Rather than continue a conversation that obviously was going nowhere, Shelley helped her mother in silence. Once everything was in the oven, she removed her apron and went to William's room.

She stood at the door of his room and watched him for a few seconds as he sat at his desk staring out the window. "William?"

He turned around and met her gaze. "Hi, Shelley. Is supper ready?"

"No, not yet. Mind if I come in?"

"You can come in." He turned back to the window and pointed. "Look at that redbird out there. I think he forgot he was supposed to fly north."

Shelley leaned over and watched the bird pecking at the food on the bird feeder Father had placed in the backyard. "Why should he fly north when he has it made right here in Sarasota?"

"Because that's where his family and friends are," William replied. "If I was a bird, I wouldn't want them to go away without me."

"But you went away without us," Shelley reminded him.

"That's different. I was upset."

"Maybe the bird is upset about something."

William watched the bird until it had its fill and flew away. He looked directly at Shelley. "Do you think Myra will ever like me again?"

"Maybe, but if I were you, I would concentrate on your job and not so much on whether or not Myra likes you."

"I want her to like me."

Shelley reached for his hand and held it between both of hers. "But why?"

He shrugged. "I don't know. I don't want anyone to not like me."

"Do you like your job?"

"Uh-huh. I like doing work and making money. And Mr. O'Reilly is very nice. He tells me I'm a hard worker, but it really isn't hard at all. I just do what he tells me to do, and that always makes him happy."

"You're supposed to enjoy your work, but that doesn't mean you have to put up with mean-spirited people."

"Shelley, is anyone ever mean to you?"

"Sometimes, but I try not to think about them too much." She thought about the few rude customers she'd had to deal with. "I have to admit that I'm glad when they leave the restaurant."

"Myra works with me, so she won't leave."

"Are there any nice people there?"

"Uh-huh. Alexander is nice. His mother bakes cupcakes, and sometimes he shares with me during break."

Shelley smiled. "That's very sweet. Why don't you ignore Myra and just be friends with Alexander?"

William thought about that and nodded. "That's what I'm going to do. I'll tell Alexander to ignore Myra, too."

"I don't think God would want you to tell Alexander to do anything like that, but I do think He'd want you to concentrate on the things you like about work."

The sound of Father coming in the door caught their attention. Shelley stood. "Why don't we go set the table and help Mother get everything ready for supper?"

"Is it okay if I come out of my room now?" William asked.

"Yes, I'm sure it's fine." She took him by the hand and led him to the kitchen, where Mother and Father were already deep in conversation.

Chapter 12

By Friday, the Burkholder family had settled back down. Shelley's only concern was Mother's increasingly gloomy mood. Each time something happened, she handled the crisis as it happened and then gradually retreated into despondency and remained in bed later than usual. Shelley was concerned about leaving her alone.

Shelley went to her mother's bedside. "Do you want me to stay with you or call someone?"

"No," Mother said. "Go on to work. I'll get up in a few minutes to help William get ready for school."

"I've already done that. He's eating breakfast right now."

In the dim early-morning light, Shelley watched her mother stiffen and then turn over on her other side. When Shelley was much younger, Mother's moods had frightened her, but now she expected them.

"I'll see you this afternoon," Shelley said as she pulled the bedroom door closed behind her.

"Is Mother sick again?" William asked when Shelley joined him in the kitchen.

"I'm not sure. Do you think you can finish and get to school without any help?"

William slammed down his fork. "Of course I can. I am not a baby. When will this family ever understand that I am almost a grown-up?"

Shelley lifted her eyebrows and glared at her younger brother. "William!"

He tucked his chin close to his chest and offered a sheepish look. "Sorry. I know God doesn't like me to get mad."

"I made your lunch, and it's in the sack on the counter."

"Thank you, Shelley." He lifted another forkful of eggs to his mouth but stopped. "I promise I won't run away again, even if Myra says mean things."

"Good. Myra is the one with the problem, not you."

William nodded. "Alexander would never be mean."

Shelley paused and then leaned over the table to look William in the eye. "Just remember that anyone can say hurtful things, but that doesn't mean you should react."

He gave her a puzzled look.

"When people say mean things in the future, either ignore them until they stop, or stand up to them and tell them to stop being so mean. Then drop it."

"Okay." A smile tweaked his lips. "Maybe Alexander's mother will make cupcakes, and he'll bring one to share."

"That would be nice. Just in case she didn't, I put an extra cookie in your lunch bag for your break at work."

Shelley left for work with a heavy heart filled with worry about her mother. She wished she knew what to do about her mother's depression, but no matter how hard she tried to cheer her mother up, nothing seemed to work.

The morning crowd slowly trickled in, and business remained steady for a couple of hours. Jocelyn arrived right before they reached their peak. Shortly after ten o'clock, the bell on the door jingled. When Shelley glanced up, she saw her brother Paul.

"Take a break, Shelley," Mr. Penner said. "Go visit with your brother, and I'll bring over some coffee."

"Good morning, Shelley," Paul said. "I took the morning off to see Mother, but she isn't home."

"I think she is home still, but she's having one of her spells." Shelley glanced around to make sure no one else could hear. "I'm worried about her, Paul. Mother is getting worse."

"I sort of suspected that might be the case since I heard about William running away."

"Who told you?"

Paul blew on his coffee and took a sip. "Father called me this morning. Fortunately, I still have some personal days I can take off from work. Is there anything I can do?"

"I don't know," Shelley admitted. "I might have made matters worse yesterday when I talked back to her." As she told him about the words she and Mother had exchanged, he nodded his understanding. "Mother wants me to agree to marry Peter, but that's not what I want."

Paul smiled and took her hand from across the table. "You don't have to marry Peter just because Mother wants you to, but we need to help her get through whatever she's dealing with."

"I wish I knew what to do."

"There's something else going on that Father told me about, and I wanted to hear your side of the story."

Shelley tilted her head and gave him a questioning look. "What's that?"

"Father says you and Jeremiah have been seeing quite a bit of each other."

She felt the heat rise to her cheeks as she looked down at the table. "Mother doesn't like him."

"It's not that she doesn't like him, Shelley. Mother is afraid of losing another child."

"But she hasn't lost a child."

"I know that, and you know that," Paul said. "But as far as Mother is concerned, she lost me when I married Tammy. And you know what happened when William came along. I think she feels she's being punished."

"Now one is punishing Mother but herself."

"Yes, I've known that for a long time," Paul said. "You were forced into being a caretaker when you were quite young, and Mother has always used whatever she could as an excuse to retreat."

"I don't want to dwell on what I can't change."

Paul nodded. "So how is everything here at work? I see Mr. Penner hired someone new."

Shelley took advantage of the change of subject and told him how hard of a worker Jocelyn was. "I like her. She's funny and interesting."

After they finished their coffee, Paul stood. "I'm going back to see about Mother. Thanks for filling me in on what's happening. One of the things I need to do is bring the kids around to see their grandmother. Maybe that'll remind her that she has gained more than she's lost."

Paul left before the lunch rush started. Jocelyn worked as hard as ever, in spite of the deeper bruises still evident on her cheek and right arm. She seemed to enjoy the fact that some of her regular customers made a fuss over her.

Business slowed quickly by midafternoon. Mr. Penner approached Shelley. "Why don't you go on home now? You have been through quite a bit over the past several weeks, and I want you to get some rest."

"I can stick around," she argued.

"Neh. I have Jocelyn here to help me now."

A stab of jealousy shot through Shelley, but she quickly recovered. "Ya, it's nice to have Jocelyn back."

"I missed this place," Jocelyn said from behind her. "Strange as it may sound, you all are starting to feel like family to me."

Shelley spun around to face Jocelyn. "That isn't strange at all."

Tears sprang to Jocelyn's eyes, but she swiped at them with the back of her sleeve. "You people came to visit me when I was in the hospital. That's more than my own family did. I appreciate it more than you'll ever know."

"We care about you," Mr. Penner said. "Just like we care about Shelley. Now go on home, and get some rest."

"Okay." Shelley pulled off her apron and hung it on the rack in the kitchen. "I'll see you in the morning."

All the way home Shelley thought about her day and how Paul had said he planned to stop by to see Mother. She wondered how their visit went.

When she walked inside, her mother called out from the kitchen. "Shelley, is that you?"

"Ya, I'll be right there." As she went to her room to put a few things away, she said a prayer that her mother was in a better mood than she had been earlier.

The instant Shelley arrived in the kitchen, she was stunned by what she saw. Rows of cookies were spread out over the countertops, and the kitchen table had tins stacked high.

"Why are you baking so many cookies, Mother?"

"Here, have one of these, and tell me what you think." Mother offered a heaping platter, and Shelley took a sugar cookie. "Paul and Tammy are bringing the children over tomorrow, and we're going to decorate cookies."

Shelley smiled. "That sounds like fun. I have to work in the morning. Do you know when they'll be here?"

"Late morning. I promised to fix them a picnic to eat in the backyard, and then we'll come inside to decorate the cookies. I'm sure we'll still be at it when you get home from work. I can't wait to tell William. He loves his niece and nephew."

Shelley moved a few tins away from the edge of the table before sitting down. "What else did you and Paul talk about?"

Mother didn't answer right away. She finished positioning cookies on the baking sheet, stuck it in the oven and then joined Shelley. "I told Paul about Peter and Jeremiah."

Shelley's insides twisted. "What did you tell him?"

"I explained how Peter broke your heart and you can't seem to forgive him."

"That's not exactly—"

Mother lifted a hand to shush her. "We talked about Jeremiah coming back to the church and trying to court you." She cleared her throat and glanced down before looking Shelley in the eye. "Paul talked to me about forgiveness and trusting that the Lord would guide you in your decision."

Silence fell between them. Shelley wasn't sure where Mother was going with this, so she remained quiet, hoping to hear more.

"I have to admit I argued with him about it, saying that you could learn to love Peter since you obviously wanted to marry him before he got. . .engaged to Clara. Paul asked me why I was so opposed to Jeremiah, now that he's returned to the church."

Mother looked directly at Shelley as if waiting for some sort of response. "I would like to know that, too," Shelley said softly.

"Paul and I talked for quite a while, and he helped me see some things. . . ." Her voice trailed off as she glanced down at the table before raising her gaze back to Shelley. "He asked what Jeremiah could do to win my favor. We all have sins that must be forgiven, so I couldn't give a good answer." Mother reached over, grasped Shelley's hand, and squeezed it. "I am so sorry for acting the way I did with Jeremiah. After having a child who will never be able to live on his own, then losing Paul, I'm afraid I put all my stock in you. Now I know that isn't the right thing to do."

"First of all, Mother, William is a wonderful brother, and he's doing just fine. Second, you didn't lose Paul."

"Ya, I know that now."

"And third, I don't think I ever truly loved Peter. He was simply there, giving me attention at a time when I was worried I might be getting too old to find a husband." She self-consciously smiled at her mother. "And I want to get married and have a family."

"Ya, I know that. I will have to get to know Jeremiah before I pass judgment on him."

Shelley lifted both hands and widened her smile. "I'm not even saying Jeremiah is the man I want to marry."

"But you're not saying he's not either," her mother teased.

"True. I really do like him, but like you, I had some reservations about him. I don't ever want to leave the church."

"I can't believe I'm saying this, Shelley, but now you're the one who needs to learn forgiveness. Give Jeremiah a chance."

After they finished their talk, Shelley got up from the table. "I think I'll go for a little walk now. This has been a difficult week."

"Go on ahead. If you want to help with supper, I'll wait until you get back to start it."

Shelley had a lot of thinking to do. As she took off down the street, she inhaled the warm air and allowed it to fill her lungs before slowly exhaling. Today had been filled with surprises—first seeing Paul at the restaurant and then walking in on her mother in such a cheerful mood. Her mother's acceptance of Jeremiah was nothing short of a miracle. But then Shelley remembered how Paul was so good at talking to her and showing her all sides of situations. Shelley wished she had that gift.

Her mind was so filled with the twists and turns in her life that she thought she was imagining the sound of someone calling her name. At first she kept walking, but when she heard it again, she stopped and glanced over her shoulder in time to see Jeremiah jogging toward her.

When he reached her, he stopped to catch his breath. "I've been trying to find you for the past fifteen minutes."

Shelley laughed. "That's not all that long. What did you need?"

"Your mother said you were out walking."

The earth seemed to shift beneath her. "When did you talk to my mother?"

"I just left your house. I stopped by to see if you were home from work yet. When your mother invited me inside, I thought you might be there."

"She invited you in?" She wondered what Jeremiah thought about that.

"Yes." He chuckled. "I was surprised, but the real bombshell was when she asked me to come over tomorrow to help decorate cookies. Any idea what's going on?"

Shelley shook her head. "My brother stopped by and had a talk with her.

Apparently, he said something that completely turned her around."

"I think she's just happy Paul is going to bring his family to the Mennonite church."

"Ya, that would make her happy. Mother has always dreamed of our whole family attending the same church together."

They resumed walking, at first without talking, until Shelley got up the nerve to ask what was on her mind. "So are you planning to join us?"

"A million wild horses couldn't keep me away."

"Oh, I bet a million horses could," Shelley said with a giggle.

"I'm pretty strong when I'm determined."

"That's good to know."

When Jeremiah reached for her hand, her tummy fluttered. "What else would you like to know?" he asked.

"How's your farm coming along?"

Jeremiah told her all about the crops he'd planted and how he was looking at lemon and lime tree varieties, trying to decide which ones to plant. "There's a whole lot more to farming than most people realize."

"Do you like it?"

"I like it much more than anything I've ever done. This feels like real life to me, and it doesn't hurt to know I'm actually doing something productive."

"I know what you mean," Shelley said. "Mary loves living on the farm and doing a little bit of gardening for canning."

"Can you see yourself doing that?" Jeremiah asked.

Shelley opened her mouth and then closed it and shrugged. She was afraid if she told Jeremiah that she dreamed of having what Mary had—a doting husband who loved the Lord and a home to take care of—she'd scare him away.

"We'll be starting on my house as soon as I choose some house plans." Jeremiah paused. "Would you like to look at the ones I'm considering?"

"I'd love to."

They arrived at the front of Shelley's house and stopped. Jeremiah dropped Shelley's hand but didn't budge from his spot on the sidewalk. "See you tomorrow?"

"I'm working, but I'll come straight home afterward."

"Your mother told me to come early for lunch, but I think I'll wait for you."

"No," Shelley said. "I'd like for you to come early and spend some time with my family."

Jeremiah smiled and nodded. "Okay, since that's what you want, that's exactly what I'll do."

"I don't always expect you to do what I want, Jeremiah."

He howled with laughter. "Trust me, Shelley, I won't."

After Shelley went inside, Jeremiah went on home. He set the table and ate dinner with his parents and then sent them out for ice cream, so he could clean the kitchen.

"Practicing, son?" his dad asked as he lingered for a moment in the kitchen while Jeremiah's mother got her wrap.

Jeremiah glanced up from the sink. "Practicing?"

"Practicing for those times when your future wife needs a hand in the kitchen?" His father winked before leaving with his mother.

That was exactly what Jeremiah was doing, now that his dad mentioned it. He could imagine himself working side by side with Shelley. Now all he had to do was plant the same image in her mind.

He went to the Glick farm early and let Abe know he was going over to the Burkholders' house to decorate cookies. Abe lifted his eyebrows. "Sounds like you are making some headway there."

"I hope so."

"In that case," Abe said, "leave early to check on your own farm, and then go back into town to be with Shelley's family."

Jeremiah hummed as he did all his tasks. Working hard with his hands kept him busy yet freed his mind. He called David to arrange for his ride, and then he let Abe know when he was about to leave.

"Enjoy yourself," Abe said. "And tell Shelley hi from Mary and me."

<hr>

Shelley left the restaurant immediately after the lunch crowd dwindled. She practically ran home. Her hands were a little bit unsteady as she opened the front door. If Jeremiah was able to get off early, she knew she'd see him soon.

Mother was in the kitchen arranging all the cookies on the counter. She pointed to the children, who were enjoying a picnic lunch on an old tablecloth. "I was hoping Jeremiah would be here to have lunch with you."

"He said he was going to try to take off early," Shelley said. "Mother, I've been thinking about your change of heart. It happened so fast—I'm confused."

Her mother put down what she was doing, wiped her hands on the towel, and faced Shelley. "Paul found me in my bedroom. At first he didn't know what to say, but when I refused to get up, he got firm with me. He said I was trying too hard to make everything go my way."

Shelley pulled back. "Paul actually said that to you?"

"Ya." Mother hung her head. "In case you're wondering, ya, it did make me mad. So mad I hopped up out of bed and gave him a piece of my mind. Once I was up, he took hold of me and led me to the living room, where he sat me down and said we needed to talk about a lot of things."

Paul sure did have a lot of nerve, and Shelley was grateful. "And all he had to do was mention that Jeremiah deserved a second chance?"

"Oh, it was much more than that, but I will spare you the details. I will say that he used scripture to remind me that the Lord wouldn't want me to hold grudges, now that Jeremiah is claiming to be sorry for what he did."

"How do you feel about Jeremiah?" Shelley asked.

Mother folded her arms and gave Shelley a stern look. "Are you asking me how I'd feel about Jeremiah courting you?"

"Well. . .ya, I s'pose that is what I'm asking."

Her mother's expression turned pleasant, and she actually smiled. "I think I would be okay with that as long as you are sure he is sincere."

Shelley relaxed. "Ya, that is important."

A knocking sound at the door got their attention. "I suspect that's Jeremiah. Why don't you get the door while I call the children in to start decorating the cookies I baked? Ask Jeremiah if he's had lunch yet. If not, I'll send the two of you out to the backyard for your own private picnic."

Three weeks later during the church picnic, Jeremiah approached Shelley as she stood with her mother. "If you don't mind, Mrs. Burkholder, I'd like to have a chat with your daughter."

The twinkle in her mother's eye let Shelley know her mother was in on something she was about to find out. "Of course I don't mind."

"I promised to help put out the desserts," Shelley said. "Can it wait?"

Both Jeremiah and her mother shouted, "No!" in unison.

"Okay then. Let's go." She turned and tucked her hand into the crook of Jeremiah's arm. "Where are we going?"

He gestured toward a waiting car. "I called David to drive us to the beach."

All the way to the beach, David kept glancing at them in his rearview mirror. Even he seemed to know a secret. "How about I drop you off here?" he asked.

"Perfect," Jeremiah said. "Pick us up in about an hour unless I call you to come earlier."

"When are you going to let me in on your secret, Jeremiah?" Shelley asked as she removed her shoes before stepping onto the sand. Then it dawned on her. She turned toward him, smiling. "You've started working on the house!"

"Well," Jeremiah said as he rubbed his neck, "not exactly, but that will be happening soon."

"Then what's so important we had to come all the way here for you to tell me?"

Jeremiah tugged her over toward a private area beside a cluster of palm trees. He opened the towel he'd brought and placed it on the sand. "Have a seat, Shelley."

Once they were seated facing the water, Jeremiah took her hand and kissed the back of it. Neither of them spoke for a few minutes.

Finally, Jeremiah took a deep breath and turned to Shelley. "I've never done this before, so I might be a little bit awkward."

She laughed nervously. "You've never seemed awkward to me, Jeremiah."

"How do I seem to you?"

"You are a very sweet, hardworking man who has asked for forgiveness... and a man who loves the Lord."

"Yes, that is true, but that's not all. I love you, too, Shelley."

A lump formed in her throat, but she managed to reply, "And I love you."

"Good. That makes what I have to say much easier. I would like for you to be my wife."

Shelley remained sitting there, stunned, for a few minutes before she turned to face him. "You've already talked to my parents about this, haven't you?"

"Yes, and William and Paul."

"What did they say?" she asked.

"William jumped up and clapped his hands. Paul said he would be happy to have me for a brother-in-law, and your father shook my hand."

"How about my mother?" Shelley asked.

"She's the only one I was worried about, but she said that if marrying me would make you happy, she'll be happy for us." He looked into her eyes. "Well, what's your answer?"

Shelley flung her arms around Jeremiah's neck and hugged him tight. "Marrying you will make me the happiest woman in Sarasota." She stopped, thought for a moment, and corrected herself. "Make that the happiest woman in the world."

UNLIKELY MATCH

Dedication

I'd like to dedicate this book to my agent, Tamela Hancock Murray.

Chapter 1

All Charles Polk had ever thought he wanted in life was to be a clown—a real clown with ridiculous makeup, baggy britches, oversize shoes, and an audience at the Ringling Bros. and Barnum and Bailey Circus. Then he'd started helping out on the Glick farm and realized he had a different calling.

"Ready, Charles?" Pop asked.

Charles stepped out into the hall of the house that had gone from being his parents' dream to their burden. "Ready."

All the way to the small Mennonite church in Pinecraft, the Polk family chattered about insignificant things to calm their unspoken fears. Even though he'd been there several times, his insides still churned with nerves.

Since most of the Mennonite families walked to church or rode their adult-sized tricycles they called bikes or three-wheelers, the Polk car was the only one in the parking lot. Charles knew his family was an enigma to the members of the church, but he prayed they'd eventually accept him without questions. Pop had assured him they would, but that was hard to imagine.

Charles walked into the church sanctuary with his parents, but Mom veered off toward where the women sat as he and Pop found a place among the men. There were so many things he needed to learn about the new life he wanted, but as the people who had come to talk to his family said, they had plenty of time.

≈

Ruthie looked over toward the younger of the two new men in church and caught herself daydreaming about his past. She found it difficult to believe some of what she'd heard, but he did have an air of mystery.

Mother cut a glance at her and narrowed her eyes. Ruthie's cheeks flamed as she turned back to the pastor, who was right in the middle of his sermon.

An hour later, as she joined the other women getting ready for the monthly potluck, she overheard some of the talk about the Polk family. Ruthie's curiosity overcame her good sense, so she edged closer to the women doing all the talking.

"I heard the boy was taking some classes to become a clown. Isn't that the silliest thing?" Sharon Bowles shook her head. "What kind of work is that for a man?"

"Perhaps that was a childish dream," Mrs. Penner said. "You know how children can be."

"None of our children ever dream of being clowns."

Shelley Burkholder Yoder scooted past with a casserole dish. "That's because they're already a bunch of clowns."

"Shelley!" Mrs. Burkholder shook her head and pretended to scowl as a smile played on her lips. "That is no way to talk about the fine young people in our community, especially since you're going to have one of your own soon."

Shelley glanced down at her growing abdomen. "Oh, I'm sure this child will fit right in with the rest of the clowns with a father like Jeremiah."

Mrs. Yoder chuckled. "My son might be a clown, but he's a smart one." She handed Ruthie a basket filled with biscuits and rolls. "Be a dear, Ruthie. Take these outside and put them on the end of the bread table."

Ruthie did as she was told, although she wished she could have remained in the church kitchen to hear what else the women had to say about the Polk family. As she walked past clusters of men, she sensed that all eyes were on the basket of bread she carried. Mennonite men sure did have big appetites. They never let more than a few seconds pass after the women gave them the go-ahead to pounce on the buffet line once the food was in place.

She glanced up in time to see Abe walking toward her. Her face burned, and her hands started shaking as they had since the time she acted out of character and boldly flirted with him before she realized he was in love with Mary. Although he wasn't interested in her in the least, he was still nice, so there was no reason for her to be so embarrassed whenever he came near.

"Hi, Ruthie," Abe said. "Looks like no one will go away hungry."

"Ya. There is always plenty of food."

"It's always nice to show off our hospitality to newcomers."

Ruthie took a chance and met his gaze. "Ya." She knew his smile was meant to put her at ease, but she still felt like a bundle of nerves.

He nodded toward the Polk family. "Perhaps you can find some time to speak to Charles. He's a very interesting young man. Did you know he used to dream of being a clown?"

She looked down and tried to stifle a giggle. "So I've heard."

"I'm glad he came to his senses," Abe said. "Charles is a very hard worker just like his father."

Ruthie glanced toward the women who were hauling more food out to the picnic tables. "I'll try to speak to him, but now I need to help take out the food."

Abe took a step back. "Then I need to get out of your way. There are too many hungry men out here, and I don't want to be the cause of their starvation."

As Ruthie scooted past Abe and made her way back to the kitchen, she thought about Abe's warmth, kindness, and good humor. Those qualities were what had attracted her to him; she wondered if anyone else could even come close. She wished her older sister Amalie were here to advise her. Amalie and her husband had gone back to Tennessee to run his family's farm.

Mrs. Penner, Mary, and Shelley quickly gave her jobs to do, one right after the other, so she didn't have much time to think about her former attraction to Abe. But she did notice how many times the other women had her running past Charles Polk. Each time she looked at him, he had a different expression—all pleasant and very animated. He was attractive in an unconventional way, with reddish-brown hair that hung a little too long in front, deep blue eyes that were impossible to look away from, and a ruddy complexion from being outdoors in the sun.

❧

"She's quiet but sweet," Jeremiah whispered.

Charles pulled back. "Who?"

Jeremiah pointed toward the shy girl who stood slightly apart from the women. "Ruthie. I've known her since she started school several years behind me, and she's always been a tad shy."

There was never any doubt the people in the church loved to matchmake. As soon as the Polk family expressed an interest in exploring the Mennonite faith, he could tell that was one of the first things he'd have to face if they ever got serious about joining.

"Have you had a chance to talk to her yet?"

Charles shrugged. "Just a few words. Not much."

Jeremiah laughed. "I'm beginning to think you're just as shy as she is."

"You know me better than that."

"Yeah, I know you from working on the farm, but this is different." Jeremiah's eyes twinkled as he leaned over and exaggerated a whisper. "This is about a girl, and they can be quite scary."

"No kidding." Charles glanced over toward the women again. Ruthie stood out with her chestnut-brown hair that was darker than most of the women's. Earlier he'd noticed her stunning blue-green eyes that were framed by long eyelashes. "She's pretty. I wonder why she's so shy."

"I get the whole looks thing, but do yourself a favor and don't make a big deal of her being pretty."

Charles cringed. He'd gotten so many things wrong that he thought he'd never fully understand how to act, even though it had seemed simple at first. "Is that not allowed in the Mennonite church?"

"Not that it's not allowed so much," Jeremiah said slowly, "more that it's not the place to put emphasis in your relationships." He chuckled. "I've always thought Shelley was the prettiest girl in town, and when I told her, she let me know there was much more to her than that."

"Thanks for the lesson." Charles appreciated Jeremiah's friendship. Between Jeremiah and Abe, he felt he had a chance of grasping the basic social aspects of being a Mennonite.

"Try to find some way to talk to her today." Jeremiah narrowed his eyes and folded his arms. "That is, if you're interested."

"I'm not sure yet." Although a handful of folks from the church wanted to matchmake, Charles had seen just as many skeptics. If any of them suspected he was even slightly interested in one of their girls, he was afraid they'd erect some sort of barrier to prevent him from getting to know her. He'd been reserved about expressing his opinions of Ruthie with Jeremiah, but he couldn't ignore the spark of attraction he felt whenever their gazes met.

After the women had all the serving tables loaded with food, Charles found his place with Pop. He lowered his head before the pastor said the blessing. As he raised his head and opened his eyes, he caught Ruthie staring at him, and his heart gave an unexpected leap.

"Go talk to her, Son." Pop nudged him in the ribs.

"I'm not so sure this is a good time. Why don't we eat first?"

Pop opened his mouth, probably to argue, but he didn't have a chance before one of the older men approached and started talking. As the men exchanged words about farming, Charles mentally lectured himself about courage. He'd always been a little nervous about talking to people, which was one of the reasons being a clown had appealed to him.

Mom and Pop had taken him to a circus when he was in elementary school. He'd enjoyed watching the high-wire performers and the animals, but the acts that had intrigued him the most were the clowns. From a distance they seemed friendly, happy, and approachable, but when he got close, he realized that the makeup made them look that way, even when they frowned. And they didn't have to talk. Clowns were mesmerizing to all—from those who loved them to people who were afraid of them.

When his parents realized his obsession, they enrolled him in a clown camp sponsored by Ringling Bros. and Barnum and Bailey, where he learned some of the basics of making people laugh. He had fun, but something still seemed to be missing. After he graduated from high school, he enrolled at the Sarasota-Manatee campus of the University of South Florida and volunteered as a clown at the children's hospital. At first it was fun, but after a year's worth of performances, it started getting old. He wasn't sure what he wanted to do with his life, so he hadn't gotten past the general education classes in college. Then Pop asked if he was interested in working part-time at the Glick farm. By the end of the first week of repairing the barn, even after the rafter fell on him, he knew he'd found work that suited him. He'd never felt such a sense of satisfaction as what he experienced after working with his hands.

⤜⤛

Ruthie couldn't stop stealing glances at Charles. At first he was engaged in conversation with some of the men, but as his father continued socializing, Charles had become withdrawn. He appeared to be deep in thought. She wondered what was on his mind.

"Go see if you can get him something," Shelley whispered. "Both of you are obviously shy, and someone has to make the first move."

"No one *has* to make a move at all."

"True." Shelley rested her hand on Ruthie's shoulder. "Why don't you take the approach of being friendly and showing your appreciation for his interest in being a Mennonite?"

"I could do that," Ruthie said. "But I still feel awkward."

"I'm sure he won't notice if you don't tell him. He'll just think you're a friendly girl who wants to welcome him."

Ruthie looked Shelley in the eye and nodded. "I'll go speak to him and ask if he's had enough dessert."

Shelley turned Ruthie around and gave her a gentle shove. "Then you best do it now before someone else does."

Ruthie took a deep breath and slowly headed toward Charles, her mind focused on putting one foot in front of the other rather than the fear that welled in her stomach. When she came within a couple of feet of him, she made eye contact and swallowed hard. "Would you like more dessert? There's plenty more over there."

A sense of numbness flooded her when he didn't immediately respond. Then a wide grin spread across his lips and he nodded. "I would love more dessert. Will you join me?"

The next half hour went by so quickly it was more of a blur than a detailed memory. After she and Charles sat down with plates of pie, he asked questions and attentively listened to her answers. If she had any doubt about her attraction to Charles, it quickly dissolved. The last call for desserts went out, snagging their attention away from each other.

"I had fun, Ruthie," Charles said softly. "W–would you be interested in getting together sometime soon?"

"Ya, I would like that."

He stood up and looked down at her. "I'd like to make a date, but I'm not sure yet when I'll be available."

"I'll be in church next Sunday."

Charles smiled. "So will I. I'll talk to Abe and Pop then get back with you." He walked backward a couple of steps. "Good-bye, Ruthie. Have a nice week." Then he turned and hurried toward the parking lot.

"That wasn't so hard, was it?" Shelley asked from behind Ruthie.

"It was the hardest thing I've ever done in my life."

Shelley tilted her head back and laughed. "Trust me when I say there will be more difficult things to come." She put her arm around Ruthie and led her to the church. "So tell me all about it. Did he ask if he could see you again?"

Ruthie explained that he needed to check with Abe and his father before committing to a time. "I hope Mother doesn't mind."

"Why would she mind?" Shelley said. "Your parents are two of the kindest, most open people I know. They were both in favor of his family joining the church."

"Ya, I know, but when it comes to me and the people I associate with, they can be quite different."

"Trust me, I know how that is." Shelley glanced over her shoulder and spotted her mother staring at her. "Fortunately Jeremiah managed to win over both of my parents, but it wasn't easy for him or me."

Ruthie remembered hearing all about what Shelley and Jeremiah had gone through. "I don't even know Charles well enough to think that much into our. . .friendship. But he is very nice."

"Yes," Shelley agreed, nodding. "He's very nice, and he seems sincere about learning the Bible."

Ruthie helped clean the tables and church kitchen. After the remaining men put everything away, she walked the three blocks to the house where she lived with her parents. Mother and Papa had gone on a walk, so she had the house to herself. It was nice to have time to think.

~

"Ruthie Kauffman seems like such a sweet girl," Pop said as he maneuvered the car out of the church parking lot. "Have you thought about asking her out on a date?"

"I'd like to, Pop, but where do Mennonite people go on dates?"

His parents exchanged an amused look before his mother spoke. "Definitely not to a bar or dance club."

That was obvious. "Do you think she'd like to go to a circus?"

"I don't see why not," Pop said. "It seems harmless enough."

Mom's eyebrows were furrowed as she studied his face. "You're not still harboring the notion of being a clown, are you, Charles?"

"No, I've been over that for a while, but I still like them." He chewed on his bottom lip for a moment. "I just hope she's not afraid of clowns."

Pop stopped at the red light and winked at him in the rearview mirror. "If she is, you'll be there to protect her, just like I did when your mother and I had our first date."

Mom playfully swatted at Pop. "You took me to a scary movie just so I'd grab you."

Pop pretended to be hurt. "If we go through with becoming Mennonite, you can't keep beating me up."

Mom looked over her shoulder at Charles. "Now he's afraid of me. Go figure."

Charles was glad his parents' relationship didn't suffer after Pop lost his job of twenty years. The plummeting economy had caused his company to downsize, and he was part of a massive layoff. At first Pop had deluded himself into thinking he'd be in high demand, and it would only be a matter of time before some other company found out he was available and begged him to work for them. But that didn't happen. Pop and Charles both had to take odd jobs just to pay the bills, and there were times when the Polk family worried the power would be shut off. Mom worked, but her income didn't come close to covering the family's bills.

After they got home and settled in the house, Mom went to her room to change and Pop mentioned some of the work they'd be doing on the Glick farm during the next several weeks. "I never realized how much work went into citrus farming. After we swap out some of the citrus trees, we have to work on the irrigation system to make sure it's adequate for grapefruit."

"Do you think Abe will be able to give me more hours?" Charles asked. "I only have Tuesday and Thursday classes this semester, so I can work an extra day."

"I'll talk to him." Pop thought for a moment then amended his offer. "Why don't you ask him if he can give you more hours? If not, maybe Jeremiah can. He's talking about planting some summer crops. I suspect he would be happy to have another pair of hands."

Mom joined them. "One of you needs to cook dinner on Wednesday. I'm going over to Esther Kauffman's house for church instruction."

Charles gave Pop a curious look before turning back to Mom. "That's Ruthie's mom, right?"

She grinned. "Yes. Why?"

He shrugged a few seconds too late. "Just asking."

Pop laughed. "You'll be able to come home with some inside information on the girl. Maybe you can put in some good words for Charles."

"Jonathan," Mom said as she leveled Pop with one of her firm looks, "our son is perfectly capable of handling his own romance. He doesn't need help from a couple of meddling parents."

"After seeing some of the meddling among other people in the church, I think it might be good for Charles to have someone looking after his interests."

"I'm standing right here, Pop. You don't have to talk about me in the third person."

Pop lifted his eyebrows with a look of amusement. "Then stop acting as though you don't have a vested interest in your love life. Take action, Son."

Charles opened his mouth to defend himself then thought better of it. Pop had enough on his mind already, between being behind on the mortgage payments and trying to make a decision about joining the Mennonite church.

~

Mondays were always busy for Ruthie. After a hectic Saturday and taking Sunday off, she had quite a bit of bookkeeping to catch up on. She generally spent most of the day in the office, so to get her out among people Papa occasionally had her work in Pinecraft Souvenirs, the family store, waiting on customers. Ruthie struggled with her shyness, and she found it difficult to talk to strangers. Fortunately most Mondays were slow.

Most of the customers were retired people—some were residents of Sarasota and others were on vacation. Ruthie didn't mind the grandmotherly types who shopped for their grandchildren. She stayed behind the counter and let them browse.

She'd barely finished lunch and had gone out to work in the store until the late-afternoon sales clerk arrived when a group of women from the church stopped by. She knew all of them except one—Charles's mother, Mrs. Polk, whom she'd seen in church a few times but hadn't spoken to yet.

"May I help you?" Ruthie asked in her quiet voice. She kept her attention focused on Mrs. Penner.

Mrs. Polk stepped toward her and smiled. "We just finished a Bible study, and they insisted we come here." The woman glanced over her shoulder at the other women. She smiled and whispered, "Now I know why."

Ruthie's lips twitched with nerves, but she managed a meager smile. "What are you looking for?"

Mrs. Burkholder glanced around and finally settled her gaze on Ruthie. "I'd like to pick something out for my grandkids."

The women began to nod and mumble their agreement. "That's an excellent idea, Melba," Mrs. Penner said. "How about those little chocolate alligators? I bet they'd like some of those."

As the women walked around the store, Ruthie caught them staring at her and whispering when they thought she wasn't looking. If Papa had been here, she would've run to the office and closed the door.

Finally a couple of them brought some small items to the cash register. After she rang them up, she noticed that Mrs. Polk was the last one out the door. Before she left, she turned, smiled at Ruthie, thanked her for being so patient, and winked.

～

Charles and his father went straight home after working on the Glick farm. Mom was waiting in the kitchen, so Pop said he'd tell her about his day before washing up. Charles took his time showering and dressing in fresh jeans and a T-shirt. When he came out to the kitchen, he heard his parents laughing.

"What's so funny?" he asked.

Pop looked back and forth between Charles and Mom. "Your mother's new friends are on a mission to make her a mother-in-law."

Charles sat down. "Oh yeah? Do I need to ask who the unlucky girl is?"

"Stop it, Charles. We're talking about that sweet little Ruthie," Mom explained. "After we finished our Bible lesson this morning, they asked me to stay for lunch. Since I'd taken a vacation day from work, I thought that sounded like an excellent idea. One thing led to another, and next thing I knew, we were going shopping."

Charles knew it had been a long time since Mom had gone shopping, even though it used to be one of her favorite pastimes. "Did you buy anything?"

"Of course not." She cast her gaze downward.

Pop laughed and gently nudged her. "Tell him what that shopping trip was really all about."

"We went to one of the little souvenir shops in Pinecraft," Mom said with a slight grin.

Charles raked his fingers through his hair. "What's the big deal about going to a souvenir shop?" His mind raced to find a connection.

"Tell him who you saw," urged Pop.

"Oh that's right. Doesn't Ruthie Kauffman's family own a souvenir shop?"

"Yes," Mom said, "apparently so."

Chapter 2

I heard you had some interesting visitors today," Mother said as she and Ruthie sat down for tea.

Ruthie looked down at the table, not wanting to look her mother in the eye. "Ya, some of the church ladies stopped by for souvenirs."

Mother laughed. "All this time living in Sarasota and suddenly they want souvenirs. Sarah Penner could have come up with something better than that."

"Business was slow today," Ruthie said to change the subject. "But Saturday's receipts were high."

"That's good," Mother said as she lifted her teacup to her lips. "What did you and the. . .church ladies talk about?"

Ruthie shrugged. "Not much. They were looking for things for their grandkids."

"I heard Lori Polk was with them."

"Ya." Ruthie set her cup in the saucer and leaned back, ready for the barrage of questions Mother would surely ask.

"She seems like a nice woman."

When no questions followed, Ruthie looked directly at her mother. "Very nice."

"Good. I'm happy we're attracting nice people to the fold. It would be difficult if someone with a bad disposition wanted to join our church." Mother stood up, carried her teacup and saucer to the sink, and turned around to face Ruthie. "If you want to see Charles outside of church, your father and I have decided we are okay with it, as long as you let us know everything."

That was such an unexpected comment that Ruthie nearly dropped her teacup. "I never asked to see Charles."

Mother smiled. "Not yet, but I suspect you will soon."

"I—I don't know what to say to him."

"Ruthie, I know how difficult it is for you to talk to people you don't know well—particularly men—but you need to get over that."

"I tried once with Abe," she reminded Mother. "And look how that turned out."

"Did it turn out bad?"

"He wasn't interested in me, remember?"

Mother sat back down, leaned toward Ruthie, and took her hands. "That doesn't make it bad. He was already interested in Mary at the time. You and

Abe are friends now, right?"

Ruthie nodded. Yes, they were friends, but she still felt awkward around him.

"Don't let one setback determine your future. Remember that the Lord is always with you."

"I know that." Ruthie let go of Mother's hands and wrapped them around her teacup. "Maybe I'll talk to him next week at church."

Mother tightened her lips as she always did when she wasn't sure whether or not to say what was on her mind. Ruthie braced herself for whatever might come next.

"I hear he's talking about taking you to the circus."

Ruthie's jaw dropped. "The circus? Why?"

Mother shrugged. "He told his father he might ask you to the circus. His father asked one of the men at the church if that would be acceptable."

"Why wouldn't it be?"

"I don't know. Perhaps he thinks there might be something the Mennonite faith would object to." Mother smiled. "I think it is very nice that he'd be so concerned. It shows his diligence and desire to do the right thing."

More than anything, it showed Ruthie another reason to be nervous around Charles Polk. She'd never been on a real date, and she'd never even had the desire to go to the circus, even though it was in Sarasota.

"Your papa thinks it would be a good place to go with Charles since you can go during the day and there will be plenty of people around."

Ruthie thought about it and agreed that going to the circus would be a safe date option—that is, if she ever went on a date with Charles.

⤳

Charles had classes on Tuesdays and Thursdays, so he got to sleep an extra hour on those days since he didn't have to report to the farm. At first he needed that extra hour after long days of manual labor. But he was used to it now. Sometimes it was difficult to stay in bed after getting into the habit of waking so early.

Mom had already gone to work, but she'd left a note on the counter letting him know his lunch was packed and in the refrigerator. He smiled as he grabbed it and dropped it into his backpack. When he first started packing his lunch, he missed the fast food he used to grab every day. Now he looked forward to a healthier meal—generally leftovers from dinner the night before.

That wasn't all that had changed in the Polk family. Until Pop lost his job, the family had three cars. It cost too much to maintain all of them, so they sold two of them and let Mom drive to work. Charles took the city bus to class. He and Pop got rides to the Glick farm with David, an acquaintance of Pop's and the man who told them about Abe needing workers. Charles never would have considered being without his own wheels in the past, but now that he didn't have them, he actually liked not having the burden. Cars were expensive to maintain, and it wasn't always easy finding a parking place. As long as the buses ran in Sarasota, he could get to just about any place he wanted to go in town.

Charles had a tough time concentrating on the professor's lecture during economics class. His mind kept replaying his conversation with Ruthie Kauffman at church. He'd had a few dates in the past, but being the class clown had put him in the position of being more of a friend than a romantic interest in girls' minds. Even on his dates, the girls had expected him to make them laugh. As much as he once thought he'd enjoy performing, he was tired of it.

After lunch he had two more classes before heading back home. And since he'd agreed to work for Abe on Friday and Jeremiah on Saturday, he needed to get his studying out of the way.

Charles had to walk a quarter of a mile home from the bus stop. Both of his parents were still at work, so he took advantage of having the house to himself. The aroma of the stew Mom had started in the Crock-Pot this morning teased his taste buds. He rummaged through the nearly bare pantry until he found a forgotten box of crackers shoved to the far corner. He pulled one cracker out, nibbled a corner, and then tossed the box into the trash when he realized it was stale.

He put on a CD and cranked up the music before settling down at the kitchen table to study. It didn't take long until the shrill music grated his nerves. Strange how that happened after being in the midst of the calmness in the Mennonite church.

He'd barely closed his book when Mom called his cell phone. "I have to stop off at Publix on my way home. Need anything?"

"We're out of milk."

"It's on my list. Anything else?"

Charles wanted to tell her to bring home some junk food, and lots of it, but he knew how tight the budget was. "That's all. Dinner smells good, Mom."

"I hope the stew tastes good. I bought some cheap meat on sale, and I'm hoping the slow cooker will at least tenderize it."

"I'm sure it'll be just fine." Charles knew how much their financial situation had devastated his parents, but at least they were still together. He knew other couples in their situation who'd split when times got tough.

"Have you called Stan about getting circus tickets?"

"Not yet," Charles replied. "But I will soon."

"Don't wait too long. After he runs out of promotional tickets, that's it. Remember what happened last year?"

"Yes, I had to buy my tickets." That totally wasn't an option this year with money being so tight.

"I'm pulling into the Publix parking lot now. I won't be too long."

After Charles clicked OFF, he thought about calling Stan Portfield, one of the clowns who'd worked with him at clown camp. The man had connections with Circus Sarasota and the Ringling Bros. and Barnum and Bailey troupes, so he could score tickets for almost any show. But as Mom had mentioned, there wasn't an unlimited supply.

He stood and started pacing as he scrolled through his phone list and found Stan's number then punched CALL. Stan answered with his standard, "Wanna hear something funny?"

Charles and Stan chatted for a few minutes before Stan asked if he needed anything. "Do you have any Circus Sarasota tickets left for one of the shows at Ringling?"

"Of course I do. How many do you need?"

"Two." Charles paused before adding, "Is there any chance of getting a weekend show?"

"Yup, I have two weekend matinee tickets left. Meet me at our usual place tomorrow afternoon, and I'll buy you a cup of coffee."

"Um. . ." Charles hesitated before blurting, "I have to work tomorrow."

"I wanna give you these tickets, but you know how fast they go. I have lots of friends, and I can't very well tell them I don't have tickets when I do. First come, first serve, ya know."

"Yes, I know." Charles's shoulders sagged as he thought about his options. "Can we meet somewhere tonight?"

"Nope. I promised the hospital I'd be there for a kids' show. Wanna come? We can go out for pie and coffee afterward, like old times."

"Sorry, I can't."

"In that case, you better figure out a way to meet me tomorrow, or I can pretty much guarantee they'll be gone."

"Um. . .I'll try to meet you tomorrow afternoon. What time?"

"Are you out of class by two?"

"All my classes are on Tuesday and Thursday, so I should be able to make it at two."

"Good. See you then."

Charles punched OFF then leaned against the wall and slid down to the floor. He sat there staring at the blank screen on his phone wondering what to do next. He knew how important responsibility was to Abe, but he didn't want to miss the opportunity to get free tickets to the circus.

The instant that thought flickered through his mind, he realized how ridiculous it was. The circus was fleeting while Abe's impression of him would last. Without standing up, he scrolled his list again and punched Stan's number. This time Stan didn't pick up. He didn't bother leaving a voice mail because he'd learned years ago that Stan never bothered checking messages. "If someone has something important to tell me, they'll call back," he'd said.

Charles tried Stan's number several times but to no avail. When his parents got home, they were so eager to talk about their days at work, they didn't even notice his silence until after dinner. He and Pop were putting away the food when he got the nerve to ask the question that had been bugging him.

"What do you think about me knocking off early tomorrow?" Charles asked.

"Is it for something important?"

"Not really." Charles thought for a few seconds then changed his mind. "Actually, it sort of is."

"I'm sure Abe will understand, but remember he needs all the workers he can get, and you did commit to being there."

Charles explained his situation and how he really wanted to take Ruthie to the circus. Pop listened until he poured out all his thoughts.

"You done?" Pop asked.

"I've pretty much told you everything."

"Why do you have to go to the circus?"

Charles thought the answer to that was obvious. "It's all I know, Pop."

"C'mon, Charles. Give yourself more credit than that."

"I'm comfortable at the circus. I don't want to look like a nerd."

"There's nothing wrong with being a nerd."

Such a Pop thing to say. "Maybe not, but I'd rather get to know a girl in a place where I'm comfortable." He cleared his throat. "So do you think Abe will give me the afternoon off to get the tickets?"

Pop let out a chuckle of disbelief. "Ya know, son, I thought you had more integrity than that. You don't tell a man you'll work for him then back out just because something better comes along."

"But everyone wants me to take Ruthie out on a date, and you and Mom both said—"

"Sure, we thought it was a good idea for you to date a sweet Mennonite girl, but we didn't intend for you to go back on your responsibilities. If you leave early tomorrow, not only will Abe think less of you, but I'll be terribly disappointed in you."

"Stan said he has lots of people wanting those tickets, and it's first come—"

"So work to earn the money to buy your tickets. I don't see the problem."

"You know how expensive the good tickets are, Pop. If I have to buy them, I can't afford the decent sections."

Pop put the last bowl in the refrigerator, closed the door, and turned to face Charles. "Remember when we took you to your first circus?"

Charles nodded. "Of course I do. How can I forget?"

"Those were the cheapest tickets I could find. You were quite a bit younger then, so your mother didn't have a job outside the house. We barely made ends meet on my salary, but we found inexpensive ways to have fun as a family."

"Those were cheap tickets?" Charles asked. He reflected on that day and didn't remember sacrificing anything. "I thought they were the best in the house."

"Only because we made you think that. Now do the right thing and let Stan know you'll have to pass, unless he can hold those tickets until you're available."

Pop was right, but it sure didn't make things easy. He'd have to keep trying to get in touch with Stan, and then he'd need to set aside the money he'd make over the next several weeks to be able to afford two tickets to the circus. Even the cheap ones put a dent in the budget.

He finally got in touch with Stan the next morning as he rode to the Glick farm.

"I already told you I can't hold the tickets," Stan reminded him.

"Yes, I realize that. Thanks for offering them to me though."

"If you change your mind in the next few hours, call back."

Charles clicked the OFF button and turned to his dad.

"You did the right thing, Son. It's just a circus."

It was *just* a circus to Pop, but at least it was a place Charles felt comfortable and he'd have something to talk about. At the circus, he could point out some of the acts and explain some of the things the clowns were doing.

Friday and Saturday were grueling. Summer had begun, and the Florida sun beat down on the field, casting blazing rays on the workers' shoulders and necks. Charles didn't mind though. Now he knew what it was like to feel manly and worthwhile.

When Sunday morning rolled around, he was ready for a day off. Mom and Pop took their time getting ready, so Charles went outside and trimmed some of the shrubs while he waited. They finally let him know they were ready to go to church.

"Don't let Ruthie get away after the services are over," Mom said once they stepped inside the church. "Since you work and go to school all week, this might be your only opportunity to ask her out."

"I'll try, Mom."

She lifted an eyebrow. "Don't try. Just do it."

Charles laughed as Mom turned and headed for the other side of the church. All his life, Pop told him that trying wasn't always good enough when "doing" was what it took to get the job done.

∽

Ruthie was about to leave the building after church when she heard her name being called. She spun around and saw Charles Polk walking briskly toward her. She reached up to tuck a stray strand of hair back under her kapp and licked her lips to keep them from feeling so dry.

"Hey, Ruthie, I was wondering if you'd like to. . .um. . .would you like to. . ." Charles had stopped about ten feet in front of her and had begun fidgeting with the paper in his hands.

"Would I like to what?" she asked when he didn't continue.

"Circus Sarasota has their big summer event at Ringling Brothers and Barnum and Bailey, and I thought. . .well, maybe. . ." He cleared his throat. "Would you like to go with me?"

Ruthie hoped he couldn't hear her heart pounding. "I've never been to the circus before."

"You'll love it. They have all kinds of fun acts. Even if you don't like one, there will be another one right afterward. I don't know anyone who doesn't like the circus."

"I guess that would be okay. When is it?"

"The end of June. I'll get the dates and let you know. Since I'm working and going to school, I thought a weekend afternoon would be best."

Since Ruthie's parents had already approved, she nodded. "I would like that."

He wiped his palms, one at a time on his pant leg, as he remained standing there. She wondered if he had anything else to say, but he obviously didn't when he said, "I'll be in touch. See ya."

How strange. Charles appeared just as uncomfortable around her as she was around him.

Even stranger was how the people in the church reacted when they found out Ruthie was going on a date with Charles. The matchmakers were delighted, but another group was so upset they stopped by to see the Kauffman family to find out if it was true. Howard and Julia Krahn led the group, followed by Daniel and Cynthia Hostetler and Clayton and Diane Sims.

"Look who's coming up the walk," Mother said. "And they don't look happy." She opened the door slowly.

Mr. Krahn had already taken the position of spokesperson. "We wanted to find out if the rumor is true. Is your daughter in a relationship with that Polk boy?"

Ruthie's face burned. Fortunately Mother spoke up. "All depends on what you call a relationship."

"You know what we're talking about. Are they dating?"

Mother opened the door wider. "Would you like to come inside and get out of the sun?"

"Mother," Ruthie whispered as Mr. Krahn turned to consult the rest of the people in the group. "I'm not so sure that's a good idea."

"It'll be fine, honey. They just have a few questions that I'm sure I can answer very quickly."

Ruthie had her doubts, but she couldn't argue with Mother. All three couples marched into the tiny house with scowls on their faces.

"Have a seat," Mother said, gesturing toward the living room at the front of the house. "Or would you be more comfortable in the kitchen?"

"This is fine," Mr. Krahn said. "And this will only take a few minutes. We need to protect our young people from the wickedness in the world."

"I believe that is what the Lord would want you to do," Mother said. "Would you like some tea or coffee?"

The visitors exchanged glances before all shaking their heads. "Neh, we don't need refreshment," Mr. Krahn said.

The demeanor of the guests had softened, but now they looked uncomfortable standing in the small living room. Mother gestured toward the sofa. "Why don't you have a seat?"

"We can't stay," Mrs. Krahn said. "We just wanted to come by to remind you how important it is we protect our children's faith. Walking with the Lord is difficult in these times."

"Yes," Mother said, still smiling, "from what I remember, it always has been. We certainly appreciate your concern."

Ruthie remained standing at the edge of the room, listening to everything. No one even bothered looking in her direction, even though they claimed to be there out of concern for her.

Mr. Krahn took a step toward the door, and the others followed. "Keep your daughter away from anyone who might cause her to stray," he advised before opening the front door and walking out.

"Thank you again," Mother called out as they filed out of the house.

After she shut the door behind the last of the group, Mother turned to Ruthie and shook her head. Her smile had faded, but she didn't look angry.

"Why do they hate the Polks?" Ruthie asked. "It's not like they're doing anything wrong. I would think they'd be happy to see another family wanting to know more about the Lord and the Mennonite life."

"I don't think they hate the Polks." Mother nudged Ruthie toward the kitchen. "They mean well. Unfortunately they're reacting to something they don't understand."

"What don't they understand?"

"The Polks' motives. Most of the naysayers in the church speak out of ignorance."

"Do you think the Polks have good motives?"

Mother sighed. "There's no way I can know for sure, but it appears they do. They seem to realize that the Lord has led them to the church by using adversity to get their attention."

Ruthie knew some of the details about how Mr. Polk had lost his job and how they were struggling to pay their bills. She admired them for turning to the Lord.

"Just remember, Ruthie, that when people say they don't want you associating with the Polk boy, they think they're protecting you."

Ruthie nodded. "I don't always know what to say."

"Why bother to say anything? They're going to believe what they want anyway, so putting up resistance will only fuel their argument."

Mother was the wisest person Ruthie knew. She never would have considered the ramifications of defending herself.

"I have to admit something else," Mother added. "Your papa and I are concerned about you dating Charles, but we don't want you to turn your back on the Polks because we don't know them very well."

"If you don't want me dating him—"

Mother lifted her finger to shush Ruthie. "I didn't say that. All I'm saying is that you need to be cautious."

"I always am." Ruthie didn't mention again how the one time she wasn't careful had backfired.

Chapter 3

C harles woke up with a flutter of excitement in his belly. Three weeks had passed since Ruthie Kauffman had agreed to go to the circus with him, and she hadn't changed her mind. He'd seen her in church Sunday nearly a week ago, and she'd even smiled at him before looking away. Her shyness intrigued him.

He'd seen a change in Pop ever since they'd known Abe Glick. Even Mom had noticed it and said she liked how he'd taken his eyes off his own plight and concentrated on his spiritual life. She'd been trying to get him to go to church with her ever since Charles could remember, but he'd always found some excuse not to go. Charles doubted she expected Pop to embrace the Mennonite life so eagerly. Between being too tired and using bad weather as an excuse for not wanting to go anywhere, Pop had managed to attend church merely a handful of times each year. As a small child, Charles had gone to Sunday school, but as he got older, he'd become more like Pop. Mom had finally given up.

Charles had to laugh about Mom's reaction when Pop started talking about going to the Mennonite church. The only exposure she'd had was when they went to Penner's Restaurant in Pinecraft. Mom and Pop had always considered the Conservative Mennonites an oddity. After Pop started working for Abe, he mentioned wanting to check out the Mennonite church to see what it was all about. At first Mom had resisted until she got to know some of the women who showed her the advantages of living a simple life wrapped around a deeply committed faith. Now they wanted to be Mennonite. Life was *so* filled with irony.

When Charles asked Abe if he could have Saturday afternoon off to take Ruthie to the circus, Abe gave him the whole day. "I want you to be rested and in a good mood," Abe had said, "not worried about something you'll have to leave on the farm."

Pop had argued and said he thought it would be good for Charles to work all morning, but Abe's wisdom and position of authority overrode anything Pop had to say. Charles knew Pop had been humbled enough to not even flinch at Abe's direction.

"Charles!" Mom's voice echoed through the hallway leading to the bedrooms. He could hear her footsteps on the tile floor as she got closer. "I can't believe you're sleeping so late. It's almost nine o'clock."

Charles sat up in bed. "I've been awake for a while."

"What are you doing still in bed?"

"Thinking."

Mom folded her arms, leaned against the door frame, and smiled at him. "There's been a lot to think about lately."

He threw back the covers and sat up. Mom laughed. "One of these days you'll grow out of those things," she said, pointing to his Batman pajama bottoms.

"Not likely. These are adult mediums, and I happen to know they come in large and extra large." He chuckled. "Which I'll need if we keep eating at the church potlucks."

Mom pulled away from the door. "I need to leave in a few minutes. I baked some muffins, so have one of those and some fruit before you go."

"Thanks, Mom."

Charles thought about the changes in Mom as he stood up and started getting ready. She'd not only accepted the idea of learning about the Mennonite church, but she'd embraced some of their culture, including the desire to bake. Last time they went to one of the church's potlucks, Mom's goal was to make a dessert that would have people coming back for seconds.

When he got to the kitchen, he spotted the note Mom left beside the basket of muffins letting him know she'd left the car for him. Beside the note was a key. Times sure had changed for the Polk family.

He spent the rest of the morning eating, watching a little TV, and getting ready for his date to the circus matinee. His nerves were frayed. Charles had very little experience with women, and he sure hoped this date didn't turn out to be a disaster.

In spite of the fact that he'd learned to pray about whatever was bothering him, he couldn't stop the jittery nerves from taking over. The time finally came for him to leave. On his way out the door, he stopped and muttered a prayer. *Lord, I appreciate everything. Now please don't let me botch this date. You know how nerdy I can be.* He paused and chuckled. *Thanks for listening. Amen.*

On the way to Pinecraft, Charles listened to a variety of music, changing the station when something annoyed him. He eventually realized all of it grated his nerves, so he punched the POWER button.

He pulled up in front of the Kauffman house and expected to have to walk to the door, talk to Ruthie's parents, and wait for her. Instead he'd barely gotten halfway up the sidewalk when she and her mother came out.

"Hi, Charles," Mrs. Kauffman said, a frown forming on her forehead. "Did you drive here?"

"Yes, ma'am." He smiled. "Mom left me the car so I could drive Ruthie and me to the circus."

Mrs. Kauffman glanced at Ruthie with a look of concern. "Are you okay with this, Ruthie? You can still change your mind."

Charles froze in his tracks. "Is there a problem?"

Both women stared at him for several seconds until Mrs. Kauffman spoke. "I didn't expect you to drive. Most of us. . .well, not many of our people. . ." She turned to Ruthie and then back to him. "Very few of the people in our church drive cars. We generally find other modes of transportation."

"Oh yeah, well, I guess we can take the bus or something, if that would make you feel better about—"

Ruthie stepped toward him. "No, I'd much rather go in the car." She glanced over her shoulder at her mother. "We'll be fine, Mother."

Charles helped Ruthie into the passenger seat and started around to the driver's side of the car before he stopped and turned to face Ruthie's mom. "I promise to be very careful, Mrs. Kauffman."

Her frown slowly faded, and she smiled and nodded. "Take good care of my daughter, Charles. She hasn't been on many dates."

~

Ruthie was so embarrassed she wanted to crawl beneath the seat. Why had Mother said so much? It wasn't any of Charles's business about how many dates she'd been on.

He got into the car, buckled his seat belt, and turned to face her. "Your mom is really sweet."

"She worries too much," Ruthie said. "I wish she'd learn to relax."

Charles laughed. "I say the same thing about my mom, but I think that's just what they do. It comes with the territory. I'm sure I'd be the same way if I had kids."

"But we're not kids. . .I mean, children. We're adults."

"Yeah, but this is our parents we're talking about. To them we'll always be children."

Ruthie thought about that and nodded. "I s'pose you're right. But it's hard to act like an adult when I'm constantly treated as a child."

Charles started the car and pulled away from the curb. "Isn't that the truth."

All the way to their destination, Charles talked about how much he enjoyed working for Abe. Ruthie felt her nerves calming as she learned more about him. To her delight, he was even nicer than she originally thought, but he still had some peculiar ways that puzzled her. Maybe if she got to know him better, she could ask questions. She didn't want to seem too nosy this early.

"So, you've never been to a circus, huh?" He stopped at a light, turned to her, and smiled.

She shook her head. "Never really had a desire to go."

"I think you'll enjoy it. There are so many different things to watch, I can't imagine not liking something about it." He counted on his fingers as he named some of the acts. "Besides the clowns, you have the high wire, trick gymnasts, the animals—"

Ruthie's eyes widened. "Does anyone ever get hurt?"

"Sometimes, but they practice enough to minimize that happening in front of the audience."

Ruthie couldn't imagine why people would put their own lives in danger, strictly for the sake of entertaining a crowd. "I know you wanted to be a circus clown. Did you ever get a chance to perform at one of these events?"

"No, I never did. I enjoyed being a clown for a while, but after doing a few volunteer shows, I realized it's not all fun and games. It's a lot of work, too, and after the show's over, you still have to face the realities of life."

"Why would you think otherwise?" she asked.

Charles let out a good-natured laugh. "That is a very smart question, Ruthie—one I asked myself years after I let everyone know I planned to be a clown when I grew up."

"That's such an odd aspiration."

"Yes, but I've never been accused of being normal."

Ruthie couldn't help but laugh. Charles was absolutely delightful company. She reached up and patted the hair around her kapp to make sure it was all in place and properly tucked.

"I've been wondering something," Charles said. "Maybe you know the answer."

She lowered her hands to her lap and faced him. "What's the question?"

"Will I have to dress differently when I take the final step of becoming a Mennonite?"

"I don't know. I've never seen anyone do what you and your parents are doing." She cast her gaze downward. "It generally happens the other way, with Mennonites going out into the world and not coming back."

They arrived at their destination. Charles parked the car and came around to help Ruthie out.

Ruthie looked around in amazement at the variety of people walking toward the huge building. "I've never seen anything like this," she said, her voice barely above a whisper.

"Just wait until you get inside. This is nothing compared to the show."

As they approached the building, Ruthie noticed a few people staring at her. She was used to tourists stopping at the shop and acting as though she was some oddity to be gawked at. Now she was doubly uncomfortable because she was out of her element.

"Does it bother you to have all these people staring? If it does, I'll tell them to mind their own business."

"No! Don't do that. People always like to watch anything they haven't seen before." She tried to hide the fact that she was pleased he wanted to protect her.

His smile warmed her. "So you're saying it doesn't bother you?"

"I'm not saying that," she replied. "I just don't want to give people cause to think I'm a bad person."

"Why would people think that?" He tilted his head and studied her face, making her tingle all the way to her toes.

"I—I don't want to make anyone defensive. Let's keep walking or we'll never get there."

Ruthie was surprised at the tingling shocks bolting up her arm when Charles took her hand and led her to the gate where he handed someone their tickets. Someone else gave them directions to their seats.

"I'm sorry I couldn't get better seats," Charles said as they sat down. "This was all I could afford."

"What are you talking about?" Ruthie pointed down to the ring in front of them. "We should be able to see everything from here."

He smiled at her and closed both of his hands around the one of hers he was still holding. "Thanks for saying that. Pop told me it wouldn't be an issue."

"What?" Ruthie had no idea what he was talking about.

"I'll tell you about it later. Right now I'd like to explain some of the things we're about to see." And he did, fascinating her with information she never dreamed existed.

Once the show started, Ruthie sat mesmerized by everything that happened, one act after another and some happening simultaneously. It was all so different and new she didn't have any idea what to ask.

Charles occasionally explained each act as it appeared, and it made slightly more sense. Then it was over. All the performers and some of the animals came out for a final bow.

"Well?" Charles turned and looked directly into her eyes. "What do you think?"

"I think. . ." She blinked, almost expecting everything to disappear as she woke up from the most confusing dream she'd ever had. "I think it's all fascinating and chaotic."

"That's the best description of the circus I've ever heard."

She pointed down toward a clown in the arena. "And you wanted to do what that man is doing?"

"Yeah, afraid so."

"But why?"

Charles shrugged as he stood and pulled Ruthie to her feet. "It's hard to explain. I've always felt as though my life was boring and no one would be interested in me the way I am. Clowns get quite a bit of attention, and they elicit reactions from people."

"They're funny, but in sort of a scary way."

"I know," Charles said. "And I liked that, too. No one really knows what to think about clowns because they do such unexpected things." He tugged her toward the aisle. "C'mon, let's get outta here. Want to stop somewhere for a snack?"

"Okay," Ruthie said.

She thought about Charles's comments about why he thought he wanted to be a clown. She understood more than he probably realized. All her life she'd felt invisible, but it never dawned on her to dress up in a silly outfit, slather pasty makeup all over her face, and throw herself around as she'd seen the clowns at the circus do. Even after seeing them, it still didn't appeal to her.

Ruthie had to shield her eyes against the late-afternoon sun as they walked outside.

"You okay?" Charles asked.

She nodded and was about to let him know her eyes were adjusting when a little boy pointed to her and asked the man beside him, "Daddy, why is that lady wearing that funny outfit? Was she in the circus?"

"No, but she should be."

Ruthie felt Charles's hand tense around hers as he pulled her toward the man and little boy. "We are not freaks. We are Mennonites."

The man snickered. "You just contradicted yourself. You religious fanatics are all a bunch of freaks if you ask me."

If Ruthie hadn't pulled Charles away, she wasn't sure what he would have done. "Come on, Charles. Ignore those people. They don't understand."

"I can't ignore them." Ruthie had managed to get him far enough away from the people, so she relaxed just a tad before he hollered back, "You need to find out what you're talking about before you teach your child a bunch of lies."

Ruthie wanted to crawl into a ditch and hide, but she couldn't. The man was heading toward Charles, his face colored with rage. "Don't you call me a liar, you—" She put her hands over her ears to block out the string of curse words that flew from his mouth.

Charles blinked and glanced back and forth between the man and Ruthie before looking the man in the eye. "Okay, calm down. I wasn't trying to call you a liar. I was just saying—"

"Is there trouble over here?"

Ruthie turned around and saw a couple of uniformed police officers. She started to say something, but Charles spoke up before she had a chance.

"No, sir. We were just trying to explain to that man and his child that we are Mennonites."

One of the officers offered a friendly nod. "I like you people. We rarely have any trouble from your neighborhood." Then he turned to the angry man and dropped his smile. "Would you like an escort to your vehicle?"

After Ruthie was fairly certain they were safe, she let out breath she'd been holding. She'd seen a few confrontations but never when her personal safety was in jeopardy.

"I am so sorry," Charles said once they were buckled in his car. "That man made me so mad I wanted to hurt him."

"Do you understand that once you become Mennonite you are not allowed to fight anymore?"

Charles gave her a goofy but apologetic grin. "That's what's so ironic about this whole situation. I've never been a fighter. In fact, the only time I was ever involved in a fight was when some kids decided to beat up on me one day after school."

"That's terrible!"

He shrugged. "It happens. Kids can be mean when they want to show off. Boys don't want anyone to think they're sissies. I guess that must be hard for you to understand—this whole thing about people being mean to each other."

"Oh no, I do understand that. I've seen my share of meanness. Just because Mennonites aren't allowed to fight doesn't mean they don't find other ways to be mean."

"Well, I haven't seen it."

"Trust me," she said, "you will. That is, if you stick around awhile."

"So now where?"

Ruthie gave him a puzzled look. "Where?"

"Where would you like to go? Remember? We were talking about getting something to eat."

"Oh." She tapped her chin with her finger. "How about Penner's? They have the best pie in town."

"Sounds good to me. To Penner's we go!"

Ruthie tilted her head back and laughed. "You say the funniest things!"

He cast a quick glance at her before focusing back on the road. "You think I'm funny?"

"Very funny. I never know what to expect from you."

"And I thought I had to dress up like a clown to get a laugh."

Ruthie shook her head. "No, you don't have to dress up like anything other than what you are."

Silence fell between them, and Charles's expression changed from smiling to concern. "Does it bother you to think I'm funny?"

"Of course not," she replied. "I like to laugh."

"Whew. I was worried there for a second."

Ruthie laughed again. "See? That's what I'm talking about. You don't even have to try to be funny, but you are."

The rest of the way to Penner's they talked and laughed. Ruthie couldn't remember the last time she'd had so much fun and been so lighthearted.

They walked into Penner's Restaurant still laughing. Mr. Penner seated them at the corner booth where they had a view from two windows. Ruthie knew that was the best seat in the place. Mr. Penner gave her an understanding grin, making her face flame. She wanted to hide her face, but that would make her embarrassment obvious.

"So did you have fun?" Charles asked once they were alone.

"I had a wonderful time!"

So Pop was right. Ruthie was perfectly content in the second-cheapest seats in the house. She even said she thought they were in the best place because they had a good view of everything. In a way, she was right. They couldn't see all the performers' facial features, but they got a good bird's-eye view of everything.

He opened the menu and perused the different sections. The desserts weren't listed, but he could see a bunch of pies in the glass display case by the register.

A server approached their table and addressed Ruthie first. "Hey there, girl. How ya been?"

Ruthie smiled at the quirky girl in the apron holding the pencil and order pad. "Hi, Jocelyn. What kind of pie do you have today?"

"The best coconut cream pie you ever tasted. Want some?"

Ruthie nodded and looked at Charles. "Mrs. Penner makes all the pies, and I love her cream pies."

"Sounds good to me." He closed the menu and slid it toward the server.

"I've seen you in here before," the server said. "You got a name?"

Ruthie laughed. "Jocelyn, this is my. . .friend Charles."

Jocelyn arched one eyebrow as the corners of her mouth twitched into a grin. "Your friend, huh?" She looked directly at Charles. "Nice to meet you. You'll love the pie. It is totally delish."

After Jocelyn left the table, Charles gave Ruthie a questioning look. She leaned forward and spoke in a low voice. "Jocelyn started working here after Mary married Abe."

"Oh that's right," Charles said. "I remember the story now."

"Jocelyn is different, but I've heard that the customers like her."

"And I suspect she's not Mennonite," Charles said.

Ruthie giggled. "Whatever gave you that idea?"

"Something about the outfit, the hair, and all the makeup." He made a goofy face that had Ruthie laughing even harder.

"You should have seen her before she toned it down."

The bell on the door jingled, so Charles glanced up. "Isn't that Peter?"

"You know Peter?" Ruthie asked.

"I do, but only because of what happened to Shelley. I was at the feed store with Jeremiah once when Peter tried to start trouble. Jeremiah did a good job of diffusing the situation. I can't say I would have done the same thing."

"Ya, I know how Peter can be."

"He's not a very nice person, is he?"

Ruthie shook her head. "No, he's not, even if he is my cousin."

"Peter's your cousin?"

Her cheeks flamed. "Ya, his mother and my father are brother and sister."

"I never would have. . . I mean, you don't seem like. . .um. . ."

"That's okay. People are always surprised when they find out."

Chapter 4

A few minutes later, Jocelyn arrived with their plates of pie. "Here ya go. Enjoy!"

"Thank you," Charles said. "It looks delicious."

Ruthie appreciated how polite Charles always was. He'd treated her with the utmost respect all day.

After Jocelyn left to check on Peter, silence fell between Ruthie and Charles. If Ruthie had any idea what to say, she would have spoken, but most of the time words didn't come easily to her.

"I had a great time today," Charles finally said, breaking the silence.

Ruthie nodded. "Ya, it was very nice. How long will the circus be here?"

"Not long. They have two sets of performances every year—one in February and the other during the summer."

"Do you always go?"

"I try to see them at least once per season. The man who spent the most time with me at clown camp still works with the troupe."

Ruthie sat up straight. "Was he there?"

"He's a behind-the-scenes guy. He used to perform as a clown, but something happened and now he helps produce the show." Charles paused before adding, "So I didn't see him."

"Oh." Ruthie didn't know what to talk about next, so she sat back.

Jocelyn stopped by their booth to check on them. "Anything else I can get you two?"

"I think we're fine," Charles said. He gestured toward Ruthie. "Unless you want something else."

"No thank you. I'm fine."

Jocelyn's eyes twinkled as she smiled. "I hope both of you have a wonderful day."

She turned toward Peter and hesitated before taking a step. Ruthie watched, waiting for Peter to act out.

"Would you like more tea?" Jocelyn asked, her voice slightly deeper than it had been seconds earlier.

Peter opened his mouth but closed it as he shook his head. Ruthie had never seen Peter hold back. He obviously realized Jocelyn wasn't easily bullied.

"Sometimes I wish I could be more like Jocelyn," Ruthie said after Jocelyn left.

"Why?"

Ruthie thought about what to say and decided she might as well be open with Charles. He'd find out eventually anyway. "It's very hard for me to speak my mind sometimes."

"Some people speak their minds too much," Charles said. "I find it refreshing to see self-restraint."

"You do?" She couldn't keep the surprise out of her voice.

"Absolutely. Have you noticed that most people in their early twenties try to copy some of the crazy celebrities they see on TV?"

Ruthie looked down at the table, cleared her throat, and looked back at Charles. "I wouldn't know. I don't watch TV."

Charles slapped his palm on his forehead. "That's right. I forgot. I am so sorry."

"What is there to be sorry about? You didn't do anything wrong."

"There are a few things I'll need to get used to about living a simple life. I've been watching TV for as long as I can remember, so that's one habit that'll be hard to break."

After they finished their pie, Charles left a tip on the table and went to the counter to pay. Ruthie stood nearby, waiting and not knowing what to do, so she looked around the dining room. She felt awkward. Mr. Penner called out and asked if they were in a hurry because he needed to get something out of the oven. Charles said that was okay, he would wait.

When her gaze met Peter's, he smiled. Ruthie didn't trust Peter enough to think his smile was friendly, so she quickly looked away.

"Whatsamatter, Ruthie?" Peter called out. "Embarrassed to be seen in public with your new boyfriend?"

Enraged, Ruthie walked straight toward Peter and glared down at him. "You are the meanest person I know, Peter. Why don't you try to be nice at least once in your life?"

Peter burst into laughter. "Don't be so serious all the time, cousin."

"I don't like all your insults." Ruthie took a couple of deep breaths and tried to tamp back her anger. Even she was surprised by her action.

"It's hard to hear the truth, isn't it?"

"Are you this condescending to everyone?" Jocelyn said, startling Ruthie. She hadn't seen Jocelyn coming.

"What are you talking about?" Peter said. "This is a family conversation, in case you didn't notice, and last time I checked, you weren't in my family."

Jocelyn placed her hand on Ruthie's arm. "Want me to get Mr. Penner?"

Ruthie shook her head. "No thanks. Peter may be my cousin, but he's not worth the effort of pulling Mr. Penner away from whatever he's doing."

Peter yanked his napkin from his lap and stood, causing the chair to screech across the floor behind him. "You women are crazy. I don't have to put up with this."

"Sit back down, Peter," Ruthie said, her voice low and deeper than usual. "You're making a spectacle of yourself. I'd hate word to get back to your mother."

He glared at her for several seconds, causing Ruthie's pulse to accelerate. She had no idea what to do next. Charles had left the counter and walked toward them. "What's going on?"

Peter grabbed his napkin and sat back down. "Your girlfriend is acting crazy."

Jocelyn placed her hand on the table and leaned toward Peter. "Who's acting crazy?"

"You heard me," Peter said. "And she's not the only one."

As Peter and Jocelyn bantered, Ruthie saw something she hadn't noticed before. Sparks of attraction flew with the words. Ruthie turned to Charles, who had clearly noticed as well.

He placed his hand on hers and tugged her back toward the counter. "Stick with me, okay? I think they need to work through this on their own. Interference from us will just complicate things even more."

"I don't want to leave Jocelyn." Ruthie looked back at Jocelyn who remained in the same position, her face about a foot from Peter's, both of them showing off and trying to get the upper hand. "On second thought, I'm sure she'll be fine."

Mr. Penner approached the counter. "Sorry it took so long. I had to move a few things off the counter before I could. . ." He looked past Charles and Ruthie at Jocelyn and Peter. "What's going on over there?"

"Just a little spat of attraction," Charles said.

Ruthie gasped. She didn't think Mr. Penner needed to be concerned with this.

Mr. Penner laughed. "That has been going on for weeks. Peter comes in here with a chip on his shoulder, and Jocelyn keeps trying to knock it off. When he leaves, he says he's never coming back, and Jocelyn says that's a good thing because she doesn't want to see him again." He rubbed the back of his neck, still grinning. "But he always comes back to do it all over again. And Jocelyn is right there to argue with him. I don't understand why, but they both seem to enjoy arguing."

Charles paid, thanked Mr. Penner for the pie, and led Ruthie to the car. "I've known couples who thrive on conflict. It might sound like arguing to most people, but it's how some people show their affection."

"I don't think I'd like that," Ruthie said, hoping Charles wasn't one of those who did. She didn't think he was, but she still didn't know him all that well.

"I know I wouldn't," he said, putting her mind at ease a bit.

"Peter has always been rather strong willed," Ruthie explained. "He knows what he wants, and he stops at nothing to get it, even if it hurts other people."

"Yeah, I figured as much after he dumped Shelley when she thought he was going to propose." Charles pursed his lips and looked at her. "Sorry. I shouldn't talk about your cousin like that. It's bad form."

"That's okay," Ruthie said. "You didn't say anything I didn't already know. The whole family likes Shelley, and they were appalled by what happened. We all assumed she'd eventually be part of our family, but then Jeremiah came along."

"Jeremiah seems like a good guy."

"I think he is." Ruthie wasn't sure what all Charles knew about Jeremiah's past—leaving the church and living a wild life before coming back. And she wasn't about to be the one to tell him.

They pulled out of the restaurant parking lot and headed toward Ruthie's house. She was content sitting in silence, watching the scenery as they rode.

Charles let go of the steering wheel with his right hand and placed it on top of hers. "Would you like to go out with me again sometime?"

She had to resist the urge to shout with joy, so she swallowed hard and nodded. "That would be very nice."

"Good. I'll need to figure out my schedule and see when I have some free time. Between school and work, I stay pretty busy. At least I know I'll see you at church."

"Have you decided to join?"

"My whole family is leaning in that direction. I have to admit I'm a little surprised. Pop wasn't much of a churchgoer. Even though Mom was, she enjoyed all the finer things money could buy. When Pop lost his job, I thought she might go ballistic and do something crazy like some of her friends did, but she didn't. In fact, she seems more at peace now than ever, even though we can barely make ends meet."

"When you said your mother's friends went crazy, what were you talking about?"

"One of them left her husband for another man, and another stopped talking to all her friends."

"That's terrible!"

Charles nodded. "I agree. It's a strong reminder that people can't control every aspect of their lives, and when they refuse to give God the reins, things go from bad to worse."

"Sounds like your parents have a solid marriage," Ruthie said softly.

"Yes, and I eventually hope to have what they have." He pulled up in front of Ruthie's house. "Wait right here. I'll get your door."

Ruthie's family rented the small house in Pinecraft, and since it was already wired for electricity, they used it, although sparingly. The front drapes were open, so she could see a tiny spark of light coming from the back of the house.

"Would you like to come in?" Ruthie asked when they reached the front door.

"I better get home. This is the only car we have, and I suspect Mom is itching to get it back."

Ruthie didn't understand, but she nodded. "Thank you for everything, Charles. I'll see you at church tomorrow."

~

Charles felt a combination of elation and peace as he drove home. Mom and Pop would no doubt fire nonstop questions at him, and he was glad to have some time to gather his wits. He created some quick answers to satisfy them without having to explain some of the feelings he'd never experienced before.

Ruthie's shyness had obviously prevented her from quite a bit in her past, including getting into romantic relationships, which was just fine with him. He hadn't exactly been Mr. Smooth Guy. He chuckled to himself as he thought about how awkward he felt with girls in the past, yet with Ruthie he had more confidence than ever. That brought back something Pop had said about when he and Mom started dating. *Your mother brought out something in me that I never even knew I possessed. That's one of the ways you'll know you're in love.*

Although Charles didn't know Ruthie well enough to say he was in love with her, he knew he loved being with her, and he wanted to get to know her better. What blew him away was that she said she'd like to go out with him again. The day couldn't have been better.

Mom and Pop didn't disappoint him. The second he walked into the house, they were both right there grinning, ready to pounce. He pretended not to notice as he walked by and hung the keys on the Peg-Board and headed to the living room, where he stopped and waited.

"Well?" Mom walked up right behind him, so when he turned around, they were face-to-face. "We want details."

"It was fun."

Mom made a growling sound, and Pop laughed as he approached. "You know what your mother is asking, Charles. Out with it."

"Let's see. We went to the circus and sat in the nosebleed section."

"Did that bother her?" Pop asked.

"Not at all. In fact, she said she thought we had the best seats because we could see everything."

"I told you." Pop appeared mighty pleased with himself. "So what else happened?"

"We watched the circus, and I explained some of what was happening when the clowns came out. After that we went to Penner's and had pie." He lifted his hands and let them fall to his sides. "That's about it."

"Charles." Mom tilted her head toward him and glared at him from beneath her eyebrows. "I know better than that."

"What else do you want to know?"

"Are you going out with her again?" Pop asked.

"I asked her if she wanted to, and she said that would be nice."

Mom and Pop exchanged a glance before both of them turned back to face Charles. "That's all?" Mom said.

Before he had a chance to answer, Pop winked. "Did you kiss her?"

Charles felt his face grow hot. "I didn't think it was appropriate. It seems awkward, ya know? I mean, she's been a Mennonite all her life, and. . .well, do Mennonite girls do that?"

Both of his parents burst into laughter. "Of course they do, Charles. They're still human."

"I just don't want to make any mistakes. I like Ruthie, and I think she likes me, too."

"Trust me, Son," Pop said. "Ruthie is just as human as you are. If you make mistakes, she'll understand."

"Do you two need anything else?" Charles asked as he backed away from Mom and Pop.

Mom stood on tiptoe and gave him a hug. "We'll let you off the hook for now."

"Then I think I'll go to my room."

After he left his parents, Charles wandered slowly back to his room, unbuttoning his shirt on the way down the hall. He paused for a moment when he heard Mom's hushed voice; then he took a few steps back so he could hear her better.

"Do you think we should say something to him about our visitors this afternoon?" she asked.

"Nah, let's let him enjoy the aftermath of his date. I'm sure he'll find out soon enough that not everyone thinks he's good enough for Ruthie."

"I can't believe what they said."

Charles strained to hear the rest of the conversation, but they'd taken it into the kitchen, out of hearing range of the hallway to the bedrooms. Whatever the visitors said must have been bad for Pop to think it would ruin his date.

❧

Ruthie stood staring at Mother, her mouth hanging open in shock. Papa's rage was evident in his bulging eyes and reddened face, but she knew he wasn't about to act on it.

"They actually said that?" Ruthie managed to ask in a squeaky voice. "Why do they think Charles is trying to use me? He's not that way. Besides, what about me would he use?"

"That's exactly what we thought," Mother said. "I expected as much from the first group, but when the Atzingers and Conrads stopped by, your papa and I were at a loss for words."

"Speechless," Papa agreed. "I had no idea there would be so many concerns about outsiders wanting to join our church."

Ruthie felt an uncommon rage welling in her chest. "They didn't seem to mind them joining the church until now. Why would the fact that Charles and I are friends affect their opinions?"

Papa's scowl turned to contemplation. "They said they're trying to protect you, but I think there's more to it than that."

"What else could it be?" Mother asked.

"No telling. I think we should just tell people to mind their own business."

"No," Mother said, "that would only anger them. Why don't we invite the Polks over and perhaps get one or two of the other families to join us? That way we can show an example of Christian love."

Papa nodded. "We can do that, but you know we can't control what anyone says. The Polks might hear something upsetting."

"Then so be it. I'm sure they've heard upsetting words before."

Ruthie was still perplexed, and she felt an intense desire to keep anyone from hurting Charles's feelings. "I think that might be a huge mistake. What if they decide not to join the church just because some people are mean spirited?"

Mother and Papa looked at each other. "She has a point," Papa said.

"It's better for them to change their minds before they join than to join and become disenchanted."

Ruthie thought about that and agreed deep down, but now she had her feelings for Charles to consider. "Why don't we just invite the Polks over first and let them see how our family is? After they know that some of us are nice, we can include others."

Mother smiled. "Ya, that might be good."

"Why don't you talk to Lori tomorrow at church?" he said. "Ask if they'd like to come over for supper."

Ruthie didn't expect him to want to invite the Polks over so soon, but she thought that sounded good. She looked at Mother, who nodded. "Okay, I'll do that if it's okay with Ruthie."

"Ya, that's just fine with me."

Mother and Papa smiled. "Then that's what I'll do," Mother said. "Ruthie, why don't you and I bake some cookies right now so we'll have something to serve for dessert?"

They didn't discuss the visitors, but Ruthie couldn't stop thinking about them. When she saw them at church the next morning, she felt their disapproving gazes as they said their good mornings.

Mother spoke to Mrs. Polk, who said she needed to consult her husband. By the time everyone left the church, arrangements had been made for the Polks to stop by for a light supper. Charles grinned at Ruthie. She knew her cheeks were flushed as she smiled back.

Chapter 5

Charles lay back on his bed, study Bible in hand. He wanted to spend some time immersed in the Word before going to the Kauffmans' house for dinner.

On the way home from church, Pop said he was uncomfortable about going because he thought they might have an ulterior motive—one other than simply getting to know each other. Mom told him he was being paranoid after a couple of people gave them the cold shoulder. Charles knew not everyone was in favor of letting his family in, but the Kauffmans were kind and open to giving his family a chance.

After a couple of hours, Charles's stomach started rumbling, so he left his room and went to the kitchen for a snack. The aroma of baked chocolate accosted him the second he entered. Mom was bent over the open oven, checking a pan of brownies.

"For me?" he asked. "I'm starving."

"No, not for you." Mom straightened. "They need a few more minutes. I'm taking them to the Kauffmans'."

"I thought they were having supper for us."

Mom rolled her eyes. "You know better than that, Charles. Never visit people empty handed."

"And since you're from Alabama, that means you'll come bearing food."

"That's right." She propped her elbow on the counter and tilted her head as she watched him open the refrigerator door. "There's some fresh pimento cheese. Why don't you make yourself a sandwich?"

"Mmm. Good idea." He pulled out the bowl of pimento cheese and carried it to the counter by the bread box to make his sandwich. "Has Pop lightened up about his suspicions?"

"No, but he has agreed that it's probably a good idea to go, even if there is an ulterior reason they invited us. At least we'll have a better idea once we do this."

"Sounds like you're a little skeptical, too."

Mom shrugged. "You have to admit, today was strange. Some of the people who were originally open and friendly basically ignored us."

"I wonder if it has anything to do with my dating Ruthie." He scooped a heaping mound of pimento cheese onto a slice of bread, spread it with a knife, and topped it off with another slice of bread. Then he lifted it to his mouth and took a bite. "This is good, Mom."

She smiled. "At least I still remember how to cook. It's hard to believe that this time last year we barely had any meals together—we were so busy with lives that pulled us apart. I actually thought it would go on like that forever, and I thought I was happy. But now I realize I was in a perpetual state of numbness."

Charles put the sandwich on the plate so he could put the pimento cheese back in the fridge. As he worked, he thought about what Mom had said.

"I'm still surprised at my reaction when your dad lost his job."

Charles put his plate on the table and sat down to eat. "Why's that?"

She pursed her lips and stared down at the floor. "I was relieved. I must have subconsciously known that things weren't working for us before." She looked back up at Charles with sadness in her eyes. "We needed something to shake us up and bring us back together as a family." Her voice cracked as she added, "After your sister died. . ."

As her voice trailed off, Charles closed the distance between them and pulled Mom into his arms. She shook as she sobbed for a few seconds before pulling away. "Things will all work out," he said.

"Yes, I'm sure they will." She dabbed the corner of her eye with the edge of her sleeve. "I can't help but think that God saved us in the nick of time."

"What are you saying? We weren't exactly starving to death."

"Not in the physical sense, but I felt empty all the time, and no amount of shopping ever filled me up."

"I didn't realize you were miserable."

Mom grinned with tightened lips. "I knew I wasn't happy, but until we were forced to come together and rely on the Lord, I didn't know how unhappy I was either."

"Are you happy now?"

"I suppose I am, but I'm still worried about things that I need to let go of."

"Are you talking about money?"

She nodded. "We still have to pay this crazy huge house payment. I don't know what we were thinking when we refinanced a couple years ago to make all those expensive updates. I hope we're able to sell soon and move into a smaller place."

"We can, but we'll have to get rid of a bunch of stuff. Giving up TV and some of the other things will be hard—at least for Pop and me."

"I'm working on your dad, but I think he'll come around soon. I think Abe's been talking to him, too. He came home a few nights ago and actually asked if we could have a quiet evening without TV."

That was a major deal. Until now, Pop had the TV on nonstop, even when he wasn't watching. He said the sound drowned out his worrisome thoughts.

Charles had heard his parents discuss the different church options, so he didn't have to ask why they'd chosen the Mennonite church. Pop admired

Abe's simple life, and Mom saw it as a way to prevent them from falling back into their old pattern of acquiring more possessions. He understood that, but he didn't want them to regret any decisions.

After he finished his sandwich, Charles put his plate in the dishwasher and turned to Mom. "What do you think we'll do at the Kauffmans'?"

Mom shrugged. "I understand that some of the families want to get to know us better, and I assume they're one of the first since you are dating Ruthie."

"Probably."

"You are okay with that, aren't you?"

"Of course," Charles said. "Why wouldn't I be?"

"You haven't exactly brought home a parade of girls in the past. I thought maybe you worried about your dad and me embarrassing you."

"No chance of that, Mom. I've always been proud of you. The reason I haven't brought home girls is I haven't exactly been a chick magnet."

Mom laughed. "They don't know what they're missing."

"I better go get cleaned up."

Mom looked him over and nodded. "Why don't you change shirts while you're at it? That one's pretty rumpled."

❧

Ruthie kept looking out the window. The afternoon dragged, and she couldn't wait to see Charles. She was nervous about his family visiting, too, because she had no idea what the two very different sets of people would find to talk about.

"They'll be here soon."

Ruthie turned around and saw Mother standing behind her. "I know."

"He must be a very nice boy to have you acting like this."

"Charles is nice, but. . ." Ruthie paused to try to think of the right words. "He isn't like anyone I've ever known before."

"That can be a good thing, Ruthie." Mother took Ruthie by the hand and led her to the sofa, where they both sat. "Did you know that my mother wasn't Mennonite when she met my father?"

"No." Ruthie remembered Grandma Abigail. "Why didn't you tell me before?"

Mother shrugged. "I guess I never saw a reason. My father was born into an Amish family. When his parents came down here, they eventually joined the Mennonite church. Mother was visiting the church with a woman who'd befriended my grandmother, and that's how they met."

"Was there ever any problem with that?" Ruthie asked.

"I'm sure there were plenty of problems in the beginning, but eventually people forgot. They were married forty years before Mother passed away."

Ruthie glanced out the window then back at Mother. "I wonder if Grandfather ever had reservations about her."

"If he did, he never told us," Mother said as she stood. "In fact, he said one of the things he loved most about Mother was how she could always see a different side of things. I knew she was different, but she loved the Lord as much as anyone."

"Yes, I remember." Grandmother was the person who used to explain confusing passages to Ruthie when she first started reading her Bible.

"So your papa and I are open to you seeing Charles as long as we feel that he is sincere in his faith."

"Of course." Ruthie thought for a moment. "How will I know he's sincere?"

Mother smiled. "Pray about it and be open to the Lord's guidance. You should always do that anyway. Come on, Ruthie, let's put some finishing touches on supper. I want everything to be good for the Polk family."

They added cheese to the broccoli casserole, prepared a platter of fresh-cut vegetables, and set the table for six. Ruthie was thankful for something to do to settle her nerves.

When they heard the knock at the door, Mother nodded toward Ruthie. "Want to get that, or would you prefer I greet them?"

"I'll go."

"Good. I'll be right behind you."

Ruthie opened the door to three smiling Polks. Mrs. Polk handed her a plate covered in plastic wrap. "Brownies."

"Thank you." Ruthie started to carry them to the kitchen, but Mother gestured toward the front room beside the front hallway.

"Why don't you have a seat in the living room? I'll go outside and get my husband."

Ruthie showed them the living room then carried the plate of brownies into the kitchen, where she left them on the counter. When she went back to join the Polks, they were just sitting there looking as awkward as she felt. For some reason, that made her relax.

"How long have you lived here, Ruthie?" Mrs. Polk asked.

"Most of my life. We came to Pinecraft from Pennsylvania."

Charles opened his mouth, but before he said anything, something behind Ruthie caught his eye. She glanced over her shoulder and saw Papa as he came toward them.

"Welcome, Polk family. We are happy you agreed to join us." He faced Mr. Polk. "Come on, Jonathan. I'd like to show you my shuffleboard court." Papa took a few steps before adding, "You can come, too, Charles, if you want to."

Charles nodded. "I'd love to see it." He smiled at Ruthie, leaned toward her, and whispered, "My mom is very excited about being here. She says you have one of the nicest families she's ever met."

Mother had already led Mrs. Polk to the kitchen, chattering the whole time. Ruthie could tell Mother liked Charles's mother based on her facial expressions. She felt her shoulders relax as she realized she was nervous for no reason.

Mrs. Polk quickly fell into conversation with Mother, discussing her lack of cooking during the past few years and how she'd gotten caught up in insignificant things. She said she was happy to focus on what was really important.

"I can see how that might happen," Mother said. "I have to admit I've been curious about some of the things we don't have, so it's probably best not to indulge."

"You are so right." Mrs. Polk sniffed the air. "Something smells absolutely delicious."

Mother chuckled. "I hope it tastes as good as it smells. I really wanted to feed your family a good meal."

Mrs. Polk laughed along with Mother. "One thing I noticed at the potluck is how the women in the church like to feed everyone. I hope I can measure up."

"Trust me, Lori. No one is measuring how well you cook. We love to eat anything we don't have to cook."

A half hour later, the two families were seated around the table. Papa bowed his head and everyone else followed. After he said the blessing, he looked all three members of the Polk family in the eye as he spoke. "We are honored to have you at our table, and we hope you enjoy your time in our home. Now let's eat."

Everyone laughed and started passing serving bowls. Ruthie kept stealing glances at Charles, who seemed as enamored of her family as she was his. Mr. and Mrs. Polk were interesting and fun, and they seemed to have an excellent rapport with Mother and Papa.

"Do you have other children?" Mother asked Mrs. Polk.

The instant she said that, Ruthie saw the distressed look Mr. and Mrs. Polk shared. Her stomach lurched.

Mr. Polk cleared his throat. "We had a daughter who was four years older than Charles. She was killed in a car accident when she was in high school."

"I am so sorry to hear that," Mother said. "We experienced the loss of a child, only he was much younger." Then she told about how the brother Ruthie never knew had drowned in a lake when the family was visiting some friends. "He was three years old and one of the most delightful children I'd ever seen. Our older daughter Amalie took it pretty hard. I never thought we'd be able to enjoy life again, but then Ruthie came along and showed us a whole new spectrum of light."

As the parents discussed their commonalities, Ruthie thought about how much sorrow both families had experienced, yet they still managed to go through each day, walking in faith.

She noticed that Charles was very quiet, so she lifted the basket of rolls.

"Would you like some bread?"

He nodded and took the basket, but he didn't say a word as he broke open a roll and buttered it. Ruthie worried that something had changed between them.

&

Charles had been able to shove aside memories of his big sister Jennifer until times like this when his parents talked about her. He'd loved and adored her, and she never failed to be there for him. She was always such fun to be around, and she brought a steady stream of friends home. He'd developed crushes on more than one of them, although he never let any of them know.

He noticed Ruthie giving him concerned glances, but he didn't feel like talking now. She'd lost a brother, but that happened before she was born, so she'd never know or fully understand the pain he felt. The memory of losing Jennifer had removed all the joy of this visit.

Mom and Pop continued chatting with the Kauffmans, and they'd already moved on, although the conversation had become much more solemn. But still, Charles didn't understand how they could continue after bringing up Jennifer.

"Would you like to see the flower garden Mother and I planted in the spring?" Ruthie asked. "We can go out there after dinner if you want."

"No, I don't think so."

Ruthie put her fork down, sat back in her chair, and stared at her food. He knew he'd snapped at her, but he couldn't help it. All Charles wanted to do was go home and be alone in his room.

Every now and then he noticed Pop giving him a stern glance, so Charles looked away. This continued throughout the remainder of dinner.

Finally, Mrs. Kauffman stood. "Ruthie and I can clean up. Why don't the rest of you go on into the living room? We can have dessert after our dinner settles."

Pop carried his plate to the sink. "I need to have a talk with my son anyway. We'll go outside for a few minutes." He darted a glance toward Mom. "Maybe you can help Esther and Ruthie in the kitchen."

She didn't hesitate to agree, but before she lifted a dish from the table, she shot Charles a warning glance. He knew he was about to get the riot act about his sullenness.

"C'mon, Son." Pop started toward the door with Charles right behind him.

The instant Charles pulled the front door closed, Pop turned around, placed his hands on his hips, and shook his head. "What are you trying to do? Sabotage our new friendship?"

"No," Charles said as he looked down at the ground. "It's just that when Jennifer came up—"

"Jennifer is gone, Son. I miss her as much as you do. . .maybe even more. She was our firstborn child, and from the moment I first saw her, she brightened every day. When she was killed, I felt as though the light had gone out and might never come back." He paused and looked Charles in the eye.

"That's how I felt, too. Still do."

"I know, and it's okay to still be sad over our loss." Pop raked his fingers through his hair and let out a shaky breath. "If I could bring her back, I would. You know that. But I can't. She's in heaven now, and we're still here."

Charles let Pop's words work in his mind, but his heart still ached. "I just wish you hadn't brought her up."

"It happens, Son. And it will for the rest of our lives. When people ask us about our children, it's natural to bring her up. In this case, we learned that the Kauffmans also lost a child, so they understand what we've been through."

Charles couldn't deny that. "That must have been tough for them, too."

"No doubt it was, but they're still here, and they're living their lives." Pop took a deep breath and slowly let it out before looking back at Charles. "Do you realize that Jennifer told your mom that she loved the Lord and she wanted our whole family to start attending the church she went to with her friends?"

"I knew she was going to church, but I didn't know the details."

"You were awfully young, so you probably didn't understand what was going on, and we didn't like to talk about it much."

"I don't get why we didn't all go to church. Wouldn't it have made things better?"

"I was so angry about Jennifer dying that I refused to go, but your mother went, and she liked it. She said it brought her peace knowing this wasn't all we had to look forward to."

Charles remembered when the women in the church surrounded Mom and brought meals on days when she couldn't get out of bed. He didn't fully understand what was happening back then, but now it made sense.

"It took losing my job and working for Abe to realize the importance of faith in God," Pop continued. "And now look at me. I'm dragging you and your mother to the Mennonite church. Who would ever have thought?"

Charles nodded. "I can see the Lord's hand in this."

"So can I, Son, and I think we need to remember that if the Lord can turn me around, he can certainly help us deal with the loss of Jennifer. She loved you, and she'd be the first to tell you to enjoy the rest of your life."

"You're right, Pop." Charles knew he still wouldn't be able to shake the sadness that had come over him during dinner, but he could at least keep reminding himself of what Pop just said.

"Why don't we go on back inside so the Kauffmans won't think we took off?"

Charles nodded. "I think I'd like to see the flower garden."

"Good idea."

❦

Ruthie heard Charles and his father come back inside the house. She could tell Mrs. Polk heard them, too, because she stopped what she was doing for a second and a look of apprehension came over her. Mother was quick to place her hand on Mrs. Polk's arm and give her a gentle squeeze, just as she did when Ruthie was worried about something.

"We've been through quite a bit since Jennifer died," Mrs. Polk said softly. "It's been especially hard on Charles. Just when we think he's better, something sets him back. The sadness seems to stay with him awhile."

Mother gave Mrs. Polk a hug. "The sadness may always be with him. Sometimes I can't help but think about our little Hans and how he found joy in everything—from wiggly worms in the ground to the birds in the sky."

Mrs. Polk sighed. "I'm sorry you all had to go through that, but it's nice to know you understand."

"We do understand. If you ever need someone to talk to and pray with you, I'm always here."

Tears misted Mrs. Polk's eyes. Ruthie had to turn away to keep from crying over the pain she saw.

Charles appeared at the door and watched the women for a few minutes before clearing his throat. Ruthie knew he was there, but she couldn't face him after the way he'd snapped at her.

"Ruthie," he said as he took a step toward her.

She looked up but didn't say anything.

"I'd love to see your garden. Would you mind showing it to me now?"

Ruthie glanced over her shoulder toward Mother, who nodded. "Good idea. Why don't the two of you look at the flowers, and when you come back inside, we can have some dessert?"

Chapter 6

As soon as they got outside, Charles took Ruthie's hand. "I'm sorry for what I did to you."

"You didn't do anything." She still didn't feel like looking at Charles, so she pointed to a row of marigolds. "My favorite colors are all the different shades of orange and yellow."

"They're very pretty, just like you." Charles turned her around so she couldn't avoid looking him in the eye. "You're not only pretty on the outside, you are a beautiful person on the inside. I should have never been so abrupt with you. I'm sorry."

Ruthie had to fight back the tears as she nodded. She didn't know why his apology brought this kind of emotion, and she certainly didn't want him to see her cry.

"So why don't we try to start over and talk about our next date?"

Now when Ruthie looked him in the eye she saw something different. His eyes were still filled with pain, but she could tell he truly wanted her to forgive him.

"Since we went to the circus last time, why don't we do something simple?" she said softly.

She loved the way the corners of his eyes crinkled when he smiled. "I would love that. Got any ideas?"

"Well. . ." Ruthie thought about the different things she did and realized it might seem boring to him. "You might not think this is fun. . ." Her voice trailed off as her cheeks heated up.

"You might be surprised. I'm not that hard to please."

"We can walk on the beach or go on a picnic."

"I love both of those ideas," Charles said. "Why don't we have a picnic on the beach? Nothing like a little sand to add texture to the picnic food."

Ruthie laughed. "And seasoning."

"Now that we've settled that, tell me about your flowers." He pointed to the periwinkles. "What are those?"

Ruthie led him along the path as she pointed out the varieties of flowers and told him what she knew about them. "I'm sad that some of the flowers are starting to wilt, but not all of them can take the hot Florida summer sun, like these impatiens."

"If I tried to grow any of them, they'd wilt, even in the best of conditions,"

Charles admitted. "I don't exactly have a green thumb with flowers." He held up his thumb. "But good thing I have a knack for vegetables and fruit. I don't think Abe would appreciate my killing his crops."

She couldn't help but smile as he made a funny face. "Mother is the one who understands flowers. I used to overwater them. She's teaching me that giving any living thing more than it needs can ruin it."

"That's true with everything. Even people and animals." He touched the tip of his fingers, counting off the different farm duties as he named them.

"Do you see yourself staying in farming?"

He looked out over the yard, paused, and turned to face her, nodding. "There's always something that needs to be built or fixed, like a barn or piece of farm equipment. I enjoy being busy all day. Makes me feel like I'm doing something worthwhile."

"Do you think you'd like to have your own farm someday?"

Charles shrugged. "I don't know yet. I'm still taking some college classes, but I'm losing interest in school very quickly. Mom and Pop used to push me to go to college, but now they're backing off."

"You know Abe went to college," Ruthie said.

"Yes, he graduated with a degree in business, which was a smart thing to do. From what I hear, he turned his family farm around from barely making ends meet to being a tremendous success."

Ruthie nodded. "That's what I hear, too." She wondered if he had any idea of the fool she'd made of herself when she threw herself at Abe. Ruthie decided to bring it out and get if off her mind. "I used to have a crush on Abe."

"You did?" Charles gave her a worried look. "What happened?"

Ruthie shrugged. "When I realized he wasn't interested, the only thing I felt was embarrassment. Since I wasn't all that brokenhearted, maybe I wasn't ready for a relationship."

"Are you ready now?"

"I don't know."

He smiled. "You'll know when it's time. . .at least so I've heard."

"Ready to go back inside?" The conversation had gotten uncomfortable, and Ruthie didn't want to stay on the same track.

When they walked into the house, their parents were already sitting around the table again, enjoying dessert. "Why didn't anyone let us know?" Charles asked.

"We didn't want to interrupt you." Mother hopped up from the table and grabbed a couple of plates. "Would you like coffee, tea, milk, or water?"

Ruthie and Charles joined their parents, who didn't waste any time resuming their conversation about the Polks' house. "It was Lori's dream house when we first bought it," Mr. Polk said.

Mrs. Polk nodded but looked wistful. "It started out being my dream house, but now that my dreams have changed, it's not so much anymore. If anything, it's become a burden."

"Then why do you hang on to it?" Papa asked.

Ruthie wished Papa wouldn't be so quick to ask that question. Everything was so simple to him—black and white with no shades of gray. But Ruthie knew most people weren't like Papa.

Mr. and Mrs. Polk looked at each other before she spoke up. "We've discussed it, but the housing market isn't all that great right now. Besides, where would we go? With my husband out of a job, we probably won't qualify for a mortgage on another house."

"Then rent," Papa said. "That's what we do, and we're perfectly happy."

"My wife. . . I mean, we never considered renting after we hopped onboard the mortgage train." Mr. Polk chuckled. "We assumed the market would continue to go up and equity would keep increasing."

"What does that matter if you feel that your house is a burden?" Papa asked. "The Lord doesn't want us to feel the burden from things on earth."

"Good point," Mr. Polk said. "That's something Lori and I should probably discuss. . .among many other things."

"Yes, think about it, discuss it, and do whatever you feel you need to do," Papa said. "Just don't allow your house to create a wedge between you and your faith. I wouldn't be able to sleep at night if I were in that position."

Mrs. Polk nodded. "We are having trouble sleeping." She gave her husband a contemplative glance. "Yes, I agree it's probably worth discussing. We can't continue as we have, worried about how we're going to come up with our mortgage payments to keep the bank from foreclosing. I wish we'd saved more money when Jonathan was working, but we never saw this coming."

"Even if you had saved money, it doesn't last forever," Papa said.

As the parents talked, Ruthie cast an occasional glance at Charles to see his reaction. He seemed to be taking it all in just as she had.

Mr. Polk finished his dessert and stood up. "We need to head home now. Thank you for everything, Esther and Samuel—the food, the conversation. . . and the advice. You've given us quite a bit to think about."

"We'll pray for you and that you make the right decision," Papa said. He turned to Charles. "I'm sure we'll be seeing more of you."

Ruthie cringed. Papa's assumption embarrassed her, but at least she knew Charles wanted to see her again, so it could have been worse.

∾

They'd barely pulled away from the curb when Mom started talking about the evening. "I've never seen you so talkative, Jonathan. You've always been such a private person—particularly when it comes to finances."

Pop nodded. "I know. The Kauffmans are easy to talk to though. They don't seem judgmental."

"I can't believe I'm saying this, but I want what they have." Mom turned and looked out the window before continuing. "Outwardly they appear to have very little, but when it comes to the important things, they're richer than anyone I've ever known in the past."

Again, Pop nodded. "I agree."

"We should probably put the house on the market soon."

They pulled up to a red light and stopped. Pop turned to Mom. "We don't need to act on emotion. Let's think about it for a few days then discuss it."

"Okay, but I'm pretty sure I'll say the same thing then."

Charles looked out his window in the back of the sedan. During the past several months, his family had gone through more changes than they had in all the years before, and his parents still seemed to have a strong marriage. He had to admit that he missed having his own wheels, but he'd adjusted and discovered the joy of eliminating unnecessary junk from his life.

But the house? This was the house he came home to right after he was born, so he didn't know what it would be like to live any other place. His room had undergone many transformations, but it was still the same room, with the same window overlooking the backyard he used to play in as a kid.

Until recently, Charles couldn't have imagined his parents even considering moving anywhere, let alone to a rental house. The thought of them joining the Pinecraft community still seemed like a stretch. Those houses were tiny enough to fit at least two, maybe three, of them in their house.

All three of them rode the rest of the way home in silence until they pulled into the driveway. "I have to run to the grocery store," Mom said. "So why don't you leave the car out?"

Mom took off a few minutes later, leaving Charles and Pop in the family room. Instead of turning on the television as he normally did, Pop turned to Charles. "Want to talk about tonight?"

Charles thought for a moment then shook his head. "Not really. I don't have much to say."

Pop smiled. "Yeah, we've pretty much said all we can for now, haven't we?" He reached for a magazine on the end table.

Charles left Pop and went up to his room to study his lecture notes, but his heart wasn't in the lessons. He had too many other things to think about.

An hour later Charles heard the sound of Mom pulling into the garage. He didn't have to be asked to help unload the car. He was out the door before she got out of the car.

Once all the bags were inside, Charles helped her put everything away. He lifted the butter out of a bag and studied it. "When was the last time you bought real butter?"

Mom smiled. "I can't remember. All I know is that food tastes much better with real butter, even though it does have way more calories than I should have." She put an armload of things into the pantry. "I've noticed that the Mennonite women don't even mention diets or calories, and most of them seem perfectly healthy."

"Remember they walk or ride those three-wheelers they call bikes, so they're working off the calories."

"True." She shoved a couple of cans into the pantry and closed the door. "I think downsizing our house and belongings will have a positive effect on us."

"It already has."

"We still have too much. Even if we choose not to give up TV, why do we need one in every bedroom?"

Charles pointed to the one attached beneath a kitchen cabinet. "When was the last time you watched that one?"

Mom poured herself a glass of water and leaned against the counter to drink it. "It seemed like a good idea when I had it installed."

Charles laughed. "I remember you saying you could watch the Food Network and cook along with your favorite chefs."

"Who has the time?" Mom finished her water and put the glass in the dishwasher before turning back to face Charles. "And that leads me to something else. Today wasn't the first time your dad and I have talked about putting the house on the market."

"So when do you think you'll do it?" Charles waited for that sick feeling in the pit of his stomach to return, but this time it didn't.

"Soon. We need to get it ready to show."

"I'll help."

"Good. We'll need to get rid of the clutter in the closets and paint. That should help make it more presentable."

"If you want me to, I can trim all the shrubs back along the front of the house," Charles offered. "I might even ask Ruthie for advice on planting some flowers."

Mom smiled. "That'll be a nice touch."

They chatted for a half hour about some of the things they could do to make the house more attractive to prospective buyers before Pop joined them. "If you fix this place up too much, we won't want to move." Pop walked up to Mom and put his arm around her waist. "We need to stay in prayer throughout this process."

"That goes without saying," Mom agreed. "And we don't need to let up afterward. I have no doubt this will be difficult on some levels, but as long as we lean on the Lord, those difficulties will be overshadowed by the blessing of doing His will."

Charles couldn't move; he was fascinated by his parents' unity in this decision. They'd always gotten along, with the exception of a short time after Jennifer's death, but this decision was clearly the most bonding experience he'd ever witnessed. Even though he'd had a sliver of doubt about his parents being able to give up so many of their worldly possessions before now, he was certain of their convictions at this moment.

"C'mere, son," Pop said, motioning Charles to join them.

Mom pulled him closer. "Group hug."

Pop chuckled as they huddled together. "I have a feeling we'll be doing quite a bit of this in the days to come. It's not gonna be easy, ya know."

"Of course it won't, and that's what'll make the experience even better," Mom said. "Working hard as a family to make this become a reality will help us as long as we're all on the same page."

Pop dropped a kiss on Mom's head. "I've been blessed."

∽

"Do you think they'll go through with it?" Papa asked Mother the next morning during breakfast.

Ruthie sat at the table and sipped her coffee as her parents discussed the Polk family. She'd wondered the same thing. Being without many of the possessions most outsiders had was never a problem for her, but she suspected it would be difficult to give up some of what they called conveniences.

Mother lifted one shoulder in a half shrug as she stood to get more coffee. "We can only pray for them and hope that the Lord keeps them on the path of His desires."

"Do you ever want anything we don't have, Esther?"

"Why would I?" she replied as she sat back down. "I have everything I need and want right here at the table." She smiled at Ruthie.

"How about an automobile or a television?" Papa asked. "Or a dishwasher or microwave oven?"

Mother's eyes widened playfully. "Can you imagine me behind the wheel of an automobile? I can barely steer the bike you bought me."

Ruthie chimed in. "Sometimes I think a television would be fun."

Mother and Papa both snapped around to face her. Papa nodded. "I imagine a little bit of television would be fun, but from what I hear, it becomes an addiction that's hard to break."

"Anything can become an addiction," Ruthie said. "But we're so busy I can't imagine when we'd fit it in anyway, so we're just as well off without it."

Papa's eyes sparkled as he nodded. "You are so right, Ruthie. We are very well off, and we need to always remember that." He stood and pushed his chair back. "I better get moving. I've got more than enough to do today."

As soon as Papa left, Mother and Ruthie cleared the breakfast dishes. As they worked, they chatted about what they had to do all week.

"Papa wanted me to come in early to finish posting the weekend's receipts before the new girl starts," Ruthie said. "I don't understand why he wants me to train someone to do what I've been doing since I was a teenager."

"He wants a backup, just in case you're not able to work," Mother reminded her. "We've also been talking about how to help you overcome your shyness."

"I don't need someone else working in the store to help me with that." She tried to hide the fact that her feelings were hurt. "I'll work on it, I promise."

Mother smiled and patted her arm. "It's time for you to experience more things, Ruthie. We understand your not wanting to have a rumspringa, but you do need to prepare for life as an adult. You never know what surprises the Lord might have in store for us."

Ruthie assumed Mother was talking about the possibility of Ruthie eventually getting married and deciding to stop working outside the home. But there would be plenty of time if and when that ever happened. She didn't say anything, though, because Mother had already started talking about her Bible group.

An hour later Ruthie was in the store's office, lining up the numbers and making sure they balanced with the actual cash receipts. Since business was generally slow on Monday mornings, Papa walked around the store checking to see what they needed to order. Rosemary, the new girl Papa had hired, wasn't due in until right before lunch. He wanted to spend some time with her showing her around before Ruthie was supposed to take her to lunch at Penner's.

Papa had informed her that he was hiring Rosemary sight unseen, simply because he trusted Rosemary's aunt and uncle who'd agreed to let her stay with them when she first moved to Florida. She was from Ohio, and she didn't know anyone outside her family, so they'd hoped she could become acclimated by working and getting to know the Kauffman family. She and Ruthie were the same age.

Satisfied with how quickly the numbers balanced, Ruthie underlined the totals. She glanced up and saw Papa watching her. "How long have you been standing there?"

He grinned. "Long enough. Rosemary should be here any minute."

Ruthie stood and stretched her arms over her head. "I've been sitting in one place too long."

"Then would you mind taking over out here while I run to the bank?" He lifted his bank bag and waved it around.

"Of course I don't mind." The store rarely got busy on weekday mornings, and sometimes they didn't have a single customer during the ten minutes it took Papa to walk the block and a half to the bank, hand the deposit bag to the teller, and walk back.

"If Rosemary gets here early, show her around the store." With that he left.

Papa wasn't back as quickly as usual, so Ruthie assumed he either got sidetracked by a friend who wanted to chat or he wanted to be away when

Rosemary arrived. He'd been commenting lately about how Ruthie needed to overcome her shyness. Normally that bothered Ruthie, but today she didn't mind.

Ruthie had just straightened a couple of the shelves where Papa had pushed some merchandise aside to count stock when she heard the door open. She glanced up in time to see a short, blond-haired woman wearing a dark gray skirt, lighter gray long-sleeved blouse, and a crocheted hair cover walk in.

"Hi," Ruthie said. She suspected the woman might be Rosemary, but she didn't want to assume anything. "May I help you?"

"Is Mr. Kauffman here? My name is Rosemary, and I think he's expecting me."

Until this moment, Ruthie didn't think she'd ever met anyone shyer than she was, but Rosemary looked frightened. Her heart went out to the woman.

"I'm Ruthie Kauffman, his daughter. Papa said if you arrived before he came back from the bank, I should show you around the store."

Rosemary's lips quivered as she smiled. "Okay."

For the first time in her life, Ruthie had the upper hand, making her feel confident and outgoing. "Have you ever worked in a store before?" Ruthie asked.

Rosemary shook her head. "No. The only work I ever did was help people with their children and some light housekeeping."

"You'll need to talk to customers if you work here," Ruthie said. "Can you do that?"

The brief hesitation let Ruthie know Rosemary wasn't sure what to say. "I...um...if you tell me what to say, I think I can."

Ruthie never thought she'd see the day when someone else asked her how to talk to people and help customers in the store. She'd always been self-conscious about doing it before, but Rosemary was counting on her, and Papa wasn't here. If a customer walked in, she'd have to act confident.

She continued showing Rosemary around. As they walked by the front window, Ruthie leaned over and glanced down the street. Papa sure was taking his time. She didn't see any signs of him.

A middle-aged couple walked in and asked if they carried anything they could bring back home to their granddaughter. As Rosemary watched, Ruthie asked how old the child was, whether it was a boy or girl, and if he liked animals. Once she had the answers, she showed the couple some children's T-shirts, an alligator pencil, and a juice cup shaped like an orange. The couple bought all the items and walked out of the store happy that they didn't have to go anywhere else.

"You make it look so easy," Rosemary said. "I'm not sure I can be that good with people."

"Sure you can. Remember that the customers aren't grading you. They're thinking about what souvenir to buy and take home to show that they've been to Florida." Papa had told Ruthie this so many times she had it memorized. "Tell you what. When Papa comes back, I can show you the books. After we go over that, we can come out to the sales floor. You can observe today, and next time you come to work, I'll let you handle the easy customers."

Rosemary blinked, smiled, and nodded. "Thank—"

Papa walked in and caught their attention. "You must be Rosemary." He smiled, but Ruthie could tell something was bothering him.

Chapter 7

Ruthie told Papa how she'd shown Rosemary around. "And now that you're back, I'd like to show her the books."

A frown replaced his smile for an instant, but he quickly recovered. "That's a good idea. I'll tend to things out here."

Rosemary cast a curious glance toward Ruthie, but she didn't say anything as they walked back to the store office. Once seated, Ruthie behind the desk and Rosemary in a side chair, Ruthie leaned over and saw Papa rubbing the back of his neck. She could tell he was worried about something, but based on how he was acting, she couldn't very well ask about it in front of Rosemary—especially not on her first day.

"Did your uncle tell you how many hours you'd be working?" Ruthie asked. "I knew you were coming, but Papa and I didn't discuss your hours."

"He wasn't sure, but your father said I'd start out part-time and work up to full-time if I like the job. . .and if you and your father like me."

"Oh, I'm sure we'll like you just fine," Ruthie assured her. "Wait right here. I'm going to ask Papa how long he wants you here today."

Ruthie found Papa in one of the aisles. He was bent over, counting items on a shelf where he'd left off earlier.

She touched his shoulder. "Papa, I have a couple of questions."

He quickly stood and grazed his head on the edge of the shelf. "Be careful when you come up from behind. You startled me." His angry tone alarmed Ruthie, and she took a step back. Even if he'd slammed his head on the shelf, he didn't typically get mad about something like that.

"I'm so sorry, Papa." She reached toward him and gently rubbed his back.

"Neh, Ruthie, I'm the one who should be sorry. There was no reason for me to talk to you like that. What do you need?"

"I've shown Rosemary the sales floor, and now we're going over the books. Is there anything else you wanted me to do with her?"

He shook his head. "I think that should be it for today."

"How many hours do you want her to work?"

Papa rubbed his chin as he thought about it. Ruthie glanced around the shelf and saw Rosemary still sitting in the same position, still as a statue.

"All depends. I would like her to eventually be full-time, but not now. How about twenty hours a week until she's comfortable working here?"

"I'll tell her."

"Have her come in five mornings a week and make sure Saturdays are included."

"I'll give her a schedule," Ruthie agreed. She started to walk back to the office but paused a few steps away. "Papa, what is wrong?"

"I can tell you later."

"At least give me a hint, okay?"

His jaw tightened before he finally nodded. "I ran into Howard Krahn at the bank. He said he and some of the others are going to see to it that the Polk family leaves the church."

"But why would they do that?"

"He questions Jonathan Polk's motives. Claims Jonathan is using the church."

"What is there to use? It's not like we're giving them anything besides friendship."

Papa gave her a half smile. "I know. But you know that the Krahns have quite a bit of clout, and Howard can be very convincing."

"Ya, I do know that, but I think the people in the church are kind and loving enough to accept those who are sincere in wanting to be part of the fold."

"Howard is coming here this afternoon to talk to me some more. I think it would be best if Rosemary left before that."

"What time?" Ruthie asked.

"He said late, so tell her she can leave at two."

"Do you still want me to take her to lunch at Penner's?"

"Ya," he said, "tell you what. Take her to lunch at one after the crowd has a chance to die down. I will pay her for the time since you will probably discuss the store and answer any questions she has."

Ruthie brought the information back to Rosemary, who still hadn't moved. Some of the fear appeared to have subsided, but she was still obviously nervous.

The bookkeeping system wasn't complicated, so it didn't take long for Ruthie to show her how to balance the numbers. "I can show you a couple of times; then we'll work together before I turn you loose on it."

Rosemary nodded. "I'm wondering something, Ruthie."

"What's that?"

"Since you have been doing this for so long, and you obviously know what you're doing, why does your father want me to learn this?"

Ruthie wondered the same thing, but she wasn't about to let on. "I think he wants backup, just in case something happens and I can't do this anymore."

"Oh." Rosemary still didn't look convinced.

"It's never a bad idea to have more than one person who knows how to do a job. We also need more salespeople to work in the store during busy seasons."

"I just hope I am able to help." She glanced down shyly. "I'm not exactly the most outgoing person."

Ruthie smiled. "After you learn the job, you will do just fine. Would you like to see the ordering process now? Papa generally handles it, but there are times when he's swamped and I have to jump in and help."

Ruthie went over how to do inventory and ordering. Rosemary didn't say much, so Ruthie assumed she understood. By the time one o'clock came, Ruthie had shown Rosemary most of the operation of the store.

"Ready for lunch?"

Rosemary gave her a shy smile. "Ya, I am very hungry."

Papa handed Ruthie some cash to treat Rosemary to lunch. "You don't need to come back to the shop," he told Ruthie. "I don't expect a crowd."

"Mr. Krahn's coming," she reminded him. "You might need me to tend the shop while you talk to him."

"I don't have anything to say to him. If I am alone in the shop, I will have work to do." He fixed her with a firm gaze. "The more I think about it, the more I know it is wrong for him to do this."

Ruthie could tell he knew what he needed to do. "Okay, I'll go home and help Mother."

Rosemary stood by the door watching. Ruthie joined her, and they walked to Penner's in silence.

⟞⟞

Charles kept watch for David while Pop packed their lunches. Mom had already left for her job, so the house was quiet. In the past, either Pop or Charles turned on the TV first thing just to have noise in the house. Over time since working for Abe, they'd gradually gotten out of the habit.

David showed up a couple of minutes early as usual. He said he'd rather wait than keep someone else waiting.

All the way to the farm, Pop and David discussed the various crops while Charles partly listened but mostly thought about something he'd been considering for a while. School had become less important to him, and he loved working on the farm. He wondered what Mom and Pop would say if he told them he wanted to quit his studies and work for Abe full-time. Abe could obviously use the help.

David occasionally glanced at Charles in the rearview mirror. "You okay back there? You're awfully quiet."

"I'm fine. Just doing some thinking."

David laughed. "Sometimes my wife tells me I think too much."

Pop glanced over his shoulder from the front passenger seat. "Are you worried about something, Charles? You've been awful quiet lately—even at home."

Charles lifted a shoulder in a half shrug. He didn't think this was the time or place to discuss his future.

"Not worried exactly," Charles said slowly. "We can talk about it later."

David cast another quick glance in the mirror before changing the subject. "Looks like we might get some rain this afternoon. Want me to pick you up early?"

"I'll call you if we do," Pop said. "Abe might need us for some chores in the house or barn."

Charles kept his eyes peeled on the farmland as they approached Abe's place. The change in scenery—from touristy beach town to the farms and land waiting to be farmed—wrapped him in a sense of peace. He felt as though he'd been living in two completely different worlds since they'd been attending the Mennonite church. Eventually he'd have to make a decision between the two, and at the moment, the simple life won hands down. It was difficult to keep his eyes focused on the Lord when his schoolwork led him in a more worldly direction. He sometimes wondered how Abe had managed to go all the way through college without losing some of who he was.

As soon as they pulled up in front of the farmhouse, Abe walked outside and stepped down off the porch. He leaned over and chatted with David while Charles and his pop got out of the car. David pulled away, and the men went into the house to put their lunches on the kitchen counter.

"I told David to come early today. We will get as much work done this morning as possible; then you can go on home. I'm taking Mary and the baby into town, so I thought it would be a good idea to make one trip instead of two."

Pop nodded. "I have plenty to keep me busy at home with some things Lori wants done around the house."

"Have you decided what to do about your house yet?" Abe asked as they started their trek toward the barn.

"We have to get caught up before we make any decisions," Pop replied.

"Ya, that is a good idea for business purposes. If potential buyers know you are behind, they might try to take advantage of you." He unbolted the barn door and opened it wide. "We have been praying that you make a wise decision."

"So have we," Pop said as he cast a brief glimpse in Charles's direction. "Lori and I pray about it every night. At first I was concerned she wouldn't be okay with moving out of her dream house, but now she says her dream has turned into a nightmare."

"That happens," Abe said. "Particularly when we try to tell the Lord what we want without listening to what He wants for us."

All morning Charles thought about Abe's words. In the past, Mom and Pop spent all their time planning for a future filled with everything money could buy. They didn't even bother waiting until they had the money either. Instead they charged everything to their credit cards, assuming the money would always be there. Although he hadn't heard his parents fighting, he sensed their tension as their concern about making ends meet increased.

What he now found amazing was the way the heated discussions had subsided. They still disagreed, but instead of letting the arguments escalate, they turned to prayer. The problems didn't disappear, but with God's direction, they'd begun to take action in lowering their debt. And instead of turning Charles down as they once had when he offered his financial assistance, they accepted. Pop had once told him he had too much pride to allow his son to pay the bills. Charles appreciated being able to help out. It made him feel more like the man he knew he was.

They broke for lunch and headed down toward one of the lakes on the edge of Abe's property. Some of the other farmhands chose to stay in the backyard, but Charles wanted to talk to Pop in private.

"What's on your mind, Son?" Pop asked as he leaned against a tree, sandwich in hand.

Charles chewed his bottom lip then decided to just let his thoughts out. "I'm thinking about dropping out of school."

Pop didn't even flinch. "I thought you might wind up doing this."

"Are you okay with it? We always talked about how important education was."

"Education is important," Pop said. "But that doesn't mean you have to stay in a college program that doesn't lead you to anything you want to do. You can't keep taking classes without a goal in mind." He turned and faced Charles. "So have you decided exactly what you want to do. . .besides being a clown?" A smile played on his lips.

Charles laughed. "That was a rather silly dream, wasn't it?"

"Not really. There are plenty of clowns who do quite well."

That was one of the things Charles always appreciated about Pop. Although in the past he'd stressed the importance of education, if Charles wanted to do something, he was able to do it without parental resistance.

"I love working on Abe's farm," Charles said. He finished the last of his sandwich and opened his bag of chips. "It gives me such a good feeling at the end of a long day."

"Yeah, I know exactly how you feel. I like it, too." Pop rolled up his empty chip bag and extracted a cookie from his lunch box. "Why don't you finish the semester and take some time off?"

Charles didn't want to finish the semester, but he understood what Pop was saying. "Okay."

"After we sell the house—that is, if we can find someone to buy it—maybe we can think about buying some land."

Charles thought about the bills they still owed. "Maybe we can live in town and continue working here until all the bills are paid off."

Pop chuckled. "Good thinking. I like the idea of not having all those bills hanging over my head."

"What's your thinking about the church?" Charles asked. He'd been wondering about this, and now seemed a good time to bring it up.

"You do realize there are some people there who don't trust us, right?" Pop said. "I don't want to impose on anyone who doesn't want me."

"The Lord wants you," Charles said, "and that's all that really matters."

Pop looked out over the horizon before turning back to Charles and patting his shoulder. "I don't know how this happened, but my son is getting smarter than his old man."

"That'll never happen." Charles closed his lunch box, stood, and dusted off the back of his jeans. "Let's get back so we can finish up before David comes to pick us up."

As they walked back to the Glicks' backyard, Charles inhaled the fragrance of plants and fresh dirt. He couldn't remember anything smelling this good.

An hour and a half later, they were in David's van heading back to town. Mary spoke quietly with Abe in the middle seat, their baby in a car seat in the middle section, while Charles and Pop stared out the side windows.

⟨⟩

Ruthie noticed how quiet Papa was during supper. Mother occasionally glanced back and forth between Papa and Ruthie, but she didn't say anything. Finally when she got up to serve dessert, Papa motioned for her to sit back down.

"I would like to discuss some things with the two of you," he said.

"Can't it wait?" Mother asked.

"Neh. I would like to do it now."

Mother folded her hands in her lap and nodded. Ruthie could tell Mother already knew what was going on. She turned to Papa. "What is so important that we have to talk about it now?"

"I spoke with Howard Krahn this afternoon. He seems to think the reason we are not opposed to the Polks joining the church has something to do with Charles courting you."

"We're not exactly courting." Ruthie glanced down at the table as her cheeks flamed.

Papa propped his elbows on the table and steepled his fingers. "That is not the way people in the church see things."

"Why would that be a problem?" Mother asked. "I would think that would make people appreciate the Polks even more."

"Not the way they look at it," Papa said. "Howard seems to think we stand a good chance of losing Ruthie to the world if she continues seeing Charles." He turned and faced Ruthie with a long gaze before shaking his head and turning back to Mother. "Our daughter has a good head on her shoulders. I don't see her leaving the church for any man. Besides, if the Polks are sincere—and I think they are—it is a decision that requires many hours of hard work and effort."

"Ya," Mother agreed. "I don't think someone who wasn't sincere would go to that much trouble."

Ruthie listened to her parents discussing the Polks and decided this was probably not a good time to continue pursuing a relationship with Charles—at least not until they were sure. If his family wound up not joining the church, she'd be an emotional mess. As it was, she liked him enough to know she'd miss him if she didn't see him again. On the other hand, if his family eventually became accepted members, she was still young and she had plenty of time to court Charles—that is, if he wanted to.

"Well?" Papa asked, staring at her. "What do you think about it?"

She blinked. "Sorry, Papa. I wasn't listening."

He leaned back in his chair, folded his arms, and feigned anger. "Not listening? What kind of daughter doesn't listen?" Before she could respond, he burst out laughing. "Thinking about the young man again? I understand." He reached for Mother's hand. "We were young once."

Ruthie needed to set her parents straight. "I like Charles, but I've decided I need to back off...at least for now. There is no point in continuing to see him if I'm not sure he'll even stay."

Papa gave her an odd glance. "Have you prayed about this?"

She couldn't lie, so she shook her head. "No, Papa, but I don't think the Lord wants me taking chances like this."

"Ruthie, the Lord wants you to turn to Him for everything, including matters of the heart, which doesn't mean you can't take chances. If you care about Charles as much as I think you do, you should turn to God and ask for guidance. Don't try to make any decisions without Him."

Papa was right, but Ruthie didn't know where to start with a prayer about her relationship—particularly since she wasn't certain how Charles felt about her. She didn't have enough experience with men to even begin figuring them out.

"That is what your Mother and I will pray for, Ruthie. And I want you to remember to do the same."

After dinner all three of them cleared the dishes. Mother filled the sink with water, and Papa went out to the backyard to check on his tomatoes that had been attacked by aphids.

"Ruthie, do you mind bringing me the saltshaker?" Mother asked. "The humidity has the holes blocked, and I need to clear them out."

They worked in silence as they finished cleaning the kitchen. Once they were finished, Ruthie went out the front door and watched the sun set.

A few minutes after the sun went down, Papa joined her on the porch. "Rosemary seems like a nice girl. Do you think she can handle the store?"

"She caught on to the paperwork fairly quickly, but she seems timid around the customers," Ruthie replied.

Pop looked down at Ruthie. "You were that girl once, remember?"

She smiled. "I still am."

"And you do just fine with the customers, so I suspect she will, too."

He had an excellent point, and she nodded. "True."

"My concern is how motivated she is to make the effort."

"I'll try to find out," Ruthie offered. "She said she likes it here."

"That's a good start. Why don't you get your office work done early and spend more time with her on the sales floor tomorrow?"

～

The next morning Charles decided to leave the house early and stop by the Kauffmans' souvenir shop before going to the campus. He was surprised to see another woman standing behind the counter. As he approached, he thought he saw fear in her eyes. His heart sank as he assumed she must be one of the people from the church he hadn't met yet.

"M—may I help you?" she asked as he got closer.

"Is Ruthie around?"

"Um. . .she stepped out for just a few minutes. Would you like me to give her a message?"

"Do you think she'll be back in the next five minutes or so?"

She nodded. "I think so."

"Good, then I'll wait."

As Charles walked around and perused the aisles, he couldn't help but smile at some of the merchandise. The store offered everything from scented, orange-shaped erasers to chocolate alligators. He imagined tourists buying some of those items and wondering what to do with them once they got home.

"Charles?"

The sound of Ruthie's voice from behind caught his attention. He turned and found himself face-to-face with Ruthie, and his breath caught in his throat. The sweet expression on her face had captured his heart, and he suspected he'd never be able to erase the image of her soulful eyes looking at him at this moment.

"Hi, Ruthie. I just wanted to stop by and see you for a few minutes before I go to class."

"Did you need something?" she asked as she took a step back.

Charles looked around, trying to think of something to say. His gaze settled on the other woman in the store. "Who is she?"

"Oh, that's Rosemary. Papa hired her to help out, and I'm training her."

"I don't think I've met her," Charles said. "Does she go to our—I mean, your church?"

Ruthie studied him for a second before replying. "She just moved here, but I think she will go to our church."

Charles was at a loss for words. In the past, he would have resorted to putting on a clown act, but he didn't want to do that with Ruthie. She'd see right through him.

He lifted his arm and glanced at his watch. "Well, I better get going. I have to catch the next bus to make it to class on time."

Chapter 8

After Charles left, Ruthie turned and walked toward Rosemary. "Did you have any problems while I was gone?"

"Neh," Rosemary said. "That man you were just talking to was the only person who came in."

Ruthie cleared her throat. "Tuesdays are generally slow. Papa should be here shortly. Once he arrives, we can place the order. I'll let you do it."

"But—"

"You'll do just fine. I'll be right there with you to make sure you don't make any mistakes."

Having someone to teach gave Ruthie confidence she didn't know she possessed, even though she sensed something else going on with Rosemary. Papa had trusted her, and now she was happy to rise to the occasion. But she made a mental note to be cautious.

After Papa came into the store, Ruthie and Rosemary spent the rest of the time going through the new catalogs and ordering merchandise. "Until you learn your way around here, it's probably best to concentrate on reorders of what we know sells," she explained. "Papa likes to add new merchandise, but he's very careful about which vendors he chooses. Some of them aren't as reputable as others, and we won't carry merchandise that doesn't fit what we believe."

Ruthie was happy to see that Rosemary paid close attention and asked questions. Occasionally she caught Rosemary giving her an odd look, but she didn't mention it. Instead she found something else to explain.

Dan Hostetler from one of the neighboring shops stopped by right before noon. "I saw the Polk boy come in here earlier," he told Papa.

Ruthie quickly stilled as she waited for Papa's reaction. It was Rosemary, however, who broke into a coughing fit. "I'll get you some water," Ruthie offered.

"Neh," Rosemary said. "I'll be fine."

Papa frowned at Rosemary before responding to Mr. Hostetler. "I didn't know the Polk boy was here, but that is fine by me. Did you have anything else to say about it?"

"No," Mr. Hostetler said, shaking his head while staring at Ruthie through narrowed eyes. "I just thought you needed to know since you weren't in the store at the time."

"He can come in here anytime the store is open," Papa said. "Is there anything else I can do for you?"

Mr. Hostetler mumbled a few words about evil trying to infiltrate the church before leaving. Ruthie noticed Papa's jaw tightening.

Ruthie wished Rosemary wouldn't stare at her. She felt as though Rosemary was judging her.

Papa went back to the office, leaving the women on the sales floor. Ruthie decided to explain stock rotation and other merchandising concepts since they were still so slow.

After a half hour, Ruthie had taught her everything she knew about merchandising. Rosemary still looked puzzled.

"Is there anything you still don't understand?" Ruthie asked.

"One thing," Rosemary said. "Is it always this slow around here?"

"No, it's just that way early in the week and during the times between our tourist seasons."

"When are the tourist seasons?" Rosemary asked.

"Holidays are generally busy. We see a lot of older people during the winter, and then families come when their children get out of school in the summertime."

Rosemary nodded. "I guess you probably don't have many customers who are from Sarasota."

"Actually we have quite a few. Some people like to buy Florida souvenirs for family and friends up north."

Ruthie hadn't realized how much she knew about her family's business until Rosemary asked all those questions. The extra confidence boost made her feel good.

"I have one more question," Rosemary said softly.

Fully expecting it to be about business, Ruthie looked at Rosemary. "What's that?"

"Why are you courting that Polk man? My uncle says he's not Mennonite, and if he has anything to do with it, he and his family won't be allowed to join the church."

For a shy girl, Rosemary sure did know how to produce a shock. Ruthie felt her blood rush as she tried to think of an answer. She opened her mouth but nothing came out. Fortunately Papa walked up and took over.

"All done here?" he asked. Instead of waiting for an answer, he gave a clipped nod toward the door. "You can go on home now, Rosemary. We'll see you in the morning."

He folded his arms and waited for Rosemary to get her bag. As soon as she left, he turned to Ruthie. "How long has she been talking about the Polks?"

"Not long," Ruthie replied. "She just asked—"

"I heard what she asked," Papa said. "She has no business coming into our store and talking to you like that."

"She surprised me."

"Next time she says anything about her uncle's opinion of the Polk family, tell me right away so I can deal with it. I would have said something this time, but I wanted to find out what you'd already told her first."

Ruthie swallowed hard and nodded. "Okay, Papa."

Fortunately the summer semester was a short one. Charles didn't think he could last much longer in the classes that had ceased to hold his interest a long time ago. He studied hard during the next couple of weeks to get good grades, in case he ever decided to go back to school.

When he first mentioned his desires to Abe, he was surprised at Abe's reaction. "Don't do anything you'll regret. I agree with your father. Finish the semester and make sure you do it on good terms. You may decide to finish your education, and getting low grades will make it more difficult to come back."

"Would you consider hiring me full-time?" Charles asked. "I mean, I like the work, and we could use the mon—"

"Ya, I need more labor. I will switch you to full-time as soon as you finish this semester." The pleased look on Abe's face overshadowed his stern voice.

Charles wanted to jump for joy, but he tamped down his excitement as much as he could. "Thanks, Abe."

The rest of the afternoon Charles had more energy than ever. Pop walked up to him and laughed. "I want some of whatever you ate for lunch. You're working circles around the rest of us."

"I don't want Abe to regret offering me full-time work after this semester," Charles said without bothering to hide his smile.

"Good job, Son. I never dreamed you and I would be working together, let alone doing farm labor."

"The Lord is amazing, isn't He?"

Pop took a long look at Charles before placing his hand on his shoulder. "Yes, He is amazing, but we still have quite a few hurdles."

"That's only because we're dealing with imperfect people," Charles reminded him. "Too bad others aren't as understanding as Abe."

"Most of them are open to our joining the church," Pop said.

"Do you think that the minority can keep us out?"

Pop shook his head. "I don't know, but one thing I'm certain of is that the Lord knows what's in our hearts. If we aren't allowed into this church, we are to ask for guidance and direction." He glanced up and pointed. "Here comes Abe."

"I've been thinking about asking Abe for advice on how to handle the people who are trying to keep us out."

"No, let's not do that yet, Charles. There's no point in creating controversy among his friends."

"Shouldn't we at least tell him what's going on?"

"He probably already knows." Pop lifted a hand and waved to Abe. "Looks like we're right on schedule," he called out.

"Ya. You are both doing a fine job. I have a good crew."

Charles felt pride swell in his chest before remembering the One to thank. He silently sent up a prayer, and when he opened his eyes, he noticed Abe watching him.

"Finished with your prayer?" Abe said.

Charles nodded, both Abe and Pop looking at him. "I sure wish I could come tomorrow, but I still have classes."

"How much longer before this semester is over?" Abe asked.

"Three more weeks."

"Good. You'll be done in time to work full-time on the fall harvest and get ready for the citrus. Jeremiah said that if you finish early he can use you over at his place."

Charles and Pop both liked working for Jeremiah, who was just as fair as Abe. Jeremiah's wife, Shelley, was working on getting their new house in order before the baby arrived. Charles occasionally wondered how difficult it had been for Jeremiah to transition back to the simple Mennonite life after being out in the world for several years.

"Looks like David's here." Abe shielded his eyes against the late-afternoon sun and pointed toward the shell-covered driveway. "I'll see you tomorrow, Jonathan." He turned and walked back toward the house.

The instant the Polk driveway was in sight, Charles saw Pop frown. "The garage door is open." They got closer and the frown turned to a look of worry. "Looks like your mother is home early today. That's odd."

"I'm sure everything is okay, Pop. She probably finished work and got sent home. Mom said they've been cutting hours."

David pulled into the driveway and stopped. "I'll be here first thing in the morning, Jonathan. Call if you need me before then."

Charles and Pop got out and made it halfway up the walk when the door flew open and Mom came running out, tears streaming down her cheeks. Pop pulled her to his chest and wrapped his arms around her, leaving Charles standing there looking on.

"What happened, Lori?" Pop asked.

"They had to let a bunch of people go." She dabbed at her tear-stained cheeks with a wadded tissue. "What are we gonna do, Jonathan? You and Charles aren't making nearly enough to support us. We have to get this house ready to sell."

Pop's worry lines deepened, but he didn't let it come through in his voice.

"We'll figure out something. Right now let's go inside and pray about it."

In the past, prayer would have been an afterthought. Pop gently helped Mom to the sofa, and he sat down next to her. Charles took the chair adjacent to them. Between sniffles, Mom told Charles and Pop how her boss had taken her and several of her coworkers to lunch. She knew something wasn't right because they'd discontinued company-funded lunches during cutbacks.

"Did he tell you before or after you ate?" Pop asked.

Mom gave him a curious look. "Afterward. Why?"

Pop shrugged. "At least he let you enjoy the food."

Her chin quivered. "Now what am I supposed to do? It's hard to get a job in these times."

Charles remembered meeting someone new at the Kauffmans' shop. "Maybe you can ask someone at church. Some of the businesses around Pinecraft seem to be doing just fine."

"All I know is office work," she said.

Pop pulled her to her feet. "We can ask around. I'm sure we'll be just fine. Take a few days and try to calm down a bit before you start looking."

⌇

The following Sunday, Ruthie went to church with her parents, determined not to get in the position of being alone with Charles. It was too risky now that she'd been with him and knew how he could make her feel.

Mother was the first to notice Mrs. Polk standing alone, looking forlorn. "She's usually such a happy person. Let's go check on her." Before Ruthie had a chance to say a word, Mother had made a beeline to Charles's mother.

Ruthie started to follow, but Charles stepped from out of nowhere and into her path. "Can we talk for a minute?"

"Um. . ." Ruthie cut her glance over toward her mother who had Mrs. Polk cornered. They were deep in conversation. "I guess that's okay."

"My family needs your prayers. Mom lost her job last week. Dad and I are both working, but without Mom's paycheck, I'm not sure how we'll pay our bills."

Prayer. That much she could do. "Of course I'll pray for your family."

"I offered to quit school so I could get more hours right away, but Pop and Abe still don't want me to drop out."

"I'm sure they have a good reason." Ruthie couldn't even pretend to understand the stress of having to pay bills. She wasn't even twenty yet, and she'd always lived with her parents, who'd always lived a frugal lifestyle.

"We want to sell the house and get out from under all our debt, but it's hard with all the bills we've incurred."

"I can imagine." But she really couldn't. She glanced over toward Mr. Polk, who was deep in conversation with Abe by the church door. "I'll pray for your family," she repeated, "but now I need to get settled in for church."

Charles pursed his lips and stepped to the side. "Yes, of course. Maybe we can talk later?"

"Maybe." She scurried toward a pew near where Mother still stood with Mrs. Polk. A few minutes later the two women joined her.

Mother leaned over and whispered, "Lori lost her job last week."

"I know," Ruthie said. "Charles just told me."

"I'm going to ask around and see if anyone is hiring. All she knows how to do is paperwork, but she's young enough to learn something new." Mother stared straight ahead for a few seconds before turning back to Ruthie with her eyebrows raised. "I wonder if your papa would want to hire her for the store."

"He just hired Rosemary, remember?"

"Oh that's right. I'm not so sure he's all that pleased with Rosemary, but I don't think he will ever send her away without a good, solid reason."

Ruthie agreed with a nod. "Rosemary doesn't seem to mind working in the back, but she's not happy about helping customers."

Mother grimaced. "That's one of the things she'll need to change if she wants to continue working in retail."

Ruthie wondered if Papa had told Mother what he'd overheard Rosemary say. He'd always been a man of his word, no matter what—even when angry—so Mother was right about him keeping Rosemary employed.

⁓

Charles thought the semester would never end, but the day of his final exams finally arrived. Abe gave him an extra day off to study, so he had no excuse not to do well. After he finished the last exam, he felt light on his feet as he walked across campus toward the bus stop.

He couldn't wait to start working full-time for Abe, and now that he was free from school—at least for now—he'd be able to do that the following week. Mom was even more stressed over losing her job. She'd taken a few days off at Pop's insistence, but now she went out every morning and applied at all the companies where she thought she was qualified to work. Charles noticed that she started out with hope, but as time went on without a nibble, her spirit had started to fade.

As he waited at the bus stop, he said a silent prayer for Mom—not only that she'd find work, but that her mood would be lifted. Mom had always been one of the most positive people he'd ever known, so this was a side of her he'd never seen. Even when she and Pop had started worrying about paying bills, they at least had hope for a breakthrough. Seeing her beaten down broke his heart.

No one was home when Charles arrived, so he went around the house and did some straightening up. He still had some pent-up energy left, so he vacuumed, ran the dishwasher, and when the dishes were clean, unloaded it. Then he thought it might be nice to start supper. He wasn't a great cook, but he could put together a basic meal. Their stock in the pantry had slowly diminished over time, making meal planning difficult.

Charles had a few dollars in his pocket, but they lived too far from a grocery store to walk. He thought about how easy life would be if they were in a community such as Pinecraft, where he could walk almost anywhere he wanted to go.

He took one more look in the pantry and decided to make a chicken casserole with the condensed cream soup, the small amount of rice in the container, and some chicken thighs he saw in the freezer. Pop had brought home some green beans and tomatoes from Abe's farm, so he could prepare a full meal.

Pop got home first. He walked in the door, sniffed the air, and shot Charles a puzzled look. "I didn't see the car. Is your mom home?"

"No, I started supper."

"Good for you." Pop washed his hands at the kitchen sink. "I hope this is a good sign for your mother. She's determined to find something even though I told her to try not to stress over it so much."

"I know but she's always worked."

Pop tightened his lips and nodded. "That's another thing I wish we'd done differently. When we first got married, she said she wanted to be a full-time mother to our children as long as they remained at home, but there were so many things we wanted, it became impossible after a while."

"Don't beat yourself up over it, Pop. You both did what you thought was right, and I turned out just fine."

Pop stepped closer to Charles and placed his hand on his shoulder. "You sure did, Son. I'm very proud of you."

Mom arrived home a few minutes before it was time to remove the casserole from the oven. For the first time in weeks, she beamed.

"Good news! I finally found a job." She cleared her throat before adding, "It's not exactly what I'm qualified to do, but it's something I should be able to learn fairly quickly."

"Are you gonna keep us in suspense all night?" Pop asked.

She grinned as she glanced back and forth between Charles and Pop. "Joseph Penner hired me to work the breakfast shift."

"Breakfast shift? As in waiting tables?" Pop asked. His jaw fell slack.

"Yep. I never thought I'd be this excited about working in a restaurant, but on a whim I decided to ask if he knew of any job openings. Apparently Shelley and Jeremiah are getting ready to move out to their farm, and it will be difficult for her to stay at the restaurant. She agreed to stay long enough to train me."

"Mom, that's wonderful," Charles said as he closed the distance between them for a hug. "Mr. Penner seems like a fair man."

"The salary isn't great, but Jocelyn said the tips are the best she's ever gotten. Apparently they have a mix of regular customers and tourists, so I'll never be bored."

Pop remained standing in the same spot, staring at Mom with a neutral expression. Charles couldn't tell what he was thinking.

"Say something, Jonathan," Mom said. "You're not upset, are you?"

He shook his head. "Not upset, but are you sure you want to do this? Waiting tables is hard work."

"No harder than anything else I've ever done. And it's something I can do and then come home and forget about it."

"That's a good thing," Pop agreed. "Ever since I've worked on the farm, I've slept like a baby."

Mom smiled at him. "That's what I'm counting on. I'm tired of not sleeping at night. And at least now we'll all have an income, so we should be able to keep our heads above water."

"We have to be careful though," Pop reminded her. "Even with all three of us working, our income is still a fraction of what it was."

"Oh," she said as she hung her purse on the hook by the door, "another perk is that I get to take home leftover desserts."

Charles grinned. "And they have the best desserts. Speaking of food, I want you two to sit down. Dinner is almost ready."

As she sat, Mom winked at Charles. "I could get used to this."

Pop said the blessing before Charles put the filled plates on the table. Mom took one bite of her chicken, closed her eyes, and visibly relaxed.

Dinnertime conversation was quite a bit lighter than it had been since Mom lost her job. Charles sent up a silent prayer of thanks.

❦

Ruthie went to church early on Sunday to set up some tables for the potluck. Mom was still preparing the vegetable platter and casserole when she left.

She arrived at the church, expecting to see only a few of the men who generally put the tables on the lawn. When she spotted Charles and his parents talking to the Penners, her breath caught in her throat. She'd managed to avoid Charles by getting lost in the crowd at church, but now, with just a few people there, it would be awkward.

The second Charles spotted her, he left his parents and came toward her. There was no way she could even pretend not to see him.

"I've missed you, Ruthie," he said. "We need to talk."

"Maybe later. I have to cover the tables and set up the condiments for the potluck."

Charles lifted his hands. "I'll help."

Each time they made eye contact or brushed hands, her heart hammered and her mouth went dry. There was no way she could deny the attraction she'd tried to push aside. After they finished their tasks, Charles brushed his hands together. "All done. See? When you have two people working, you can get everything done in half the time. Now can we talk?"

She couldn't very well say no so she nodded. Charles led her over to a bench beneath the shade tree on the edge of the church lawn.

"I'm working full-time for Abe now," he said.

She looked him in the eye. "You quit school? For good?"

He shrugged. "Maybe. Abe said I might want to go back later, but for now I've decided I prefer working on the farm all day."

"You've really taken to farming, haven't you?"

He nodded. "I love everything about it."

"Even more than being a clown?" she teased.

"Way more than being a clown. It feels more like a calling from the Lord."

Ruthie studied his expression as he explained all the things he enjoyed about working on the farm—from the physical labor to the beauty of the land. There was no doubt in her mind that he was sincere.

"Ruthie," he said softly before pausing. When she met his gaze, he took one of her hands and covered it with his. "I really like you. . .a lot. Is there any way we can hang out more and see where our relationship can go?"

Chapter 9

She hadn't expected such a direct question. "I. . .uh, I'll have to talk to Mother and Papa." She already knew her parents would be fine with her seeing Charles, as long as she did so in a cautious manner, but she'd already decided to back off.

He nodded. "Of course I want to date you with their blessing. It wouldn't be right to do it any other way."

Ruthie wondered if Charles was aware of the people who disapproved. But not everyone was against it. In fact, some of her parents' friends who'd arrived at church early had seen her talking to Charles and were grinning. She knew it wouldn't be long before the matchmaking resumed. And the heated discussions would continue.

"I hear you're having a birthday soon." Charles met her gaze with a grin. "Would you like to do something special?"

Ruthie had always had a quiet birthday dinner at home. "I don't know what Mother and Papa have planned."

"I wouldn't want to interfere with whatever it is, so perhaps you and I can go out on a different day?"

His persistence flattered her, and she couldn't resist her heart's desire. "What would you want to do?" she asked. "I enjoyed the circus, but I don't think I want to do that for my birthday."

Charles looked away then back at her. "To be honest, I'm not sure what all we're allowed to do."

Ruthie's heart warmed at his admission. "We could go on that picnic we talked about or. . ." She hesitated for a moment. "I've always wanted to go to an art gallery."

"Then let's do that," Charles said. "The Ringling Museum of Art is one of the best I've ever seen."

In spite of her resolve, Ruthie decided right then and there to throw caution to the wind. "I would love to go!"

⌒

As soon as the words left Charles's mouth, he regretted asking Ruthie to go to the Ringling Museum of Art. Money was tight, and although he'd never considered the admission price too high, it was money they needed to pay bills. But there was no way he could retract his offer now that he'd made it.

They chatted a few more minutes until it was time to go into the church.

Pop nudged him. "So how's Ruthie?"

Charles cleared his throat. "Fine."

Pop leaned away from Charles and narrowed his eyes. "What's wrong, Son? Did you two have an argument?"

Charles didn't want to mention his concern about asking Ruthie to do something he couldn't afford. "No, we had a nice talk." He gestured toward the pastor who had walked up to the front of the church.

As they worshipped and prayed, Charles tried to focus on the service. Every once in a while a sense of dread washed over him. He couldn't back out of his offer to take Ruthie to the art museum, but his family needed every penny he earned at the Glick farm, so he had to figure out something else.

After church Mr. Penner chatted with Mom and Pop and said he was happy to have her working in his restaurant. The chasm between the groups who were for and against the Polk family joining the church had become wider and more obvious. Those who didn't like the idea of outsiders becoming one of them walked a wide berth around all three of them, while those who welcomed them didn't hesitate to surround them and offer prayers. Charles could see that these people weren't as different from outsiders as he used to think.

Charles sought out Ruthie after the service was over and asked if she would sit with him. Her brief hesitation made his stomach ache. He wanted her to feel something for him, and he was still confused by her reactions. Sometimes when he caught her looking at him, he thought she might feel an attraction, but other times—like now—he wondered if she was simply being kind.

After the pastor said the blessing, everyone crowded around the buffet tables. Ruthie helped serve some of the children so Charles waited until she was ready to prepare her own plate. Together they walked to the picnic table farthest from the church.

"Any idea who cooked the ham?" he asked.

"Probably Mary. She generally brings the meat, and her grandparents bring desserts."

"It's seasoned just right." Charles tasted a few other things on his plate. "What did you bring?"

"Mother made the vegetable casserole." She glanced down at his plate before looking at him with a grin. "Looks like you're not big on vegetables."

He wrinkled his nose. "You caught me. Mom used to have to puree my vegetables and put them in sauces, but I have gotten better." He lifted a green bean from his plate. "See? I eat green stuff now."

She laughed aloud. "At least it's a start. Here, try some of my mother's casserole. It's really good." She scooped some of the food off her plate and put it on the edge of his. "Go on, try it."

He studied the blob of food and turned it over with his fork. "Are you sure it's good?"

"It just happens to be my favorite food."

"Okay, then in that case I'll try it." Charles slowly scooped some of the food and lifted it to his lips. "Down the hatch." He put it into his mouth, chewed it, and grinned. "Yeah, for vegetables it's not half bad. And coming from a veggie-phobic, that's a compliment."

A shadow moved over the table so Charles spun around and saw that Jeremiah and Abe had joined them. "Don't look now," Jeremiah said, "but you two have half the congregation staring at you."

Naturally Charles looked up and saw that Jeremiah was right. "Um. . . yeah."

Abe sat down beside Charles. "Everyone is interested in what is going on between you two. Enjoying the food?"

Charles cast a quick glance toward Ruthie whose cheeks were flaming red. He felt bad that she was so embarrassed, but at this point there was nothing he could do to change it.

"Yes, the food is delicious. I even tried some vegetables and liked them."

Jeremiah gestured toward someone behind Charles. "Over here, Shelley." He looked down at Charles. "Want me to bring you some dessert?"

Ruthie hopped up. "I can get it. What would you like—pie, cake, or cookies?"

"It all sounds good," Charles said. "Bring me whatever you're having."

Jeremiah's wife, Shelley, and Abe's wife, Mary, joined them and sat across the table from Charles. They instantly started chatting about the baby in Mary's arms and the one Shelley was pregnant with. He was relieved he didn't have to think of anything to say. Jeremiah talked quite a bit, too, but Abe was his usual silent self. He rarely had much to say, but when he spoke, most people listened. For as young as Abe was, Charles could see he garnered a tremendous amount of respect.

For the first time in his life, Charles felt as though he was part of something big. He was surrounded by people who sincerely respected and cared about each other. But when he leaned over and glanced beyond the circle around him, he also saw the doubters—who sat there with pursed lips watching, waiting for the "intruders" to make some sort of misstep.

Ruthie brought him a plate heaping with a variety of desserts—German chocolate cake, red velvet cake, two kinds of pies, and an oatmeal raisin cookie. He raised his eyebrows and his eyes widened.

Jeremiah laughed. "Better get used to it. These women like to make sure their men are well fed."

Ruthie's face once again turned bright red. Instead of making a big deal over the massive amount of dessert, Charles stabbed a piece of cake and tried it. "This is the best cake I ever had."

"Try the red velvet," Jeremiah said. "You'll like that even better."

Charles had no doubt he'd wind up putting on some weight, which he could stand to do. Most of his life he'd been too skinny anyway, in spite of all the food he put away.

He lost track of time with Ruthie, Abe, Mary, Jeremiah, and Shelley, but eventually the crowd started to disperse. Some of the younger men began breaking down the tables so Charles and his new pals joined in. Ruthie, Mary, and Shelley scurried back and forth carrying bowls and casserole dishes to the kitchen, trying to stay a few steps ahead of the men.

Finally it was time to leave. Ruthie's parents had already gone home so she was there alone.

"Would you like a ride home?" he asked. "I'm sure Mom and Pop won't mind."

She nervously glanced around then shook her head. "Neh, I can walk."

"Are you sure?" he asked.

"Ya. I like to walk."

He watched her walk toward home before joining his parents, who stood near the car patiently waiting. Pop placed his hand on Charles's shoulder, but neither Mom nor Pop said a word about Ruthie all the way home.

Once they were in the house, Charles went straight to his room to try to figure out how he could afford to take Ruthie to the Ringling Museum of Art without sacrificing any of the money his family needed. His gaze settled on his sizable collection of video games. He instantly knew what he needed to do.

It had been a while since he'd been on an Internet auction site, but it didn't take long to list the first batch of items. Rather than list everything at one time, Charles decided to start with a couple dozen CDs and DVDs to see how they'd do. Some of them were rare, so he suspected he'd do well with them. By the time he finished, he already had bids on the first few. He sat back in his chair and stared at the computer screen. A year ago he couldn't imagine himself considering giving up all his electronic gadgets. Now he was eager to move on to a simple life without all the distractions that prevented him from living in the moment and developing a stronger relationship with the Lord.

Later that night as he and his parents sat at the kitchen table eating sandwiches, Pop asked him what he'd been doing all afternoon. "Once we got home, you disappeared."

"I went on an auction site and listed some of my stuff." Charles noticed his parents exchanging a glance as he took another bite of his sandwich. He decided right then to let them in on what he was doing. There was no reason to keep it to himself. "I asked Ruthie to go to the Ringling Museum of Art for her birthday. I can use the money from the sales for that."

Mom's forehead crinkled. "Are you sure you want to do that? I know how much you enjoy your music and movies."

Charles put his sandwich on the plate and leaned back in his chair. "I used to enjoy them, but this whole Mennonite thing. . ."

Pop chuckled. "Yeah, this *whole Mennonite thing* has me shifting my priorities, too."

"I just hope I get enough to pay for our admission and take Ruthie out for dinner afterward."

Again, Mom and Pop looked at each other before Mom reached for his hand. "We appreciate everything you do, Charles. I don't think we tell you often enough."

Warmth flooded Charles as he smiled back at her. "You are the best parents a guy could have."

"We're not perfect parents though," Mom reminded him.

"Perfect parents would be boring." Charles shoved the last bite of sandwich into his mouth and pushed his plate back. "After you're done, why don't you two go for a walk or something? I'll do the dishes."

Pop jumped up from the table and pulled Mom to her feet. "Let's go, Lori, before he changes his mind."

Once Charles was alone in the house, he did the dishes, wiped the countertops, and swept the kitchen floor. In the past, he dreaded the times when Mom asked him to do anything around the house, but now he actually enjoyed it. Once the kitchen was clean, he went to the doorway, turned around to see the fruits of his labor, and smiled. He couldn't remember feeling better about his life.

⌒

Ruthie met Rosemary on the sidewalk in front of the shop the next morning so they walked in together. Papa was already inside behind the counter, jotting something onto a notepad.

He glanced up. "Ruthie, I need to talk to you for a few minutes. Rosemary, why don't you mind the floor while my daughter and I meet in the office?"

A panicked look crossed her face. "I. . .um. . .okay."

"If you need one of us, just knock on the door," Ruthie said.

Rosemary nodded. She turned her back so Ruthie couldn't see her face anymore, but she knew Rosemary was miserable about being left alone on the sales floor.

Once Papa came into the office and closed the door behind himself, he turned to Ruthie. "I've been thinking it might be a good idea for you to work for someone else for a while."

"But why?"

Papa shrugged. "This is all you've ever been around. I think another job will give you more perspective."

"What kind of job?"

"Rolf Fresh will be opening a frozen yogurt shop soon, and he's looking for part-time help."

Working in that environment sounded like a nightmare to Ruthie. Not only was she self-conscious out of her element, but she also tended to be klutzy when she was nervous. An image of accidentally dropping a cup or cone of frozen yogurt down a customer's shirt made her shiver with horror.

"I've never done anything like that before," she argued.

"That's exactly why I want you to do it." Papa pointed to the chair and waited for her to take a seat before he sat down. "I'm not saying you have to do it forever. I just want you to have more experience than you can get in this store and the housework you do at home. I told Rolf that you'll be there tomorrow for an interview."

"Tomorrow?" Ruthie's voice squeaked.

"Ya." Papa folded his arms. "You'll start next week—that is, if he thinks you can do the work."

All Ruthie could do was nod. After Papa dismissed her, she walked back out to the sales floor where Rosemary remained behind the counter while a couple of customers browsed. Relief replaced Rosemary's panic when she saw Ruthie and her papa coming out of the office.

Since Ruthie was certain her new job was inevitable, she had Rosemary do all the bookwork while she supervised. Papa spent some time telling Rosemary a few simple phrases to use with customers until she became more comfortable.

After lunch, Papa asked Rosemary if she could stay an extra hour. She nodded but Ruthie could tell her heart wasn't in it. Ruthie wondered if Rosemary was as miserable as she was.

⁓

By Wednesday, Charles had made enough money off his auctions to take Ruthie to the Ringling Museum of Art and to dinner wherever she wanted to go. And he had money leftover that he could give his parents. He was eager to make plans, but now that he worked every day at the farm, he didn't have time. At least he could tell his parents the good news.

"You don't have to give us the money," Pop said. "Keep it for yourself."

"No, Pop. That wouldn't be right. I'm part of this family, too, and I want to share in the responsibility."

Pop started to argue, but Mom shushed him. "Jonathan, I think this is important to Charles. He's a grown man, and it makes him happy."

After looking back and forth between Charles and his wife, Pop finally nodded. "Yeah, you're right, Lori." He looked Charles in the eye. "You are a much better man than we raised you to be, and that's even more proof that the Lord is active in our lives."

Charles didn't want to take anything away from his parents, but he knew Pop was right. "The best thing you ever did for me was lead me to Christ."

Tears sprang to Mom's eyes so Charles decided to change the subject.

He'd changed quite a bit lately, but since Mom rarely cried, his gut clenched.

"Where do you think I should take Ruthie for dinner?" he asked.

Pop thought for a moment before replying, "Why don't you ask her where she wants to go?"

"I don't know if she's been many places outside of Pinecraft."

"He's right, Jonathan," Mom said. "Let me give this some thought. In the meantime, you can ask Ruthie what some of her favorite foods are. That should help narrow the list."

<hr>

When Sunday arrived, Ruthie was out of sorts. She'd applied for the job at Fresh's Yogurt Shop and gotten it. Mr. Fresh told her she'd start the following Monday, helping set up before their grand opening. The very thought of it sent her into panic mode.

"Why aren't you ready yet?" Mother asked as she stood at Ruthie's bedroom door. "We need to leave in five minutes."

"I can't get the kapp on right." Ruthie felt as though her hands had become detached from her arms as they shook.

"Here, let me help you." Mother walked right up to her, spun her around, and adjusted the kapp in a matter of seconds. "There you go. All your hair is in place, and your kapp is just right."

"Thanks." Ruthie looked down at the floor to avoid her Mother's gaze.

"Ruthie, stop worrying about tomorrow. You'll do just fine."

"I'm not so sure," Ruthie said. "You know how I can be when I'm nervous." She pointed to her kapp. "Even in the privacy of my own room, my hands are shaking. Can you imagine how embarrassing it'll be if I'm like this tomorrow?"

"Perhaps it won't be so embarrassing if you stop thinking about people looking at you. Consider yourself the Lord's servant and serve the frozen yogurt for Him."

Mother always did have a better perspective than she had. "Ya. You're right."

"You've always worried about offending people or doing something others don't approve of. The only thing you need to concern yourself with at this stage in your life, Ruthie, is following His calling." She backed toward the door. "Now take a deep breath, say a prayer, and meet your papa and me outside."

After Mother left, Ruthie did exactly as she said. When she finished her heartfelt but brief prayer, she felt much better. Her nerves hadn't completely calmed, but she felt more anchored.

The instant she arrived on the church lawn, she spotted Charles and his parents. Charles grinned at her and mouthed that he wanted to see her after church. She nodded.

Ruthie had to force herself not to let her mind stray throughout the service. She stared at the pastor during the sermon and tried to absorb what he said.

Afterward she followed Mother toward the door. Charles stood outside waiting. Her pulse quickened as she stepped closer to him.

"Good news!" he said, his face lit up.

Ruthie couldn't help but smile at the obvious joy he exuded. "Tell me. I'm ready to hear good news."

"If you'll accept, I'm taking you to the Ringling Museum of Art and out to dinner afterward. The only thing I need to know is what kinds of food you like or don't like."

"We can always go to Penner's," Ruthie said. "They have a wide variety."

Charles looked disappointed at first, but he quickly recovered. "If that's where you want to go, I'll take you there, but I thought. . .well, maybe. . .I don't know. How about we go somewhere different?"

"I haven't been to all that many places," she admitted. "So it's hard for me to suggest a place."

"Do you like seafood?"

"Ya. I like fish and crab cakes."

"Then I bet you'll like lobster. I know the perfect place."

Ruthie had never tasted lobster, but she knew it was pricy. "Isn't lobster awful expensive?"

Charles pursed his lips and nodded. "It can be but this is a special occasion, and I really want to treat you to something you'll always remember."

Ruthie didn't need lobster to remember being with Charles, but he seemed so excited she didn't want to poke a hole in his joy. Instead she said, "We can go wherever you want to take me."

"Perfect!" He shifted his weight from one foot to the other. "Mom and Pop are waiting for me. Your birthday's on Friday, right?"

She nodded. "Ya, but if that's not a good night for you—"

"I don't want to interfere with your family's plans. . . ."

"My parents won't mind celebrating on a different day."

She was delighted to see him smile. "If your dad will let you off early, I can pick you up at two thirty. Abe has already given me the afternoon off."

"Um. . .well, I'm starting a new job."

"I heard. Mr. Fresh told me you start tomorrow, but the shop doesn't open for another week. He said you don't have to work on Friday afternoon either."

Ruthie wasn't sure how she felt about everyone making arrangements without consulting her, but this wasn't the time to bring it up. "Okay, then we can go at two thirty on Friday."

As soon as Charles left with his parents, Ruthie joined hers. Mother was the first to speak up.

"Did I hear Charles ask you out on your birthday?"

Ruthie nodded. "He's taking me to the Ringling Museum of Art and out for dinner afterward."

"Where is he taking you for dinner?"

"Someplace that has lobster."

Papa laughed. "In other words, someplace fancy."

"Have you ever had lobster before?" Ruthie asked.

"Once," Papa said as he closed his eyes and rubbed his belly. "It was absolutely delightful. It's one of those foods you can't get enough of."

Mother tilted her head back and laughed out loud. "Samuel, I haven't met a food yet that you can't get enough of."

He grinned. "I do like to eat."

"You sure do," Mother said before turning her attention back to Ruthie. "I've never had lobster, but I've heard it tastes sort of like crab, only better."

"Then I'm sure I'll like it." Ruthie decided to change the subject. "I have to be at Fresh's first thing tomorrow morning. Mr. Fresh wants all the workers to help him set up, and he says we'll need to learn how to use the machines."

Mother cast a concerned glance at Papa. "Our Ruthie has never operated machines before. What if she doesn't like that job?"

Papa tightened his jaw. "I didn't think about that. Remember that you don't have to work there forever. I just want you to have the experience of working for someone outside the family."

Ruthie didn't bring up the fact that she was just as concerned about how Rosemary would cope in the souvenir shop as she was about herself working at a job she didn't like. Papa appeared deep in thought, so perhaps he was thinking the same thing.

Chapter 10

Some of the men from the church had volunteered to come over and fix the Polks' house up to make it more attractive to potential buyers. All week the house was filled with workers painting and making small repairs. They painted the outside of the house, and they prepped the inside to be painted the following week. Abe had brought over a couple of fruit trees that would bear fruit in another year or two so they could add that to the listing, which the realtor said would help attract buyers.

Mom went straight home from work on Friday so Charles could have the car for his date. He tried to explain that Ruthie would be just fine riding the bus, but Mom reminded him they'd be getting rid of their car soon and this would probably be one of the last times he'd be able to use it. They'd decided to rent a house in or close to the Mennonite and Amish community of Pinecraft as soon as their house sold.

Charles came home from the farm before lunch. The men were still at the house working, and some of the women had come by bus with food. Mrs. Penner invited Charles to join them, so he did.

"The men have a meeting at the church this afternoon so they will likely leave early but come back to finish their work," Mrs. Penner said.

"We appreciate everything."

Mrs. Penner's eyes twinkled with a knowing look. "I hear you're taking our Ruthie on a date this afternoon," she whispered.

"Yes," he replied. "She said she's always wanted to go to an art gallery, so I figured I'd take her to the Ringling Museum of Art."

"That is the best one," she said. "When Mary first came to live with us, we took her there, hoping she'd find some joy here." Mrs. Penner shook her head. "But unfortunately it didn't work. She was always quiet and kept to herself until Abe came along. We prayed for something, and the Lord delivered Abe."

Charles hadn't known that about Mary. "Abe and Mary seem very happy now."

"Ya," Mrs. Penner agreed. "Mary has turned into a joyful young woman with a sunny disposition. We never thought that would happen."

"I guess I still have quite a bit to learn about the people in the church," Charles said. "I used to assume everyone was happy all the time."

"Neh, not always." Mrs. Penner placed her hand on his arm and looked him in the eye. "Remember that even Mennonites have troubles. We need the Lord as much as anyone."

A comfortable silence fell between them before Charles nodded. "Thank you for reminding me."

"Ya." She let out a deep sigh. "We have problems, but we handle them differently from outsiders. Before we make any decisions, we are called to first turn to the Lord for direction. Only then should we act, and when we act, it is never in anger. . .or at least it shouldn't be." She chuckled as though she thought of a private joke. "But trust me when I tell you we still feel anger."

After Mrs. Penner left him to help serve food to the other men, Charles reflected on all the things she'd told him. Now that he thought about it, he could see some of the anger that brewed beneath the surface in some people who didn't want to give his family a chance. He looked around at the dozen and a half people working on his family home and knew that those people weren't among those who resisted allowing the Polks into the church fold. These were the folks who took Mom, Pop, and himself at their word and accepted them for who they were right now rather than who they were in the past.

Charles bowed his head, thanked the Lord for all He'd done to take his family to this Christ-centered church, and prayed for guidance and direction on all their future decisions. When he opened his eyes, he saw Mrs. Penner watching him. She smiled and quickly turned back to what she'd been doing while warmth and a sense of joy came over Charles.

After a busy morning, Mrs. Penner shooed him away. "You have something very important to do this afternoon. Go on inside and get cleaned up."

❧

Ruthie paced as she waited for Charles. Since she'd been given the day off at Fresh's, she went to the souvenir store and offered to help, but Papa told her he didn't need her. Rosemary was holed up in the office, which didn't surprise Ruthie. Although Papa hadn't verbally expressed his dissatisfaction with his new employee, Ruthie could tell by the way he averted all discussion of Rosemary.

"You have a big date this afternoon, so go home and get yourself ready," Papa said.

"There isn't much to do. I've already bathed."

Papa leaned toward her and lowered his voice. "I'm not talking about the outside. Go home and spend some quiet time with the Lord. You should always seek guidance when you are considering a relationship with a man."

She met his firm gaze and nodded. "Okay."

"Your mother wants the family to celebrate your birthday tomorrow night, so start thinking about what you want for supper."

Ruthie smiled. "She already knows."

"Roast beef hash?"

"Is there anything better?" she asked.

"You are a very unusual young woman," he said. "Almost too easy to please sometimes."

Ruthie finally left the store and went home. She was relieved that Mother wasn't there because her nerves were on edge, and talking only made her condition worse.

As the time slowly passed and the time for Charles to arrive drew closer, she felt as though she might get sick. Papa's words about spending quiet time with the Lord rang in her head, so she closed her eyes and prayed for her nerves to settle.

At two twenty-five, she peeked out the front window and saw Charles sitting in his car parked at the curb. She inhaled deeply, slowly let the air out of her lungs, and opened the front door. He looked up and smiled. Her belly did one of its drop-roll motions, but she managed to smile back at him.

Charles got out of the car and helped her into the passenger seat before getting into his side of the car. "Mom and Pop wanted us to enjoy the car while we still have it."

"You're getting rid of it?" She studied his face, half expecting to see regret, but he seemed perfectly fine.

"Yeah. After hanging out with people from your church, we see how unnecessary it is."

"Will you miss it?"

"Absolutely, but once we get used to not having it, I'm sure we'll be just fine. Even having one car was an adjustment, but now that I look back, I realize it was insane to have three cars. We justified it by saying we were scattered in three different directions, and it wasn't always convenient to have to take a bus or catch a ride with someone else."

Ruthie didn't know about such things. "I've always had to ride buses, and I've never found it inconvenient."

"Oh, I'm with you on that. We didn't realize how much money we actually spent on the cars until we didn't have two of them." He held up one hand and used his fingers to count. "First, there's the cost of buying the car. Second, you have to put gas in it and change the oil. Then you have to maintain it, which can be quite costly. After you add the price of insurance, you're talking some major bucks."

Ruthie nodded. "That sounds like a lot of money."

"Even though it's not cheap to hire a driver, we're still coming out ahead." When they stopped at a red light, he turned to her. "Let's not talk about money today. This day is all about you and your birthday. It's your twentieth, right?"

"Ya." Ruthie never liked all the focus and attention to be on her, but she appreciated Charles's interest. "I find it hard to believe that I'm this old."

"Turning twenty-one did that to me." He slowed the car and took a turn before speeding back up. Ruthie watched the road as he maneuvered the car on the busy Sarasota streets, amazed that he seemed to instinctively know what to do. "So how's the new job?"

"Different. We haven't officially opened yet, which is good because I have so much to learn. I have to admit I'm nervous about messing up."

"I bet. At least you'll be dishing out something good."

The sound of sirens blared in the distance. Ruthie heard them but only gave them a brief thought.

Charles pointed up ahead. "We're here." They pulled into a parking lot and found a spot not far from the entrance. "I hope you enjoy this place as much as I have."

Ruthie accepted Charles's hand as he led her toward the main entrance. As they strolled through the museum, she was spellbound by the sculptures and fountains.

Charles pointed out some things he was familiar with. "That's the *Fountain of Tortoises*, a replica of one in Rome," he explained.

"Rome," she repeated softly. "That is like another world."

"It is," Charles agreed as he tugged her toward a room with a special exhibition. "Some of the art is permanent, but this will only be here another week."

Ruthie remained captivated by everything she saw. "I've never seen anything like it."

"Same here," he replied.

They walked through the museum and stopped at whatever interested her. Charles knew more than she thought he would about art, but what he didn't know, he enjoyed reading on the plaques next to the exhibits.

Finally he glanced at his watch. "We have another fifteen minutes before they close. If I'd known you'd enjoy it this much, I would have suggested coming earlier."

"Oh no, we've been here two hours, and I've seen as much as I can handle in one day. It's all so beautiful and. . .different."

Charles stopped, turned her around to face him, and gazed down into her eyes. "Just like you, Ruthie."

In spite of her cheeks blazing, she couldn't budge. Having Charles so close and giving her such an intimate look had rendered her incapable of moving. She felt as though they were the only living creatures in the world until she heard a man clearing his throat behind her.

"Sorry to interrupt, folks, but we're closing in a few minutes."

Charles licked his lips and nodded. "We were just leaving."

≈

As they stepped outside, Charles thought about what had just happened. He'd almost kissed Ruthie. What would she have done? Before being involved with the Mennonite church, he wouldn't have had to worry about it, but he didn't know if he was allowed to show affection, and if he did, if it would be okay to kiss her in public.

Ruthie was being awfully quiet, which had him worried. "What are you thinking?" he asked.

She shrugged but didn't answer. He opened her door and helped her into the car. As he walked around to his side, he tried to gather his thoughts enough to discuss what had just happened, but his mind had been rendered incapable of rational thinking.

So he decided to just come out and share with Ruthie the first thing that popped into his head. He took her hand and looked her in the eye. "I wanted to kiss you, Ruthie."

She blinked but still didn't utter a word.

"Would that have been okay?" he asked. "I mean, I've never dated a Mennonite girl before. . . . Well, I haven't dated much at all, and. . .well, I. . ." He didn't know what to say, and now he feared he might totally blow any chance at all of Ruthie liking him.

Ruthie looked as perplexed as he was. "I'm not sure."

"Do Mennonites. . .well, do they kiss?"

"Of course we do." Her lips quivered into a smile. "But I've never. . .well, I haven't kissed anyone before."

Her simple admission drove his attraction to her through the roof. If he managed to get the nerve to kiss her tonight, he'd be her first.

Instead of pursuing this line of conversation, Charles decided to change the subject. "Ready for some lobster?"

She nodded. "Papa seems to think I'll like it."

He sure hoped she did. Fortunately, some of his old video games and gaming systems had brought in quite a bit of money. Mom and Pop had been shocked when he gave them several hundred dollars in cash and said he still had plenty to take Ruthie on their date. Mom actually started to cry. He forced himself back to the moment.

"I think you will, too. Lobster is one of my favorite foods."

"What else do you like?" she asked.

All the way to the restaurant, they discussed their favorite foods. He noticed that most of the items she named were simple dishes that could be found in most homestyle restaurants. Mom had never been a great cook, but he'd eaten enough meals out to know a good meat loaf when he tasted it.

They'd barely reached the restaurant parking lot when his cell phone rang. He lifted it to see who was calling, and when he saw it was Pop, he answered.

"Are you in a position to talk?" Pop asked with a gravelly voice.

"Yes," Charles said as he glanced at Ruthie, who sat looking straight ahead. "We just got to the restaurant. What's up?"

"Um. . .I hate to do this to you, but you might want to take Ruthie home now."

Adrenaline shot through Charles's veins. "Why? Did something happen?"

"Yes." Pop coughed.

"Is it Mom?"

"No, it's the house." He coughed again. "We had a fire. Someone tried to call you, but you must have turned off your phone."

"I left it in the car when we went into the art museum."

"It doesn't really matter because there was nothing you could do. Now we need you here."

"So tell me what happened."

Charles glanced at Ruthie as Pop explained that the house had been consumed by fire and nothing was salvageable. As he tensed, he noticed the concern on Ruthie's face.

"After you take Ruthie home, come on over to Penner's," Pop advised. "We have some decisions to make."

He punched the OFF button and put the phone down on the console. Ruthie laid her hand on top of his. "What's wrong, Charles?"

"My family's house burned down. We lost. . .everything."

She gasped. "I am so sorry."

Charles looked at her and saw that she was sincere. "I hate to do this to you on your birthday, Ruthie, but I need to take you home now. My parents really need me."

"Of course," she said. "You don't have to apologize. I would be disappointed if you didn't go to them."

He drove straight to Ruthie's house, where her parents stood on the front lawn. Mr. Kauffman came to the car window and leaned over. "We heard what happened. If you need us, don't hesitate to call." Ruthie's mother looked Charles in the eye. "We waited here, in case you decided to take Ruthie home. Would you like us to go with you?"

"I appreciate the offer, but I think we'll be fine."

"We would like to help in any way we can."

After Charles thanked him, he headed for Penner's, praying all the way there. The restaurant was still open, but there weren't many cars in the lot.

Charles didn't waste a minute. He hopped out of his car and took off for the front door that was opened for him before he got there. Mr. Penner gestured toward the corner. "Your parents are in the corner booth."

To Charles's surprise, the place was packed with people—most of them not eating. Immediately after he made his way to his parents' booth, Mr. Penner walked up with a pot of coffee, and without asking if they wanted any, poured a cup for all three members of the Polk family.

Pop looked exhausted but resolved. Mom, on the other hand, appeared distraught. "Everything I owned was in the house. I don't think there's anything left."

She shuddered but relaxed when Pop put his arm around her. "Everything that matters is right here. No one was hurt."

Charles was numb and had a difficult time wrapping his mind around the whole situation, so he didn't say anything. Some of the people standing nearby discussed who was going to do what to help them.

Mr. Penner placed the coffeepot on the table and sat down next to Charles. "Most of us live in small houses, so we don't have room for your whole family. That's why you're staying with my wife and me, and your parents will stay with the Yoders."

Charles glanced at Pop, who nodded. "What about clothes?" Charles asked.

Mr. Penner spoke up. "Some people from church have already brought some things over to the house—clothes and other personal items. They should do for the time being. My wife is putting your things away right now."

When Charles looked back at Mom, he tried to picture her wearing the clothing from other Mennonite women. It was hard to imagine, but she didn't have much choice at the moment. Then he remembered the money he'd planned to spend on Ruthie's dinner.

"I still have a few bucks," he said. "We can go shopping if you want."

Mom shook her head. "No, keep that money for now. We might need it later." Then she turned to Mr. Penner. "Would you mind if I had my son drive me to the Yoders' house now? I'm tired."

Charles stood. "I'll come right back after I drop her off."

People in the restaurant moved aside to make a path for Charles and his mom. Pop stayed behind.

Once they were in the car, Charles looked over at Mom as he turned the key in the ignition. "Any idea what happened?"

She leaned back against the headrest and closed her eyes. "No idea whatsoever."

"I'm glad no one was home." Charles shuddered to think about the disaster that could have been much worse.

"Oh, I didn't say I wasn't home. In fact, I was in the kitchen when I heard some popping sounds in the back of the house."

Charles stopped the car before pulling out onto the road. He turned to Mom. "What did you do?"

"I ran toward the sound, but by the time I got there, the whole bedroom area was engulfed in flames. So I did what any normal person would do. I ran out of the house screaming." She opened her eyes and offered a hint of a smile, but it quickly faded. "I can't remember ever being that scared before."

He lifted his foot off the brake and pulled out onto the road as he visualized Mom running from their burning house. "How long before the firemen arrived?"

"One of the neighbors must have called because I don't think I was outside more than ten minutes before they came. By then every room in the house was on fire."

When they arrived in front of the Yoders' house, Charles could see a roomful of people through the picture window. "Looks like you won't be alone."

Mom groaned. "I tried to talk your father into getting a hotel room for at least one night, but with everyone insisting we stay here, he didn't want to offend them."

"I'll go in with you." Charles made it to Mom's side of the car as quickly as he could so she wouldn't have to take a step without him by her side. She latched on to his arm and leaned into him as they walked up the sidewalk.

Mrs. Yoder opened the door, and they were quickly embraced by the crowd that consisted of Jeremiah and Shelley Yoder, Jeremiah's parents, Shelley's parents, and a couple of other people from church whose names Charles couldn't remember. He could tell they'd been involved in a heated discussion by the way they acted when he and Mom walked in.

Jeremiah's mother quickly took Mom by the hand and led her away. "I'll show you where you can get cleaned up. I have some clothes out on the bed in the room you and your husband will be sleeping in."

After they left the group, Jeremiah walked up and put his hand on Charles's shoulder. "Tough situation," he said quietly. "Don't let anything anyone says bother you. Some people can't handle change, but they'll eventually come around."

Charles wasn't sure exactly what Jeremiah was talking about, but he had a pretty good idea. He nodded. "I'm too worried about Mom to let other people bother me."

"Don't worry too much. My parents will take good care of her."

Charles knew enough about Jeremiah's past of leaving the church and coming back to open arms from his family to believe his mom and dad would be welcome in the Yoder home. However, some of the other people in the room continued to scowl their disapproval as they chatted with Jeremiah's father.

"Is something going on that I need to know about?" Charles asked Jeremiah as softly as he could.

Jeremiah looked at Shelley, who nodded. "You better warn him," she whispered.

"Okay." Jeremiah tilted his head toward the kitchen then turned and headed in that direction. Charles followed. Once they were in there, he pulled out a chair and motioned for Charles to sit down, then he sat adjacent to him. 'I'm sure you already know there's a small but vocal group that is trying to keep your family from joining. This might be all they need to reinforce their argument."

Charles's breath caught in his throat, so he coughed. "What?"

"It's not the general consensus of the church, Charles," Shelley said. "It's just a few who always fight change."

"Yeah, tell me about it," Jeremiah said as he raked his fingers through his hair. "When I came back, the same bunch told my family I'd never change."

"I've never been in a situation like this before," Charles admitted. "I have no idea what to do next. I guess I'll need to go to the house tomorrow and see if I can salvage anything."

Jeremiah shook his head. "No, you can't do that. The authorities have the area roped off." He cut a glance in Shelley's direction before leaning toward Charles. "You're not allowed to cross the tape until after they investigate."

Chapter 11

On Saturday, Abe sent word to Charles and his pop that he wanted them to take the day off and not even consider working on the farm. Charles drove over to the Yoders' and picked Pop up to take him to the charred remains of the house. Mom wanted to go, but Pop told her he'd rather she didn't, and Mrs. Yoder convinced her she should stay.

The acrid smell of smoke hung in the air so strongly, Charles could smell it when they were a block away. Pop's jaw tightened, and he didn't say a word as they pulled up in front.

"It's hard to believe this is all that's left," Charles said, his voice hoarse with emotion. "Even the front porch roof is burned."

"You should see the backyard," Pop added. "Even the oak tree caught fire, and it'll need to be cut down."

Charles felt his throat constrict. Mom had planted the oak tree in Jennifer's honor the year she died. Even though they'd planned to sell the house soon, they'd always assumed the tree would remain standing for decades. Mom had chosen an oak for longevity.

"One of the things the authorities are considering is arson," Pop said, his voice husky with emotion. "There's even a rumor that we might be responsible, since we were planning to sell in a tough market."

"I can't believe anyone would think we'd do something like this to our own place," Charles said as they walked around the perimeter of the yellow tape. "We have so much of our lives in there, and now most of it's gone."

Pop started to say something, but he stopped, squeezed his eyes shut, shook his head, and shuddered. Charles hadn't seen Pop like this in a very long time.

Some of the neighbors gawked, but no one came to see how they were doing. Charles thought about how with the three-car garage, he, Mom, and Pop pushed the remote on the garage door opener, pulled in, and closed it without getting to know any of the people on their street. There was never any reason to converse with the neighbors so they didn't.

"It's such a shame," Pop said. "I know that all the stuff we lost was unnecessary, but I wanted to be the one to get rid of it."

"Yes, I know, Pop." Charles flung his arm casually over Pop's shoulder, and together they walked back to the car. "What do we do now?"

"We have to find a more permanent place to live. I appreciate the Yoders and Penners, but I don't want to impose on them any longer than we absolutely have to."

"I agree." Charles automatically went to the driver's side of the car and got in. Pop looked at him for a moment then opened the passenger door.

"Now that we don't have much left, why don't we just go ahead and sell the car?" Pop said.

"Are you sure?"

With only a brief hesitation, Pop gave a clipped nod. "Positive. Once we do that, we'll have nothing left to lose."

Charles couldn't argue that point, so he didn't even try. He'd gotten used to the idea of paring down, but he obviously never expected it to happen so abruptly.

All the way back to Pinecraft, they discussed what to do next and where they'd live. "The insurance company should cover the cost of a hotel room until we find a more permanent place," Pop said. "However, the claims adjuster said he needed an official report from the fire inspector to make sure it wasn't. . . um. . ."

"Arson?" Charles said.

Pop didn't answer right away, so Charles looked at him. He'd buried his face in his hands, and if his shaking shoulders were any indication, he was crying. Charles had only seen Pop cry once before, and that was the day after Jennifer's funeral. He'd managed to remain stoic for Mom until then.

He took his right hand off the steering wheel and placed it on Pop's hand. "We'll get through this. I'm just glad Mom was able to get out before. . .well, before the whole house was consumed."

Pop removed his hands from his face to reveal blotchy cheeks and reddened eyes. "I can't stop thinking about what would have happened if I'd lost your mother."

Charles steeled himself against his own emotion to be strong for Pop. "Don't do this to yourself. Remember that the Lord is in control, and He chose to send her to safety. Now He wants us to pick ourselves up and do what we have to do to bring some normalcy back to our lives."

Pop cleared his throat and stared straight ahead for a few seconds. "Normal has changed for us."

"And that's what we wanted, right?"

"Yes." Pop closed his eyes again, only this time Charles could tell he was praying.

When they got to the Yoders' house, Mrs. Yoder ran outside, clearly eager to tell them something. Her eyes were lit up, and she was smiling, so Charles assumed the news was good.

"We found a small house for you to rent," she said. "It's a few blocks from here, and you will be within walking distance from almost anything you need."

"That's good, but I wonder how long it'll be before we can sign a lease. The insurance company needs to investigate before they give us any money."

Mrs. Yoder continued smiling. "You don't have to worry about that for now. We've already taken up a collection for the first month's expenses, so you can move right in."

Charles almost couldn't believe what he was hearing. Most of the people in this community had modest incomes, so their generosity had to come from deep in their hearts.

"We can't accept something like that," Pop said, although he was clearly as moved as Charles was. "It's too much."

Mrs. Yoder appeared crestfallen. "But this is something we do for our own. Don't let pride prevent you from accepting something the Lord wants us to do."

Charles stepped closer to his father. "Pop," he said softly, "I think we should accept."

"I've never. . . Well, no one has ever been that generous with us, first of all, and secondly, I've always been the one to do the giving," Pop admitted.

"That's all the more reason we should take what they're offering," Charles said. "I remember you saying how good it felt to give to others."

"Yeah, you're probably right, and my pride is too big for my own good." Pop swallowed hard, looked at Mrs. Yoder, and forced a smile. "Thank you."

Mrs. Yoder beamed with joy. "We love serving." A momentary cloud seemed to hover, and she added, "Most of us do, anyway."

⤲

The grand opening for Fresh's Yogurt Shop was on Saturday. Although Ruthie had mastered the machines and learned all about the ingredients so she could answer customers' questions, her nerves were frazzled.

Mother tried to calm her during breakfast. "You'll do just fine, Ruthie."

"What if I spill something or I dump a cone of yogurt onto someone?"

"I doubt that'll happen, but if it does, think of the worst thing that can happen." Mother had used this throughout Ruthie's life, but it still didn't ease her worries. "Now go on to the shop. We'll be praying for you."

As Ruthie left the house, her thoughts wandered to her date with Charles. She couldn't remember ever having such a wonderful time. The art museum was delightful, but even better was the feeling she got from simply being with Charles. He looked at her in a way that reminded her of how Papa looked at Mother, and the mere memory of it made her tingle. She felt safe and secure with Charles, even though they were in a place she'd never been. Ruthie had always had trouble adapting to new situations, but this one time was different. She sighed. Too bad the evening ended on such a sad note.

Ruthie had to walk past her family's souvenir store on the way to Fresh's, so she looked inside. Papa leaned against the counter talking to some men, and again, Rosemary was nowhere in sight. Acting on impulse, she pushed the door open and walked in. She had left the house a half hour early, so she had a little bit of time.

The men instantly stopped talking when they heard the bell on the door. Papa looked up at her and tried to smile, but she could tell he was unhappy about something.

"Is everything okay, Ruthie?" Papa asked.

Ruthie nodded. "I'm on my way to work. We have our grand opening today."

Papa lifted a yogurt shop flyer from the counter and showed it to her. "I'll hand these to all our customers today. Business should be good—at least on your first day."

"I hope so," she said, although a part of her wanted no one to walk through the doors. "I just wanted to stop by and see you since you left before I got to the breakfast table." She leaned around the counter and looked toward the office, the door barely ajar. "Where's Rosemary?"

Papa pointed. "She stays in the office most of the day. I try to get her to come out, but she doesn't like being on the sales floor."

Ruthie understood how Rosemary felt, but she suspected there was something more to Rosemary's reluctance to help customers than shyness. "Does she come out when you have to leave?"

Papa nodded. "Ya. That's the only time she does though."

What Ruthie wanted more than anything at the moment was for Papa to tell her he needed her to come back and that it was all a mistake to send her to another job. But he didn't. She'd just have to put in her time, and hopefully he'd ask her to return when he was satisfied that she had enough experience away from the family business.

"Have a good day, Ruthie, and don't worry. You'll do just fine."

Right before she got to the door, the men started talking again. When she overheard one of the men lambasting Papa for being so welcoming to the Polks, her stomach churned. She'd already heard about how a small handful of people from the church had gone to the authorities and claimed they had reason to believe the Polks had set the fire.

Anyone who spoke to Charles, Mr. Polk, or Mrs. Polk for any amount of time and got to know them would know that wasn't true. There was no doubt in Ruthie's mind that they were sincere in their quest to learn about the Lord. She'd also seen Charles's face when he heard about the fire, and based on how lost he suddenly appeared, he clearly had nothing to do with it.

Ruthie arrived at Fresh's at the same time as Zeke, another part-time worker, who was just as nervous as she was. "Part of me wants to be busy, but if we're too busy, I'm afraid I'll mess up," Zeke said. "But I suppose we should pray for a successful grand opening so we will be able to keep our jobs."

The thought that she didn't want to keep this job flickered through her mind. Papa had tried to explain how she needed to get out and experience something besides their family business for a while, but she didn't get the point. Why change something that didn't need to be changed? She also had a bad feeling about Rosemary. She'd overheard Papa telling Mother last night that he always had to go over the books after Rosemary finished because she made so many mistakes. Ruthie had seen Rosemary in action, and she knew that Rosemary was competent in math. She didn't think Rosemary was sabotaging the shop, but her mind and heart obviously weren't in what she was doing.

Fortunately, early morning grand-opening business trickled in slowly and gradually increased over the course of the day. By midafternoon, they were packed, but Ruthie had gained enough confidence to handle the crowd. She even enjoyed helping customers decide what flavor to choose. Fortunately her boss encouraged them to offer samples.

Mr. Fresh staggered the workers' breaks, letting two of them take off fifteen minutes at a time. She was glad she had her break with Zeke. She'd known him since high school, when his family moved to Sarasota from Tennessee. Zeke's family was different from most of the other Mennonites in Pinecraft, and he had a way of making Ruthie laugh. As they sat in the back room talking, he cracked a few jokes then asked her if it was true that she was seeing the Polk boy. The way he asked was matter-of-fact rather than accusatory, so she didn't mind answering. And he always had a silly grin that she found endearing.

"He seems like a nice enough guy," Zeke said. "But I find it interesting he's trying to break in at a time in his life some of us are trying to get out."

Ruthie tilted her head in confusion. "Break in?"

"Ya, break in to the simple life. I've always wondered what it would be like to be out there in the world."

"That's what rumspringa is for," she said.

"My parents never went for that, and I didn't want to upset them since my father has a bad heart." He dropped his crooked grin as he reflected. "I don't recall you having rumspringa either."

"I never had the desire," Ruthie said. "We better get back to work so the others can have a rest."

Her shift was supposed to end at three, but Mr. Fresh asked her to stick around another hour if she didn't have any other commitments. "You're doing such a good job, Ruthie. The customers like you."

He couldn't have said anything to make her happier. Her last hour on the job flew by.

Mr. Fresh approached her with a wide smile as she took off her apron. "You did a wonderful job, Ruthie, and I hope you work here for a very long time."

She smiled back. "Thank you, Mr. Fresh. I did the best I could."

"Customers appreciate your quiet demeanor. You're not pushy and they trust you."

That small amount of flattery brightened her day. She hung up her apron and started her walk home. As she drew near her family's store, she slowed down a bit but decided not to stop. Papa was inside talking to a customer, and she was pretty sure she could see the light on in the office at the back of the store, meaning Rosemary was still there. Papa never left lights on that he wasn't using.

Mother glanced up from weeding the front flowerbed when she got home. "Oh hi, Ruthie. How was your first day on the job?"

Ruthie stopped and talked about the grand opening and how the crowd had been steady. Mother seemed pleased as she went back to her weeding. Ruthie went inside to wash the stickiness off her hands, arms, and face from the frozen yogurt that had splashed on her.

She still hadn't heard anything about the Polks' house. Mother might know something, so she decided to ask her.

❦

Charles drove his pop to Penner's, where they picked up Mom. Mr. Penner had told her she didn't need to come to work, but she said she needed something to get her mind off the fire. She came out to the car looking haggard.

"I take it you had a rough day," Pop said.

She closed her eyes and leaned back against the backseat. "I don't know why I thought working would help me get my mind off all we're going through. Seems like everyone who came in today—at least the locals—asked what we planned to do."

Pop glanced at Charles. "Tell you what. I'll take you back to the Yoders', and Charles and I will go look at the house we're about to rent."

Mom's eyes opened as she bolted upright. "What?"

"The people from the church found us a house to rent, and they're getting it ready for us. I'm surprised no one told you."

Mom rubbed her forehead. "They might have, but the way I've been all day, it wouldn't have registered unless someone came right out and handed me a set of house keys. Tell me about it."

"All we know is that some of the people from the church found us a house, and they're getting it ready for us to move into."

"Did you get the insurance money yet?"

"No, not yet," Pop said. He explained how generous some of the families were by paying all the house-related expenses for the first month. "I plan to pay them back, of course, but at least we won't have to worry about things for a few weeks."

Mom sat staring out the window in a daze as Pop told her that the fire marshal had promised to expedite the investigation so they could deal with the insurance company and move on with their lives. "What if they find something suspicious?" she asked. "Will we have to prove our innocence?"

"Don't worry so much, Lori," Pop said. "Let's continue to pray about it and trust that the Lord will protect us."

"I don't want to go back to the Yoders' now," Mom said. "I'd rather go with you and Charles."

Charles made a quick decision to do something he'd been wanting to do all day. "Tell you what. The two of you can go to the house, and I'll visit Ruthie. I'd like to see how her new job went."

Mom and Pop agreed, so he drove straight to the new frozen yogurt shop, where he got out so Pop could take over at the wheel. After Mom got in the front passenger seat, he closed the door and waved as they pulled away from the curb. Then he went inside to see Ruthie at her new job. But she wasn't there. Frustration welled in his chest. Seeing Ruthie could make all his worries seem less. . .well, less worrisome.

"She's not on duty now," Mr. Fresh said. "Would you like to try one of our delicious flavors? We're giving samples."

"I'd like to later," Charles replied. "But right now I want to see Ruthie."

"Come back when you have time. And bring your parents. I'm sure a little frozen yogurt will help cheer them up."

Charles had to pass the Kauffman family's souvenir shop on the way to their house, so he slowed down and glanced in the window. Mr. Kauffman was talking to Rosemary, who hung her head and occasionally nodded. It didn't appear to be a friendly conversation, so he quickened his pace so they wouldn't see him.

A few minutes later he arrived at Ruthie's front door. He was about to knock, but Mrs. Kauffman flung open the door before he had time to lift his hand.

"I'm so happy to see you, Charles," she said. "Come on in and join us for some coffee cake."

Between dealing with the house fire and wanting to see Ruthie, Charles still had so much on his mind he hadn't thought about food much. The mere mention of coffee cake sent his stomach rumbling as he followed Mrs. Kauffman to the kitchen. She turned and smiled.

"Sounds like you could use a good meal. Why don't I make you a sandwich?"

"I don't want you to go to any trouble," he said.

"Oh it's no trouble at all. In fact, I enjoy feeding people." She walked into the kitchen and motioned toward the table, where Ruthie sat. "Have a seat and I'll bring your sandwich in a minute."

His pulse quickened as he saw Ruthie. "So how was your first day on the new job?"

Ruthie shrugged. "Okay I guess but busy."

"That's a good thing, right?"

"Ya. I guess it is." Ruthie took a sip from the cup in front of her. "How are your parents?"

Before Charles had a chance to say a word, Mrs. Kauffman glanced over her shoulder. "Did you have a chance to see the house you'll be moving into yet? My husband took over some dishes and cups. They might not be as nice as you're used to, but they'll work until you can find something you like better."

"I haven't, but that's where Mom and Pop are now. That was such a nice thing for everyone to do for us."

Ruthie raised her eyebrows, giving him the impression she didn't know what they were talking about. But she didn't say anything. Instead she sat and waited.

"It's not too much when several families participate," Mrs. Kauffman said as she cut the sandwich and carried the plate over to the table, where she set it in front of Charles. "I hope you like ham."

The ham was good but even better was being with Ruthie. Charles felt an odd combination of excitement, warmth, and security when he was with her. No matter what else was going on, looking at her sweet face gave him the feeling that all was right in the world.

Mrs. Kauffman joined them at the table with her cup of coffee. "The Penners are stocking the pantry. We weren't sure what your family liked to eat, so they're putting a little bit of everything in there. The Yoders brought bedding, and the Burkholders' older son had some extra furniture he wasn't using."

Charles listened in amazement as she rattled off all the things people had done for his family. They'd thought of everything. "I just hope we can repay all of you, but it'll be hard as generous as you are."

"The way to repay anyone is to live for the Lord," Mrs. Kauffman said. "That is what most of us are trying to do." She stood. "I think I'll leave you two alone for a little while. I'm sure you have some talking to do after last night."

Ruthie blushed as her mother smiled down at her. Charles wanted to reach out and touch her red cheek, but instead he clasped his hands together on top of the table.

Once Mrs. Kauffman left the kitchen, Charles leaned toward Ruthie. "I had a really nice time yesterday until we got the news."

"Me, too." She started to smile but caught herself. "I am so sorry about what happened to your house. Any idea what caused it yet?"

"Pop and I talked about it, and we can't come up with anything. We've always been so careful, so I can't imagine what happened. Mom was in the kitchen, but according to her, it didn't start there."

"I hope the authorities find the cause soon," Ruthie said.

As their gazes met, he felt unsteady even though he was sitting. The desire to leap toward her and plant a kiss on her little bowed lips nearly overwhelmed him, but he didn't want to startle her. Instead he took a deep breath, shuddering as he exhaled.

"Once all this fire business is settled, I would like to take you someplace nice."

She offered a shy smile. "That would be very nice."

"As soon as we get settled in our new place, we can make plans. Pop wants to sell the car, though, so we might have to take the bus or call for a ride."

Ruthie beamed. "You already know I don't mind riding the bus."

Chapter 12

After Charles left the house, Mother enlisted Ruthie's help in the kitchen. As they worked, she chatted about a variety of topics, from the souvenir store to Ruthie's new job.

"The Polks are taking this whole thing extremely well," Mother said. "I'm sure it's difficult, but with the prayers and community support, they can get through this."

"Ya." Ruthie didn't know what else to say, so she just bit her lip.

Mother stopped stirring and smiled at Ruthie. "You and Charles seem to like each other very much." She turned back to the pot on the stove but continued talking. "Did you know that your papa and I didn't know each other very well before we decided to get married?"

Ruthie abruptly turned to Mother. "I thought you lived on neighboring farms."

"We did but that was only after your father moved in with his grand-parents after his parents were killed in a horse and buggy accident."

Ruthie knew Papa's parents had died young and that he and his brothers moved in with his grandparents, but he was born in the same general area as Mother. "Didn't you know him before that?"

"Well," Mother began slowly, "I'd seen him, and I knew who he was, but he is quite a bit older than me. It wasn't until his older brother asked me on a date that he even noticed me."

Ruthie blinked in shock. "You dated Uncle Paul?"

Mother giggled. "No, of course not. I wasn't interested in Paul. In fact, after I turned him down, your papa came to see me to find out what was wrong with me. It didn't take long to realize he and I were more suited for each other."

"I had no idea," Ruthie said. Her parents rarely discussed their past, so she assumed they knew each other for a long time, courted, and got married when Mother was old enough. "Uncle Paul is such a sweet man, but I can't see you and him. . .together."

"Ya, he is very sweet, and fortunately there were no hard feelings when your papa told him he wanted to court me."

"How long did you date Papa before you agreed to marry him?"

Mother gave her a sheepish grin. "Six weeks."

Ruthie was speechless. She couldn't imagine marrying someone after only dating for six weeks.

"I know you are in the early stages of your relationship with Charles, but I can see the sparks between you," Mother said. "While I realize love can happen quickly, I would like the two of you to wait a bit longer than your papa and I did. At least we shared similar backgrounds and faith. You and Charles don't have that."

"Mother! I haven't even thought about marrying Charles!" *At least not until now.* Ruthie placed the salt shaker back in the cabinet, pulled a fork from the drawer to turn the meat in the skillet, and turned her back so Mother couldn't see her face.

Before Mother had a chance to respond, Papa walked into the kitchen. "Rough day," he said. "I had to let Rosemary go."

Ruthie dropped the fork into the pan. "What are you going to do now?"

"I have no idea. Do you know someone who needs a job and is good with numbers?"

"I would like to come back to the store, Papa."

He shook his head. "No, you've got a job, and from what Rolf Fresh has said, you are very good with the customers." He smiled at her. "I'm proud of you, Ruthie."

"But—"

"I hear Lori Polk needs more hours, but Joseph Penner can't give them to her," Mother blurted. "How about hiring her part-time?"

Papa's eyebrows shot up, and he nodded. "Ya, that might be a good idea. Lori is apparently very good with numbers, and she seems to have a good head on her shoulders. I'll talk to her after they get settled in their new house." He chewed on his bottom lip for a moment as silence settled in the kitchen. Then he turned to Ruthie. "Since you're working part-time at Fresh's, I would like you to come in for a little while until we get Lori trained. . .that is, if she takes the job." He paused as he looked at Mother. "Is that okay with you, Esther?"

"Of course it is. I can handle things just fine around here."

As her parents chatted, Ruthie's thoughts went straight to Rosemary. She wondered what had happened—if Papa had another reason for letting her go. Something about Rosemary seemed suspicious.

⁓

Sunday morning, Charles woke up feeling out of sorts. He was still at the Penners', in Mary's old room. He sat up in bed and thought about all the things he and his parents needed to do, on top of working for Abe. Fortunately, Abe offered them extra time off when needed to get things in order. However, when Charles and Pop talked about it, they came to an agreement that they'd do as much as they could on their own time because there was so much work to be done on the farm.

The sound of Joseph Penner's booming voice rang through the tiny house. "Breakfast is ready for anyone who wants it."

Charles wasted no time getting out of bed, dressing, and straightening the room. He arrived in the kitchen ten minutes later.

Mr. Penner belted out a hearty laugh. "I knew you'd be hungry. Have some biscuits and ham. If you want jam, there's plenty in the cupboard."

"Don't dillydally," Mrs. Penner said. "We like to get to church in time to help the pastor, and since you are our guest, we expect you to join us."

"Yes, of course." Charles nodded. "I would be honored."

He saw the exchange of glances between Mr. and Mrs. Penner. "Good boy," Mr. Penner said. "I suspect you want to see Ruthie, too. She's a sweet girl but awful quiet."

"Joseph," Mrs. Penner said in a warning tone. "Don't embarrass our guest."

Charles gobbled down a couple of ham and biscuit sandwiches, took a few sips of Mrs. Penner's notoriously strong coffee, and left to brush his teeth. He joined Mr. and Mrs. Penner on the front lawn for their weekly trek to the church.

As they rounded the corner, Charles caught sight of Ruthie pedaling her three-wheel bike, her parents right behind her on theirs. He grinned as she kept one hand on her skirt to keep it from billowing in the breeze.

Charles could tell when she saw him because her expression completely changed. His heart hammered as her eyes twinkled with recognition.

"The girl is smitten," Mr. Penner said, jolting Charles and reminding him he wasn't alone. "And apparently so are you."

Struck speechless, all Charles could do was smile. Mr. Penner laughed until Mrs. Penner shot him a look that quieted him down.

Throughout church, Charles cast glances in Ruthie's direction. He hoped Mr. Penner was right about Ruthie being smitten. He was certainly on the mark with Charles. The more he saw Ruthie, the more he wanted to be with her. Seeing the brightness of Ruthie's smile made the fire seem less disastrous.

Pop stood up after the service was over and pointed toward Mom. "I have the keys to the house now," he said. "Let's go get your mom and take a walk to the new place."

Ruthie stood by the church door. At first he thought she might be waiting for him, but when he saw her mother chatting nearby, he realized that was only wishful thinking.

As soon as Mom and Pop joined him, they headed toward the door. An expectant look crossed Ruthie's face, but it quickly faded as he walked past. *Maybe she was waiting for me.*

"Go talk to your girl," Pop said. "We can wait."

Charles spun around and headed straight for Ruthie, who now had her back to him. When he said her name, she turned to face him, and the instant they made eye contact, everything else around him blurred.

"I thought you left," she said softly. "Did you forget something?"

His mouth went dry as he nodded. "Yes. You."

She frowned in confusion. "Me?"

"I came back to see if you wanted to go look at the new rental house with my family."

"I. . .I, uh. . ."

Ruthie's mother turned around, touched his arm to get his attention, and smiled at him. "She would love to."

"But my bike—"

"We'll get it home. Don't worry about it," her mother told her before addressing Charles again. "And afterward why don't you and your parents come to our place for dinner?"

"I'll have to ask Mom and Pop."

"No you don't," Pop said from behind. "We'd love to come, if it isn't too much of an imposition."

"It's never an imposition," Mrs. Kauffman said. "Take your time. I'll have dinner waiting for you when you get there."

❧

At first Ruthie felt awkward tagging along with the Polks to the house they were about to rent. However, Mrs. Polk chatted and made her feel at ease.

Ruthie wasn't sure if Mrs. Polk knew Papa was going to offer her a part-time job, so she didn't say anything. When they got to the house that had been set up for the Polks, Ruthie gasped. It was on the edge of Pinecraft so she rarely went by it, but last time she saw the place, she remembered weeds that had gotten so unruly they'd worked their way into the front window screens. Now the house appeared neat, tidy, and freshly painted. The lawn was mowed and the bushes trimmed. The screens had been replaced, and there was a WELCOME sign on the front door.

Mrs. Polk's voice shook with emotion as she lifted her hands to her face. "This is such a sweet little place, Jonathan. I love it."

Mr. Polk put his arm around his wife, and she buried her face in his shoulder. She and Charles quietly stood there, waiting to go inside.

Finally, Mr. Polk pulled a key from his pocket and led Mrs. Polk to the front door. After unlocking and opening it, he stood back to let everyone else in first. As they walked through the house, Ruthie recognized various pieces from other people's homes.

"I want to see the kitchen," Charles said.

His father winked at Ruthie. "Of course you do, Son. That's always been the most important room in the house to you." He pointed in the opposite direction. "Your mother and I will take another look at the bedrooms, and we'll meet you in the kitchen in a few minutes."

Ruthie followed Charles to the back of the house, the most logical place for the kitchen. Once they found it, she studied Charles as he surveyed the small but functional room with a cooking station on one side and a wooden kitchen table that seated four on the other, divided by an island with a butcher-block counter. Two walls were covered with cabinets. A narrow pantry took up the small space beside the archway leading to the rest of the house. "Mom will love this," he said. "She always said she felt lost in the big kitchen in our old house."

"I hope you're right," Ruthie said. "Even if she doesn't like it, you'll have a place to stay until you figure out what to do next."

"I like it," Charles said as he leaned against the counter, folded his arms, and locked gazes with her. "After we get everything settled, I might think about striking out on my own."

Ruthie imagined herself striking out with him, but she quickly squelched her thoughts. She had no business harboring such ideas.

"I can't believe it," Mr. Polk said from the door. "The whole place has been furnished from one end to the other. We don't need to get anything to move in."

His wife ducked into the kitchen beside him. "Someone even put a few outfits in the closet."

Ruthie knew that Mrs. Penner had gotten some clothing donations from women who were the approximate size of Mrs. Polk, but she couldn't imagine Charles's mother wearing whatever she'd found. But Mrs. Polk was polite, and she didn't let her opinion be known.

"Yeah," Mr. Polk added. "There are a couple pairs of work pants and shirts in there, too." He paused. "Go look in your closet, Son."

"C'mon, Ruthie," Charles said. "I want to check everything out."

Charles flipped the light on in the bathroom and pointed to the counter where a basket filled with toiletries lay. "Whoa. Someone thought of everything."

"You might not have all the things you're used to, but. . ." Ruthie's voice trailed off as she noticed Charles watching her. She shrugged. "It'll get you started."

"Looks like we have what we need." Charles leaned against the wall and extended a hand toward Ruthie. "Come here, Ruthie."

She followed his command and took his hand in hers. To Ruthie's surprise, he pulled her all the way to his chest and wrapped his arms around her. She didn't know what to do, but she liked the way it felt being in his arms.

"Uncomfortable?" he asked.

Slowly she shook her head. He turned her around to face him then tucked his hand beneath her chin and tilted her face upward until their eyes met. She could feel her pulse in every inch of her body, from her head to her toes.

"Mind if I kiss you?"

Before she had a chance to respond, he'd lowered his head toward hers, and their lips touched—a feather-light touch at first then a more pressing kiss. The sound of voices drawing closer alerted them, so they pulled apart.

"Son. . ." Mr. Polk had just come into view of them standing in the doorway of the bathroom.

Mrs. Polk had caught up with her husband by now, and her eyes twinkled with acknowledgment. She grinned at Ruthie. "This is such a sweet little house. I think we'll be very happy here."

Ruthie was grateful that Charles's mother hadn't called them out on the embarrassing situation, but she was still humiliated by the fact that his parents saw what they did. Years ago a boy had tried to kiss her, but their teacher caught them. Embarrassed, he'd teased her about it on the playground later. Ruthie was all of twelve when she vowed never to kiss a boy again. Although she knew better than to hold herself to that promise, the old humiliation made her feel like a preteen again.

She cast a furtive glance in Charles's direction and noticed that he didn't seem to be the least bit embarrassed. If they'd been her parents, she would have wanted to crawl into a hole and not come out for a very long time. Not even Mother and Papa had public displays of affection, although she knew they loved each other deeply.

Chapter 13

Charles heard footsteps coming through the house. He glanced at Pop. "Are we expecting anyone else?"

"No, but plenty of people know we're here, so it's probably someone from a welcoming committee," Pop said. "I'll go check and see who it is."

Ruthie still wouldn't look him in the eye since the kiss, and he wanted to give her time to recover. "I guess we're ready to move in."

"Charles," Pop said as he approached, "can you come outside for a minute?"

Mom started to follow, but Pop held up his hand. "Why don't you stay here with Ruthie?" He gave her a look unlike any Charles could remember.

When Charles got to the front door, he understood why. Mr. Krahn, Mr. Hostetler, and Mr. Atzinger were all on the front porch, glaring at him as though he'd committed a crime.

Charles tried not to assume anything, so he forced a smile and nodded. "Hi there, gentlemen. This is a very nice house the people from the church found for us."

"We didn't find it," Mr. Hostetler said, his voice gruff and unwelcoming. "That's why we stopped by. In case you haven't noticed, this community is made up of fine people who attend one of the Mennonite or Amish churches. We don't think outsiders would appreciate our way of life."

"We do," Pop said.

Mr. Hostetler glared at Pop as Mr. Krahn stepped forward to assume the lead. "You don't understand what he was saying. Pinecraft doesn't offer what people like you need. You are still outsiders to us."

Pop stepped forward with a finger lifted, but Charles took him by the arm and gently nudged him back. Charles spoke up. "I do understand what you're saying, but in case you haven't heard the news, we're seriously considering joining your church. Our needs have changed."

The men looked at each other and all nodded at the same time. "We don't feel that you are coming to our church for the right reasons."

Charles narrowed his eyes and looked directly at Mr. Krahn, who appeared to be the leader of the group. "Exactly what reasons do you think we'd attend your church if not for the right ones?"

"That is what we would like to know." Mr. Krahn folded his arms, and the other two men followed his lead. "Maybe it is for business purposes"—he turned to Mr. Hostetler before looking back at Charles—"or maybe you want to have our blessing to court one of our young women."

"No," Charles said softly as he placed his arm around Pop's shoulder. "You're mistaken. We've come to know the Lord through your church, and we've decided to embrace everything about it."

Charles could feel Pop's body tense even more as they waited for the men to say something else.

Finally, Mr. Atzinger spoke up. "I for one don't believe you, but I'm sure the truth will come out soon enough. . .after the fire marshal gives us the report."

"Ya, we have reason to believe—" Mr. Krahn started.

Pop yanked away from Charles, pointing to the street. "I would like for you to leave our property now."

"This isn't—"

Mr. Krahn tugged on Mr. Atzinger's arm. "Let's leave now."

Charles was angrier than he'd ever been in his entire life, but he had no desire to do anything but pray for the Lord's light to shine on what was right. Pop, on the other hand, seemed to have forgotten some of what he'd learned.

"Let it go, Pop. We can't make them believe us."

In spite of the fact that Pop closed his eyes, apparently in prayer, Charles saw his father's fists clenched by his sides. If the majority of the church felt the way these men did, they wouldn't even want to be part of this church family. But most people were loving, accepting, and willing to help. The furnished rental house served as proof that there were enough kind people committed to encouraging the Polk family to make the effort worthwhile.

Pop opened his eyes and nodded. Charles could tell that he was still tense, but he'd done exactly what he'd been taught—to pray whenever sinful urges threatened.

⤚

Ruthie and Mrs. Polk had gone outside to see what was going on. While Mrs. Polk joined hands with her husband, Ruthie stood in stunned silence as the men from her church walked away without another word. She'd always known that Mr. Krahn was an angry man who resisted all change. But Mr. Hostetler and his wife had been friends of her family's until about a year ago, when Papa caught their nephew shoplifting from the souvenir store. They'd tried to defend the boy, but since Papa caught the boy walking out of the store with the merchandise stuffed under his coat, there wasn't much they could say. Even though Papa had decided not to call the police, the Hostetlers had pulled away and become tight with Mr. Krahn.

Charles tugged at Ruthie, pulling her from her thoughts. "I am so sorry they did this while you were here."

Ruthie cast her glance downward. "That was terrible. I don't know what to do."

"There isn't anything you can do," he said.

Perhaps there was, Ruthie thought. Maybe she should heed Mr. Hostetler's words and back away from Charles—at least for now—to give the Polks time to prove themselves. She feared that she was making the Polk family's transition to the church more difficult than it needed to be, simply by being involved with Charles.

Ruthie saw Charles's parents cast a curious glance their way before Mrs. Polk took her husband by the hand and led him back into the house. She looked up at Charles and saw the concern on his face.

She took a step away from him. "I should go home now."

Charles frowned. "I can take you home."

"That's not necessary." She swallowed hard as she continued putting more distance between herself and Charles. "Bye."

In order to break through the tug of her heart, she took off running as soon as she stepped onto the sidewalk. When she reached the edge of the block where she needed to turn toward home, she thought she heard someone calling her name, so she slowed down and glanced over her shoulder, expecting Charles to be right behind her. But he wasn't. He wasn't even in sight.

Ruthie gripped the STOP sign next to where she stood and bent over slightly while she caught her breath. She should have known better than to get involved with Charles—particularly at this time, with his family trying to join the church and with so many uncertainties that would cloud any relationship they could have.

The Polks' rental house was as far from her house as it could be in Pinecraft, so it took her a while to get home. She was glad, though, because it gave her time to regroup.

~

"Where's Ruthie?" Pop asked when Charles stepped back inside. Before Charles had a chance to answer, Pop gave Charles one of those concerned, narrow-eyed looks. "What just happened?"

Charles's mind still reeled from her abrupt departure. "I—I don't know. She told me she needed to go home, and after I offered to take her home, she took off running."

"Did you run after her?"

"No."

Pop shook his head. "You should have found out what she was thinking while it was still fresh. Now she'll wonder if you even care."

"What?"

"I've been married to your mother long enough to know that there are times when she needs me to show how much I care by working hard and digging for answers."

"I didn't think. . ." Charles cleared his throat. "I guess I just didn't think.

Should I go after her now?"

Mom jumped into the conversation. "Your father is right, but now that you've let her go, why don't you give her a little time to think? That might be all she needs."

"But what if—"

"She's not going anywhere, Son," Pop said. "If you don't see her sometime this coming week, you'll see her at church on Sunday. Maybe you can talk to her then."

Charles nodded and tried to consider Ruthie's perspective. He doubted she'd ever faced this kind of situation in her past, so giving her some space to mentally process what had just happened was probably a good idea.

"So what do we do now?" Charles asked. "Looks like the place is ready for us. Are we staying here tonight?"

"I think so," Pop said. "But it would be a good idea to go by and thank our generous hosts for putting us up and making this possible."

After dinner at the Kauffmans', they went to the Yoders' and Penners' houses to express their appreciation. They went to their new home with baskets of food the women had prepared so they wouldn't have to cook for a while. Charles announced that he was hungry again, so Mom pointed to the baskets on the counter.

"Help yourself. You can help me put everything away after you're finished."

Charles filled a plate with baked chicken, mashed potatoes and gravy, green beans, a tomato and cucumber salad, and chocolate cream pie. Mom ate another piece of pie before patting her tummy and making her usual comment about needing to go on a diet. Pop laughed as he took her plate to the sink. "You look good to me no matter what, Lori. Don't worry if you put on an extra pound or two."

Before they went to bed, Pop called David to let him know they'd moved. "Yes, I know that," he said. "Abe gave me your new address. See you tomorrow."

Early the next morning, Charles and Pop waited for David on the front porch in the dark. Mom stepped out and informed them that she wanted to sell the car as soon as they finalized everything with the insurance company.

Charles looked at Pop, who nodded his agreement. "Yeah, I think that'll be a good idea. Then we can sell the vacant land and be done with it."

Mom leaned in for a kiss from each of her guys. "Have a good day at the farm," she said before darting back inside to get ready for her job at the restaurant.

Once she was inside, Pop shook his head. "Your mother seems much happier than she was before. I think she likes waiting on tables."

"I didn't see that coming," Charles said with a chuckle.

"Neither did I." Pop pointed to the road where a pair of headlights came toward them. "Looks like our ride is here."

Each day that passed when Ruthie didn't see Charles felt darker than the one before. "If I thought you would tell me, I'd ask if you were in love," Papa said.

Ruthie didn't respond. She'd just stopped by the shop to see if she could help, since Papa hadn't replaced Rosemary. He'd already prepared the bank deposit, so he handed the pouch to her to take to the bank.

"I've spoken to Joseph Penner about asking Lori Polk to work here a couple of hours in the afternoon," Papa said. "He said he'd send her over this afternoon."

Ruthie looked down at the floor. She had no doubt Mrs. Polk would do an excellent job. She had people skills as well as experience balancing numbers. If she agreed to work at Pinecraft Souvenirs, Papa wouldn't ever need Ruthie to return. Too much in her life was changing at once.

"Go on to the bank, Ruthie. I don't want you to be late for work."

Ruthie scurried out of the store and stopped by the bank on the way to the yogurt shop. The teller smiled as she took the pouch. "I'll have the transaction receipt waiting for your father tomorrow," she said. "Have a nice day."

With a nod, Ruthie went to work, feeling as though nothing was right in her world. She'd been displaced from her family business, and she had a job that was still uncomfortable for her, even though Mr. Fresh continued praising her. A group from the church had made it very clear that they were making it difficult for the Polks to become members because of her, and not wanting to stand in the way of what was really important to them, she'd had to pull away from Charles.

Even thinking about him made her stomach ache. Papa was right. She had fallen in love with Charles. Until now she never understood what a romantic relationship was all about. She loved the strange sensations she had from being with Charles, and he acted like he enjoyed being with her, too. But being apart from him was painful.

Ruthie wished she had someone to talk to—someone who would understand what she was going through. She racked her brain trying to think of anyone who'd fallen in love with an outsider until she remembered how Shelley and Jeremiah had gotten together. He wasn't completely an outsider like Charles, but he'd left the church long enough to create controversy. Maybe she could talk to Shelley.

That would be difficult for Ruthie, though, because Shelley had as much confidence as Ruthie lacked. When Shelley wanted something, she didn't stop going after it. The more she thought about the similarities and differences between herself and Shelley, the more she realized confidence was the key.

Ruthie's shyness had prevented her from stepping out and doing what she really wanted to do. Until now she preferred the safety net of hiding in the family home and business. But everything had changed. She didn't have that safety net any longer. It was time to bust out and take charge of her own life. Papa had probably seen that, which was why he was pushing her outside her comfort zone.

Before she did anything though, she'd try to talk to Shelley. Since Mrs. Polk was still officially in training at Penner's, Shelley continued working there, so Ruthie knew where to find her. Maybe she'd run over to the restaurant during her break.

Mr. Fresh greeted her at the door, but the instant she walked in, he frowned. "Are you not feeling well today?" he asked.

"I'm okay."

"If you want, you can do the prep work for a little while. . .until you feel like facing customers."

Ruthie forced a smile. "I'm really fine."

"If you're sure. . ."

She nodded as she brushed past him to get her apron. Without another word, she took her place behind the counter and took the next customer's order. Although she still didn't feel 100 percent confident, she was getting better and less fearful of messing up each day.

The shop was so busy, time flew by until break time. She tossed her apron onto the counter and ran down to Penner's where Shelley stood by the coffee station, waiting for a pot to finish brewing. She glanced up and smiled at Ruthie.

"Hi there. Did you need a menu?"

"Not today," Ruthie said. "I just wanted to know if you could talk to me sometime soon."

Shelley frowned with concern. "Is there a problem?"

"Sort of, but I'm on break now, and I don't have time to discuss it."

"What time do you get off work today?" Shelley asked.

"Three."

Shelley glanced over at Mrs. Polk, who was waiting on a table. "I'm supposed to work through cleanup after the lunch shift, but Mrs. Polk is doing so well, I think Mr. Penner will let me go early. I'm meeting Jeremiah at his parents' house after work. Why don't you stop by, and we can walk together?"

"Thanks!" Already Ruthie felt a load being lifted. She was glad Jeremiah's parents lived a block from her.

The rest of Ruthie's shift went by very slowly, so when Mr. Fresh said it was time to leave, she was ready. All the way to Penner's Restaurant, she prayed that Mr. Penner would let Shelley leave an hour early. To her delight, Shelley was outside waiting for her. However, as she got closer, she saw the sadness on Shelley's face.

"Did something happen?" Ruthie asked.

Shelley hesitated then nodded. "Ya. We just heard bad news about the Polks."

"What?" Ruthie couldn't have heard right.

"Mr. Hostetler came by after you were here and said he talked with one of the people at the fire department. They said it appeared that someone had started the fire intentionally. They found evidence of some accelerant chemicals that could have been used to start the fire."

"Did the authorities actually find something, or is this conjecture on Mr. Hostetler's part?" Ruthie asked as numbness crept over her entire body.

"That's what Mr. Penner asked. Mr. Hostetler reminded him that it is difficult to sell a house these days, and the Polks were struggling to keep up with their bills."

"But. . ." Ruthie didn't have any idea what to think, let alone say. All the questions she'd planned to ask Shelley were now irrelevant. Then she thought about the fact that Mrs. Polk still worked at Penner's.

Chapter 14

So what did you need to discuss?" Shelley asked.

"Is Mrs. Polk still working at Penner's?"

Shelley nodded. "Mr. Penner said he didn't want to do anything drastic until he sees the final report, but I suspect he'll have to let her go. Oh, by the way, did you know that your father wanted her to come by and see him this afternoon?"

"Ya."

"I guess you better let your father know about the Polks."

Ruthie nodded. "I will."

"What else is on your mind, Ruthie? I'm sure you didn't want to talk to me about Mrs. Polk working at Penner's."

"It doesn't matter now," Ruthie said. "I think my problems have just taken care of themselves."

They walked in silence for a few seconds before Shelley spoke up. "So it's true, isn't it?"

"What's true?"

"You and Charles Polk have fallen in love."

Ruthie couldn't lie but this wasn't the right time to admit something she couldn't do anything about. So she didn't say anything.

"That's okay if you are, Ruthie. Granted, if Charles was responsible for the fire, you'll need to learn to get over him, but if he wasn't, the Lord will see a way to bring you together—that is, if it is His will."

"I don't know, Shelley. This whole situation has gotten so complicated. I don't think it's meant to be that way."

Shelley laughed out loud. "Trust me when I tell you that this isn't any more complicated than when Jeremiah and I fell in love."

"But you knew what to do."

Shelley stopped and turned to face Ruthie. "Is that what you think?"

"Ya. You always know what to do."

"Not at all. In fact, I had no idea what to do. Between my little brother pulling his disappearing act all the time, my mother's depression, and my father being at work most of the time, I thought there was no way I could fall in love with someone who'd left the church and been so. . .wild."

"But everything worked out for you and Jeremiah," Ruthie reminded her.

"Ya, and that was all the Lord's plan and His work. I didn't see how

Jeremiah and I stood a chance for a very long time."

Ruthie found some comfort in Shelley's words, but that still didn't negate the fact that the Polks were suspects in their own house fire.

"If I have any advice to give," Shelley continued, "it would be to continue praying and let the Lord lead the way. The truth will most likely come out, and once you have the facts, He'll show you what you need to do." She offered a comforting smile. "And I'll pray for you along the way."

⌦

Abe walked out to where Charles, Pop, and a couple of temporary workers were plowing a new section for some fall crops. Pop lifted a hand in greeting but continued working. Charles had to do a double take at Abe, whose expression didn't change. Normally he offered at least a hint of a smile.

"Jonathan and Charles, I would like to speak with the two of you for a few minutes."

"Sure thing, Abe," Pop said as he straightened and brushed the dirt off his hands. "When?"

"Now." Abe turned and walked back toward his house, leaving Charles and Pop to wonder what was going on.

One of the other workers said he'd take care of the equipment so they could follow Abe. All the way, Charles tried to figure out what could be so urgent.

Once they arrived at the picnic table beneath the shade tree, Abe gestured for them to sit. After they were in place on one side of the table, Abe sat down across from them.

"I just heard that there's some reason to believe the fire at your house was caused by arson."

Charles and Pop both gasped. "What?" Pop said. "Who would do something so terrible?"

Abe's temple pulsed, and he nodded. "According to Mr. Hostetler, you are the prime suspects. Some of the little explosions were from aerosol cans throughout the house and a case of craft finishing spray in the attic."

"Mom got a good deal on craft supplies, but she never used it all, so I put it up in the attic to get it out of the way. How can they think—"

"Ya, but that's not the biggest concern. Mr. Hostetler claims that the authorities are most concerned about the chemical accelerant you purchased the day before the fire. They found it in the bedroom where the fire started."

"Chemical accelerant?" A sick feeling washed over Charles. "Where does Mr. Hostetler get his information?"

"I am not certain, but I have heard he's been talking to the firemen. Unfortunately, they are merely speculating on limited information they've received."

There was no way he would have or could have started the fire. First of all, nothing like that ever crossed his mind. And secondly, he wasn't even home when it happened. Abe couldn't possibly believe they were guilty. "I was with Ruthie when the house burned," he said.

"True," Abe acknowledged, "but your mother was home."

Pop tensed but he didn't move. Charles had no doubt his father was as confused and enraged as he was.

Abe stood. "I'm not saying I believe them. In fact, I don't. I just wanted to let you know what is going on so you aren't surprised when you go back into town this evening."

"Do. . .do you want us to continue working?" Charles asked.

"It is up to you. If you feel that you are capable of working after getting this news, please continue. If not, I will understand."

Charles turned to Pop who had buried his face in his hands. He wanted to wrap his arms around the man who'd raised him to always do the right thing and let him know that everything would be all right. But at this point, he wasn't sure about anything.

Charles looked back up at Abe. "Can you give us a few minutes alone?"

"Ya. Just come to the house and let me know what you decide."

After Abe was out of hearing range, Charles looked at Pop. "What do you want to do?"

Pop rubbed his neck and sighed. "If all we had to worry about was us, I'd say let's stay here. But your mother is in town by herself. No telling what she's having to deal with."

"Good point." Charles thought about it for a few seconds. "How about if I stay and you go be with Mom?"

A hint of a smile flickered on Pop's lips as he nodded. "Good thinking, Son. I like that idea."

Together they went to Abe's house to let him know what they'd decided. "Abe, I can promise you that no one in our family did a thing to start that fire. I have no idea what the authorities found, but we didn't do it."

Abe held his gaze then looked at Charles before he nodded. "I believe you. Let's say a prayer together before we call David to come for you."

⌒

Shelley's talk helped Ruthie get through the remainder of the day. When Ruthie and her parents sat down to supper, Papa didn't waste any time talking about the Polks.

Papa had offered Mrs. Polk the job, in spite of the warnings from Mr. Krahn and Mr. Hostetler. "I don't believe she had anything to do with the fire," he said firmly when Mother questioned his judgment.

"But the authorities said—"

Papa's glare stopped Mother midsentence. "Mr. Hostetler is the one who said that, not the authorities. Jonathan came into the store this afternoon,"

Papa added. "He looked worried sick about his wife, and I can't blame him."

Mother shook her head and clucked her tongue. "This has to be difficult on the whole family. If they're found innocent, I can't imagine them wanting to continue attending our church."

Papa shook his head. "Don't forget the power of the Lord, Esther. He's in control, not us. If He wants them to stay with our church, they will."

Ruthie remained quiet, although she agreed with Mother. If she were in Charles's position, she would seriously consider running as far away from the accusers as she could.

"Remember that those doing the accusing are still in the minority. There doesn't appear to be conclusive proof that the Polks did anything wrong," Papa added. "Most of us still don't believe they're guilty."

Mother tilted her head and raised her eyebrows. "According to the sewing group, a lot of people are changing their minds now that there's some evidence."

Ruthie jumped at the sound Papa made. She'd never heard him growl like that before.

"Samuel!"

Papa exchanged a glance with Mother before turning to Ruthie. "I found out that Rosemary has been reporting back to her uncle, who has joined the group against the Polks. I don't understand how a girl raised in the Word can do something so deceptive. She didn't want to work for me, so she tried to use this tragedy to convince her uncle she should leave." He shook his head and lowered his gaze to the table before looking Ruthie directly in the eye. "Sorry, Ruthie, but this is so frustrating. I wish there was something I could do to make everything right."

That was one of the things Ruthie most admired about Papa: his sense of justice. He had a very strong sense of right and wrong, and the line between them was bold. Ruthie had all sorts of questions about Rosemary, but she knew how Papa was about letting things go.

"When does Lori start the new job?" Mother asked.

"Tomorrow," he said. "She's coming in immediately after she finishes her shift at Penner's."

Mother frowned. "I can't imagine wanting to work two jobs."

"She said she's thankful for the work," Papa said. "Her family needs the money to pay off some of their bills. That's one of the reasons I believe in their innocence. The Polks don't seem to mind hard work. In fact, Abe says Jonathan and Charles are very industrious, and they are an asset to his team of workers." He looked at Ruthie. "Do you have plans to see Charles soon?"

"Neh." Ruthie looked down. "I don't think I'll be seeing him anymore."

"Do you think they're guilty?" he challenged.

"No! I don't believe for one minute they're guilty, but if I continue seeing

Charles, Mr. Krahn and the other men will never leave the Polks alone."

"That is not a good enough reason to stop seeing someone you love, Ruthie," he stated firmly. "That is, if they're innocent."

"Correction." Mother grinned and winked. "That is, if you love him."

Papa leaned back and folded his arms. "Ruthie, are you in love with Charles?"

Both of her parents watched her without blinking. Ruthie had never lied to them before, and she didn't plan to start now. She slowly nodded. "Ya, I believe I am." She cleared her throat. "Or at least I was."

⊸

Pop stayed in town the next day to talk with the fire marshal. Charles went to the farm with the understanding that he'd come home if needed. Mom went to her job at Penner's because she felt she was better off busy than trying to help when she didn't have any idea what she could do to help.

Throughout the morning, Charles glanced up toward Abe's house to see if there was any sign of news. When lunchtime rolled around and no one came to get him, he headed to his favorite spot under the shade tree. He'd barely opened his lunch bag when David's van came rolling up the sandy road.

Charles started to pull out his sandwich, but when he saw what appeared to be Ruthie sitting beside Pop, he paused. No, that had to be his imagination. What would Ruthie be doing here?

David pulled to a stop, but no one got out of the van right away. That was odd. Pop generally hopped right out so David could get to his next fare.

Charles put his lunch bag down, got up off the picnic bench, and walked toward the van. He was about twenty feet from the van when he saw that his eyes hadn't played tricks on him. Ruthie really was sitting next to Pop, and they were talking with David about something.

He paused for a moment until Ruthie turned and looked directly at him. His heart felt as though it would pound right out of his chest. Instead of waiting, he ran toward the van and yanked open the door.

"What are you doing here, Ruthie?"

Pop shook his head and chuckled. "Why are you talking to your girlfriend like that, Son? After I got some good news, I went to tell her and her parents. She wanted to see you, and who am I to stand in the way?" Charles noticed the joy on the faces of both Pop and Ruthie.

"But—"

"I spent the morning with the fire marshal, and we've been cleared of any wrongdoing. The chemicals they found were paint thinners used on the exterior of the house."

"Do the authorities know how the fire started?" Charles asked.

"Some faulty wiring that got out of control when sparks ignited the materials we used for painting," Pop said. "Now that they know we had nothing to

347

do with it, the insurance company is going to come through and settle everything." He got out of the van and helped Ruthie out.

Ruthie smiled at Charles. "I am so glad that's all over with."

Charles wasn't sure what to do next, but Pop was right on top of the situation. "Don't let this girl get away, Son. Make sure she knows how you feel." Pop gave him a gentle nudge with his elbow. "Do it now."

"Um. . .Ruthie, I like. . .no, I love you, and I'd like to spend the rest of my life with you."

"Whoa, Son," Pop said with a chuckle. "That's not exactly what I was talking about. Slow down and wait until the timing is right. . .and you're alone."

"You said not to let her get away."

Pop didn't try to hide a goofy grin. "I did say that, didn't I?"

"See?" Charles heard David laughing in the background, but that didn't bother him. "And she went to all this trouble to come out here with you, so I'm not wasting another minute. I love Ruthie, and she's the girl I want to marry."

"Well. . ." Pop got David's attention and motioned to follow him to the tree. "Since I can't control my son's sense of urgency, why don't we go over there and give them some space?"

"You don't have to do that," Charles said. "I don't care if everyone in the world knows how I feel."

David was still laughing as he and Pop left him and Ruthie alone.

"Well?" Charles said as he turned back to face Ruthie, whose face was flaming red. "Do you feel the same way?"

She looked down for a few seconds then slowly raised her gaze to meet his. He held his breath until she finally nodded. "Yes, Charles, I do feel the same way."

"Okay then." He sucked in a breath. "I guess I should have asked your father for your hand first, right?"

"Probably," Ruthie gave him a shy grin, "but I think he'll understand."

❧

Ruthie's nerves were a tangled mess as she rode back home in silence. Occasionally she caught David glancing at her in the rearview mirror, but once she looked at him, he turned his attention back to the road. After he pulled up in front of her house, he hopped out and ran around to open her door.

As soon as Ruthie's feet hit the ground, David leaned over and whispered, "Congratulations. I'm glad Charles found such a sweet girl."

Ruthie felt her cheeks grow hot, but she didn't look away as she would have in the past. Instead she met his gaze and said, "Thank you."

Before entering her house, she stood facing the front door and inhaled the air that had started to cool down a bit. Charles said he would be here after he got home from work because he wanted to talk to her parents. She knew it would be difficult not to say anything to her parents, so she hoped Mother wasn't home.

The instant she walked inside, she heard Mother puttering around in the kitchen, so she went straight to her bedroom. Mother must have heard her because she was there in a matter of seconds.

One look at her, and Mother narrowed her eyes. "What's that funny look about, Ruthie?"

Ruthie just smiled.

Mother's eyebrows shot up. "I heard the news about the Polks' innocence. Your father and I are very happy."

"Ya. Me, too." Maybe Mother wouldn't guess the rest.

"I need your help with supper. Your papa will be home early tonight. He said we're having company for dessert."

Ruthie's heart thudded. Tonight wasn't a good time to have company. "Who?"

"The Polks, of course. We have a wedding to discuss." Mother smiled as she closed the distance between them and gave Ruthie a big hug.

"You know?"

"Of course I do." Mother chuckled as she captured a stray strand of Ruthie's hair and tucked it beneath her kapp. "I am so happy for you, Ruthie. Charles is a very sweet boy, and his family is so nice."

Ruthie couldn't keep the tears from falling. Mother dabbed at Ruthie's cheeks with her sleeve.

"Why don't you freshen up and change clothes before everyone arrives?"

Ruthie was in her room changing when she heard Papa walk in the front door, so she hurried to join her parents. Papa motioned for her to join them for a family discussion.

"I want you to know that the church is demanding a public apology from the troublemakers," he said.

"Have they apologized to the Polks yet?" Mother asked.

"Mr. Hostetler is over there right now, doing just that. I pray they find it in their hearts to forgive him."

"Even for us it would be difficult, after those terrible accusations," Mother said.

"What if the Polks can't accept their apology?" Ruthie asked.

Papa placed his hand on her shoulder. "Do not worry about what you cannot control, Ruthie. This is in the Lord's hands now. The church council is going to meet with all the families who tried to prevent the Polks from joining."

～

Charles was nervous as he and his parents took off on foot for the Kauffmans' house. Pop hadn't wasted any time letting Mom know, and Charles had spoken to Ruthie's father when Abe sent him home early. This would be the first time the two families would come together knowing they'd eventually all be part of one big family.

"Mr. Hostetler seemed very sorry," Mom said. "I feel bad that he and the others have to speak in front of the church about what they did wrong."

"I believe it's the right thing for the church to do." Pop smiled. "It reinforces my decision that we're doing the right thing." He turned to Charles. "You okay, Son?"

Charles cleared his throat. "I'm very nervous."

"Relax, Son," Pop said as they started up the walkway to the front door. "Everything will be just fine."

Before they got to the door, Mr. Kauffman flung it open and pulled Charles into a bear hug. "Welcome to the family, Charles." Then he turned to Mom and Pop with only slightly less enthusiastic hugs. "Esther and I are very happy."

Charles saw Ruthie appear at the front door, her sweet, smiling face lighting up the near darkness.

"Go on, Son," Pop said as he nudged him toward the house. "She's waiting for you. Go make some memories."

Without wasting another second, Charles ran toward Ruthie and pulled her into his arms. He leaned down and whispered, "Okay if I give you a kiss?"

She nodded. As he kissed her, their parents let out deep sighs, reflecting what Charles felt in his heart. He pulled away and looked into Ruthie's eyes.

"I love you," he whispered.

"I love you," she said without an ounce of reservation. Yes, this was a moment he'd never forget.

Epilogue

Ruthie stood in the churchyard with her brand new husband of half an hour, watching Mary and Abe take turns chasing after their toddler. Her heart overflowed with joy, love, and peace like she'd never felt before.

"That'll be us in a few years," Charles whispered.

She turned to face the man she loved and trusted with all her heart. "I certainly hope so."

As if on cue, Shelley approached and opened the blanket so Ruthie and Charles could get a better look at the bundle in her arms. Ruthie's heart did a little flip. "He smiled at me."

Shelley offered a beatific grin. "He senses your joy."

Ruthie sighed. She couldn't ever remember a time when she was this happy. She had a husband she adored, parents who loved her, in-laws who were happy to share their son with her, and friends who were a few steps ahead of her so she would have someone to ask questions when she and Charles started their own family.

"C'mon, Mary," Abe called from the edge of the lawn. "Grab Elizabeth and let's go. David will be here any minute."

As their friends left the churchyard one by one, Ruthie and Charles hugged them and accepted their best wishes. They soon found themselves alone.

"Ready to go home now, my sweet wife?" Charles asked.

Ruthie's eyes misted as she nodded. "Yes, my loving husband. I am ready to go to *our* home."